Praise for the novels of Diane Farr

"A delightful debut." —Mary Jo Putney

"Signet introduces another sparkling talent in the form of Diane Farr. . . . Ms. Farr beguiles us. . . . Put this writer's name on your list of authors to watch." —*Romantic Times*

"The author's feel for the era is excellent, as is her writing craft, and she caps it all with a wonderful note of humor." —Romance Communications

"A definite keeper. Imagine *Gigi* transported to Regency England and done much better. . . . *Fair Game* has the emotional intensity of Mary Balogh at her very best." —*The Romance Reader*

"[Farr's] stories are delightfully charming." —The Belles and Beaux of Romance

"A superbly written book. I enjoyed every word." —Julia Quinn

"Delightful . . . a wonderful blend of romance and humor." —All About Romance

"*Once Upon a Christmas* is another of this author's engaging love stories. . . . I've always found Diane Farr's Regencies delightful reads, and this fourth book is no exception." —Romance Reviews Today

"I found it to be one of the sweetest and romantic stories I have read." —Huntress Book Reviews

Under the Wishing Star

Diane Farr

A SIGNET BOOK

SIGNET
Published by New American Library, a division of
Penguin Group (USA) Inc., 375 Hudson Street,
New York, New York 10014, U.S.A.
Penguin Books Ltd, 80 Strand,
London WC2R 0RL, England
Penguin Books Australia Ltd, 250 Camberwell Road,
Camberwell, Victoria 3124, Australia
Penguin Books Canada Ltd, 10 Alcorn Avenue,
Toronto, Ontario, Canada M4V 3B2
Penguin Books (N.Z.) Ltd, Cnr Rosedale and Airborne Roads,
Albany, Auckland 1310, New Zealand

Penguin Books Ltd, Registered Offices:
80 Strand, London WC2R 0RL, England

First published by Signet, an imprint of New American Library,
a division of Penguin Group (USA) Inc.

First Printing, September 2003
10 9 8 7 6 5 4 3 2 1

PUBLISHER'S NOTE
This is a work of fiction. Names, characters, places, and incidents either are the
product of the author's imagination or are used fictitiously, and any resemblance to
actual persons, living or dead, business establishments, events, or locales is entirely
coincidental.

BOOKS ARE AVAILABLE AT QUANTITY DISCOUNTS WHEN USED TO PROMOTE PRODUCTS OR
SERVICES. FOR INFORMATION PLEASE WRITE TO PREMIUM MARKETING DIVISION, PENGUIN
GROUP (USA) INC., 375 HUDSON STREET, NEW YORK, NEW YORK 10014.

Margie, I miss you so.

Chapter One

June 1803

Her roses were gone. Natalie halted in midstride and stared out the library window, too shocked to move. Her rose bushes, the plants she had lovingly tended since she was fourteen, were simply not there. Ugly gashes in the turf marked the spots where they had stood.

For a few moments she stood frozen, aghast. Then her bewilderment ignited into anger. *Why* this barbarous act had been committed she could not imagine, but *who had done it* she surely knew. She spun on her heel and flew out of the library, heading directly for her sister-in-law's quarters. Only Mabel would order her beloved roses dug up. Only Mabel was capable of such a crime.

By the time she reached Mabel's morning room—which she would forever think of as *Mabel's* morning room, since the newest Mrs. Whittaker had insisted on choosing and refitting a room that had never before been used for that purpose—Natalie was pale with anger. She burst in without bothering to announce herself.

Mabel cringed at her sister-in-law's hasty entrance.

"Please," she whimpered, dramatically lifting one limp hand to her brow. "My head."

Natalie felt her jaw clench with the effort to control her temper. She wanted, oh, she wanted to be fair. It was hard to be fair to Mabel. She was one of the most infuriating persons on the planet—Mabel's husband being another—but she was, after all, in a delicate condition. One must remember that. At the moment she was stretched languidly on a chaise longue, so perhaps her head really did ache.

On the other hand, Hector was perched sullenly at her feet, rubbing her puffy ankles. So it was more likely that Mabel was simply playing to her audience. Judging by the sour expression on Hector's face, her performance wasn't very convincing.

He paused in his task to shoot Natalie a glance of dislike. "You might knock before barging in," he snapped.

Natalie's control broke. "You might ask permission before destroying my roses," she countered hotly.

Guilty looks flashed across their faces. It was instantly plain to Natalie that they had both been in on the scheme, and that both had known it to be cruel. The slyness of Hector's smile, poorly hidden, told her that he took a perverse delight in her reaction.

He immediately assumed an air of superiority, saying, "*Your* roses? I like that! The Hall belongs to me now."

It was a difficult tone to take from one's loathsome little brother. Natalie took a deep breath, fighting to appear calm. "The estate belongs to you," she said, steadily enough, "but the roses were mine."

Papa had given her those roses. A pang of loss shot through her. Papa had given her so little over the years. His strange gift of rose bushes, brought home from one of his journeys, had taken on an emotional significance it would not otherwise have had. She knew it was ridiculous to feel so attached to a set of plants, but Natalie had loved those bushes the way some children love a pet. And Joe Willard, their old gardener—gone these ten years now—had taught her how to care for them during the last few months of his life.

Hector's expression turned ugly. "You've been ruling the roost here for too long, sister dear. Your precious roses were planted on *my* land, and if I want them dug up, they'll jolly well be dug up."

Natalie's hands curled into fists, but she managed to keep her voice level. "You did it to vex me," she said in a low tone. "You did it purely to vex me. You ruined something beautiful just to cause me pain. For shame, Hector! How much of Crosby Hall will you deface with your spite?"

His eyes narrowed. "As much as I choose, Natalie. As much as I choose."

"But there's no *sense* in doing so! Since the estate is yours, you should care for it."

An angry red spot appeared on each of Hector's cheekbones. "I intend to take excellent care of what is mine, thank you, but if I want to make changes, I will. I'll do what I please, and you may keep your nose out of it. I don't know how Mother put up with your interference. I've only been home six weeks, and I'm sick of it already."

"Your mother took no interest in Crosby Hall, as well you know." Despite her best efforts, Natalie's voice was shaking. "Even when Papa was alive, Lucille kept you in London for most of the year. Since he died, I don't believe I've seen her above twice. Or you, until now."

"That's neither here nor there," sniffed Mabel, apparently deciding it was time to draw the attention back to herself. "Crosby Hall belongs to Hector, and *I* am mistress here. Just because he didn't rush back the instant he inherited doesn't mean he deeded it to *you*. Hector was only a boy at the time. Well, he's a man now, and married. You aren't the lady of the house any longer."

"In point of fact, she never was," said Hector cruelly. "She was barely five when her mother died and my mother took the reins. Mother did choose to live in London after Father died—why wouldn't she? This is a godforsaken place!—so Natalie started putting on airs around here. Fancying herself the lady of the manor." He gave Natalie an overly sweet smile. "Old illusions die hard, it seems."

Natalie swallowed past a lump in her throat. What he said was true, but it was difficult to hear. "I never meant to . . . usurp your mother's authority. Or yours. But someone had to take charge. A house as large as Crosby Hall won't run itself." She took a deep breath to steady her voice. "With Lucille in London, there was no one else to manage things. I merely . . . stepped into the breach."

"Well, you may step out," said Mabel rudely. "I may be young, but I have very decided ideas."

"Both those facts are abundantly clear." To her dismay, Natalie felt tears rising. She cleared her throat and lifted her chin defiantly. Hector and Mabel would *not* get the better of her. "I do try, you know, to hold my tongue. I do try to stay out of it, even when I think . . ." Her voice trailed off. She mustn't express her opinion yet again; she had already pleaded in vain too many times, unable to help herself when Mabel had plunged ahead, changing things just for the sake of asserting her youthful authority. The worst had been when Mabel sacked most of the staff and replaced them with strangers—but she mustn't think of that; it was too distressing. She was thankful that Mabel's pregnancy had led her to keep Nurse, at least. Nurse was the only rock left for Natalie to cling to.

She tried to appear reasonable. "You are mistress here. I realize that. But I am asking you, in simple charity, to refrain from destroying my personal property."

Mabel pouted. "If you *must* know, the roses haven't been destroyed," she said in a voice of long suffering. "They've only been moved."

"Moved?" Natalie stared. Relief flooded her . . . then doubt. "But you can't transplant mature rose bushes in this heat. They'll never survive it. Moved where? And why?"

Mabel waved a vague hand. Her voice rose into a whine. "Hector, pray explain it to her," she begged. "Oh, my aching head! I don't know why every unpleasant task should fall to me."

Hector looked annoyed. "A bee flew in the library window yesterday," he said shortly.

Natalie wasn't sure she had heard him properly. His words made no sense. "A bee. Yes?"

He shrugged. "Mabel dislikes bees."

Natalie was speechless.

Mabel folded her arms across her ample chest. "I am terrified of bees," she announced. "I can't bear insects at any price, but a bee is worse than anything. Except, perhaps, a wasp. Or a snake. Yes, Hector, I know a snake is not an insect, so kindly take that look off your face."

Natalie closed her eyes for a moment. "Let me be sure I understand this," she said carefully. "Mabel ordered my roses taken out because she is afraid of *bees*?"

Hector snickered. "It may be difficult for you to understand, Natalie, having lived in the country all your life—"

Hector's snicker apparently hit a nerve; Mabel sat up. "Don't you dare make excuses for me," she cried. "I can't help how I feel. It's nothing to be ashamed of, whatever you may think. Many people are afraid of bees. They *sting!* And you needn't look down your nose at me just because I'm a Londoner. You're practically a Londoner yourself! Why are you forever harping on that? What's that to do with a fear of being stung?"

"Nothing," said Hector hastily. "For pity's sake, Mabel, be calm."

Wasted breath, thought Natalie, but she did not say it aloud.

"It's not just the bees," Mabel complained, the rising note in her voice warning of impending fireworks. "I don't see what is so wonderful about your beastly country life. You promised I would like it here. Well, I don't, and I don't believe you do, either! There's nothing to do, and nobody to see, and I can't sleep a wink. There's a perfectly frightful row all night long from those horrible crickets, and another in the morning from the ghastly birds! No wonder you haven't lived on your precious estate since you were a boy! If I weren't expecting a baby in the autumn, I daresay we wouldn't be here at all."

"It's a safe bet *you* wouldn't be," said Hector nastily. "For I wouldn't have—"

He choked off his sentence with a visible effort. The unspoken words, *married you,* hung in the air. Natalie gave a tiny gasp, and Mabel's eyes grew round. She burst into an impassioned medley of tears and shrieks.

Well. There it was. Natalie eyed her half brother in disgust. She had wondered why he had saddled himself with a wife—and, all too soon, a child—at nineteen.

Now she knew. The newlyweds' hasty removal to Hector's country seat, and Mabel's rapidly rounding belly, had been very bad signs . . . but in such cases, whatever one suspected, one naturally hoped that one was wrong.

She sighed and covered her eyes with her hand while Mabel's tantrum raged. The storm was directed at Hector, for which Natalie could only be thankful. At times like this, she told herself grimly, her only comfort was the general knowledge that Hector Whittaker was her *half* brother. With luck, when the villagers shook their heads and whispered about his hasty marriage, they would blame Lucille for her boy's behavior. And for his dreadful choice of bride.

She knew she should be ashamed of these uncharitable thoughts. Somehow, however, she could not summon the energy to scold herself any more. She had been fighting to suppress her feelings, one way or another, ever since Hector and Mabel had arrived at Crosby Hall six weeks ago. She opened her eyes again and looked at them. Mabel's tears were streaking the powder with which she had caked her plump cheeks, and Hector's sneering features were beet red with fury. They made an unlovely pair.

For once, she gave up the everlasting struggle to give them the benefit of the doubt, and admitted the truth to herself: She honestly had no doubts to give them the benefit of. Hector and Mabel were both nasty pieces of work and, God help her, she disliked them. That was the stark reality. They were her family, but family or not, she disliked them.

Natalie slipped out of the room. Hector and Mabel were too engrossed in their tiff to notice her departure. Now that her anger had dissipated, depression settled on her spirits. She went in search of Mabel's new gardener, or groundskeeper, or whatever he called himself.

She found him outside the kitchen door, passing the time with a dirty-faced wench in a mobcap whom Natalie did not recognize at all. More new staff, she supposed. The girl ducked back into the scullery the instant Natalie appeared, and the gardener straightened and tugged sullenly on his forelock.

"How do you do?" she said briskly. "I've come about my roses."

His expression became wary. "Aye? Wot about 'em?"

She forced herself to remain pleasant and businesslike. It wasn't easy. "Where are they?"

He jerked a dirty thumb. "Back o'the garden." In response to her obvious bafflement, he amplified this statement. "Last row. Be'ind the carrots."

Her eyes widened. "You've put them in the *kitchen* garden?"

An oily smile spread across his face. "Bless me, miss, the roses don't care. Wot they need's a bit o'sun and a drop o'water from time to time."

"Yes," said Natalie faintly. "Of course."

It wasn't, she thought detachedly, the fact that her roses had been moved to the vegetable garden that was pushing her over the brink. It was the steady drip-drip-drip of little digs and stings that had been her lot since Hector and Mabel's arrival. Everyone has a limit, and she was rapidly approaching hers.

Well, she promised herself, she wouldn't lose her temper in front of the new gardener. She could salvage that much of her pride. She took yet another deep breath and began yet another inward litany of reminders. First she reminded herself that this latest insult wasn't the gardener's fault; he had merely followed Mabel's instructions. Then she reminded herself that the roses—if they survived the move—wouldn't care whether they stood beside orchids or onions. They would not feel slighted. It was Natalie who felt the slight. As, no doubt, she was meant to.

This train of thought failed to make her feel better.

She did not trust her voice, so she gave the gardener a nod and a strained smile, then turned to walk back into the house. She would look at the roses later. After she had had some time to grow accustomed to the idea of visiting them in the row behind the carrots.

The instant she reentered the house, the sound of Hector and Mabel's quarrel assaulted her. She could not make out the words, but the angry, high-pitched voices carried past the flight of stairs and the closed doors between herself and the newlyweds. It seemed, to her, the last straw.

Overwhelmed, Natalie halted inside the cool, dark passage between the kitchen and the main portion of the house and closed her eyes. Grief swamped her. It wasn't just that her roses had been uprooted so rudely; they were mere symbols. It was her life that had been uprooted, ripped up with an unforeseen abruptness when Hector brought Mabel back to Crosby Hall. The pervasive changes were permanent, *permanent,* and none of them were pleasant.

Now that it was gone forever, she realized how much she had valued her tranquil existence. She had loved the peaceful days when she could order things exactly as she wished. The smooth running of a large house had given her quiet pleasure.

She had done it well, she thought wistfully. Unfortunately, it was not her job. It had never been her job. What Hector said was true: Crosby Hall, the home she had lived in all her life, had never truly been hers. And now that the rightful mistress of Crosby Hall had taken possession, Mabel was rubbing Natalie's nose in that sorry fact.

Upstairs, the rightful mistress of Crosby Hall could be heard working herself into a fit of strong hysterics. Her maid would soon be summoned, and the house would be set on its ears. Again. How could Mabel bear to make such a spectacle of herself?

Natalie could stand it no longer. She had to get away. She wanted air. She wanted exercise. She wanted a little solitude.

She did not stop to brush her hair or change her dress. She had always kept a stout pair of walking shoes and a deep-brimmed hat in the kitchen passage; she donned these homely articles, pulled on her gloves, and headed for the fields. Ten steps from the kitchen door, she could no longer hear Hector and Mabel's quarrel. With every step she took, she left them farther behind. Her heart soared with relief.

A fresh wind out of the west heralded a possible end to the heat wave. The breeze rattled her hat, and she paused at the first stile to tie the ribbons more tightly beneath her chin. Standing on the stile, she took a moment to gaze across the lush patches of green and gold spread neatly as a quilt over the gently undulating terrain. In the distance, a field of flax in bloom shimmered with blue like a sheet of cool water. The peace of summer settled on her spirit. She felt better already.

"Natalie Whittaker," she murmured, "you should spend more time counting your blessings and less time feeling sorry for yourself."

Her lot in life was not such a bad one. She had a roof over her head, for heaven's sake, and a fine roof at that.

There were many people in the world who never knew where their next meal was coming from. There were women who were beaten and abused, starved, or made to work themselves to death. She ought to be grateful for her life of comparative leisure and prosperity, and stop bemoaning her lack of freedom. Stop resenting her powerlessness.

Ah, but it chafed her.

She frowned and jumped down into the next field, tramping fiercely through the sheep-clipped grass. There was no point in denying reality. She was sick of telling herself a string of optimistic lies. She was sick of trying to pretend she was lucky. She wasn't lucky. Her life was *small*. She felt as walled up at Crosby Hall as those nameless wretches in the Bastille, overlooked and forgotten by the world. While a girl she had dreamed of romance and adventure, but romance and adventure apparently had better things to do than visit an obscure gentlewoman in a country backwater. At any rate, neither romance nor adventure had ever come calling. And a proper young lady wasn't allowed to leave her home and seek them out.

On days like this, thought Natalie crossly, she could almost kick herself for turning down Jasper Farnsworth. Anne seemed happy with him, so he evidently had redeeming features Natalie hadn't quite glimpsed. And Squire Farnsworth took his wife to London every year or two. It was galling that plain little Anne Farnsworth had experienced far more of the world than Natalie had. Children, too! Really, it hardly seemed fair.

Natalie sighed and shook her head. No sense regretting what couldn't be changed. And besides, every time she saw the squire's broad, beaming face she remembered why she hadn't married him. Jasper was a kind and jovial soul, but . . . shouldn't a lady *welcome* her husband's kisses? Natalie couldn't imagine kissing Squire Farnsworth with any degree of enthusiasm. So that was that.

Four-and-twenty years! Christmastide would mark her twenty-fifth birthday. Why, she had been alive for nearly a quarter of a century. All that time wasted. It was maddening. Wasn't there *something* she could do with her life? No husband, no child, no house of her own, no useful employment of any kind. She was nothing but a charity case, really; a worthless parasite. And without the management of Crosby Hall to occupy her, she would be bored to tears as well.

If only Derek were home! Thanks to the peculiarities of Crosby Hall's entail, Hector was the brother with all the power, so there was little that Derek could actually *do*—but he would have stood up for her, defended her, shielded her from Hector's spite and Mabel's aggression. And when he couldn't defend her, he would have joked her out of the megrims. She missed him every day, but especially now, when she felt so friendless. Relinquishing the reins of Crosby Hall to Mabel Whittaker was the hardest trial Natalie had ever had to face.

She emerged from her brown study to discover that her restless feet had carried her nearly to Hitchfield. She paused. Everyone in the village knew her, and she was reluctant to be seen in the old hat she used for gardening. After tramping across the fields, she must look windblown and bedraggled, too. But just as she was about to turn and retrace her steps, a bright splash of blue caught her eye.

A beautifully dressed little girl, a stranger, was standing in front of the village's sole inn. She was a tiny, doll-like thing, only five or six years old, yet she seemed to be quite alone. It was the color of her cloak that had drawn Natalie's attention. What held Natalie's attention was the fact that the child was apparently in the midst of a spirited conversation with nobody.

The little girl tilted her head, arguing earnestly. She shook her finger in the air as if scolding a dog, then took three little hops to her right and halted, one foot in the air. She balanced solemnly for a few moments, then slowly lifted the hem of her cloak as if trying to catch the breeze and fly away.

Natalie smiled. Something about the little sprite tugged at her heart. She walked forward, but the child was so intent on her imaginary world that when Natalie finally spoke to her, she jumped and gasped.

"I beg your pardon," said Natalie politely. "I didn't mean to startle you."

The little girl carefully returned her foot to the ground and dropped the edges of her cloak. The face she lifted to gaze at Natalie was deeply serious, almost fearful. "I didn't hear you coming," she said gravely.

"No," agreed Natalie. "You were busy." She smiled. "May I ask what you were doing?"

Fear and guilt flitted across the child's face. "Nothing," she whispered.

Natalie was immediately sorry she had asked. Was the little girl ashamed of her imaginativeness? On impulse, she squatted beside her as if confiding a secret. "When I was about your age," she said softly, "I had an imaginary kitten. Her name was Clara."

The child looked both interested and wary, as if she very much wanted to believe Natalie—but didn't quite dare. "Did you? Really?"

"Indeed I did. Clara was almost as much fun as a real

kitten. And she always came when I called her, which is more than a real kitten would have done."

The tense little shoulders relaxed a tiny bit. "Did she purr?"

"Oh, yes. She purred beautifully. Shall I tell you a secret?"

The girl nodded, her eyes huge in her small, pale face.

Natalie winked. "Clara could talk."

The child squirmed with delight. "Kittens can't talk."

"Imaginary kittens can. Why, there were days when Clara talked so much I could hardly hear myself think."

The smile disappeared from the little girl's face as suddenly as if Natalie had wiped it off with a rag. "Did you make her sit in the corner?" she asked fearfully. "Did you tie her up?"

Natalie was startled. "Certainly not. I loved Clara."

"Even when she was naughty?"

"Especially when she was naughty," said Natalie firmly. "She was my very own. Whenever Clara was naughty, who was to blame? Tell me."

The little girl thought for a moment. A sparkle lit the back of her eyes. "You were."

"That's right. She was my imaginary kitten, and no one else's."

"What became of her?"

Natalie was surprised for a moment. The child had asked the question so seriously, she felt as if something momentous hung upon her answer. "Well," she said carefully, "I don't quite know. I haven't seen Clara for a long, long time."

"Perhaps she's dead," said the little girl in a low tone.

What a life this child must lead, to have such thoughts! Natalie impulsively reached for her and gently held her by the elbows. "No, my dear, that cannot be.

Imaginary kittens live forever. I'm sure she is alive and well." Inspiration struck. "Shall I call to her? Do you think she would come? Even after all these years?"

A nearly invisible smile curved the edges of the little girl's mouth. "You said she always did."

Natalie straightened and looked down the street. "Here, Clara," she called softly. "Here, puss-puss. Here, kitty." She glanced around the inn's small yard. "Heeeere, Clara." She bent and pretended to peer beneath the scraggly shrubs that stood near the doorway. "Clara? Is that you?"

She was tickled when the little girl came and stood beside her, bending nearly double to look beneath the branches. "What color is she?"

"White. A pure white kitten with green eyes. Do you see her?"

The child stared with fierce concentration. "I see something white," she breathed. She held out her fingers as if inviting a kitten to come to her. "Clara? Come, Clara," she crooned. "Come, kitty."

A sharp voice sounded behind them, causing both Natalie and the little girl to jump. "What's all this, then?" said the voice.

Natalie straightened, blushing a little. The woman addressing them was clearly a servant, but she had an air of outraged authority that made one feel instantly guilty. "I'm so sorry," said Natalie politely. "My little friend, here, is helping me find my imaginary kitten."

She was hoping to reassure the woman that she and the child were only playing. Reassurance, however, was not the effect she achieved. The woman looked seriously annoyed. The little girl was standing motionless, looking for all the world as if she had frozen in place from pure dread.

There was something dark in the air, something wrong here. Natalie felt compelled to fill the charged silence, even at the risk of babbling. "I hope you don't mind," she blurted. "I certainly meant no harm to the child."

"I'm sure you did not, miss," said the servant. Her words were courteous, but the tight lines around her mouth indicated displeasure. "But I had *hoped* that Sarah knew better than to bother a stranger with her nonsense."

So it was the little girl who had angered the woman. Dismayed, Natalie rushed back into speech. "Oh, but I'm afraid you have misunderstood me. Sarah didn't bother me in the least. I found her play quite charming."

Now the woman looked even angrier. Her hand shot out quickly, and for a moment Natalie thought she was going to strike the child. Instead, her fingers closed like a vise on Sarah's little arm. Sarah made no sound, but she visibly shrank at the woman's touch. Natalie almost cried out with distress; the expression on the child's face was pathetic.

"Oh, no!" said Natalie quickly. "I approached Sarah, not the other way round. Pray do not be angry! We were only playing, you know. I assure you there was no harm done."

The servant gave Natalie a look so venomous that she fell back a step, startled. "I'm sure you meant well, miss, but Sarah knows that there are rules she must follow. It's my duty to see that she follows them."

Heavens, what a gorgon. It was clear that Natalie must appeal to the woman's superiors; she would get nowhere pleading Sarah's cause with this harridan. "Perhaps I might speak with the child's mother?" suggested Natalie, doing her best to sound polite. "If I could only explain myself, I feel sure that—"

"That won't be possible. Good day."

She began half dragging the frightened child back into the inn. The expression of despair on Sarah's face indicated a certainty that she was about to be punished, and the woman's disproportionate anger seemed to bear this out. Natalie still could not fathom why. Baffled and alarmed, she instinctively followed them, trailing in their wake as they moved from the sunlit yard into the comparative darkness of the inn's interior. She had a vague notion of intervening, should the woman actually move to hurt the little girl, but before she had gathered her wits to speak the two came to an abrupt halt in the passage. Natalie nearly caromed into them from behind.

A voice spoke out of an open doorway to her right. "What seems to be the trouble, Mrs. Thorpe?"

It was a masculine voice, dark and sonorous and filled with quiet authority. Its tone was polite but implacable, investing the commonplace question with an unspoken warning: *You had better have an excellent answer ready, Mrs. Thorpe.* A burden seemed to lift from Natalie's shoulders; here, surely, was a powerful ally. Sarah seemed to think so, too. She pulled free of Mrs. Thorpe's grasp and ran to the shadowy figure in the doorway.

As her eyes adjusted to the dimness, Natalie's initial impression of a massive presence resolved into a truer picture of the man who stood there. He was tall, but not the giant her imagination had conjured from his deep voice. He was dark, but his face had the pallor of recent illness or grief. Grief, she guessed, since the austerity of his clothing suggested mourning. His eyes were hooded with shadow, but she sensed a keen and watchful focus there. He stooped slightly, whether out of habit or merely from fitting his tall person into the low door frame she could not tell. Sarah, meanwhile, clung to his legs with the fervor of a plaster saint clutching at the

Savior's robe. He placed one hand lightly on the child's head, but his attention remained fixed, unwaveringly, on Mrs. Thorpe.

Mrs. Thorpe gave him a strained smile. "There is nothing amiss, sir," she said, brightly but firmly. "Nothing that I cannot handle."

"And who is this?" The man's head swiveled and Natalie felt herself pinned by his shadowed eyes. They were the color of ice long-frozen, their blue gaze as penetrating as winter's chill. His scrutiny made her feel vulnerable, as if he could see into the depths of her being.

It occurred to her for the first time that her position was awkward. Why on earth had she pursued these strangers into the inn? Whatever dynamic was operating here, it was none of her business. She must seem a perfect busybody. To her annoyance, she felt herself blushing.

Mrs. Thorpe's lips thinned. "I don't know her, sir. One of the local women, I should think. She was outside with Sarah just now, but I can't imagine why she has followed us in." She added her basilisk glare to the gentleman's scrutiny, but it was the gentleman's gaze that disconcerted Natalie.

Natalie opened her mouth to apologize, then closed it again. It seemed dishonest to apologize for behavior she did not, in fact, regret. The inn was a public place, for pity's sake. She had every right to walk in if she chose. She ignored Mrs. Thorpe and offered the man a tiny curtsy. "My name is Whittaker," she said stiffly.

The gentleman's expression did not change. He continued to regard her fixedly. Natalie gave him back stare for stare, but said nothing. She owed no one an explanation of her conduct. Let him stare.

Out of the corner of her eye, she saw Mrs. Thorpe smirk. "As I say, sir, I've no idea who she is."

An interruption came from an unlikely source. Sarah spoke, in the thread of a voice. "Papa."

The man's attention immediately shifted to the child's tense face. Sarah looked up at him and bravely whispered, "She is my friend."

Natalie's heart melted.

The tall man looked at Natalie again, and she saw a flicker of some powerful emotion—understanding? Gratitude? Before she could decipher it, he bent his head and shadowed his expression. "I see" was all he said. But Natalie felt, in a flash of certainty, that he really did.

Chapter Two

The young woman met his gaze fearlessly, lifting her chin and regarding him with a level scrutiny that matched his own. The gesture seemed neither defiant nor insolent. Despite her outmoded gown and battered hat, she had a self-possessed air that suggested quality. Malcolm was amused in spite of himself—and intrigued as well.

"Miss Whittaker, would you join me in the coffee room?" He said it as mildly as he knew how, and even stepped back to let her pass before him. Still, her clear brown eyes clouded with doubt.

Mrs. Thorpe interrupted with an angry sniff. "Forgive me," she snapped, "but I *hope* you don't mean to dignify this young person with a private audience. I see no need to reward her for what seems, to me, nothing more than vulgar curiosity. It's obvious that she's trying to meddle in something that simply doesn't concern her."

Malcolm felt a stab of irritation. "I shall give your opinion the consideration it deserves, Mrs. Thorpe," he said dryly. He quirked an eyebrow at the newcomer and again indicated the coffee room. "Miss Whittaker?"

He thought he saw a spark of appreciative laughter in

the back of the young woman's eyes. He smiled, pleased by this evidence that she had caught the veiled insult in his words to the redoubtable Mrs. Thorpe. Whatever Miss Whittaker was, she was no slowtop. His smile seemed to make up her mind for her; she relaxed and smiled back.

The effect was extraordinary. Her face lit with a swift, sudden beauty he had not before perceived. The mouth that had struck him as too wide and straight to be pretty curved into a delicious, inviting shape that proved him wrong. The difference her smile made was astonishing— much like those April days when the sun suddenly emerges from behind a cloud and you realize that the hills are a more brilliant green, the flowers a brighter yellow, the entire world a more lovely and pleasant place than you had imagined.

She spoke, then, shaking her head in polite refusal. Her voice was pleasant and musical. "Truly, sir, I'm sure it's very kind of you, but I don't think—"

Sarah's little hand reached out and fastened on the lady's sleeve. Miss Whittaker looked down, startled. Sarah's eyes were wide and pleading. "Please stay," she said. "Please?"

Mrs. Thorpe made a huffing sound. "Sarah Chase, we've heard quite enough from you," she said sharply. "I think you had better come with me."

"On the contrary, Mrs. Thorpe," said Malcolm gently. "I believe it is you, not Sarah, from whom we have heard enough. I'm sure you have duties to perform elsewhere. We won't keep you from them any longer."

Without waiting for a reply, he smoothly guided Sarah and Miss Whittaker into the coffee room and closed the door in Mrs. Thorpe's outraged face. Miss Whittaker, he was glad to see, was a well-brought-up female. When push came to shove, she did as she was bid. She looked a little dazed, but she did, in fact, walk into the coffee room without further protest.

"My word," she murmured, apparently to herself.

Closing the door on Mrs. Thorpe acted like a tonic on Sarah. She gave a little skip of happiness and seized Malcolm's hand, swinging it. "She stayed!" exclaimed Sarah. "Look, Papa. She stayed! I didn't think she would. How long will she stay? Will she have dinner with us? Papa, only fancy—she has an imaginary kitten. She purrs *and* talks."

Malcolm looked at Miss Whittaker with renewed interest. "Really? How extraordinary. I've never met a lady who purrs *and* talks."

Miss Whittaker had turned a becoming shade of pink. Her lips pursed repressively. "It is the kitten, sir, who purrs and talks," she said severely. "Sarah, you disappoint me. I told you about Clara in the strictest confidence."

Sarah looked puzzled. "Do you mean it wasn't true?"

"No, I mean it was a secret."

Sarah beamed. "But it was true. You didn't say it wasn't true. Papa, did you hear? I wasn't to tell you about Clara because it was a secret. But it was a *true* secret."

"Yes, I heard. But I hope you will not divulge any more secrets. It's very bad form, you know. Miss Whittaker will think you are not to be trusted." Sarah's face fell, and he inwardly cursed himself. He had forgotten, again, that she was too young to discern a jest from a real rebuke. He gentled his voice and leaned down to her. "Never mind, poppet. I've brought down Mrs. Mumbles and Blinky for you. They're in the corner, with your doll house."

"Oh, thank you," cried Sarah, with as much pleasure

as if he had offered her the keys to fairyland. He watched her scamper over to the corner and plop down among her toys. Such a simple thing, to bring her so much joy. Why was she so surprised by even the smallest of treats? His heart ached with a love for her that was tinged with sorrow.

He returned his attention to Miss Whittaker in the nick of time. She was glancing around the room with the nervousness of an unbroken colt. He almost expected to see her eyes roll and her head toss. One more second and she would have been gone. As it was, she met his eyes askance. "I see that you have brought me to a private coffee room. I must not stay," she said firmly.

He offered what he hoped was a disarming smile. "For a few minutes only, Miss Whittaker. Sarah will be with us, you know. Your reputation is quite safe."

She looked uncertain. He bowed, indicating two wing chairs that flanked a table near the window. The table should appeal to her. Nothing safer than to place a piece of furniture between them. The window was a nice touch, too. He saw her shoulders relax as she decided she was being overly prudish. Good.

She walked slowly to the farthest wing chair and sat, but perched on the edge of the seat as if poised for flight. He noticed that the hem of her dress was damp and flecked with mud. She tucked her feet beneath it as if ashamed of her shoes as well. Her hair was as brown as molasses, and springy with natural curl. It threatened to burst from its confines; a few tendrils had already worked loose and coiled into ringlets in a haphazard pattern around her face. The effect made a man itch to touch them, if only to tuck them back under her hat. Her demeanor, however, did not second the invitation issued by her wayward curls. Her back was very straight; her chin, above the frayed strands of her hat strings, perfectly level. Never mind that she looked as if she had just tramped cross-country with the gypsies; Miss Whittaker was the picture of primness.

"What is it you wish to discuss, please?" she asked.

He settled into the chair opposite hers, leaning back to make himself comfortable, and studied her wary face. "My daughter," he said softly. "As you have probably guessed." He watched as several emotions chased each other across her expressive features, then added, "In fairness, I must tell you that I watched you through the window."

She looked surprised, but not offended. "If you are so concerned for her safety that you watch her through the window, I wonder that you allow her to play all alone. She was very near the public street. I suppose you will say that is none of my business—"

"I wouldn't dream of it," murmured Malcolm.

"—but it seems to me that she is too young to be left unattended. Such a little girl, you know, is unaware of danger. She may behave imprudently."

"You seem to know a great deal about little girls."

Her amazing smile flickered again. "I used to be one."

He couldn't help smiling back. "I see. Well, there you have the advantage of me. I must bow, therefore, to your superior knowledge."

Her eyes twinkled. "So I should hope." She seemed to catch herself, then, and sobered at once. "I shouldn't presume to advise you, however."

"Don't apologize. I told you I wanted to discuss Sarah."

"With a complete stranger?" She shook her head, looking amused. Another tendril of hair escaped and curled, fetchingly, beside her temple. "I can't imagine why."

"It's not hard to fathom. You look to be exactly the sort of young lady who dispenses excellent advice. I wouldn't be surprised to learn that most of your circle seek you out when they are in trouble and beg for your assistance. Am I right?"

Some of her wariness returned. "Perhaps. Every circle of friends contains at least one individual who plays that role. You and I are not acquainted, so it would be extremely odd of you to confide in me. I suggest you seek out whichever of your own friends you rely upon for guidance."

He chuckled. "Allow me to point out that despite our short acquaintance, you have just given me a piece of first-rate advice."

She flushed. "Then I trust you will follow it. Good day."

She started to rise from her chair. Without thinking, he reached to stop her. His hand closed on her wrist. "Please," he said. "Don't go."

She stared at him in obvious astonishment, and he felt himself coloring. "It's important," he said gently. He had to let go of her wrist; otherwise she would think him either mad or lecherous. But it was, in fact, so important she stay that it went against the grain to free her hand. "Please," he repeated, and indicated the chair where she had been sitting.

She lowered herself back onto it with obvious reluctance. "I hope you will explain yourself," she said severely. "For you seem quite addled to me."

"I suppose I must." He glanced over at his daughter. She appeared oblivious to the adult conversation—but one never knew with Sarah. She could be damnably precocious at times. Malcolm leaned forward, one forearm on the table, and addressed his companion in a lowered tone. "As I say, I happened to be watching Sarah through the window when you approached. I was much struck by what I saw. I must tell you, Miss Whittaker, that Sarah is not a child who talks easily to strangers. It seems that you and she have a . . . rapport, for want of a better word."

A slight smile crossed Miss Whittaker's features. She looked over at Sarah, and he could have sworn he saw affection in her glance. He could have kissed her for it. She seemed unaware of his gratitude, however; her liking for Sarah was apparently genuine. All she said was "Yes. I suppose that's a fair assessment."

He nearly had to bite his tongue to keep from telling her how long and hard he had searched for someone, anyone, who felt a rapport with his little girl. The best reaction he had encountered thus far was pity. And as for Mrs. Thorpe—

"What is your impression of Mrs. Thorpe?" he asked abruptly.

Her clear brown eyes flew back to his, startled. "Mrs. Thorpe? Why, she's—" Miss Whittaker halted in mid-sentence and visibly struggled to keep her opinion to herself. "I'm sure it's not my place to say."

"If it *were* your place to say, what would you tell me?"

She bit her lip. "Really, sir, this is the most outrageous conversation—"

"Just tell me."

She pressed her lips together, studying his face. She seemed to decide he was in earnest, for she eventually unclosed her lips enough to ask, "What is Mrs. Thorpe's relationship to Sarah?"

"That of governess."

"Governess! Surely she is too young for that?"

"I believe her to be nearly forty."

Miss Whittaker gave a spurt of laughter. "I meant Sarah."

"Sarah is . . ." he paused. There were so many reasons why he had hired a governess rather than a nurse. But he must pick and choose among the many reasons, and only reveal one or two. For now. "Sarah is unusually intelligent. And I had hoped to achieve a certain . . . stability in her life. In hiring either a nurse or a governess, one is hiring the child's chief companion. I had hoped to select one individual to fill both roles. Sarah becomes extremely attached to the few people she allows within her circle. I wanted to make her passage from babyhood to girlhood"—he stopped for a moment and searched for the right word—"painless. Or, at least, easier. If I could."

He hadn't told her everything, but nevertheless he saw understanding flicker in her eyes. "I think I see," she said quietly. "It was a kind thought."

His mouth twisted wryly. "It hasn't turned out as well as I had hoped."

"No," said Miss Whittaker absently. Her eyes returned to Sarah, playing quietly in the corner of the room.

He waited for her to elaborate, but she did not. "Mrs. Thorpe came with excellent references," he offered, hoping to prompt her. "But I think she had always worked with older girls."

An expression of scorn settled briefly on Miss Whittaker's features. "I cannot imagine her methods working well with any child," she said briskly. "They certainly would not have worked with me."

"At Sarah's age, do you mean?"

"At any age." She gave him a rueful smile. "But I

spoke without thinking. My comment is unjust. Mrs. Thorpe may, in fact, be an excellent governess. Some children do respond best to a firm hand. I never did, but few girls are as headstrong as I was." She looked hesitant for a moment. "Based on the interaction I witnessed, my impression is that Mrs. Thorpe is a strict disciplinarian. Am I mistaken in that?"

"Hardly," said Malcolm dryly. "From the moment I engaged her, a battle of wills has raged between her and my Sarah."

Miss Whittaker frowned. "That will never do. Why do you not intervene?"

"I would, but my position is delicate." He tried not to laugh. "I haven't yet decided which of them I side with."

"Dear me." She bit her lip again. "That *is* a dilemma."

"My instinct is to side with my daughter."

"That's only natural."

"But I find myself in sympathy with Mrs. Thorpe as well. After all, I hired the woman to teach Sarah. It seems unfair for me to quibble with her methods. What do I know of teaching young girls? A governess, I suppose, must be allowed to govern."

"My dear sir," she exclaimed, "this is no time for fence-sitting. Mrs. Thorpe's methods may be doing more harm than good. Your child's future may be at stake."

"Yes, so I think." He gazed thoughtfully at the young woman on the other side of the table. Her cheeks were flushed and her eyes sparkled with indignation. She was clearly a passionate person. Miss Whittaker formed opinions quickly and defended them with gusto—and yet she had a kind heart. The more he saw of her, the better he liked her. "I realize you are familiar with none of us," he said, trying to sound diffident. "But frankly, your opinion will be more valuable to me for that reason.

I need the opinion of an unbiased stranger. How would you advise me?"

"Regarding your Sarah?" She looked tempted, but shook her head. "I couldn't. I have nothing to base an opinion on. I would be relying solely on intuition."

Malcolm held up one finger. "And rapport," he reminded her softly. "Do not forget that. I am inclined to respect your intuition. Tell me about my daughter."

She stared at him. "How intense you are," she said. Her voice shook a little. "It can't possibly matter that much—what a stranger thinks."

Her eyes were so clear. He felt as if he could look straight through them to the bottom of her soul, where he saw only the sweet, grave light of goodness. The notion was nonsensical, of course, but he could not shake it. What this unknown young woman thought, what she felt, *was* important. Somehow, it did matter. He felt it in his bones. If he told her so, however, she would probably think he was a lunatic. So he merely said, "Indulge me."

She took a deep breath, then looked away from him. "Very well," she said. "I will tell you what I think." Her gaze focused thoughtfully on Sarah, still absorbed in an incomprehensible game with her toys. Sarah was whispering and singing to herself, moving the dolls in a pattern that only she could decipher. Miss Whittaker did not appear to find this either disturbing or funny; the little smile that touched her lips was one of understanding. "I think Sarah is a highly imaginative child."

That was an understatement. "Yes, she is."

"Such children tend to be sensitive, yet difficult to discipline. I imagine that Sarah rarely follows orders and doesn't respond well to threats or punishment."

"That's true."

"On the other hand, an appeal to her emotions or reason will almost always have the desired effect."

"Right again."

He must have sounded amazed, for she laughed a little. "It's only logical. Imaginative children are skilled at putting themselves in another's place. If she behaves badly, ordering her to stop or punishing her may make matters worse. But I fancy that if you tell Sarah how her behavior *affects* you, she understands at once why you want her to stop—and stops, out of love for you."

Malcolm realized he had been holding his breath. He let it go. "Miss Whittaker, you have hit the nail squarely on the head."

She blushed. "I've only told you what anyone might have told you."

"How do you know so much about children?" He hoped it wasn't because she had a brood waiting for her at home. He'd assumed she was single, but, come to think of it, she hadn't been specific. He glanced at her hands. If she wore a ring, her gloves concealed it.

She caught his surreptitious glance and looked amused. "I don't know anything in particular about children. But people in general interest me, and children are people. What motivates them isn't much different than what motivates the rest of us, I should think." She tilted her head as if considering. "I don't believe I've changed much, simply by growing older. Have you? I think we are all, most of us, the same person throughout our lives. It is only the exterior that changes."

Now, there, she was wrong. He felt his jaw tightening and looked away from her, afraid that such an intuitive woman might read his thoughts in his eyes. "Some of us, I daresay, change very little," he said shortly. "Others are not so fortunate."

A tiny silence fell. She must have understood that she had touched a nerve in him, for she eventually said, with an attempt at lightness, "I dare not press the issue, since I have already told you what a headstrong child I was."

He gave himself a mental shake and smiled, grateful to her for breaking the awkward moment. "Still headstrong, are you? No, you need not answer that! At any rate, it seems you would advise me to sack Mrs. Thorpe."

She gave a choke of startled laughter. "Did I say that?"

"It's what you meant, I think. And I'm inclined to agree with you. Mrs. Thorpe's ways are unsuited to Sarah's temperament. She has spent several months attempting to instill obedience in my daughter through a system of strict orders and harsh punishment. She has not succeeded, and I am more certain every day that she will never succeed. It has reached the point where Mrs. Thorpe dislikes Sarah, even despises her. And Sarah is miserable."

"Poor lamb. Perhaps when she is older—"

"No." Malcolm rubbed his chin. "I think you are right that some people do not alter. I think Sarah will always be a dreamer. Not to the extent she now is, I hope, but I cannot imagine her ever embracing an organized, regimented kind of life."

Miss Whittaker nodded in agreement. "You should try to find someone more sympathetic. Clever children are often difficult to handle, but with the right approach they can be delightful. Someone more gentle, with a vivid imagination of her own, could easily turn Sarah's imaginativeness into an asset."

"Someone who feels a rapport with Sarah."

"That's right."

He looked at her. "Someone like you."

Her eyes widened, dilating in surprise—and alarm. His hand shot out and closed over hers, stopping her before she could speak. "Please. Do not say no. Hear me out."

Her eyes, Good Lord, her eyes. They were huge. And beautiful. Not that that had anything to do with it, but still . . . he couldn't let her get away.

Providence must have led him here, to this spot where he would meet her. Heaven may have forsaken Malcolm long ago, but surely, surely it watched over his little girl. He was meant to find Miss Whittaker. For Sarah.

Chapter Three

"You're mad," said Natalie faintly. "You know nothing about me."

Her response was automatic. What else could she say? It was crazy for him to ask such a thing. And it was even crazier for her to feel so tempted when he did! But his ice-blue eyes held hers, their intensity overwhelming. She had never encountered such mesmerizing eyes. She felt unable to look away.

"I know you are an honest, forthright, plainspoken woman, and God knows there is nothing more valuable on earth than that." His voice was deep and sure. And persuasive.

Persuasive? Ridiculous! Was she so hungry for approval that a few words of praise from a stranger could overcome her common sense?

But he wasn't done. "Your intelligence is obvious," he said. "You have the voice and manner of a lady of quality. You have a kind heart. And you like my Sarah." Emotion quivered in his voice. "I cannot tell you what that is worth to me. Miss Whittaker, I beg of you, consider my offer. Do me the courtesy of thinking it over. Do not dismiss it out of hand."

If he only knew. She gave a shaky little laugh. "I'm not dismissing it out of hand. That's what worries me." Hope flared in his eyes, and she shook her head, frowning. "I don't mean that I accept your offer. I cannot. The idea is preposterous."

She moved to pull her hand out from under his, but he seized it more strongly. "I haven't yet told you what it is."

"I assume you want me to accept a position as governess to your child. That's very flattering, I suppose—"

"Not flattering enough. There is a stigma attached to the label of governess. You may call yourself whatever you choose: companion or teacher or what-you-will. I want you to come and live with us, and your only duty will be to act as Sarah's companion and teacher. Not only for reading and drawing and French and such things; I want you to teach her whatever skills you think a gentlewoman needs. Dancing and comportment and the art of conversation. Everything. I am prepared to pay you handsomely, Miss Whittaker. You will have a suite of rooms—"

"Stop, stop." She felt a little dizzy. "You don't understand. I am not a governess."

"I beg your pardon." His gaze flicked down her person. "What are you?"

She opened her mouth to tell him what she was: a gentlewoman. Chatelaine of Crosby Hall; Mainstay of her family. But the words wouldn't come out.

What, in fact, was she? A nonentity, even in her own home. She wasn't the chatelaine of Crosby Hall, she was nothing but a spinster half sister—and fast dwindling into an aunt. Needed by nobody. Wanted by nobody. Soon her days would be spent dancing attendance on

Hector's infant, she had no doubt: *Let Natalie mind the baby. She has nothing better to do.*

No wonder this stranger's offer of employment had unexpectedly struck a chord. No wonder she longed, against all reason, to say yes. Hadn't she spent most of the morning dreaming of escape?

She pressed one hand to her brow, trembling a little. "I—I don't know how to answer you. I'm not alone in the world, if that's what you think. I don't need to earn my bread. I have a home. I have a family."

He looked disappointed. "A gaggle of younger siblings, I suppose, who all depend on you."

She had to smile. "Not quite. Two brothers—both younger than myself, but not by much. And as for depending on me . . . alas, the shoe is on the other foot." She sighed.

She should have known she couldn't slip that sigh past him. He quirked a brow and fixed her, again, with that keen and penetrating gaze. "Are you content with your lot, Miss Whittaker?"

She shrugged and looked away. "I lack for nothing," she said evasively.

"That's not the same thing," he said quietly.

Natalie looked down at her hands, clasped lightly in her lap. It was difficult to speak past the sudden constriction in her throat. "Whether I am content or not is entirely beside the point," she said. Her voice sounded strained but composed. "Most people—certainly most women—have little choice in such matters. We must bloom where we are planted."

She felt, rather than saw, his body lean forward beside her. His deep voice rumbled again, softly and much nearer to her. "Miss Whittaker, you do have a choice. I just offered you one."

Her eyes flew to his, startled. His face was nearer than she had guessed; disturbingly near. His eyes were very blue indeed, she thought, distracted. She could smell the sandalwood scent of his shaving soap. It drove whatever she had been about to say directly out of her brain. For some reason, her toes were curling. Gracious.

He didn't appear to guess the direction of her thoughts. Amusement lifted the corners of his mouth. "All I need do, it seems to me, is ensure that my offer is better than the life you currently lead. You have just given me hope that my task is not impossible."

"H-have I?"

He rubbed his chin and squinted at her, in the manner of a man sizing up a horse. "Let me see. What is the source of your discontent? I don't pretend to share your powers of intuition, but I wonder if I can deduce something about you from the information you have given me."

She tensed. This was a dangerous game. "Don't be absurd."

He leaned back in his chair, stretching out his long legs and crossing them lazily at the ankle. "No, no, it shouldn't be that difficult. Hmm. Two brothers, close in age to yourself. I have it! You fill the role of an unpaid housekeeper. Your brothers work you to death and take you for granted."

Natalie bit back a laugh. "Wrong." *Thank goodness.* "The elder of the two doesn't even live at home. He acts as secretary to the Earl of Stokesdown, so we seldom see him these days."

The gentleman looked impressed. "Stokesdown! He's a man of influence."

"Yes. We're very proud of Derek."

His eyes narrowed in thought once more. "Eldest son

of the house employed by a nobleman. Your father is still living, then. You didn't mention him."

"No." She hesitated. It went against the grain with her, to divulge the details of her family's peculiar situation. On the other hand, it wouldn't do to let him assume that her family had no property. He might think that she was, after all, a suitable candidate for a governess post.

"If you *must* know," she said stiffly, "Derek accepted a position with Lord Stokesdown because my father's estate passed to my youngest brother."

His brows flew up in an expression of surprise—and sympathy, she thought. "What a pity. Your father and Derek had a falling-out, I suppose, and the estate was not entailed."

"Wrong again," said Natalie, trying not to laugh. The game was rather fun after all. "The estate was entailed. But the eldest son did not inherit."

She watched him, mischief bubbling in her as she waited to see what he would make of that. But then she saw the doubt in his eyes. He had thought of a reason why the firstborn might not inherit. Oh, dear—she couldn't let him think what he was thinking. She blushed, holding up a warning finger. "If you are thinking that there was something *untoward* about Derek's birth, you are wrong yet again. So pray do not think it."

He looked at her very hard. "Miss Whittaker, I think you are making a May game of me."

"*Still* wrong! Astounding." She shook her head with mock severity. "Really, sir, I think you had better give over. You've taken shot after shot, and you've missed every time."

He threw up his hands in a gesture of defeat. "Very well. I give up. Now explain to me how an entailed estate could bypass the eldest legitimate son."

Her eyes twinkled. "It could, and did, because my great-grandfather had an amazing ability to hold a grudge—and eccentric ideas about how to exact revenge. He was the youngest son of a prominent family, and he loathed his eldest brother. Alas, the hateful eldest brother, in the way of great families, inherited everything, and Great-grandfather, as a younger son, was given nothing. So he went to India, made a fortune of his own, came home, purchased Crosby Hall, and set up a most peculiar entail. Crosby Hall always passes to the *youngest* legitimate son."

"Why, I've never heard of such a thing," he exclaimed. "It hardly sounds legal. In medieval times, I daresay the first-born son would eliminate his brothers one by one as they arrived."

"Yes, but Great-grandfather set up the entail during the Age of Enlightenment," said Natalie demurely. "So far, no male infants have met a mysterious end."

"You astonish me." He scratched his chin in bafflement. "So your unfortunate brother Derek must make his own way in the world."

"Yes. Having missed his chance to smother Hector in the cradle."

"I daresay he was a little young, at the time, to think of it. Did he not have an embittered uncle who might have assisted him in the endeavor?"

She choked. "No, alas. My father was the *only* son of his parents, so there was no help to be found in that quarter."

"And I suppose your mother could hardly be expected to act on Derek's behalf, under the circumstances."

Her smile faded. "No, but not for the reason you suppose," said Natalie softly. "My mother did not live to see her only son displaced."

He looked chagrined. "I am sorry," he said gently. "I should not joke about such things. I didn't know that you and Derek had lost your mother."

She inclined her head in acknowledgment. "Never mind. And you are right, of course. We should not joke about murdering Hector." Her mouth twitched mischievously. "Although I will admit that this is not the first time I have done so. Sometimes one simply *must* laugh. It seems to me that the more dire your circumstances, or the more wretched you are, the more you need it. Derek and I . . ." She halted in midsentence, vexed with herself. She had no business talking so freely to a man she had just met.

While she cast about for a new train of thought, he studied her again, compassion in his face. "I've done a poor job of unraveling your mysteries thus far, Miss Whittaker, but I feel disposed to take another stab at it," he said softly. His deep voice rumbled in his chest. "I have now deduced that you live at home with your younger brother. Your half brother. And I would bet that he has a wife, or a mother, or both."

"Both," she agreed reluctantly. Having told him so promptly when he was wrong, it was only fair to let him know when he was right.

"And I think you are fonder of your brother Derek than you are of—what was the name? Hector."

"Right again," she acknowledged, even more reluctantly. "Much fonder."

"Aha." He rubbed his hands together. "I think I have the picture now. Parents gone. Stepmother very much alive. Favorite brother far from home. Half brother uncomfortably near at hand."

She felt her cheeks burning and sat very straight in her chair. "My dear sir, I am not Cinderella."

"No, but Derek's departure from the family scene has isolated you. Circumstance has taken from you your closest ally, perhaps your only ally. I imagine you now live in a tense and hostile household, filled with people who . . ." He stopped and thought for a moment. "Resent you, perhaps? Yes, I think a young woman of intelligence, a woman with such quick and decided opinions, would encounter resentment from her stepmother or her sister-in-law—or both. Do they belittle you? I wonder. Do they quarrel with you outright, shout you down, and remind you that you are not the lady of the house? Or are they, perhaps, more subtle than that? I have known women who were highly skilled at making others miserable while appearing, outwardly, mild and sweet. Tell me, Miss Whittaker. Are your in-laws shrewish or simply mean?"

Natalie pressed her palms against her cheeks to cool her face. "Neither," she said unsteadily. "I have no complaints. I want for nothing. I am a very fortunate woman."

He straightened in his chair, then leaned forward, elbows on knees. "I am not persuaded," he said softly. "Try again."

She dropped her hands and looked away, willing her voice not to shake. "Nonsense. I've nothing to prove. You may believe me or not, as you choose."

He snapped his fingers; another idea had occurred to him. "A fortunate woman who wants for nothing! Now I have it. You live on the largesse of others. This would be an idyllic life for some, but not for you. You, Miss Whittaker, are a woman of ability. You are forced to hang on young Hector's sleeve—the brother of whom you are *not* fond—and you dislike it. You are strong and capable and intelligent and active. You pride yourself on accomplishments and hate being idle. Ergo, you are unhappy in your current situation. Your life lacks meaning. You feel . . . useless."

He had hit so near the mark this time that she did not dare to reply. All she could do was lift her chin and stare straight ahead, stubbornly refusing to meet his eyes.

"My dear Miss Whittaker." His voice was deep and rough. "I am offering you a supremely useful life. And independence, which I think you will prize nearly as much."

Independence. Heavens! He was right. *Independence.* What a lovely word. For a moment she imagined herself free of Hector and Mabel, earning a living on her own merits, her days filled with things to do and problems to solve. A reason to get out of bed every morning. A chance to see some part of Britain other than the parish she had lived in all her life.

She knew it was ridiculous to picture it that way—a governess's life was notoriously hard. But a tiny voice whispered to her that she, unlike the majority of governesses, would love it. Perhaps the women who hated that life had bad employers. Bad employers and, of course, nowhere else to go. Perhaps they weren't cut out for teaching. Perhaps they disliked their charges. Too many women became governesses out of necessity rather than choice. There were so few respectable options for a woman who did not marry . . . but Natalie had options. She could choose to be a governess on a whim, if she liked. *Why not?* If she found that it wasn't to her taste after all, she had somewhere else to go. She could always come back to Crosby Hall. And perhaps Hector and Mabel would respect her more. Perhaps they would learn to value her during her absence. Stranger things had happened.

Oh, but this was fantasy! She couldn't accept a governess position on a lark. She had no experience. She had no references. She wouldn't know where to begin. Besides, she didn't even know this man—or the child, for that matter. And what she had seen of them was hardly reassuring. The little girl was obviously eccentric, and the father might be dangerously unbalanced. What sort of man offered to hand his child into the keeping of a chance-met stranger? No. She had to decline.

She turned to tell him so . . . but when her eyes met his the words died on her lips, unspoken. There was stark need in his eyes. She saw a proud man, a man accustomed to command, humbling himself for the sake of a beloved daughter. She saw pain there, a torment deeper than anything she had experienced. There were depths to this man, facets she had not yet glimpsed but sensed nevertheless, a complexity of raw emotions held on a tight leash. She saw darkness and trouble and grief, and her heart went out to him.

He seemed to sense her compassion. All he said was "Please." His voice was hoarse with emotion. "Please help me."

Oh, dear. His words hit her where she was weakest. He needed her. How could she refuse?

She couldn't think straight when she looked at him. She tore her eyes away, but they fell on Sarah, still playing quietly in the corner of the room. Poor Sarah. Even in play, her pinched little face was too pale. Natalie remembered the sadness and fear she had seen flashes of. Surely Sarah displayed the confusion of a child who had lost her mother while still too young to understand it. She may have been punished, too, for reasons she did not understand or infractions she could not help. Could

Natalie wash her hands of Sarah—leave her to the harsh rule of Mrs. Thorpe?

Natalie closed her eyes in anguish. "What should I do?" she murmured to herself. "I can't agree to this. I can't possibly."

"Yes, you can."

She opened her eyes and threw the man a look of exasperation. "I've never done such a thing before. I'm not an impulsive person."

His smile was disarming. "I'm glad to hear it. I wouldn't like to lose you to the next needy family you encounter."

"I have no references," she warned him.

"No? Ah, well. You have an honest face."

She choked. "I'm not even particularly well educated. If you advertised, you might find someone who had attended one of the best schools. Or someone who had had a top-flight governess of her own."

"Such women rarely answer advertisements. They are generally too busy dining with dukes and dancing at Almack's."

She bit her lip, then went gamely on. "If you treat me shabbily or make me unhappy in any way, I shall not hesitate to give my notice."

"Then I must try very hard to treat you well."

She threw up her hands in despair. "Is there nothing I can say to make you see reason?"

He pretended to think for a moment, then shook his head with the appearance of regret. "I'm afraid not." His smile slipped out again. "Come, Miss Whittaker. Give me your hand on the bargain, and we'll work out the details later."

He stretched out his hand to her. It was a large hand, well kept. It looked strong and warm and confident. He had the long, lean fingers of a pianist. *Or a strangler,* she told herself sternly, trying desperately to remind herself how crazy this was. But it was no use. Her own hand, seeming to move of its own volition, reached out. As if in a trance, she placed her hand in his. Those long, strong fingers of his closed around it. For a moment she stared bemusedly at the sight of her hand in his, then lifted her eyes to his face.

A frisson of feeling shot through her—surprise and warmth and something half remembered, like a dream she had just woken from.

She should be frightened. Why wasn't she frightened? It felt right, being with him. It felt like . . . coming home.

A slow smile crept across her face. "When I was a little girl," she murmured, "my grandmother used to tell me that the stars control our destiny."

An answering smile softened his features. "It's a pretty thought."

"She said they dance in the heavens, charting the course of our lives here on earth. I always thought it was just a fairy story . . . but now I wonder."

He smiled outright. "Did the stars bring you to me, Miss Whittaker?"

She tilted her chin saucily. "I rather thought it was the other way round. They brought you to me. I've been here all my life." *Waiting.*

"You may be right." He seemed to realize, then, that he was still holding her hand. He dropped it hastily and rose from his chair, appearing disconcerted. "Pray excuse me for a moment. I must let Mrs. Thorpe know that her services are no longer needed."

She watched him depart, her thoughts in a whirl. What a strange encounter. She was glad, now, that she had not told him the rest of the story. Grandmama had told her that the stars, as they dance, pull on the heartstrings of mortals below. And that sometimes, when the celestial music swells, you can feel the tug of the dancing stars.

Natalie felt the tug.

She looked across the room at Sarah. Sarah had watched her papa leave the room and was now looking gravely toward Natalie, a question in her face.

She walked over to Sarah and knelt beside her. "Sarah dear," she said gently. "Would you like it if I were to teach you, instead of Mrs. Thorpe?"

Sarah's face lit with a joy that was almost blinding. She scrambled into Natalie's lap and buried her face in Natalie's shoulder, as if afraid to show her face. As if someone might steal the happiness from her if they saw it written on her features. "Yes, please," she whispered into Natalie's shoulder. "I would like it very much."

Natalie closed her arms around the tense and trembling child and surrendered to the stars. Let them lead. She would follow the dance as best she could, learning the steps as she went. The adventure would be well worth it.

Chapter Four

First came the sound of a sharp female voice, ranting in some distant room at an increasingly elevated pitch. One sentence floated down to the coffee room, crisp and clear: "Frankly, my lord, I'll be happy if I never see you or that wretched child again!"

My lord. Good heavens. Natalie, startled, suddenly realized she did not know her new employer's name. Somehow, incredibly, it had never come up.

She was distracted from these thoughts by the sound of a slammed door, followed by footsteps overhead. The footsteps had the brisk and noisy ring of well-shod feet carrying a furious human being, and they were interspersed with the unmistakable sound of drawers being opened and shut with unusual force. *Bang, bang, bang. Rasp-thump. Rasp-slam. Bang, bang, bang.* Mrs. Thorpe had obviously been sacked and was packing her bags in a flurry of outrage.

Natalie felt oddly guilty. Sarah, however, did not seem to attach any importance to the storm raging upstairs. Even when they heard the angry footsteps pounding down the wooden stairs perilously close to the coffee room—evidently Mrs. Thorpe, on her way out the front door—Sarah paid no attention. She sat happily beside Natalie on the floor, prattling away and showing Natalie her toys.

Mrs. Mumbles turned out to be a porcelain-headed doll with a human-hair wig, dressed in a lavishly detailed court gown. She must have cost a pretty penny when new, but she no longer looked her best. The golden hair had been diligently brushed and combed by Sarah's busy hands until there was little left of it, the court dress was looking much the worse for wear, and almost all the paint had been scrubbed from her china features.

Natalie hazarded a guess. "You call her Mrs. Mumbles because she hasn't any mouth?"

Sarah looked surprised. "No. I call her Mrs. Mumbles because that is her name." She handed Natalie a small block of crudely carved wood, sanded and polished as if it were a work of art. "And this is Blinky," she announced, beaming.

Blinky. Natalie turned it over in her hands, trying to distinguish what sort of animal it was supposed to be. A bear? A dog? A buffalo? Before she could decide, the door opened and her employer walked in. He looked at her with unruffled calm, as if hiring and firing governesses at a moment's notice was nothing out of the ordinary. Natalie scrambled to her feet.

The corners of his eyes crinkled with amusement. "Pray don't get up on my account. I consider you quite one of the family now."

She hoped she wasn't blushing again. "Hardly that, my lord," she said primly, folding her hands before her. He didn't bat an eye when she called him "my lord," so she must have heard Mrs. Thorpe aright. She abandoned her servile pose and looked accusingly at him. "It is 'my lord,' isn't it? Forgive me, but you haven't told me your name."

He looked startled. "Haven't I? How extraordinary."

"This entire morning has been extraordinary," she muttered, brushing the carpet dust from her skirt.

A smile of genuine pleasure lit his face for a moment. "So you accepted my offer of employment without even knowing who I am. I call that flattering."

"Do you? I call it rash."

"Whatever possessed you, Miss Whittaker?"

"Lunacy, I suppose."

"In that case, I hope you are mad enough to forgive the omission." He bowed. "Malcolm Chase, at your service."

She began a curtsy, but froze. *Chase.* She had heard Mrs. Thorpe call Sarah by that name, but it had not rung a bell. Until now.

"Chase," she repeated faintly. "Malcolm Chase. Not—not *Lord* Malcolm Chase? The Duke of Oldham's son?"

"The same. Are you acquainted with my family? We have a small property in the neighborhood—"

"My lord, I am your neighbor! My family's property adjoins your land."

He did not look at all perturbed. "Well, well. What a coincidence."

"Coincidence! It's a calamity." Natalie pressed one hand to her cheek, appalled. "I can't work for a neighbor."

He looked puzzled. "Why not?"

"Well, I—I—I don't know." She felt foolish, but only because she didn't know how to explain her dismay. "I suppose it won't matter, really, since you reside at your father's estate. That's in Lancashire, isn't it?"

"It is, but I no longer reside there. I reside here."

She stared at him. "Here? In this inn?"

"No, I mean Larkspur. I have come to take possession of my estate. Larkspur traditionally houses the second sons of my family, and I am my father's second son." When she continued to stare at him, nonplussed, he added patiently, "Larkspur, Miss Whittaker. The property that adjoins your family's."

"Yes, yes, I know Larkspur well, but—but no one has lived there for years! Oh, heavens. Why now? I don't believe I've ever seen a Chase at Larkspur."

His lips twitched. "Not a very effusive welcome, I must say."

"Well, for pity's sake!" She placed her hands on her hips, exasperated. "It's not that the neighborhood won't be glad to see you, for they will. And I'm very pleased to make your acquaintance at last. But, Lord Malcolm—you have just *employed* me!"

"What's wrong with that?"

"Everything! I never would have agreed to such a mad bargain had I known who you were—and that you meant to make your home here!"

His brows snapped together in a swift frown. "Miss Whittaker, I hope you do not mean to break your word."

Natalie stared helplessly at him. "Of course not," she said lamely, then rallied. "There is no question of my breaking my word. You employed me under false pretenses, my lord."

"Now, see here—"

"False pretenses," she repeated firmly. "I had thought you would take me somewhere far away. I assumed you must live at a great distance."

His brows lifted in incredulity. "I never said anything to make you think so."

"Well, no, you did not, but when one encounters a

stranger in the local inn, one assumes that the stranger is en route from one place to another! The business of an inn, in case you were not aware, is to temporarily house persons who live at some distance *from* the inn. It naturally did not occur to me that you might, in point of fact, be my nearest neighbor!" Her eyes narrowed. "In fact, sir, why *are* you stopping at the inn, if you truly have a house nearby?"

"Because the house is not ready for me, of course." His frown was formidable. "Sarah and I are dining here so that the caretakers need not trouble themselves putting a meal together for us. We will, however, spend the night at Larkspur."

"You did not send ahead to have the house made ready? Gracious! You must have come here on the spur of the moment."

His frown darkened. "If I did, Miss Whittaker, what is that to you?"

"Why, nothing. I am in a poor position to criticize anyone for behaving impulsively." She sank onto the nearest chair, shaking her head in despair. "This is the stuff of nightmare."

"I don't know why it should be," he said stiffly. "What possible difference can it make to you where I live? I would think that taking you far from your home would be an inconvenience, not the other way round."

Men. Why couldn't they perceive the obvious? Natalie shot him a darkling glance. "Very well," she grumbled. "I will explain." Her reasons did not cast her in a flattering light, but she supposed she had to give them. She took a deep breath.

"I was looking forward, in a perverse sort of way, to telling my detestable brother that I preferred life as a governess to life beneath his roof. But that was when I was picturing a hasty exit directly after the conversation." She felt her cheeks reddening. "And an immediate departure for some unknown, but distant, destination."

"Ah." He rubbed his chin in a rueful manner. "I see. You are not expecting your family to greet the news of your employment with enthusiasm."

"Naturally not. And the neighborhood will be scarcely less scandalized. My conduct will be viewed, and rightly so, as inexplicable—*and* as a shocking indictment of Hector and Mabel. You know as well as I do that only the direst circumstances force a gently born lady from her home."

Something sly gleamed in his shadowed blue eyes. "I rather fancy that the neighborhood's ill opinion of Hector and—Mabel, was it?—distresses you not at all."

"You're right," Natalie admitted, trying not to laugh. "It doesn't. But you are asking me to stay in the parish while disapproval rains down upon *me*. I had rather leave the neighborhood, quite frankly, and let them all exclaim and shake their heads while I am miles away." She bit her lip. "It's all very well for you to chuckle at my cowardice—"

"I wouldn't dare."

"Well, whatever you are laughing at, you may stop," said Natalie tartly. "This situation is deadly serious, sir, for you as well as for me. You have just sacked Mrs. Thorpe. I suggest you rehire her at once."

If her purpose was to nip his amusement in the bud, she succeeded. The frown settled back on his features immediately. It struck her that a grim expression appeared more at home on his face than the lurking smile had.

She felt a set of small fingers close on the edge of her sleeve. Natalie looked down into the anxious face of

Sarah. "Mrs. Thorpe is gone," said Sarah plaintively. "I heard her go. Is she coming back?"

Oh, dear. Natalie hesitated, at a loss, and Lord Malcolm's deep voice rumbled into the breach. "Mrs. Thorpe is not coming back, little one. I doubt if I could call her back now even if I wanted to. I didn't ask where she was headed."

"She can't have gone far," said Natalie stubbornly. "I won't be boxed into a corner by such a trifle."

Sarah's hand tightened. "Aren't you staying after all?"

Natalie glanced back down at Sarah. Her gray-green eyes were huge in her pale, pinched face. The child's whisper was so woebegone, her expression so pleading, Natalie could scarcely bear to disappoint her. "Oh, dear," she murmured ruefully, this time aloud. She placed one hand on Sarah's hair and gently stroked the silky strands of pale brown, baby-fine beneath her touch. "Sarah, sweetheart, it's not that I don't want to stay with you. I can't."

Sarah looked hurt. "Why not?"

Natalie sighed. "Your papa will explain it to you."

"No, he won't," said Sarah's papa. "For he doesn't understand it himself."

"Sir, if you would but think for a moment—"

"You were prepared to leave your home and take up residence with strangers in an unknown place. Now you find you need only move next door, and you suddenly wish to renege. I confess, I do not understand it. You can stay here among your friends and family, close to everything you know and love. You hardly need bother with packing, let alone traveling. My dear Miss Whittaker, this is an advantage, not a disadvantage—"

She held up one hand to stop him. "Hold a moment. It

has just now occurred to me . . . Merciful heavens! Will the household consist of only you and your daughter?"

"Certainly. A small household, but—"

"A bachelor household!"

He looked uncomfortable. "I suppose so," he admitted grudgingly. "If you call a widower a bachelor."

Natalie covered her eyes with her hands and moaned.

"This is pure foolishness." Lord Malcolm's voice was crisp with exasperation. "Do you think I would expose my little daughter to—" He stopped midsentence. "Mine will be a respectable household," he finished grimly. "No one will gossip about you."

She dropped her hands to glare at him. "Of course they will gossip. About both of us. For heaven's sake, your sudden return to Larkspur will cause a sensation! It will be the main topic of conversation here for weeks. If your arrival coincides with my moving in with you, I shudder to think what conclusions will be drawn."

He looked haughtily at her. "Does it matter what people say? Let them talk. We will know the truth."

She flushed. "Spoken like a duke's son! I daresay it needn't matter, to you."

"Do you think being born among the aristocracy shields one from gossip?" His voice sharpened. "Quite the opposite, I assure you. The minutia of our daily life is endlessly fascinating to others, for reasons that quite escape me. I often feel that I live beneath a microscope. One learns to ignore it."

"People may *talk* about you—in fact, I know they do; I am not an imbecile. But their criticism has no real effect. At least, not on the male members of the aristocracy. I daresay it may damage the ladies from time to time." She lifted her chin at him. "You don't feel the evil effects of gossip, my lord, because you are a man."

His eyes narrowed. "I am a man who cares about upright conduct."

"But not appearances?"

"No." His nostrils flared with scorn. "I have known too many people, Miss Whittaker, who cared *only* for appearances. I know how deceptive appearances can be."

"I don't care only for appearances!" she cried, stung.

"You shouldn't care for them at all. God will judge us, Miss Whittaker, not our neighbors."

She eyed him askance. "You obviously haven't met Mrs. Beasley."

A glint of laughter returned to his eyes. "Certainly I have. There's one in every parish. But I promise you, Miss Whittaker, the Mrs. Beasleys of the world need not concern us."

Natalie had to look away; the laughter lurking in his voice tempted her, against all reason, to smile. "I wish that were true." She sighed and shook her head. "I confess, I don't know what to do." She was suddenly aware of Sarah, leaning against her knee and regarding her gravely. The child had been listening intently, trying to follow the twists and turns of the adults' conversation.

It did seem cowardly, to abandon and disappoint Sarah just because she was afraid of what people might say.

Lord Malcolm seemed to sense her wavering. She heard his booted feet cross the floor, and suddenly, to her surprise, he knelt beside her chair. Now she had two faces to contend with, both too near to escape, and both focused on winning her over. Lord Malcolm slipped one arm around Sarah. The little girl leaned back against his broad chest, but her solemn gaze was still fixed on Natalie. The tableau of entreaty they made tugged anew at

Natalie's heart. She felt her defenses crumbling. "Oh, unfair," she said, rueful laughter in her voice.

Lord Malcolm smiled at her over Sarah's head. "We need you," he said softly. "Don't we, Sarah?"

Sarah nodded obediently.

"Come, now, Miss Whittaker. You promised to help us. And I know you won't go back on your word."

"Oh, that's not it at all—"

"What would your grandmother say?" He almost winked at her. "Remember the stars."

"The *stars*?"

"Terrible things happen to those who defy the stars. Haven't you read your Shakespeare?" He shook his head with mock solemnity. "Really, Miss Whittaker, I think you can hardly say no."

A reluctant smile tugged at her mouth. She liked Lord Malcolm. And she liked Sarah. And, come to think of it, she didn't like Hector and Mabel.

Would her choice really come down to that? Was it really so simple?

An irresistible vision flashed into her mind, one of bidding Hector and Mabel farewell. Even if she only moved as far as next door, she would be out from under their roof. She wouldn't hear their bickering. She wouldn't be the constant target of their petty digs and snide remarks. It would almost be worth it just to know she wouldn't have to *dine* with them every day. And, of course, if anything untoward occurred at Larkspur, she could dash home again in the twinkling of a bedpost. She would be quite safe. Lord Malcolm was right. There were some advantages to his living in the neighborhood.

"Look, Papa." Sarah pointed at Natalie, pleasure lighting her face. "She's going to say yes."

Natalie rolled her eyes, but laughed. "I suppose I am. But only because I am too lily-livered to defy the stars."

"Very wise," said Lord Malcolm approvingly. "We thank you—Sarah, the stars, and I."

Not long after, Natalie was tramping briskly back across the fields. Amazing, she thought, what a difference a few hours could make. The breeze had ushered in a few swiftly scudding clouds and the temperature had dropped dramatically. The landscape, the colors, the smell of the air, all the world seemed fresh and new. The cold wind spanked color into her cheeks and lifted her spirits.

Lord Malcolm had offered the use of his carriage but Natalie had declined it, saying she needed the walk in order to compose her thoughts and plan what she would say to Hector and Mabel. Now that she was involved in that exhilarating task, an irrepressible smile played across her face. She only wished Derek were home to witness her rebellion. She knew he would egg her on; he always did when she was at her most outrageous.

She was certainly at her most outrageous today. She could remember a dozen minor mutinies in her girlhood, but nothing to equal this colossal nose-thumbing.

Natalie searched her soul and waited for a guilty feeling to creep up on her. It didn't. Her heart was light as a feather. She went over, in her mind, all the reasons why she should feel alarm at the prospect of becoming Sarah's governess. Alarm failed to surface. She felt *good* about this decision, wholehearted and unafraid. Had she run mad? Possibly, but even that bogey failed to frighten her. It seemed that all her objections, all her hesitations, all her resistance to the idea had poured out in her conversation with Lord Malcolm. She had none left.

She did like Lord Malcolm. *And* Sarah, she amended hastily. She liked them both. How well did one really need to know a person before deciding that? Sometimes one just knew. After all, she had disliked Mabel within a few hours of making her acquaintance. And her instincts had certainly been right on that one.

Farewell, Mabel. Fare thee well, Hector. She could hardly wait to tell them.

She entered the house giddy with pleasurable anticipation, flung her hat onto the peg in the kitchen passage, and, humming under her breath, marched up the stairs to beard the dragons in their lair.

Chapter Five

"No," said Hector flatly. He crossed his arms over his thin chest for emphasis. "You can't."

Natalie's pleasant smile did not waver. "On the contrary, I can. I am joining the Chase family at Larkspur directly after dinner."

My, it felt good to defy them. She had found Hector drinking tea with Mabel in her morning room, and had simply walked in and told them. Their tea had grown cold while they listened, apparently in shock, to Natalie's brief, but pithy, tale. Neither had said a word until she finished her announcement and rose to leave. She paused now, one hand on the doorknob. She had seldom felt so powerful. "If you need me, Hector, I will be in my rooms." Her smile broadened. "Packing."

"Wait a moment!" Hector rose, his expression turning ugly. "I'm still the head of this family. You will listen to what I have to say."

Mabel picked pettishly at the fringe of her shawl. "Let her go, Hector. She may shock the world if she wishes; it's all one to us. I'm sure we do not care one way or the other what Natalie chooses to do."

"I care." Hector's nostrils flared with anger. "It will

reflect on me. On you, too, if that's all that matters to you. People will say we drove her to it."

"They won't say that of *me*. Why, I only met her a few weeks ago."

"That's why they'll blame you," said Hector rudely. "It'll look as if everything was fine at Crosby Hall until *you* arrived on the scene. Which it jolly well was."

Natalie almost laughed aloud. "I assure you, Hector, Mabel is no more odious to me than you are. And I'll be happy to tell people that, if you like."

"Thank you," said Hector sarcastically. "But it won't be necessary. You aren't leaving this house to take a governess position, and that's my final word on the subject."

It was not a tone of voice that Natalie cared to hear, especially from Hector. Anger shot through her. Her hand left the doorknob. "Are you threatening me?" she scoffed. "With what?" She stepped back into the room to face him down. "My dear Hector, I am not your chattel. You have no power over me. I am of age and may do as I please. It's not your concern."

Hector's face was turning an interesting shade of purplish red. "No you can't, and yes it is," he spluttered. "I am the *head* of the *family*."

"You are not the Grand Turk! What will you do? Cut off my pin money? Remove me from your will? I'm very sure my name does not appear there, at any rate! Or will you take away the pittance Papa left me?"

"Do you think I can't do that? You're wrong. I can."

"You are welcome to try," she replied cordially. "Because I don't care if you do. I shall earn enough in a twelvemonth to replace every penny of my meager inheritance. It will be worth it to me, *well* worth it, to be out from under your mean little thumb. There's nothing you can do or say to stop me."

Victory surged through her in a heady rush. Is this what men felt in battle? No wonder they were forever starting wars. There was nothing like it—provided you were winning. Mabel's eyes were round with angry astonishment, and Hector's glittered like obsidian, hard and black. Frankly, after all they had put her through, it was a pleasure to see.

Natalie was almost to the door again when Hector's flat voice stopped her once more.

"There's Derek."

A frisson of apprehension shivered through her, but she swiftly quelled it. Derek would understand. He always understood. And he always stood by her, through thick and thin. She lifted her chin scornfully. "A fig for that! Derek will not interfere, if that's what you think. He certainly won't side with you against me. And by the time you get word to him, I will be entrenched in my new life."

She did not like the calculated look that had crept onto Hector's face. She had liked his flustered rage better. He still looked angry, but now he had a cat-at-the-creampot look about him. A cunning little smile curled his mouth. "I am referring, sister dear, to the fact that your purse strings are not the only purse strings I control. You may choose to spurn what I give you, but Derek cannot afford to."

She cocked her head, puzzled. This didn't smell right. "What do you mean? What do Derek's purse strings have to do with it?"

"If you do not follow my orders, Natalie, I will cut off Derek's allowance as well as yours."

She stared at him. His audacity fairly took her breath away. Had he punched her in the stomach, she could scarcely have felt more stunned. But he couldn't mean it. He must be bluffing. It made no sense.

She forced herself to take a breath, then spoke. "I do not understand. Are you joking? Derek has done nothing to you. He doesn't even know what my plans are. Why would you do such a ghastly thing?"

Hector's smile grew even oilier. "Because it is the best way to control you."

The full import of Hector's villainy struck her, sickening her. "You *worm*." Her voice quivered with emotion. "You wouldn't dare."

He folded his arms across his chest again, grinning. "Why wouldn't I?"

"It's monstrous! You will not stoop so low."

His grin vanished, and his eyes narrowed. "Try me," he snarled. "If you leave this house, Natalie, I will stop Derek's allowance. And not just until you return. I will stop it for good."

So much for her short-lived victory. Natalie curled her hands into fists, trying to stop their trembling. She did not doubt for a moment that Hector would do it. This was just the sort of underhanded scheme he prided himself on. He had always been a devious child, forever pitting members of the household against each other to his own advantage. "Derek will take you to the courts if you do," she said defiantly. Even in her own ears, the threat sounded hollow. "And he will win."

"He might win in Chancery Court—eventually. How many years will it take, do you think?" Hector pretended to ponder the question, rubbing his chin.

"You are hateful," she exclaimed. "Despicable. You know his income from Lord Stokesdown is inadequate. What sort of man would beggar his brother to punish his sister? Don't you care what people would say of you?"

Hector placed his fists on the low back of a chair and leaned forward, almost hissing with fury. "No more than you do, apparently. For I might ask the same of you! Don't you know what people will say of *you,* if you leave my roof unmarried? Don't you care?"

Mabel chimed in from the sofa. "Natalie, it just isn't done. Spinsters don't leave the family home. Not respectable spinsters, at any rate."

"Nonsense," said Natalie crisply. "There's nothing disreputable about becoming a governess. The way you two are carrying on, anyone would think I was eloping, or running off to join the circus."

"You might as well be." Mabel looked smug. "You may not be of noble birth, but you are hardly a member of the servant class! A gentlewoman can't reside with a single man unless he is in his dotage, and even then, people will gossip about her. Besides, even if it were respectable—which it isn't!—it's extremely odd. Nobody *chooses* to be a governess. Hector's right; people will talk."

"They won't talk, because Natalie isn't going anywhere. Don't push me, Natalie. I'll cut Derek off with a shilling."

The feeling of power was draining completely out of her. Natalie stared helplessly at Hector, trying to think. How could she reason with him? She couldn't. And she would not beg. Either tactic would be useless; she knew Hector well enough to be certain of that.

Her eyes narrowed as an idea occurred to her: a breathtaking, masterful idea. "What is Derek's allowance?" she asked slowly. "How much do you give him?"

Hector seemed about to answer her but stopped himself. "Why?" he asked, his voice cold with suspicion.

"Just tell me. You know I can look it up in Papa's will."

"You don't have a copy of Papa's will. And besides, it wasn't a specific amount. He left it all to my discretion—which is why Derek would have to drag the matter through Chancery Court if I changed my mind and gave him nothing."

"Are you going to tell me?"

"No, dear sister, I am not." Hector's cat-at-the-creampot look returned. "Why don't you write Derek and ask him?"

"Very well, I will," said Natalie defiantly.

Hector's mouth stretched in an ugly grin. "Do you think you can make it up to him out of your wages?"

"Sneer away, Hector. I know you think I won't be able to, but you're wrong." Lord Malcolm's words rang in her memory: *I am prepared to pay you handsomely.* She was confident that whatever Hector gave Derek every quarter day, it couldn't be much. Hector would begrudge every penny. And Natalie was used to doing without. What would she do with her "handsome" salary? Why, she'd give it to Derek, to add to what Lord Stokesdown paid him. Soon they would *both* be free of Hector.

So why was Hector still smiling that nasty smile?

A stifled giggle from Mabel caught her attention. "What is so amusing?" demanded Natalie.

"You are," said Mabel snidely. "Fancying you can pay Derek's stipend."

"Why? Is it such a princely sum? I can't imagine Hector parting with anything more than a token amount—especially since Derek has joined Lord Stokesdown's household."

"It's not the *amount,* silly."

"Hush, Mabel," ordered Hector. "Let her find out for herself." He grinned again. "I daresay it will occur to her when she sits down to frame her letter."

Natalie looked from one to the other. They seemed to be sharing a nasty, funny little secret. She was too angry to care. "I don't know what you are talking about," she said, disgusted. "But I can hardly wait to be rid of you both. I'm going upstairs to pack."

She slammed out of the room. The instant the door closed behind her, it hit her; she knew why Hector and Mabel had been sniggering. She couldn't pay Derek's stipend. Not because she wouldn't have the means, but because *Derek wouldn't let her.* Derek would starve rather than take her wages from her.

Just as Hector had suggested, she tried to mentally frame the letter she would write Derek, and failed. If Derek suspected her purpose, there were no words she could employ that would convince him to tell her what Hector gave him every quarter day. Accepting a son's portion from his father's estate was one thing. Accepting largesse from a sister was quite another. And if that sister were working as a governess to *earn* the money she gave him . . . ? Oh, no, impossible.

But she would find a way. She *must* find a way. She couldn't let Hector win.

Fighting back angry tears, Natalie started for the stairs. A tall, rawboned figure faced her on the landing, looking at Natalie over the tops of her spectacles. Natalie sighed. There was no point in explaining to Nurse what was wrong; she would already know everything. Nurse always knew everything. When they were children, Natalie and the boys used to think her omniscient. Now they realized she simply listened at doors—

though none of them would ever dare accuse her of such a thing.

"Well?" said Natalie challengingly. She straightened her spine and dashed the tears defiantly from her cheeks.

"Hmpf." Nurse managed to look severe and kind at the same time. "Look at you, thrown into high fidgets by that boy's antics. Ought to know better by now, Natalie. Shouldn't give him the satisfaction of seein' you upset."

"I shan't for much longer." She pushed past Nurse and started up the stairs. "I've accepted a position at Larkspur."

She heard Nurse's tread, surprisingly heavy for such a thin woman, following up the stairs behind her. "I know you have," said Nurse.

Natalie knew that tone. She rounded on her at the next landing, taking advantage of the extra height her stairtop position afforded. "I hope you don't mean to take Hector's side in this," she said accusingly.

Nurse looked up at her former charge, no more intimidated by Natalie's challenge than she was by her advancing years. The look on Nurse's face was exactly the same as if Natalie were four years old and had been caught sneaking jam from the jampot.

"I mean to look out for you," she said sternly. "Just as I always have. While there's breath in my body, Natalie Whittaker, I can't stand by and let you run headlong into danger. Don't ask it of me."

"Danger! That's absurd." Frowning, Natalie swept into her bedchamber and opened her clothespress. She would *not* be deterred. Not even by Nurse, on whose judgment she usually relied.

"There are all kinds and conditions of danger, and well you know it." Nurse stood in the doorway, arms akimbo. "At the very least, you're putting your reputation in danger. Living in sin! Or as close to it as makes no odds. What would your dear mother say?"

"I'm sure I don't know. And neither, by the way, do you." Natalie pulled several frocks out of the clothespress and tossed them onto her bed. "Do I own a valise? I can't bear to ask Mabel for the loan of her trunks."

"Natalie, child." Nurse's voice was uncharacteristically gentle. "You've been such a brave lass, dearie. Don't think I haven't noticed. The way those two treat you would try the patience of a saint. I don't blame you for wanting to run away. But you mustn't do something you know you will regret."

Natalie stopped packing. She collapsed onto the low stool at her dressing table, burying her face in her hands. "It's been ghastly," she said tiredly. "You don't know the half of it."

"I've eyes in my head." Some of the tartness returned to Nurse's voice. "And ears as well. Come! Sit up and tell me. What really happened this morning?"

Natalie told her. By the time she finished her tale, Nurse was sitting on the window seat, looking inscrutable. It was the expression she donned when thinking hard.

"Well?" said Natalie nervously. Nurse's opinion truly did matter to her. "I can't disappoint little Sarah. And Lord Malcolm has dismissed Mrs. Thorpe. It would be unconscionable for me to abandon them now."

Nurse still said nothing.

"I've given my word," added Natalie, with a touch of desperation.

Nurse shot a look at her that caused her to hold her tongue. "You want me to tell you you've done the right thing. Well, I can't say you have, and I can't say you haven't. Time will tell."

Relief flooded Natalie's heart. "Then at least you agree that I must go."

"Hmpf. I agree that you can't abandon them, after giving your word." Nurse gave a single brisk nod of decision. "I'll go."

"What?" Natalie's eyes widened in surprise.

Nurse rose and shook out her skirts. "I'll go to Larkspur and take care of wee Sarah."

Natalie gave an incoherent cry of gladness. "Oh, that's famous! *Dear* Nurse!" She leaped up and impulsively embraced her old friend. "No one will gossip about me if you are there. And I did hate to leave you behind at Crosby Hall. It can't be pleasant for you here, even with the baby coming."

Nurse's bony shoulders were unresponsive. "You are staying here, Natalie. And I won't hear any argument about it, so you may save your breath. You are staying at Crosby Hall, and I will go to Larkspur."

Natalie froze in horror. "No! You can't. You can't leave me here! Nurse—dear Nurse—you're my only ally! Mabel's dismissed all the familiar faces. You're the only friend she's left me. Crosby Hall would be insupportable without you."

"You should'a thought o'that before runnin' amok, makin' promises you can't keep," scolded Nurse. Her speech always lost a little polish when she was agitated. "Tsk! You know you can't leave your home to move next door with a bachelor. I never heard the like! And costin' Derek's allowance, too. You can't do it, child."

It was not to be expected that Natalie would acquiesce without a struggle. She argued and pleaded and ranted . . . in vain, however, since even Natalie had to acknowledge the good sense of Nurse's plan. Natalie herself had balked at the idea of taking up residence in a bachelor household, as Nurse patiently reminded her. Well, she had been right to feel that there was something scandalous about it. There *was* something scandalous about it.

In the end, Natalie buried her head in Nurse's skirts and wept like a thwarted child, then sat up resolutely and scrubbed her face with her handkerchief. "You're right," she said glumly. "As usual."

Nurse patted her kindly on the shoulder. "Ah, well. I knew you'd see the sense of it. No, don't apologize for cryin'—you're only human, dearie, and you've had much to bear these latter days."

Natalie gave a disconsolate sniff. "The irony is that in trying to escape I've pulled the chains tighter. I'm in a worse fix now than I was before. I not only have to face life with Hector and Mabel; I have to face it without you."

"Pooh! I'll be just the other side of the brook. You can wave to me from your window."

Natalie chuckled, then sighed. "Small comfort. And, oh, dear—what will Lord Malcolm say?"

"Daresay we'll find out soon enough." Nurse gave her a final pat, then rose. "Well! I'm off to do my packin'." She looked down at Natalie, her eyes twinkling behind her spectacles. "Shall I ask Cook to send up a couple of trays for us?"

"Yes, indeed," said Natalie fervently. "I'm famished. And I couldn't bear to dine with Hector and Mabel. Not tonight."

After Nurse had gone, Natalie wearily rose and returned her garments to the clothespress. It did seem hard, to lose her only companion through sheer stupidity. On the other hand, she supposed she must be glad that Nurse was willing to bail her out, leaving to take up residence at Larkspur and care for a child she had never even met. Her no-nonsense willingness to save Natalie's face spoke volumes for her loyalty.

But what *would* Lord Malcolm say?

Chapter Six

Sarah clung tightly to his hand as they stepped into the foyer. Light streamed through the tall windows on either side of the door behind them, firing the single chandelier with dancing radiance overhead. The oncoming sunset flushed the cream-colored walls with a mellow, pinkish glow. They seemed to be stepping into a cloud of roseate, reflected light shot with sparkles. It made a lovely welcome, in Malcolm's opinion. He looked about him with pleasure.

He had seen Larkspur only once before, when he had been not much older than Sarah was now. His memory of the place was sketchy. As a boy, the entrance had not impressed him. As a man, it did. He liked the clean lines, the pristine austerity, and the chapellike effect of the streaming light. He hoped Sarah's silence was not due to disappointment. She had lived all her short life at her grandfather's ducal palace, and might have expected her new home to have a similar magnificence. Larkspur was elegant, but built on a much smaller scale.

He glanced down at his daughter. She was staring solemnly up at the ceiling. When he looked at her, she lifted the hand that was not clutching his and pointed at the chandelier. "Fairy lights," she whispered.

His gaze followed her pointing finger. He had to admit that when you squinted, the sunlight caught in the dangling crystals seemed to take on a life of its own. With a little imagination, one could picture fairies hovering overhead. "Very pretty," he agreed.

A discreet cough drew his attention back to the long-suffering caretakers. The Howatches stood before him in an attitude compounded of nervous apology, exhaustion, and resentment. Mrs. Howatch, anxiously watching his expression, broke into speech. "I did hope to have things just so, my lord, when you took possession. I'm sorry for the state the house is in—under holland covers, mostly, and everything at sixes and sevens. But the bedchambers have been set to rights."

"That's all I require at present," said Malcolm mildly. "I've put you to a great deal of trouble, arriving on such short notice."

Howatch looked embarrassed. "It's your house, my lord," he said gruffly. "Ought to be able to arrive on short notice if you choose."

"Shall I show you round the house, sir? Or would you rather I merely took you upstairs?"

It seemed clear that Mrs. Howatch would prefer the latter. Malcolm had no objection. But as they were about to begin the climb, they were interrupted by the unmistakable sound of another set of wheels coming up the graveled drive.

The caretakers' gaze shifted in surprise from Malcolm to the windows behind him. He turned and had an excellent view of Miss Whittaker driving a pony cart toward his house. His spirits lifted at the sight. He had been half afraid that she would change her mind, but the back of

the cart contained a neat stack of bandboxes, a Glaston-
bury bag, and a small trunk. So Miss Whittaker was
staying. Thank God.

He was startled, however—and a little taken aback—
by how prosperous Miss Whittaker looked. Gone were
the battered hat and mud-flecked round gown. She was
wearing a lightweight pelisse of what appeared to be
silk, and her nut-brown curls had been prettily arranged
and topped with a rather fetching little hat. It sat at a
dashing angle and sported a feather dyed to match the
pelisse. Beside her was a gaunt woman of indeterminate
age, clutching a reticule in her lap. This woman looked
to be a maid or some other sort of trusted personal servant. Her presence at Miss Whittaker's elbow added to
the general impression that Miss Whittaker was a
woman who employed others, rather than a woman who
was, herself, available for employment.

For the first time, Malcolm felt a few qualms about
what he had done. Miss Whittaker had told him she had
a family—she had even told him that her family owned
an estate of some sort—but the import of her words had
not struck him until now. He had let her windblown appearance, the way she was dressed, and the fact that
she was walking about unaccompanied, persuade him
that she had exaggerated her station in life. He had assumed that, at the very least, the Whittakers must have
fallen upon hard times. But the pony cart looked stylish
and well maintained . . . and so, in fact, did Miss Whittaker. His initial impression must have been flat-out
wrong. She looked to be exactly what she had told him
she was.

Mrs. Howatch, with a barely audible grumble, vanished to parts unknown while her husband moved to
greet the arrivals. Bemused, Malcolm watched as Miss

Whittaker pulled the pony cart to a neat halt, handed the reins to Howatch, and allowed herself to be handed down. She then floored him with that devastating smile of hers. It looked even better topped with the well-combed curls and natty hat.

"How do you do?" she said cordially. "Shall I go away again? It seems you have only just arrived."

"We have, but we are very glad to see you. Your timing is impeccable." He strolled toward her, Sarah's hand still clutching his. "I would offer you tea, but I've no idea whether there's any tea in the house. Howatch? I'm sure I may rely on you."

"Aye," said Howatch gruffly. "There's tea. I'll speak to the missus."

Malcolm reached to shake Miss Whittaker's hand. "Welcome to Larkspur," he said, remembering to smile. "I hope you'll be very comfortable here."

Miss Whittaker blushed and pulled her hand quickly away. "Thank you, but I'm afraid I must— That is, I think it only fair to tell you—"

"Come in, come in. Both of you," he added, since the servant accompanying Miss Whittaker showed no sign of following Howatch.

"Oh!" said Miss Whittaker nervously. "My lord, may I present—" She gulped and waved a hand to indicate her companion. "My lord, this is Mrs. Bigalow. She was my nurse."

Mrs. Bigalow dropped a curtsy. He noticed that her eyes, sharp with appraisal, were on Sarah. Malcolm felt his hackles rise; something was going awry. He felt it in his extremely reliable bones. "How do you do?" he said grimly.

Miss Whittaker bent down to Sarah's eye level. "Sarah," she said gently, "this lady was my nurse, once upon a time. I have brought her here to make your acquaintance."

Sarah studied Mrs. Bigalow, then offered a tiny curtsy. "How do you do?" she said, with solemn courtesy. "My name is Sarah."

Mrs. Bigalow nodded, kindness glinting in her eyes. "I'm pleased to meet you, Sarah." Her voice was nearly as gruff as Howatch's. "Miss Whittaker tells me you helped her search for her lost kitten."

"But we didn't find her," said Sarah, her regretful demeanor as serious as if they were discussing a real kitten instead of an imaginary one. "I'm frightfully sorry."

"Hmpf. I daresay she'll turn up," said Mrs. Bigalow. "That Clara was always underfoot when Natalie was your age. Miss Whittaker, I *should* say."

Natalie. Her name was Natalie. Despite his increasing sense of foreboding, Malcolm felt a tiny rush of pleasure at learning Miss Whittaker's given name. It suited her—feminine, but unusual. There was nothing commonplace about Miss Whittaker. He should have known she wouldn't be a Jane or an Anne.

Natalie was smiling, her attention on Sarah. "It's a wonder Clara survived my childhood," she remarked. "People were forever stepping on her."

Mrs. Bigalow's lips twitched. "And why not? Pesky creature was invisible."

"Not to me," said Natalie indignantly. "I saw Clara very clearly. And I fancy Sarah will see her, too—if we ever find her."

For a moment, Sarah looked a little lost. She peered anxiously up at Natalie. "Miss Whittaker, she's an imaginary kitten, is she not?"

Natalie's swift smile returned. "Yes, my dear. You will

see her in your mind's eye. Do you know about your mind's eye?"

Sarah shook her head, but looked relieved. Even a child with Sarah's active imagination apparently preferred a boundary between the real and the unreal. Natalie reached across and placed one hand gently on Sarah's shoulder. "Your mind's eye is what we call the part of you that sees invisible things. The things you imagine, like Clara, and also the things we know to be real but cannot see. When you look into a person's heart, for example, you look with your mind's eye."

Sarah's rare smile bloomed. Malcolm cleared his throat. "Now that we have cleared up that point," he said dryly, "I suggest we hunt for the elusive Clara indoors. Ladies?" He included Mrs. Bigalow in his bow and indicated the open door behind him.

Natalie slanted him an apprehensive glance. "My lord," she said, "I wonder if I might have a word with you in private."

Aha. His instincts had been right. Miss Whittaker was going to renege. He had known this would happen the moment he saw that hat. "Of course," he said, hiding his disappointment behind his blandest smile. "If Mrs. Bigalow has no objection to watching Sarah for a few moments."

"None whatsoever, my lord," said Mrs. Bigalow, as he had known she would. Still, he reminded himself, there was no need to jump to conclusions. It was possible that Miss Whittaker was *not* going to wriggle out of their bargain. She might very well have brought along her trusted old nurse for advice. Anything was possible.

Malcolm opened a door at random and ushered Natalie into the first room he found, directly off Larkspur's smallish entry hall. It turned out to be some sort of sitting room that bore signs of a recent, rather hurried, setting to rights; it smelled strongly of lemon oil and the bric-a-brac on the mantelpiece, although free of dust, were slightly askew. The windows all faced west. The heat was stifling.

As he closed the door behind them, Natalie remarked, in a falsely bright tone that did not fool him for a moment, "Sarah certainly went off willingly with Mrs. Bigalow, did she not? You told me she does not generally like strangers. But Nurse has always had a gift for dealing with children."

"I'm sure she has," said Malcolm. His tone was not meant to sound encouraging. He saw dismay flutter across her features and knew that she had guessed his suspicions. "What was it you were wanting to tell me?"

Natalie faced him squarely and took a deep breath. *Here it comes,* thought Malcolm. "Lord Malcolm, I have no intention of letting you down. Or of letting Sarah down." She hesitated.

"But?" he prompted.

"But we shall have to rethink our arrangement a trifle." She looked embarrassed but did not back down. "A few . . . adjustments . . . may be necessary."

He was not going to make this easy for her. "Why?"

She swallowed. "Well, the reasons that initially caused me to hesitate still apply. But I'm afraid that Hector and Mabel—you do recall Hector and Mabel?—have added additional impediments." She fanned herself with one hand, wrinkling her nose. "I'm sorry, but is there somewhere else we might go?"

He shrugged. "Probably." He stepped to open the French windows at the other end of the room. They led to a veranda that ran the length of the north side of the house. She followed him gratefully into the cooler, less odorous air.

Once outside, he pinned her with a glare. "Pray enumerate for me the adjustments you think will be necessary, Miss Whittaker. And then I will tell you whether I find them acceptable."

She faced him, distress in her eyes. "Oh, pray do not be disagreeable," she cried, disarming him with her directness. "Indeed, I dislike this as much as you do. But you must know that my leaving Crosby Hall to come to Larkspur was purely a fantasy. My family will never allow such a thing. Common sense will not allow it. At least, not my *living* here. I own, I had not anticipated the lengths to which Hector would go to stop it, but I should have known he would take steps of some kind. And so he has. My lord, it will not be possible for me to leave my brother's protection. But I think—I *hope*—that I have a solution to present to you."

Malcolm sighed and rubbed the knot that had formed at the bridge of his nose. "What is it?" he asked wearily. "I have a feeling I am not going to like it nearly as well as I like the idea of you living here."

She favored him with that blinding smile of hers. "Thank you," she said warmly. "Nor do I. But it will be the next best thing. My lord, I think you do not realize how very near to you I already live." She reached, as if on impulse, and took his hand, dragging him to the end of the veranda. He felt vaguely disappointed when she dropped it to lean over the railing and peer back past the front of the house. "Oh, how vexatious," she exclaimed. "You cannot see it from here. But do you see that wooded area, where the land dips? A brook runs there, between our two properties. And the land rises again on the other side of it, and Crosby Hall sits at the top of the

rise. It took me ten minutes to reach you by pony cart,
and I think I can walk it in even less time. Going down
the hill and across the brook, you know, rather than
using the road."

In her enthusiasm, she spun to face him, her lips
parted to say something more—but she halted, freezing
in place with the words unspoken. She must have known
he was standing directly behind her, but it seemed that
their nearness when she turned round took her as much
by surprise as it did him. For a tiny space of time they
stared at each other, unmoving. They were only inches
apart.

The long rays of sunset struck the side of her face, lining her cheek with fire and painting her brown hair with
streaks of gold. Malcolm was acutely aware of how
long, how terribly long, it had been since he had stood
this close to a woman. Her heat, her softness, her very
femininity were overwhelming. A subtle perfume
seemed to cloud the air, teasing his nostrils with the
musky scent of honey and the sweetness of jasmine. No
matter how near their two houses stood, he thought, it
would not be near enough. He wanted this woman beneath his own roof. He wanted to inhale her fragrance on
a regular basis and catch that breathtaking smile as often
as possible. It was a refreshment to his spirit just to stand
beside her. He wondered, for a crazy moment, what it
would be like to kiss her.

As if sensing his thoughts, Natalie shivered and
crossed her arms protectively beneath her breasts. A tentative smile wavered across her face. "At any rate," she
said rather breathlessly, "it will be easy for me to spend
most of the day here. With Sarah."

Had she felt compelled to add that clarifying remark?
With Sarah, indeed. Malcolm almost smiled. Her contact

with men must be nearly as limited as his had been, lately, with women. Perhaps he was affecting her senses almost as much as she was affecting his. He could hope so, at least.

Hope so? He frowned and gave himself a mental shake. Good Lord, he was having a completely inappropriate physical reaction to Sarah's governess. Her governess! *Get a grip, imbecile,* he told himself disgustedly. The last thing he wanted to do was frighten off the most promising candidate he had encountered yet.

He stepped back, clearing his throat. "I see. You propose to spend your days at Larkspur, but not your nights. And Mrs. Bigalow . . . ?"

"Can remain at Larkspur, with your permission, to see to the day-to-day tasks. Putting Sarah to bed and getting her up in the mornings. Looking after her things, seeing that she is fed and dressed properly, and so forth." Natalie pressed her hands together beseechingly. "It's dreadful of me to foist yet another stranger upon you, but I couldn't think what else to do."

Stepping away from her had helped marginally, but Malcolm was still struggling with an overpowering sense of Natalie's closeness. He managed a frown, but for some reason it did not come as easily as it should have. "So the things in the back of the pony cart belong to Mrs. Bigalow rather than to you. You must have been very sure that I would agree to this."

"Oh, dear." She gulped, shamefaced. "That was bad of me, I know. But indeed, indeed, there was no other choice. I could not stay tonight, and I knew you had dismissed Mrs. Thorpe, so—"

"So at least you did not leave me entirely in the lurch."

"Yes. That is what I hoped you would realize, at any rate."

Again her frankness disarmed him. He felt his manufactured frown fading. He made an effort to hold on to it. He must have succeeded, for Natalie still looked anxious.

"You must take my word for it, I suppose, but Mrs. Bigalow is truly a wonderful nurse. I am confident that Sarah will love her. And if it's any consolation, I will confess that I have brought her here at great cost to myself. We kept her on at Crosby Hall all these years as a sort of hired companion for me. And I only recently fought an enormous battle to keep her on the staff. Mabel wanted to let everyone go and replace our staff with her own people. I was only able to convince her to keep Nurse on because . . . well, because Mabel is expecting a child in the autumn. I hate to let her leave, even temporarily, but until we can come up with something better for Sarah . . ." She shrugged helplessly.

It was confoundedly difficult to follow what she was saying. In her anxiety to persuade him, she kept moving closer. It rattled him. She was backlit now, the setting sun haloing her with gold and pink. A current of air fluttered the feather in her hat. A tendril of her molasses hair curled frivolously beside her cheek and danced in the breeze. He longed to touch it. When he spoke, his tongue felt thick and clumsy, as if he had been drugged. "What you are telling me is, you are reneging. Fobbing me off with Mrs. Bigalow instead of yourself."

"No," she said quickly. Passionately. She stepped even closer, placing an urgent hand lightly on his sleeve. "You shall have both of us."

He stared at her, mesmerized by the barely felt hand on his arm, the perfume, the rosy, otherworldly light.

Her curls. That dratted hat. Everything about her conspired to fuddle his wits. She seemed to misinterpret his silence as disapproval, for she looked apologetic. "You did say, sir, that you meant to pay me handsomely."

Was she blushing? Adorable.

Her dark eyes lifted to his, pleading. "Whatever you meant by that remark, I ask you to cut my wages. I am determined that acquiring the services of both of us will not cost you a penny more than hiring my services alone. That is only fair, since I am not strictly abiding by our agreement. I shall still act as Sarah's teacher, during the days, and you may house Mrs. Bigalow in my place."

When he still did not speak, her blush intensified. "Or," she stammered, "if you insist—and I suppose you have every right to insist—I could pay Nurse out of my wages. Or—" Her voice faltered to a halt. Her eyes searched his. She looked bewildered; he must be wearing a very odd expression. "Please, Lord Malcolm, I beg you to be frank. Tell me what you are thinking."

Out of nowhere, seemingly, he heard his own voice, sounding hoarse and strange. "I am thinking," he heard himself say, "that all these little difficulties would simply disappear if you married me."

Her jaw dropped. For an instant she stood as if petrified, still with one hand laid beseechingly on his sleeve. Then she removed it. "That's not funny."

"I'm not laughing."

She took a step backward, away from him, staring at him incredulously. He watched as anger gradually replaced her bewilderment, narrowing her eyes and tightening her jawline. "Either you are making a very poor joke at my expense," she said in a clipped, furious voice, "or you are a lunatic."

He hoped the rosy light would camouflage the embarrassed flush he feared was stealing up his neck. *Good God.* She was right. He had blurted out his thoughts like a gawky schoolboy, with no regard for the effect his careless words might have. "Well," he muttered defensively, "you told me to be frank."

She stared. "Do you mean you were actually *thinking* that?"

He grinned weakly and shrugged. "I'm only human. Haven't you ever had a crazy thought?"

She continued to back away from him. "Not that crazy."

She backed into the railing and was forced to stop. He could not suppress a chuckle. "You shouldn't ask what a man's thinking if you don't want to know."

"I shall bear that in mind from now on," she said. She sounded honestly shaken.

He shouldn't be enjoying this, but now that the humor in the situation had struck him, he couldn't help it. He advanced on her, moving leisurely. Her eyes dilated. She clutched the railing behind her with both hands, bracing herself. He cornered her and grinned down into her startled face.

Surely she wasn't frightened. Not *really* frightened.

He deliberately placed one hand on either side of her, holding the railing, trapping her between his arms. His thumbs brushed her wrists, but that was the only point where they touched. She leaned so far backward to avoid bringing their bodies into contact that she almost tumbled over into the shrubbery. Her fragrance teased his senses again, warm and faint, the barest whiff of musk and sweetness.

He waggled his eyebrows like a villain in a melodrama. "Ask me what I'm thinking now."

"No," she said hastily. "I've learned my lesson."

"What a pity." He let her go and moved away, still grinning. "Sorry! I shouldn't have teased you. But it was irresistible."

An expression of relief replaced her fright as she straightened her body and let go of the railing. A scowl descended on her features, but—as he had hoped—most of her anger had evaporated with the fear. She now looked merely annoyed. "You are the most peculiar man I have ever met."

"Well, you know what they say about the aristocracy. We're all a bit potty."

"You shouldn't joke about such things," she scolded. "What if I had truly thought you were offering marriage? What if I had *accepted* you?" She shook her head in disgust. "Dangerous! I never heard anything to equal it."

"Oh, come now." Since she was half reclining against the railing, he seated himself on a stone bench against the wall. He gave her his most disarming smile. "I knew I could rely on your good sense."

"You knew nothing of the kind." She looked very severely at him. "You know nothing about me! For all you knew, I might have been perfectly *desperate* to marry, and ready to jump at the first offer I received. What would you have done then, I wonder?"

"Marry you, I suppose." He stretched out his legs and crossed them at the ankle, leaning back against the wall of the house. "Would that have been such a dreadful fate?"

She bit back a laugh. "Do not expect me to answer you with the same frankness you have shown."

"No need. You have already warned me about your true nature," he assured her. "First you told me you were a willful, uncontrollable child, and then you told me that you haven't changed much as you matured." He winked.

This time, she laughed outright. "I might have known my candor would come back to haunt me. So now you know why I am still single at four-and-twenty. No man will have me."

"Four-and-twenty is not such a great age. Who knows? Your luck may turn."

She tapped her chin with one gloved finger, regarding him in skeptical amusement. "I wonder what you mean by that? Do you mean that I might suddenly become lucky—or unlucky?" She held the finger aloft in a gesture of warning. "Be careful, sir."

He chuckled. "I dare not reply."

"Hm! That's the first sign of prudence I have seen you display."

They smiled at each other in the gathering darkness. The sky was turning a soft purple and the first stars were visible. He could have picked a worse moment to blurt out something stupid. In the dreamy luminosity of a summer's evening, his momentary lapse into madness seemed forgivable. Even amusing. He shuddered to think what her reaction might have been had he abruptly proposed marriage in the harsh glare of noontime, to a woman he had known for only a few hours. He doubted that they would be smiling at each other so warmly, ten minutes later. *Timing is everything,* he thought wryly, and had to smother another grin.

She looked inquiringly at him. He waved her off, a rueful twinkle in his eye. "No, Miss Whittaker. I'll keep my thoughts to myself this time."

What he was thinking was, he couldn't remember the last time he had smiled this much.

Chapter Seven

They strolled back into the lamplit house. Natalie was brought up short by the sight of Nurse calmly drinking tea, not far from the windows that looked out onto the veranda. She was sitting out of earshot—thank heaven—but her expression was a bit *too* neutral. The glance she sent from Natalie's face to Lord Malcolm's was just a shade too bland for Natalie's comfort.

Natalie was well aware that she had rarely, if ever, spent time alone in the dark with a single gentleman. Nurse was aware of it, too. It was impossible to believe that she could refrain from speculation after witnessing such an interesting event.

She tried to send her henchwoman a warning frown, but Nurse ignored her. Instead, she rose politely from her seat and addressed Lord Malcolm in deferential tones, informing him that she had taken the liberty of putting Sarah to bed.

Lord Malcolm looked startled. "Did she allow it?"

"Certainly, my lord." Nurse permitted herself a tiny smile. "Allow me to compliment you, sir, on your daughter's sweet disposition. She's a very well-brought-up, prettily behaved child."

Lord Malcolm actually flushed with pleasure. Natalie was both amused and touched to see how strongly he was affected by Nurse's simple words of approval for his little girl. It was heartwarming, really. Endearing. In Natalie's experience, men did not care deeply for their daughters.

It occurred to her that he must have loved Sarah's mother a great deal. That thought gave her a strange little pang.

She returned her attention, with difficulty, to Lord Malcolm and Nurse. They were conversing quite amicably. It seemed that he was reconciling himself to the notion of hiring Mrs. Bigalow. This, also, gave Natalie a pang. She couldn't remember a time when Nurse had not slept in the room next to her own, forever within call. It would feel lonely to know she was no longer there.

She sat and poured herself a cup of tea. It was cold. She pulled a face and set it down again. Lord Malcolm and Nurse were shaking hands, apparently well pleased with each other. Natalie had to suppress a sigh. She had made her bed, she reminded herself, and now must lie in it.

"It's all settled, then," Lord Malcolm was saying. "I'll send word to my solicitor to put both of you on my books as of today's date." His bow was nicely calibrated to include Natalie as well. "In the meantime, Mrs. Bigalow, I hope you have arranged to have your baggage removed from the pony cart? Yes, very good. In that case, I imagine you have some unpacking to do."

Nurse acknowledged it, but seemed reluctant to leave the room. She looked fixedly at Natalie. Her inscrutable expression had returned. "Daresay we should have brought young Daniel with us, to see you home. Should have thought of that. It's full dark now."

Natalie waved this off. "No matter. I am unlikely to get lost between here and Crosby Hall."

"I will escort you, of course," said Lord Malcolm.

Nurse looked over her spectacles at him, as if trying to read his intentions. Fearing that she was about to launch into a scold, Natalie stood up hastily. "Thank you, my lord, but I do not require an escort."

She was sure that Nurse had been about to mortify her by admonishing Lord Malcolm for his improper suggestion. But, to her amazement, Nurse folded her hands before her and said placidly, "Don't be a goosecap, Natalie. If Lord Malcolm is kind enough to offer his escort, you should take it."

Natalie stared at Nurse, astonished. "I wouldn't dream of putting him to so much trouble."

"No trouble at all," Lord Malcolm assured her.

"The distance is ridiculously short!"

"As Mrs. Bigalow points out, however, it is dark now. I couldn't let you drive home alone."

She would look foolish if she protested further. Natalie tried to smile. "What a to-do over nothing! Very well, Lord Malcolm, I accept. Thank you."

She did her best to ignore the nervous flutter that had begun when he offered to escort her home. If Nurse saw nothing wrong with Lord Malcolm escorting her home, she told herself firmly, then she was surely safe. Nurse had always been overprotective of her. She would never send her into danger.

Of course, Nurse was unaware of the more bizarre aspects of Lord Malcolm's behavior. Hiring strangers at the drop of a hat, without references, was the least of it.

She stood in the entrance hall, smoothing her gloves and trying to appear composed, while Lord Malcolm called for the pony cart. She attempted to quell her ner-

vousness with common sense. There was nothing extraordinary about this situation, nothing out of the way. Just
a simple visit to the house next door. Just a short ride
home with a friendly escort. Lord Malcolm was only
being neighborly.

Then he appeared in the doorway, driving gloves on
and hat at a jaunty angle. She felt an undeniable, almost
overwhelming, pull of attraction.

Heavens! This would never do. The butterflies in Natalie's stomach fluttered anew. She gave him an apprehensive smile and allowed him to lead her to the cart. He
handed her up into it. She was glad it was too dark for
him to see her blush. She looked away, feigning indifference, as he hopped up and sat beside her.

The pony cart had never seemed so small.

She slanted a look at him. "Shall I drive?"

"Certainly not." He headed the pony toward the road.
"What would the neighbors think?"

She smiled. "I am 'the neighbors.'"

"In that case, I depend on you to direct me. Crosby
Hall is to the south, I think you indicated?"

"Correct."

Night was a long time coming in June. Despite
Nurse's comment that full dark would have arrived by
now, the horizon was still rimmed with orange. However, Larkspur's long driveway was lined with trees. As
they headed toward the road, the trees met overhead and
plunged them into true darkness. Natalie shivered.

"Are you cold, Miss Whittaker?" He sounded concerned.

"No," she said quickly. "Not at all." It was the intimacy of sitting next to him in the blackness that had
made her shiver. She dared not let him guess that. She
cast about in her mind for something to say. "After you

set me down, you must drive the pony cart back to Lark-spur, of course. I can send our Daniel to fetch it in the morning."

"Very well."

His voice was so deep. At the sound of it, she nearly shivered again. She was glad when the tunnel of trees ended and they emerged into the comparative brightness of the summer evening. The gates stood open before them, and then the pale ribbon of road. There was not another soul in sight.

"I don't remember ever seeing the gates of Larkspur standing open," she remarked, trying desperately to make conversation. "It is wonderful to have you here at last." That sounded oddly familiar. She added hastily, "I mean, it will be pleasant for the neighborhood to have the house occupied, after it has been empty for so long."

"I understood you the first time." Amusement quivered in his voice. Natalie felt herself blushing again. Odious man! She would sit mute rather than subject herself to his teasing.

He turned the cart left onto the road. After a few seconds of silence had spun out, he spoke. His deep baritone held a tentative note she had not heard in it before. "Miss Whittaker, I have been wrestling with a question. I wonder if I ought to speak with you—and Mrs. Bigalow as well—about Sarah. Before we begin."

She looked at him and was surprised to see his brows drawn low over his eyes and his mouth set in a troubled line. "Is there something you think we should know?"

"Perhaps. I am wondering if it would help you deal with her, to understand her a little better. Sarah is"—he paused for a moment—"different. On the other hand, I hesitate to say anything, for fear it would prejudice you.

I think I may have inadvertently done that with Mrs. Thorpe."

"How so?"

"I warned her that she might find Sarah a little odd. And now I wonder whether it was my well-intentioned warning that poisoned her mind against Sarah. She seemed to take her in instant dislike."

His confession seemed to be causing him pain. Natalie had to quell an impulse to lay her hand on his arm, to comfort him. Her voice was very gentle as she said, "Lord Malcolm, I can safely promise you that I will not take Sarah in dislike."

His expression lightened a bit. He looked down at her with the glimmer of a smile. "This," he said softly, "is why I found you irresistible." His words seemed to strike him as ill chosen. He cleared his throat. "I mean, your rapport with Sarah is what made me want to hire you."

"Lord Malcolm," she said demurely, "I understood you the first time."

He laughed, recognizing his own words flung back at him, and she smiled, pleased to have her jest understood. The night seemed a little brighter, and she relaxed a bit.

"Why don't you tell me what you think I should know, and then I can tell you whether I think we should share the information with Nur—Mrs. Bigalow."

He scratched his chin. "Hm. How much time do I have?"

"Five minutes. When we round the next bend you will see the turning to Crosby Hall."

"Then there is time to tell you this much. Sarah has an overactive imagination, as I think you have guessed. I asked Mrs. Thorpe to do what she could to break her of her . . . daydreaming habits. I believe that is why Mrs.

Thorpe was so harsh with her. It may have been the wrong approach, but she was trying to teach Sarah to live in the real world rather than a world of her own making."

Natalie was puzzled. "Does she have imaginary playmates and so forth? I believe it is normal for a child of her age to—"

Lord Malcolm was shaking his head. "That is not what I mean. I don't know how to describe it. She . . . retreats. She seems to have enormous powers of concentration, and unless she is checked in some way, she spends the majority of her time in her own little world."

Natalie hesitated. She hoped she was not asking too personal a question, but she had to ask it. "Is she lonely?" she said softly.

He shot her a keen glance. There was pain in his shadowed eyes. "Ah," he said quietly. "I had forgotten how perceptive you are. Yes, I think she may be." He sighed. "I suppose you have deduced that her mother is no longer with us."

"Yes," said Natalie gently. "I am sorry."

"Thank you." His voice was toneless. "Not that Sarah knew her well. Catherine has been gone for three years now. But Sarah is such a sensitive child. She never seemed to recover, as a more resilient child might have done. I think she still feels the loss—although she may no longer be able to give it a name. This is why I had hoped, as I think I explained to you, to find someone for her who would act as a companion as well as a guide and teacher. A mother figure, I suppose." His voice dropped until it was barely audible. "Had Sarah been a boy, things would be different. I am unequal to the task God has set for me."

Natalie held her breath; she felt she was hearing private thoughts he had not intended to share. Then he seemed, with an effort, to return to the moment at hand. "Is this the turning?"

"Yes," she said absently, "we are nearly there." Now she wished they had walked rather than driven. "Tell me, does Sarah have any friends?"

He frowned, seeming to focus enormous attention on turning into the drive. Natalie was not deceived. She was well aware that the pony knew the way by heart.

"No," he said at last. "My brother, Arthur—Lord Grafton, you know—has five daughters. But he and his family live most of the year in London. When we see them, Sarah's spirits noticeably improve, even though Arthur's girls are older than Sarah. He is my elder by nearly twelve years."

"I see." They were pulling up to the house. The lamp by the door had not been lit in anticipation of her return, and Mabel's new butler was nowhere to be seen. Natalie felt a stab of embarrassment. She hoped Lord Malcolm did not notice anything amiss. She did not expect the butler to make an appearance; he would know it was only Natalie who was arriving, and he seemed to labor under the impression that waiting on Natalie was not part of his duties. Mabel, of course, had done nothing to correct this impression.

The pony stood quietly while Lord Malcolm hopped down and crossed to Natalie's side of the cart. She almost told him that she didn't need his assistance to alight. She really didn't. She could jump down perfectly well on her own. Still, it would look churlish to refuse his outstretched hand. She placed her hand in his.

His fingers closed around hers, and even through their gloves she felt his warmth. She moved to jump, and suddenly felt his other hand at her waist, steadying her. She was too startled to do anything other than finish her movement and jump—and ended up jumping almost into his arms. He set her on her feet and stepped back. She had to remind herself to breathe. "Thank you," she said in a strangled voice.

"Shall I see you to the door?"

"No," she said, a little too vehemently. She then managed a weak smile. "You have already done so, my lord."

"Good night, then."

"Good night." She moved quickly up the shallow steps to the door. Behind her, she heard the creak of the pony cart as Lord Malcolm climbed back into it. She turned when she reached the safety of the door and waved to him. He saluted her and drove off.

Natalie entered the house feeling more unsettled than she had any right to feel. Nothing untoward had happened; Lord Malcolm had done nothing improper. Unless one counted that ridiculous marriage proposal, which hadn't been a real marriage proposal at all.

As she lit a candle and mounted the stairs, she remembered that she had a right, after all, to feel rattled. Her entire life had unexpectedly changed today. Nurse was gone, perhaps forever, and she was beginning employment of her own tomorrow. Anyone might feel a trifle off balance under these circumstances. She supposed she would toss and turn all night, a prey to hopes and fears.

As it turned out, however, she neither tossed nor turned. She fell asleep immediately, slept deeply, and woke feeling refreshed. This seemed so odd, after the previous day's turbulence, that when she opened her eyes to the clear and sunny morning, she wondered briefly if she were dreaming. She felt too marvelous to be awake.

Perhaps it was foolish, but she could not help feeling that the brilliant sunshine and blue skies were an omen. She must be doing the right thing after all, she thought, or she wouldn't feel so calm about it. Calm? She felt downright cheerful.

One of the maids brought chocolate to her and she took it to her window seat, sipping it while drinking in the fresh, clean air. Every nerve in her body seemed to be humming with anticipation. She was actually *excited* about her new role. She laughed a little, shaking her head. Her life had turned upside down . . . again . . . and, this time, she was loving it. How strange.

As she looked out over the landscape, movement caught her eye. Two figures were moving down the grassy hill on the other side of the brook. Good heavens. It was Lord Malcolm and little Sarah, heading toward Crosby Hall. She pulled back from the window, her heart beating a little faster. They must rise early at Larkspur! She set down her chocolate and flew to close her bed-room curtains, calling to the maid for assistance with her toilette. Her new employer must not be allowed to think her a layabout.

She dressed in record time and ran out to meet them as they were climbing up the rise. Father and daughter both looked up and smiled at her call, and Lord Malcolm returned her wave. Natalie felt her spirits rise even further. She ran lightly toward them, laughing.

"I thought I was supposed to come to Larkspur, not the other way about. Good morning," she added, extending her hand.

Lord Malcolm shook it, smiling. "Good morning. Sarah was up with the chickens today, so I thought we would go exploring."

Sarah hopped up and down with excitement. "Are you

coming back with us? Miss Whittaker, there's a river with a little bridge. Papa let me throw a penny in the water for luck."

"A halfpenny," said Malcolm, correcting her. He gave Natalie a crooked grin. "We no longer need a penny's worth of luck."

"I'm glad you found the bridge, at any rate," said Natalie, wondering why his words made her feel so ridiculously happy. She fell into step beside them as they turned back toward Larkspur. "The path to the footbridge is used so seldom that it's hard to make out in places."

"Did you picture us fighting a raging current? Even without the bridge, I might have carried Sarah across and suffered nothing worse than a pair of wet boots."

She laughed, wrinkling her nose. "This time of year, I'll grant you, the brook is not formidable."

"Formidable," whispered Sarah.

Natalie glanced down at her with interest. It seemed that Sarah was trying the word on for size. She touched her lightly on the shoulder. "Fearsome," she explained.

"Like a bear? Could a bear be formidable?"

"A bear is almost always formidable."

Sarah nodded, then gritted her teeth in a ferocious scowl. "Formidable," she growled, bearlike. Then her brow cleared and she danced away into the grass, humming.

Natalie said, in a low tone that Sarah would not overhear, "That's a good sign, I think. She seems to have a natural interest in learning."

"Some things, yes," he said dryly. "Some things, no."

She chuckled. "I thought you told me she was different? That sounds like every child in the world."

Nevertheless, as they walked, slowing their steps to

suit their small companion, Natalie saw a glimmer of what Lord Malcolm had meant by "different." His daughter gamboled and frisked like a puppy beside them, running ahead and trotting back, dropping on all fours to examine the flowers, dancing in circles, singing nonsense syllables, and paying the adults no mind. It was not her energetic behavior that was so unusual, but the utter concentration in her face. Something in her expression gave the impression that she was unaware she was being watched, even though she knew the adults to be with her. Sarah was able, somehow, to utterly exclude them and play as if she were quite alone.

Natalie supposed it was her job, now, to restrain the little girl, but Lord Malcolm seemed unconcerned about Sarah's exuberance. He claimed Natalie's full attention by tucking her hand into his elbow—to steady her steps as they crossed the grass, she reminded herself sternly; a courtesy any man might have shown her; there was no reason in the world to feel so self-conscious about touching him—and focused his smiling blue eyes on her face as if she were the only person in the world. It felt very flattering, but she was amused when she realized it reminded her of Sarah. As they chatted, Natalie saw Sarah's powers of concentration mirrored in Lord Malcolm, and said so.

Some of the pleasure left his expression. "You are right, of course." His eyes shifted to Sarah, filled with trouble now. "She has inherited some of my temperament. And some of her mother's."

Natalie was surprised at the sobering effect her light words had had. "That's not a bad thing, is it?"

He seemed about to answer her when Sarah, down the hill ahead of them, suddenly tripped and fell facedown in the grass. With an exclamation, Natalie ran toward the little girl. Sarah lay so still and silent, she was afraid for a moment that the child had been seriously hurt.

Lord Malcolm reached Sarah at the same instant she did. He reached down and gently turned her over. Sarah's eyes were wide open but filled with fear. "Am I all right, Papa?" she whispered.

"That's for you to say. Do you hurt anywhere?"

She seemed to think for a moment, as if taking inventory. "No."

"Can you sit up?"

Another pause. "Yes." She still did not move.

"Then pray do so."

Sarah obediently sat up.

"What happened?" asked Natalie.

Sarah's eyes turned to her. They still seemed unnaturally wide, as if the little girl were straining to see through darkness. "I fell in the grass."

"Yes, sweetheart, but why?"

Fear flickered across Sarah's face, and something that looked like shame. "I don't know. Did I tear my stockings?"

Natalie inspected them. She had been struck yesterday by how expensively Sarah was dressed, and her clothing today was equally fine. The stockings, she noted, were silk. Was that why she was anxious about them? "No, my dear. A little grass stain at the knee, but nothing torn."

"Come," said Lord Malcolm roughly. He seemed once more to be hiding strong emotion. He extended his hand, and Sarah took it. He pulled her to her feet. "Are you able to walk?"

"Yes, Papa." She looked anxiously up at him. "Papa, I did not tear my stockings."

"So I heard. Stay beside us from now on, and let's see if we can get you home with no more mishaps."

Sarah hung her head and said something inaudible. Natalie bent down to hear her. "What did you say, sweetheart?"

Sarah's eyes met hers, filled with shame and distress. "Must I sit in the corner when we get home?"

Natalie was startled. She straightened, looking at Lord Malcolm for guidance. He was frowning at Sarah, evidently as perturbed as she was by Sarah's expectation of punishment. "I don't think you need sit in the corner," said Natalie gently.

"Will you put me back in leading strings?"

"Certainly not. You are far too old for leading strings."

Sarah looked relieved. Natalie tried again to catch Lord Malcolm's eye, but he was still frowning in an abstracted way at the top of Sarah's head. She took Sarah's other hand and, together, they walked sedately back to Larkspur. Sarah made no attempt to pull away. The high-spirited child who had frolicked around them vanished; her affect was now completely subdued.

There was an odd dynamic operating in this family. Natalie could not put her finger on it. Whatever it was, it definitely muted the happiness she had felt earlier this morning. It was all very strange. There was something deeply troubling about Sarah's quirks and fears, and she was also at a loss to understand the abrupt shifts in Lord Malcolm's mood. At times he grinned and teased like a boy, and at other times he had a haunted look, as if he would never smile again.

Was he still grieving for his lost Catherine? She could think of no other explanation. But what of Sarah? She did not believe, as Lord Malcolm claimed, that Sarah was grieving for a loss suffered three years ago. She was too young.

When they reached Larkspur, Natalie took Sarah upstairs so Nurse could change her stockings. Nurse took the opportunity to draw Natalie aside for a moment. "There's somethin' amiss with the child," said Nurse, looking grim. "She spilled her milk at breakfast and flinched as if she thought I would strike her."

"Yes," said Natalie in a low tone. "She expects to be punished at every turn. Mrs. Thorpe must have been a worse tyrant than Lord Malcolm knew."

Nurse looked skeptical. "From what you told me, the woman was only with them for a few months. How could she break the wee thing's spirit in such a short time?"

"I don't know," said Natalie, troubled. "Sarah is more sensitive, perhaps, than most."

Nurse's skeptical expression deepened. "Hmpf. At any rate, I'll change her stockings. It's a miracle they weren't ruined. Silk! Pure silk. Most unsuitable for a child her age."

"Why is she wearing silk stockings? Did you let her choose them?"

Nurse snorted. "She has nothing else. Would you believe it? I unpacked for the mite, and she has pair after pair of silk stockings. Not a woolen nor a cotton pair among 'em. And as for her little frocks and hats and boots and such—tsk! Never seen anything to equal it. You should see her nightgown; the trim alone is worth a month's wages to the likes of me. I know Mechlin lace when I see it. Real lace, on a scrap of muslin the child will outgrow within a year!" She shook her head in dour disapproval.

"How odd," said Natalie, feeling a twinge of unease.

Then she rallied. "But, after all, Lord Malcolm is a wealthy man. Why shouldn't he buy the best for his only child?"

"Waste is waste, if you ask me." Nurse looked sharply at her. "You be careful, Natalie."

"I?" To her vexation, she felt a guilty blush stealing across her face. "It has naught to do with me."

"Hmpf. See that you remind yourself of that from time to time."

With that cryptic utterance, Nurse bustled off to take charge of Sarah. Natalie watched her go, tapping her foot in annoyance. She hadn't meant to fire up in defense of Lord Malcolm. It had just happened. She didn't need Nurse, or anyone else, to remind her that it was none of her business. And Nurse was a fine one to talk! Hadn't she just expressed her opinion in no uncertain terms? Why shouldn't Natalie do the same?

Be careful, indeed! She was in no danger. No danger at all.

Chapter Eight

Malcolm knocked softly before opening the nursery door. One end of the large room had been set up as a makeshift classroom, and Sarah was seated at a low table with Natalie bending over her shoulder, watching her draw. The pencil looked enormous, clutched in Sarah's small fingers. She held it very carefully, moving it slowly and with great precision. Natalie looked up immediately when Malcolm entered, but Sarah neither blinked nor budged. Every fiber of her tiny being was focused on guiding the pencil.

Natalie's eyes met his, and her face lit with that phenomenal smile of hers. If she could bottle that smile, she'd make a fortune. She looked different—softer, somehow. Prettier. Then he had it: This was the first time he had seen her hatless.

Her hair was the warmest of browns, and wonderfully thick. She had piled it neatly atop her head in a complicated arrangement involving a knot at the back and two plaits laid along her hairline, framing her face. The style was both flattering and feminine, but it looked to Malcolm that she had gone to a deal of trouble for nothing. No amount of ruthless plaiting and stuffing and tying was going to tame those curls. Three or four rebellious tendrils had popped loose already and were coiling naughtily against the slender column of her neck.

She lifted a finger to her lips to signal silence, flashed the smile again, and returned to her work. He had no objection to remaining silent. Of course, he could have told her it made little difference to Sarah. When she focused on a task—or a game, for that matter—nothing short of a trumpet blast would distract her.

He quietly closed the door behind him and leaned against the wall, watching them. Natalie had placed a flower on the table before his daughter. Sarah was evidently attempting to sketch its likeness. From the look of contained excitement on Natalie's face, it appeared that whatever Sarah was doing, it struck her as fairly amazing.

"Sarah, that is excellent!" she exclaimed at last. Sarah made no reply; it was doubtful she had even heard. She was still putting the finishing touches on her masterpiece. Natalie looked at Malcolm. "You did not tell me how talented your daughter is."

"Is she?" Malcolm crossed the room to stand beside them. He looked over Sarah's other shoulder. On the paper before her was a pencil drawing of what was, unmistakably, a daisy. Several of the lines were blurred where Sarah's sleeve had rubbed against them, and others were slightly crooked. Some of the lines wavered where she had drawn them too slowly. Still, a daisy it definitely was. "It's a daisy, all right and tight," he agreed.

"It's not just *a* daisy," said Natalie indignantly. She pointed at the flower lying before Sarah. "It is this daisy."

He looked from the drawing to the daisy and back

again. A daisy was a daisy, as far as he could see. "*This* daisy," he repeated, at a loss. "Very good."

Natalie gave a little choke of laughter. "Do you not see? Look here. And here." She pointed at a section of the daisy where one petal had a broken tip, and at a place on the stem where someone had evidently bent the thing until it creased. Sure enough, Sarah had faithfully replicated both the torn petal and the fold on the stem. Amazement dawned in him. His little daughter had observed details that had escaped his adult eye, details that set this particular daisy apart from its fellows. It was ridiculous, he supposed, to feel proud of her for such an insignificant accomplishment . . . at least, he supposed it was an insignificant accomplishment . . . but pride swelled his heart anyway.

Natalie touched Sarah's shoulder. "Sarah, that is very good work."

Sarah's eyes seemed to come back into focus. She set down her pencil and gave Natalie a shy smile. "I like to draw."

Mrs. Bigalow appeared in the doorway that led to Sarah's bedchamber. "Beg pardon," she said mildly, "but the kitchen has sent up Sarah's luncheon."

"Then she must eat it," said Malcolm promptly. "Miss Whittaker, will you join me on the veranda?"

She looked a little surprised, but pleased. "Certainly, my lord." He offered his arm and she took it, allowing him to lead her downstairs and out to the shady end of the veranda. A light repast had been set out for them on a table set for two. He made a mental note to thank Mrs. Howatch; the food and the setting looked very inviting.

Natalie exclaimed when she saw it. "A picnic! How fashionable."

He pulled out a chair for her, smiling. "Well, to be

strictly fashionable, we would have to sit on the grass. But my ambition was not to be modish; I simply wanted to be private with you. And I thought you would decline an invitation to eat alone with me in the dining room."

She gave a little spurt of laughter. "Quite right," she agreed, sitting where he bade her. "Although I don't know why you would doubt your ability to persuade me. You have had little difficulty thus far in convincing me to do outrageous things."

"I dare not assume that my luck will hold."

"I see. Very wise." Her eyes twinkled. "Ladies are taught, you know, to avoid going behind closed doors with single gentlemen."

"So I have found." He sat across from her and shook out his napkin. "Now that I have disarmed you by bringing you out of doors, tell me how your morning went."

Her eyes lit up. "Oh, I am so pleased with your Sarah!"

She launched into an enthusiastic recital of Sarah's accomplishments. Bracing himself against the disappointment he feared was inevitable, he leaned back in his chair and listened, watching her expressive face.

He expected praise, of course; she would view it as her duty to find something positive to say. But Natalie seemed to be going far beyond the call of duty. As she listed all the evidence she had discovered of Sarah's quick mind and creativity, ticking the points off on her fingers, she fairly glowed with sincerity. There was no false note, no evasion. Her praise was lavish and obviously genuine. It was like a miracle. Emotion rose in him as he listened. He found he had to look away, clearing his throat to hide it.

She seemed unaware of the effect her words were having. Her lilting voice continued. "What is more important, I think, than her reading and drawing ability is the *pleasure* she takes in them. A child who genuinely enjoys learning will be easy to teach."

Malcolm cleared his throat again. "You are confirming my own impressions." He looked back at her, a wry smile twisting his features. "Until this moment, however, I believed that my natural partiality had blinded me. You are the first person I have met whose opinion marches with mine. In fact, I have it on the authority of the most prominent physician in the midlands that Sarah is feeble-minded."

Natalie's eyes widened in shock. "No. How can that be? Sarah's intelligence must be obvious to anyone who spends five minutes with her."

He regarded her in cynical amusement. "The only thing obvious about Sarah, from what I can gather, is her eccentricity." He felt a familiar tightness in his chest as unpleasant memories clamored for his attention. He looked away to avoid her eyes. "It is her oddness, not her cleverness, that strikes most people."

When she did not reply at once, he glanced back at her. She was frowning absently at her plate. "Well?" he said challengingly. "You can't have spent a morning with her and not noticed it."

"She is different," conceded Natalie. "As you told me she would be."

"You don't think her stupid, and for that I am grateful. But doesn't she strike you as lazy? Willful? Disobedient?"

His voice sounded sharper than he had meant it to. She looked up from her plate, reproof in her gaze. "No, sir. She is gentle and shy. There is nothing abnormal in her behavior. Nothing except—" She halted in midsentence, biting her lip as if vexed with herself. "Nothing at all," she finished lamely.

The silence spun out while Malcolm meditatively selected a peach from the fruit bowl in the center of the table. "Nothing abnormal at all," he repeated at last. "And yet you agreed with me that she is different."

The color fluctuated in Natalie's face. She diligently applied butter to a slice of bread, refusing to meet his eyes. "She is, as I expected, highly imaginative. This is coupled with a remarkable ability to shut the world out when her attention is fixed on something that interests her. I daresay this combination of traits—particularly the latter—might be construed as laziness or disobedience. Or feeblemindedness, for that matter."

"How so?"

"Easily. If one gives her a direct order when her mind is elsewhere, she appears not to hear it. If one assumed that she did not understand, one might think her slow-witted. If one assumed that she chose not to obey, one would think her lazy or willful." She paused, looking a challenge at him. "But many people feel hostility toward anyone they do not understand. I think what perturbs people about Sarah is that the matters occupying her attention are frequently invisible to the rest of us."

"You don't call that abnormal?"

"No, sir, I do not." Natalie sat straighter in her chair. "If you insist on knowing my thoughts . . ." She raised an eyebrow at him.

"Yes, Miss Whittaker. I do."

"Very well. I am less disturbed by the fact that Sarah imagines things than I am by *what* she imagines. Not always, but often." She was turning pink again, but her gaze met his levelly. "Too frequently, she seems to imagine that she will be punished—for the tiniest of infractions. I own, I would like to know the source of her fears before tackling any behavior problems she may have. In my view, it is her profound anxiety, not her overactive imagination, that is harming her."

Whatever insights he had hoped—or feared—she would express, he had not expected this one. Anguish clutched him in a swirl of rage and guilt. He rose from the table and crossed to the railing of the veranda, his back to her as he fought for composure.

What a mess he had made of everything. He had no one to blame but himself, but knowing that only made it harder to find a solution. How could he expect this inexperienced girl to mend matters? And yet, he realized in a bitter flash of self-knowledge, that was exactly what he had expected. Irrationally, unreasonably, he had pinned all his hopes on Natalie Whittaker's kind heart and intuition. Now he must pay the price for following his instincts. She was a little *too* perceptive. And far too frank.

"Miss Whittaker." His voice felt tight. "The past cannot be changed. Looking backward accomplishes nothing. We must look forward." He turned to face her. "I have brought Sarah here to . . . begin a new life. You are right; she has formed a habit of expecting terrible things to happen to her. We must work together, you and I, to change Sarah's expectations. Then, and only then, will she lose her fears."

And become a normal child. No. No, that was too much to hope for. He must confine his goals to what was attainable.

Natalie was regarding him gravely, studying him as if she could find answers to her questions in his face. He kept his expression carefully neutral, praying she would probe no further. When she spoke, her words surprised him. "You love her very much," she said.

Knocked off balance, he said exactly what was in his heart. "She is the most important thing in the world to me."

He scrubbed his face with one hand, annoyed with himself. He was ashamed to have shown so much emotion over nothing. At least, it must seem like nothing to a stranger. But Natalie's face betrayed no contempt or embarrassment over his unmanly outburst. She nodded her acceptance, compassion in her eyes. "I am glad," she said simply. Then, after a moment, she added, "I will do whatever I can to ease Sarah's fears. Consistent kindness will, I think, go a long way. But if you think of any specific thing I can do, or anything you think I must avoid doing, pray tell me at once."

How calm she was. How competent. He shook his head, humbled by his good fortune. "Providence has surely sent you to me, Miss Whittaker," he said. He tried to say it lightly, but his voice shook a little.

She shot him a mischievous look. "The stars, I think you mean."

Some of the tension left him. "Something celestial, at any rate." He returned to the table. "I hope your afternoon goes as well as your morning did. May I escort you home at the end of the day?"

She looked a little nervous. "Certainly. If you like."

"By the way, you needn't worry about your abrupt departure this morning alarming your relatives. I took the liberty of sending word to Crosby Hall regarding your whereabouts. I promised to return you after dinner."

Natalie smiled, but the smile did not reach her eyes. "Unnecessary, but thank you. If my family missed me at all—which I doubt—they would have known where to look for me." She held her fork aloft, studying the bit of chicken it held. "Although, I suppose it's a good thing you acted," she mused. "Hector might have assumed I was gone for good; we were that angry with each other yesterday. Heaven knows what mischief he might have tried, had he assumed that. He might have sent at once for Mr. Brownbeck."

"Mr. Brownbeck?"

"Our solicitor." She popped the bit of chicken in her mouth, chewed, and swallowed. "He lives in the village," she said helpfully, seeing that Malcolm was still puzzled by her remark.

"But why would he send for his solicitor?"

She opened her eyes at him. "Why, to punish me, of course. Didn't I tell you?"

"Good Lord." He paused in the act of slicing his peach. "Your brother would have punished you using a *solicitor*?"

"Yes, indeed."

"It sounds extreme."

"Oh, it would have been," she agreed, serenely salting her chicken. "But since you sent over a note, we needn't worry about it."

Malcolm finished slicing his peach. "Forgive me," he said at last, "but I am expiring of curiosity. Exactly what would your brother have asked the solicitor to do? I think you had better tell me, if only to prevent my imagination running wild."

She looked embarrassed for a moment, then shrugged. "I suppose I've no objection to telling you. In fact, I hope it will make you understand why I decided—with the utmost reluctance, I assure you—to stay at home rather than move to Larkspur after all." She sighed. "Had I left home, Hector was planning to do several things. First, stop all my income—"

Malcolm, startled with his mouth full of peach, made

a sort of choking sound. She looked at him, her eyes twinkling. "Oh, that was no great loss, believe me. He also threatened to write me out of his will, as I recall, but I paid little attention to that either. I'm quite certain he was bluffing."

"Even were he not, any solicitor worth his salt would have advised against it."

"I doubt he would need to, since it's difficult to remove what doesn't exist in the first place."

"I see." Malcolm swallowed. "You realize, of course, that we never negotiated a salary for you. Under the circumstances . . ."

But Natalie was shaking her head, looking very serious. "No, my lord. I am not trying to squeeze a higher wage out of you. I will not mislead you into thinking that my income is large. Hector has no ability to take from me anything worth having. The only reason why I caved in to his demands . . ." Emotion swept across her face. She looked away. "The only reason why I decided *not* to leave Crosby Hall was that Hector threatened to cut off Derek's income as well as mine." She cleared her throat. "I could not allow that, of course."

Malcolm stared at her. "Far be it from me to disparage your near and dear, Miss Whittaker, but your brother Hector sounds like a complete rotter."

She gave a little choke of laughter. "Hector may be near, but he is not dear. You may disparage him with my good will."

He leaned back in his chair, thinking. "If Derek is employed by Lord Stokesdown, he can't be receiving much from Hector. If I paid you a sufficient amount to live here with us—"

"No." She looked regretful. "And pray do not think I hadn't thought of that! I did, but it will not do. No degree of generosity on your part will suffice, I am afraid. Imagine yourself in Derek's place. You are a man of honor, sir, and not without your pride. Would you accept money from your sister, knowing she was earning it with her own labor?"

"I suppose not," he said resignedly. "What a pity."

"Yes. It is, actually." She sighed. "I would dearly love to be free of Hector. To free Derek from him, too, would have been heavenly."

Natalie toyed with her fork, looking wistfully past him at the daisy-spangled lawn. It was clear her mind was elsewhere—probably with Derek, who seemed to be the only member of her family she loved. A breeze ruffled the wispy ringlets that had worked loose from her coiffure. She looked pensive and pretty and sad. Something about her brought out the protective instincts in a man. He wished he could do something to help her.

It occurred to him again how many problems would be solved at one stroke if he just married her. It would solve her problems as well as his, apparently. What a bother these modern notions about courtship were! A hundred years ago, nobody insisted on being well acquainted before tying the knot. Nowadays, a man looked like a lunatic—or, at the very least, a boor—if he proposed matrimony to a woman he had just met. Malcolm had barely managed to get away with it last night. In the clear light of day, he'd be lucky to escape with nothing worse than a slapped face.

He wondered what her reaction would be if she knew the contents of the letter he had posted to his solicitor this morning. He almost winced, picturing the fireworks. No lady would be pleased to learn that an investigation into her background had been set in motion. But a man in his position couldn't be too careful. If he really intended to consider Natalie Whittaker as a marital prospect—and the more he saw of her, the stronger his inclination grew—he had to know more about her. In the meantime, he would try to soften her up. Because if Patterson returned with a good report, that would seal the thing . . . at least as far as Malcolm was concerned.

Finally, after years of failing Sarah, he would do something right. He would give her a mother.

Chapter Nine

L ord Malcolm had offered to walk her home. For
some strange reason, that thought preyed on Natalie's mind all afternoon. Reading with Sarah, walking
with Sarah, playing games with Sarah, her thoughts kept
straying to the fact that Lord Malcolm would walk her
home this evening. And every time she thought of it, a
shiver of nervous excitement ran through her.

She could not decide whether she was dreading it or
looking forward to it. And either way, she could not
fathom why. Why dread it? Why look forward to it? Either reaction was ridiculous. Besides, the walk was
short; she would doubtless be alone with Lord Malcolm
for less than a quarter of an hour.

Unless, of course, they dawdled.

At that thought, the shiver went through her again.
What on earth was the matter with her?

To her relief, dinner went quite a way toward easing
her mind. It was an informal affair; since Natalie had
nothing to change into, Lord Malcolm also wore morning dress. Sarah joined them at table, and they shared a
surprisingly merry meal. It warmed Natalie's heart to see
Sarah so animated. She was glad, too, to confirm that

Lord Malcolm was not the sort of parent who insisted on silence from his child. Sarah chattered happily about her day, and Lord Malcolm listened with an indulgent smile. The evening sun poured through the tall windows of the dining room, seeming to bestow heaven's blessing on the threesome gathered there.

It was delightful to dine *en famille* with the Chases, but it made Natalie feel a little sad, too. Dinners at Crosby Hall had not been this pleasant since the barely remembered days when her mother had presided over them. She mentioned as much to Lord Malcolm while tying her bonnet strings in the hall. "Not that I mean to complain," she added hastily, catching his eyes in the mirror.

"I didn't think you were." The brooding look had returned to his features. "I'm glad you had your mother long enough to remember her. Sarah was not quite three when we lost Catherine. I doubt she has any memories of her at all."

Natalie felt a swift stab of sympathy. "You mustn't despair of it," she said gently, turning to face him as she pulled on her gloves. "Many children retain memories from their toddler years. I imagine some of mine date from about that age."

"I hope you are right." He gave her a rather strained smile. "May I ask how old you were when you lost your mother?"

"I was five years old. Derek was barely four, but I believe he remembers her, too." She finished with her gloves and smiled at Lord Malcolm. "Ready," she said brightly. Thank goodness her voice betrayed no nervousness.

He held the front door for her and they stepped out into the golden evening. Lord Malcolm slanted a look at her that she could not quite interpret. "I'm sorry for your loss," he said quietly.

For a moment, Natalie didn't know what he meant. Then she remembered that they had just been speaking of her mother. She inclined her head in acknowledgment. "Thank you. It was a long time ago."

"Yes." Their feet crunched on gravel. "Had she been ill a long time?"

"Oh, no. It was a carriage accident. She lingered for a few days only." Natalie heard the constriction in her voice and cleared her throat. "We were not allowed to see her. She had been thrown from the gig and evidently her injuries were not a pretty sight. I suppose they thought it would be too upsetting for us."

"I'm glad someone showed that much consideration for the children."

She gave him a twisted smile. "Unfortunately, the result of that kindness was that Derek and I persisted for a long time in believing that our mother would return. Papa remarried quickly. I wonder, now, how much of our hostility toward Lucille stemmed from our confusion about Mama's death. We did not truly understand what had happened to her."

His features darkened in a swift frown. "That's a pity. But it's hard to know what course to take in such a situation, when the children are very young."

"Yes, I'm sure it is."

She suddenly realized that he had had to make a similar decision when his own wife died. She wondered what had taken Catherine, and whether Sarah had been allowed to say good-bye to her mother. She dared not ask. The subject was obviously still a painful one for him. She attempted a lighter tone. "I'm not sure whose idea it was to protect us from harsh reality. It seems very unlike

Papa; my father was not known for his tender heart. Quite the opposite, in fact."

As she had hoped, he looked amused. "Was he cruel, or merely selfish?"

"Selfish, for the most part."

"Ah. How proud he must have been of Hector. A chip off the old block."

She chuckled. "There is a resemblance," she agreed. "But you mustn't think too harshly of them. Every family has its good eggs and bad eggs."

"In your family, the good eggs seem to consist largely of you and your brother Derek."

She laughed. "Well, that's certainly how it seems to *me,* but you would hear a different view from Hector."

"I devoutly hope I never hear Hector's views. I have no interest in them. I cannot remember ever taking a man so strongly in dislike, merely by repute. Generally one requires familiarity with the actual human being, to form the sort of antipathy I feel for your Hector."

"Napoleon," suggested Natalie.

Lord Malcolm pretended to think for a moment. "It's not the same," he stated. "At least I understand his motives. Hector's villainy defies comprehension."

Natalie peeped up at him uncertainly. "I hope you are joking," she said. "It reflects very poorly on me, if my tale-telling has so prejudiced you against my brother."

"Nonsense," he said firmly, but she saw the glimmer of a smile in his eyes. They turned to start down the grassy slope toward the brook. "Take my arm, Miss Whittaker. The ground may be uneven."

Natalie felt her pulse flutter. How annoying. She toyed with the idea of informing Lord Malcolm that she had tramped up and down these hills all her life, but discarded the impulse as rude. It wasn't his fault she was cast into fidgets by the prospect of touching him. Pasting a look of unconcern on her face, she took his arm. "Thank you."

"My pleasure."

He immediately slowed his steps. Alarm bells rang all through her. *He's dawdling,* she thought—then sternly banished the mischievous notion. He probably slowed his pace as a courtesy to her, something any gentleman might do. She mustn't read anything more into it. Why was she having such crazy thoughts?

While she was still gathering her scattered wits, he segued smoothly back into their conversation. "Tell me more about your family," he suggested. "Does Hector have redeeming features?"

The question startled a laugh out of her. "Oh, dear. Let's see. He's a fairly decent shot, and I've heard he rides very well to hounds."

"Ah. A man of sporting proclivities."

"I suppose so. And he can be charming when he wants to be—or so I am told. He naturally doesn't waste his charm on me." She chuckled, shaking her head. "He must have something to offer. He was able to win a wife."

Lord Malcolm quirked an eyebrow. "From what you have told me, you don't think much of his wife."

"No, but you mustn't judge her by my impressions. I'm afraid my view of her is completely jaundiced. My dislike of Mabel is no reflection on Hector's abilities as a suitor. She brought a large dowry with her, so despite her flaws she is considered quite a prize." Natalie suddenly realized how waspish her words had been and gave a tiny gasp. "Oh, pray do not laugh! I should not have said such a dreadful thing."

Lord Malcolm's shoulders were shaking. "Too late! I

am picturing a cow with a blue ribbon round its neck. Sorry."

Natalie was mortified. "I hope you are able to put the picture aside when you meet her, sir. It would be *fatal* for you to think of a cow. I very much fear you would laugh out loud."

"Resembles one, does she?"

"Well, yes," Natalie confessed. "But she is in the family way, you know. Her appearance may improve once the ordeal is behind her."

He threw back his head and uttered a crack of laughter. "Poor Mabel! So you will soon be an aunt. For his sake, I hope the child takes after his aunt and uncle rather than his parents."

Natalie began to suspect that Lord Malcolm, for some unknown reason, was emptying the butter boat over her. She looked accusingly at him. "You are talking a great deal of nonsense, sir. You haven't met the baby's parents. Nor its uncle Derek, for that matter."

His blue eyes smiled down at her. "I stand corrected. I hope the child favors his aunt, and only his aunt."

She stared up at him, now certain that he meant to compliment her. "I think—I think you are trying to flatter me," she stammered. A few moments ago, his shadowed eyes had been cold and bleak. Now they were warm, lit with teasing laughter. The abrupt shifts were very unsettling.

He pressed a hand to his heart as if in pain. "Why would I do that?" he exclaimed, the picture of injured innocence.

She tried to look stern. "I'm sure I don't know, but I wish you would stop. It puts me out of countenance."

"Your wish is my command." He adopted a more respectful air, but simultaneously tucked her hand more snugly under his elbow. It wasn't really a familiarity, she told herself. It couldn't be. His intentions were, must be, completely innocent. Really, she must stop reading too much significance into their contact. She had walked this closely with other gentlemen, arm in arm, and it had never crossed her mind that there was anything unseemly about it. But somehow, when Lord Malcolm touched her, it felt improper. Why had she suddenly turned skittish?

"Did you go away to school, or have you lived all your life at Crosby Hall?"

"What! Another question?" She shook her head, torn between amusement and exasperation. "You seem to want my life history. I can't imagine why it would interest you."

"You interest me."

Natalie almost stumbled, and Lord Malcolm hastened to correct himself. "I mean," he said, "that I need to understand your background, since you are acting as my child's governess."

Natalie had the distinct impression that that wasn't what he had meant at all. Her pulse kicked up a notch. The difficulty with Lord Malcolm was that one never knew what he would say or do next. He was generally perfectly charming and gentlemanlike, but every so often he would blurt out the strangest things! Or touch her in a way that made her feel . . . unsafe. He certainly seemed to be a creature of impulse. She tried very hard to banish the memory of his peculiar mention of marriage yesterday, but it *would* intrude. Repeatedly. Oh, dear.

When she did not immediately reply, he spoke again. "I was asking about school, actually, because I wasn't sure how long Hector has been the master at Crosby

Hall. I imagine life was easier for you while your father was living."

It was a question disguised as a statement, but his tone was friendly enough. She could hardly refuse to answer. The safest thing to do was reply, she decided, and then turn the subject.

"The estate has belonged to Hector for eight or nine years, in point of fact, but he only took up the reins lately. When he married. He used to live in London with his mother." They had reached the bottom of the hill and were heading into the wooded area where the stream ran between their properties. Natalie pointed. "The path is to our left," she said, glad that their slight misdirection gave her an excuse to let go of his arm and lead the way. He trailed in her wake until they reached the path, narrow but clear, that meandered toward the footbridge. A low-hanging branch partially blocked the entrance to it and he lifted it for her, saying, "Allow me." She gulped her thanks and ducked beneath his arm.

Coolness and a woodsy scent immediately enveloped them. It was like walking into a cave of green. Lord Malcolm breathed deeply. "What a pleasant spot," he said, pleasure warming his voice. "Even better in the afternoon than it was this morning. I am thinking of putting in a bench of some sort. Perhaps overlooking the stream. What say you to that?"

"I?" She lifted her brows in surprise. Why on earth would he consult the governess on such a question? How odd. "You must do as you see fit, of course. Do you fish, my lord?"

"A little. Is there any sport to be had in this brook? I had thought it too small."

"Well, perhaps there is more sport to be had by the very young," she admitted with a laugh. "I have fond memories of summer days spent down here with Derek, getting exceedingly wet and dirty. But now that I think about it, I believe most of our haul consisted of tadpoles and frogs."

"You know, I begin to feel a twinge of sympathy for Hector after all," remarked Lord Malcolm. "Where was he, while you and Derek were off playing?"

Natalie refused to rise to this bait. "I know what you are implying, but I assure you, you are wrong," she said, with mock severity. "We did not blight his life by excluding him, and there was nothing deliberate about it. He was simply too young to play with us."

She saw the query forming in his eyes and pretended to cover her ears. "No more questions, I beg of you! I will volunteer the information. I was nearly six when Hector was born. Derek is only thirteen months younger than I, so we were natural companions. People frequently assumed we were twins. And pray bear in mind that Hector was a baby in those days."

"Thank you, I will," he said meekly, and she smothered a laugh.

They had reached the little wooden bridge. Natalie ran lightly to its center and leaned over the rickety rail, peering into the slow, muddy stream. "There!" she exclaimed, pointing. "Tadpoles."

It had been a mistake to stop. He immediately came up beside her, his arm brushing hers. The contact sent a tingle all through her. Most inappropriate! She dared not let him guess how crazily his touch affected her. If she pulled away from him, he would surely wonder at it. So she stayed where she was, pressed lightly against him from shoulder to elbow, and endured the tingle.

It was an interesting sensation. One could even grow to like it.

"I see them," he said, and the bass rumble of his voice seemed to resonate down his arm and into her, vibrating the length of her body. "We must show them to Sarah sometime."

We. The word sent another jolt of electricity through her. Oh, this was madness. She had to pull away. "Yes," she said brightly, taking a step back. "We must."

He glanced curiously at her, but made no objection to leaving the bridge and continuing their stroll. He insisted on handing her over the fallen log that blocked the path on the other side of the brook, but that was the only nerve-wracking moment she faced until they emerged back into the sunshine on the other side of the narrow band of woods. At that point, as if it were the most natural thing in the world, he took her hand and tucked it back in the crook of his elbow. She would look like an idiot if she objected, she thought. So she did not object, but docilely clung to his arm all the way up the grassy rise to Crosby Hall.

"I don't know what the protocol is in this situation," he remarked as they approached the house. "It seems a bit cavalier to drop you at the door and walk away. On the other hand, I haven't sent my card round. And even if I had, I am unsure of my welcome at Crosby Hall. Your brother and sister-in-law may regard me in the light of a kidnaper."

"Pooh! Do you imagine that Hector and Mabel will turn you away? They will not dare." Natalie's eyes twinkled with mischief. "Although, I suppose it would be helpful to decide what your role is. Are you visiting a neighbor, paying a courtesy call on the local gentry, or merely seeing one of the servants home?"

"Ouch," muttered Lord Malcolm.

She laughed. "In all seriousness, there is no need to come in unless you wish to."

"In that case, I will postpone meeting Mr. and Mrs. Whittaker until another time. Much as it pains me to delay the treat, of course."

He took a very polite leave of her, pressing her hand in both of his and smiling in a way that puzzled and alarmed her. Her experience of men was limited—well, it was almost nil—but had any other gentleman looked at her in such a way, she would have thought he was deliberately trying to charm her.

She wouldn't go so far as to call his manner flirtatious . . . no, he did nothing that went beyond the bounds of common courtesy. But she could not shake the feeling that Lord Malcolm was up to something.

She frowned as she climbed the stairs to the small sitting room that adjoined her bedchamber. If she hadn't walked to the village yesterday, and hadn't encountered Sarah and Lord Malcolm at the inn, she wouldn't be in this tangle. She would have noticed the increased activity at Larkspur through her windows, discovered when everyone else did that His Grace's second son was in residence, paid a perfectly normal social call, and made his acquaintance in the ordinary way. Under *those* circumstances, she had to admit, the notion that Lord Malcolm might be flirting with her would be . . . well . . . exciting.

But those were not the circumstances in which she found herself. Instead of meeting Lord Malcolm as a social equal—or something very near it—she had placed herself in a situation where, to him, she was little better than a servant. And she had no one to blame but herself.

And, of course, Sarah. At the thought of Sarah, her lips curved involuntarily. Sarah was a darling, and she had loved her at once. She could not regret taking on the monumental task that loomed before her. Had she refused, Mrs. Thorpe would be in residence at Larkspur, and Sarah's new life would be as miserable as Natalie suspected her old life had been.

No, she did not regret her choice, she thought tiredly, sinking into her favorite wing chair. *Not yet,* a tiny voice whispered in her mind. *Not yet, and perhaps not ever,* she told herself firmly. But the tiny voice of unease still nagged at her, warning her that if the inappropriate flashes of attraction she felt toward Lord Malcolm continued, she could come to regret it very much indeed.

Chapter Ten

By the time Patterson reported to him, more than a fortnight had gone by. The long summer days had formed a lazy, contented pattern. Every morning, Malcolm and Sarah walked to Crosby Hall, met Natalie, and brought her back to Larkspur for breakfast. If the weather was fair, they spent the rest of the day mostly out of doors. When it was too hot, or on the days when it rained or blew, the party moved indoors—but it always felt like a party. In fact, it felt more like a party during inclement weather than fine weather, because they were less likely to be interrupted by Malcolm's social obligations. During fair weather, people made calls.

The circle of local gentry in the neighborhood was small, so the visits were not numerous, but Malcolm naturally did not want to slight those who did call on him. During these visits, and the calls that Malcolm paid in return, Natalie always withdrew.

This, more than any other single factor, illustrated for him the awkwardness of her situation. These people were her acquaintances and friends, but when they called she took Sarah and disappeared.

It seemed wrong that she felt she must hide when people she knew arrived on his doorstep, but he understood her reasons. He could imagine the gossip that would begin if she were caught "visiting" him every single time one of the local ladies called. Natalie said nothing about it, but she formed a habit of working with Sarah in the park behind the house. It was very pleasant in the park. It was also well out of sight of anyone coming up the drive to call on Malcolm. He wished he knew which consideration had most influenced her choice.

Social calls, though a nuisance, were infrequent. It was business that took him most often from Sarah and Natalie. He chose a room at the back of the house for his study, so that even while interviewing staff or poring over invoices his eyes could stray to the window and follow Natalie and Sarah in their summer frocks, bright splashes against the backdrop of green. Their favorite spot was beneath a certain chestnut tree that happened to be in full view of his study window. Natalie would spread a cloth on the shady grass and sit there with Sarah for hours. The sight of their heads bent together over a book, or Natalie's hands guiding Sarah's as she taught her penmanship or instructed her in needlework or drawing, always made him smile.

It was going well, he thought. It was going very well. It was going so well, in fact, that when he was greeted by the sight of Patterson one morning in July, bowing and smiling and rubbing his plump hands together, he was strongly inclined to send the fellow away again. Still, arrangements had to be made for paying Natalie and Mrs. Bigalow, as well as the other staff members he had hired. The solicitor's visit would not be a complete waste.

Malcolm waved him to a chair. Patterson looked around him at the neat bookshelves and comfortable furniture, beaming. "Very snug, my lord, very snug, indeed. I congratulate you. High time you took up residence at Larkspur, if you don't mind my saying so."

"I don't." He gave the man a tight little smile. No point in being sensitive about it; Patterson had known him all his life. "I'm sure you have wondered what was taking me so long."

Patterson looked embarrassed. "Oh, well, as to that, I'm sure it was nobody's business but your own."

"Quite," said Malcolm dryly.

Patterson hastily changed the subject. "I hear you have been able to secure a number of excellent employees on short notice."

"Yes, I have," said Malcolm, easing into the leather chair he had placed behind his desk. "Not due to my own ingenuity, I'm afraid. It was sheer luck. My neighbors at Crosby Hall dismissed most of their staff only a few weeks before I came here."

"You don't say!"

"Amazing, isn't it? They are all experienced, highly qualified individuals—and local. They naturally viewed my arrival on the scene as providential. And, I need hardly say, I viewed their availability for immediate hire in the same light." His eyes twinkled. "I find there is nothing like mutual gratitude to put employer and employee on an excellent footing."

"But how extraordinary," exclaimed Patterson, his small, round eyes wide with curiosity. "Really, almost inexplicable. A competent staff is extremely difficult to retain, especially so far from London. Why do you suppose . . . ?" He left the question delicately dangling.

Malcolm quirked an eyebrow. "There is a new bride at Crosby Hall."

Enlightenment appeared to dawn. Patterson chuckled.

"Ah. Just so. Well, let us hope that the young lady does not come to regret it. Very rash, upon my word! But a lucky stroke for us, as you say." He fumbled in his satchel and pulled out a sheaf of papers. "Shall we get down to business, then, my lord?"

Patterson whipped through the details of salary and banking arrangements with his usual efficiency, Malcolm signed his name a good many times, and by morning's end everything was complete—or nearly everything. Patterson finished by stacking the papers with a practiced hand and peering kindly through his spectacles at Malcolm.

"There was one other matter, my lord." His voice dropped to a conspiratorial whisper. "I have the results of those inquiries you asked the firm to put forward on your behalf."

Malcolm leaned back in his chair, a faint smile lifting the corners of his mouth. "I am fairly confident that you discovered nothing shocking in Miss Whittaker's background."

Despite his confidence, it was a relief when Patterson replied, "Nothing whatsoever, my lord. A very respectable family, originally from Lincolnshire. Landholders for many generations. Not of the nobility, you understand, but solid stock, very solid. She has a brother who presently acts as secretary to Lord Stokesdown, and he speaks most highly of the young man. As for the lady herself, I uncovered not a breath of scandal, not a single rumor. I found nothing that might lead you to think her unfit for . . . for any position you might have in mind." Patterson almost winked. It was evident that he had guessed the meaning behind Malcolm's inquiry. "Is it too soon to offer my felicitations?"

"You are a little ahead of yourself," Malcolm acknowledged. "Pray keep the matter confidential for the time being."

"Certainly, my lord. As you wish." The little man rose and gathered his things. "But if I may take the liberty of speaking frankly, sir, I have known you many years, as boy and man, and it gives me great satisfaction to see you at last where you should be, here at Larkspur—and appearing to enjoy life a trifle."

Malcolm's smile became strained. He shouldn't be enjoying life. Not after the terrible mistakes he had made. But he knew the solicitor meant it kindly, so he thanked him. Patterson bowed himself out and Malcolm, frowning, returned his gaze to the scene framed by his study window.

Natalie was laughing, bending over Sarah and helping her disentangle the crochet work she had begun. Sarah giggled, leaning against Natalie's knee with such a confiding air that Malcolm felt his heart constrict at the sight. Sarah adored Miss Whittaker. It would break her little heart if anything went wrong . . . if something, or someone, took Natalie away. He could not allow that to happen.

Thank God, Patterson had found no scandals in Natalie's past. No suitors, either, but that went without saying. Had there been suitors, she would hardly be free at her age; a woman of her station would naturally have married had an opportunity arisen. The opportunity had evidently not arisen. Malcolm counted that as a stroke of almost miraculous good fortune. In fact, he had never experienced such an amazing run of luck in his life as he had enjoyed since meeting Miss Whittaker.

Such extraordinary luck could not last forever. He was made painfully aware of that fact that very evening, at a dinner party given by Squire Farnsworth and his wife.

The party consisted of the three Whittakers, the Farnsworths, the ancient vicar and his widowed sister who kept house for him, Squire Farnsworth's two married sisters and their husbands, and himself. Among the dozen present, he was the only eligible gentleman and Natalie the only single lady, so he suspected a little good-natured matchmaking on the part of Mrs. Farnsworth. Buoyed by the satisfactory report from Patterson, Malcolm had no objection to this whatsoever. What gave him pause was that *Natalie* appeared distressed by it.

The Whittakers were the last to arrive. Hector and Mabel made a grand entrance, dazzling the gathering with their London-bought attire. Natalie trailed in their wake, less resplendent in a modest dinner dress of peach-colored silk. While Mr. and Mrs. Whittaker circled the room, bowing and chattering, Natalie hovered quietly by the door. He watched her, pleased by her appearance; she was neat and elegant from head to toe. This was the first time he had seen her in a social setting, and he planned to observe her closely. He owed it to his family to be sure that his intended bride carried herself well in public.

As he watched, Mrs. Farnsworth fluttered over to her side and greeted her with affection. Natalie smiled, but her eyes darted worriedly around the company. She said something to Mrs. Farnsworth in a low tone. Mrs. Farnsworth laughed. It was a false, self-conscious laugh, and the airy wave of the hand that went with it seemed to indicate that Natalie had expressed a concern that Mrs. Farnsworth was attempting to dismiss. Malcolm tried to catch Natalie's eye, but she studiously avoided him. Instead, she approached the vicar's pinch-faced sister and engaged her in conversation.

He guessed at once that the source of Natalie's dismay, and her avoidance of him, was the conspicuous position Mrs. Farnsworth had placed her in. At first, Malcolm was rather pleased by Natalie's reticence. He considered it one more proof of her innate good breeding, and he ticked off one more item on the mental list he had prepared. Really, the more he saw of her, the more pleased with her he was.

Ten minutes later, however, Mrs. Farnsworth publicly asked him to lead Natalie down to dinner. Malcolm almost winced. This move was so transparent that it could not go unremarked by the rest of the party. *Clumsy,* he thought. But at least it gave him an excuse to do what he wanted to do anyway—spend time at Natalie's side. He bowed and smiled, acknowledging his hostess's request. The curious glances and half-hidden smiles that followed him as he crossed to Natalie disturbed him not a whit, but Natalie's reaction did. She flushed scarlet and threw Mrs. Farnsworth a look of burning reproach. He actually overheard her murmur to Mrs. Farnsworth, "Anne, how *could* you?"

He pretended not to hear.

Natalie suffered herself to be led down to dinner by him, but he had the definite impression that she did so only to avoid creating a scene. She kept herself at as much of a distance from him as she could. He had to remind himself that any well-bred woman would react this way to such blatant matchmaking. Surely that was the only reason she was behaving so stiffly.

As they descended the stairs, he leaned down to her and whispered, "Buck up, Miss Whittaker. I think she meant it kindly."

Natalie gave a tiny, mortified shake of her head. To his amusement, a curl sprang eagerly out of her coiffure and danced beside her ear. "I should not have been accorded this honor," she told him. "It's not proper. You should have Anne on your arm—Mrs. Farnsworth—not me. Or perhaps Mabel, since she is still a bride."

"Heaven forbid."

There wasn't time for more; the dining room was reached and places taken. Their brief exchange had relieved his mind somewhat; perhaps it was only her sense of propriety that had been offended. Meanwhile, Natalie was placed almost directly across from him. This was better, in some ways, than having her beside him. He liked watching the candlelight play on her features. And he enjoyed watching the tiny curls work loose from their confines, as they always did. It tickled him to observe the ongoing battle she waged with her rebellious hair. There was something delightful about the fact that she never quite succeeded in taming those curls.

Natalie soon lost all signs of the agitation she had displayed in the drawing room. She looked perfectly calm. Miss Whittaker had poise, he thought, his admiration kicking up another notch. He knew his father would be disappointed that he had chosen a woman with respectable, rather than exalted, connections, especially since her fortune appeared insignificant. But the more he saw of her, the more confident he was that Natalie would soon win Father over.

These complacent reflections continued almost all the way through the soup course, until they were rudely interrupted by one of the squire's sisters. She leaned toward Natalie, her expression an unpleasant blend of avidity and malice, and said, "Only fancy, Miss Whittaker, there is a rumor going round of your *working* at Larkspur."

Her words somehow cut through the babble and clink

that filled the room. A hush fell. Malcolm could sense the ears pricking up, all around the table.

Mabel Whittaker gave an angry little titter. "Oh, there is no limit to what impertinent people will say."

Natalie's calm expression did not alter, but he thought he saw a pink spot appear high on each of her cheekbones. She swallowed her soup and touched her napkin lightly to the corners of her mouth before replying. *Stalling,* thought Malcolm approvingly. *Very good.*

"Fancy that," she murmured, in a tone of mild surprise. And returned to her soup.

It was a masterful set-down. She neither confirmed nor denied the rumor; she simply made it clear that the woman's curiosity was as vulgar as the gossip.

Snubbed by her intended prey, the squire's sister turned determinedly to Malcolm, a false smile wreathing her face. "I wonder how these rumors get started?" she remarked.

Malcolm gave her a bland smile. "Do you? I wonder *why* they get started. It seems almost malicious." He shook his head, feigning bafflement. "Very strange."

The vicar's mild voice chimed in. "I hope you will not think our little community is overly interested in one another's business, Lord Malcolm. On the whole, I would say we are rather *less* inclined to gossip than most neighborhoods. This is the most welcoming and kind-hearted parish it has been my pleasure to serve. I shall never forget my experience in Worthing, when I was quite a young man . . ." At that, he launched into a gentle tale, bless him, that completely changed the subject and diverted all attention from Natalie and Malcolm.

Still, it had been a narrow escape. The sooner he secured Natalie's hand, the better. That was the only sure way to silence any wagging tongues.

He waited impatiently through the interminable dinner, barely able to concentrate on the idle conversation required at such functions, watching Natalie out of the corner of his eye and trying to think how best to get her alone. His opportunity came at last, when the gathering reconvened in the squire's drawing room. He strolled over to her with a casual air, bowing, for the benefit of any prying eyes, as if they were mere acquaintances rather than friends.

"I wonder if you would join me for a breath of air, Miss Whittaker? It's a bit stuffy in here."

Her expression was wary, but she nodded her assent. "Just while the card tables are being set up," she said. She added, under her breath, "We must remain in full view of the others."

"Very well. We'll step out on the balcony." He held the French window open for her and she passed out ahead of him. She crossed her arms before her, clutching her elbows as if instinctively guarding herself, and halted by the low balustrade. He joined her and she averted her face, offering only her profile.

"I am sorry," she said in a low tone. "What a ghastly evening."

"Yes, it is," he agreed. "But I don't see why you should apologize for it."

"Mrs. Farnsworth is a friend of mine. I should have known she would try to . . . I should have known she would embarrass us tonight."

"I'm not embarrassed in the least." He leaned casually against the balustrade, trying to get a better view of her features. "Not by her matchmaking attempts, at any rate. I own, hearing the rumors concerning your employment unnerved me a trifle."

She looked dispirited. "Yes. That unnerved me as well."

He frowned. "It is I, not you, who must apologize for that. I had not anticipated the awkwardness we would encounter at affairs such as this. It has been painful to me to watch you efface yourself whenever a neighbor comes to call. This is even worse."

She gave a mirthless little laugh. "Much worse. I cannot escape."

"You must not distress yourself, Miss Whittaker. And pray do not blame Mrs. Farnsworth. Your friend believes that pairing you with me would be doing you a favor." He paused, trying to gauge her reaction, but she appeared too mortified to look at him. "I do wish you agreed with her," he said softly.

She hugged herself more tightly, closing her eyes as if in pain. His instinct was to touch her, but he dared not. The French windows stood open just a few feet behind them and they were, as she had requested, in full view of the others. He suppressed his inclination with difficulty, and waited respectfully for her to speak. When she did not, he swore under his breath.

"I have placed you in an intolerable situation," he said ruefully. "The fault is entirely my own. I heartily beg your pardon. I ought to have foreseen all this."

"Yes," she said again, almost inaudibly. She opened her eyes and faced him, then, her expression bleak. "I did foresee it, and still I agreed to become Sarah's governess. It was wrong of me."

"Oh, come now—"

"Wrong of me," she repeated firmly. "Even though I have remained at Crosby Hall rather than join your household, my position is impossible to maintain. I see that now. I cannot have a foot in both worlds. I cannot serve on your staff during the day, and dine with you as your equal at night. One role or the other must be discarded. It is useless to pretend otherwise."

Good Lord, what a perfect opening. He took a deep breath and smiled. "Miss Whittaker, you are right, as usual. I believe I have a solution for this dilemma. May I tell you what it is?"

She held up one hand to stop him, looking miserable. "Pray let me finish. Had you taken me back with you to Lancashire, where the name Whittaker means nothing, our arrangement might have been possible. Here, in this parish, my status is unalterable. My brother is the largest landholder in the community. I cannot change that, and if I could, I wouldn't. You must take me off your payroll, Lord Malcolm. I cannot work for you."

"I will take you off my payroll on one condition. Will you—"

"No conditions." She frowned, tight-lipped. "What must be, must be. I realize I gave you my word. You needn't tell me; I know how unconscionable it would be for me to walk away from you, and from Sarah, without a backward look."

"I'm glad we agree on that much, at least. I don't think you should walk away. In fact—"

"Good, for I don't intend to do so." She looked relieved. "I will still come to Larkspur every day. I will still teach Sarah, as we agreed. I am saying only that I cannot accept *payment.* I cannot be your employee. I will come to you as your friend. As Sarah's friend."

He almost laughed aloud. "I can't allow you to do that," he said. "It would put me under too great an obligation. Would you do all the work of a governess but receive nothing in return? It's absurd."

"It's not absurd," she said defensively. "I'm very fond of Sarah. I enjoy teaching her."

"Miss Whittaker, I am delighted to hear that. More delighted than you know. But even the Bible says that the laborer is worthy of his hire. Teaching is labor. And despite your affection for her, Sarah is not an easy pupil."

"Nevertheless, I—"

"Miss Whittaker." He knew he sounded exasperated. He couldn't help it. "Pay attention. I am asking you to marry me."

She stared at him, the color draining from her face. "What?" she said faintly.

He took her firmly by the arms and turned her to face him. "I can find another teacher. But *you* I cannot replace. You are already far more to Sarah than a governess, and I want to ensure, quite frankly, that no matter what the future may bring, you will not leave us to go elsewhere."

She looked dazed. She closed her eyes as if gathering strength. "Lord Malcolm," she said, her voice dangerously calm, "pray take your hands off me."

He could not bring himself to unhand her; he was afraid she would turn and run. His hands tightened on her arms. "Did you hear what I said? Miss Whittaker— Natalie—I want to make you my wife."

Her eyes flew open, sparkling with anger. "Let me *go*."

He was baffled by her response. Let her go? He couldn't. She hadn't said yes. He slid his hands down to her elbows, trying not to hurt her, trying not to frighten her. "Listen to me," he urged. "I suppose this seems sudden to you. But I have been thinking of it for days—since the first day I met you, in fact. My dear girl, it would solve all our problems at a single stroke. Think! You could leave Hector's roof forever. The gossips would be silenced. Your future would be assured; you would be safe and respectable."

"And rich," she said, irony salting her voice. "And well connected."

"Those, too. I know material considerations mean nothing to you—"

"They mean less than nothing. For heaven's sake, Lord Malcolm—"

"Malcolm. You may stop 'lording' me."

"And you may take your hands off me. *Now.* I am not joking."

"Neither am I," he said, bewildered. But he dropped his hands. "What's amiss? You act as if I just insulted you."

"You did," she said crisply. She still looked pale. "You care nothing about silencing the gossips. You want to marry me because you want a mother for Sarah."

Was *that* all? He almost laughed with relief. "Of course I want a mother for Sarah," he said impatiently. "There's nothing ignoble about that. And why shouldn't you accept my offer? It's a better bargain than working as a blasted governess—even if you let me pay you, which now you tell me you won't."

"It's certainly a better bargain for you," she said, trembling with indignation. "A wife can't hand in her notice, can she? No matter what."

His jaw dropped. "What the deuce! Do you think I would mistreat you?"

"How can I tell what you would do?" She hugged herself again, shivering. "You seem to be ruled entirely by impulse! I've never seen anything like it. 'I think I'll move to Larkspur . . . I think I'll fire this highly recommended governess and hire a stranger with no experience . . . oh, and, while I'm at it, why not *marry* her? No point in doing the thing by halves.' Frankly, Lord Malcolm, I fear you are deranged."

She spun on her heel and marched back into the Farnsworths' drawing room, head held high. He stared after her for a moment, completely nonplussed. Deranged! Of all the cheek! Of all the outrageous—

His inward splutterings halted as he recognized the kernel of truth at the heart of her assertions. Thunderation, the woman was right. Viewed from her perspective, his actions must seem maniacal. She didn't know what had come before. She didn't know his reasons. And he wasn't entirely sure whether, or how much, he wanted her to know.

Fuming, he returned to the drawing room. Mrs. Farnsworth pounced on him, beaming and giggling, and tried to lure him to join Miss Whittaker's table. He resisted with great firmness. He would play whist with the vicar. He would be *delighted* to play whist with the vicar. He would play rational, meticulous, entirely sane whist, and prove once and for all, to anyone who cared to notice, that Malcolm Chase was of sound mind.

Ruled by impulse. Deranged. Hah! He wasn't deranged. But he had to admit, she might have a point about the impulse nonsense.

Chapter Eleven

Natalie leaned lazily back on her elbows and watched Lord Malcolm's line dangling in the shady water. A rowboat on a warm afternoon was utterly relaxing. Sarah had already fallen asleep on a cushion placed in the floor of the boat, her head pillowed on the seat nearest the prow. Natalie sat toward the stern, elbows propped comfortably on the sides of the boat. Lord Malcolm was fishing from the center of the boat, but not seriously. Had the small lake been teeming with fish, which it probably wasn't, midafternoon was not the likeliest time to catch any. Fishing was merely a pretext, an excuse to float out on the cool water, drift in the shade nearest the shore, and listen to nature's melody. A breeze rustled the trees overhead, birds called sweetly to each other, and occasionally cattle lowed in the distance. It was heavenly, in a drowsy sort of way.

A breeze tickled the back of her neck, and Natalie let her head drop back, savoring the feel of it caressing her face. "Mmm," she murmured. "I do love summer."

"It has its charms."

His voice was unusually soft, obviously in deference to his sleeping daughter. Heavens, what a voice the man had. It made something deep inside her loosen and melt. Dangerous. Delicious. Who would have thought a mere voice could evoke such powerful feelings? Natalie opened her eyes and lifted her head again, trying to keep herself from liquefying before his very eyes. This turned out to be a mistake. He was looking at her, the intensity in his ice-blue eyes weakening her even further.

"I think I have to thank you," he said, still in that soft, low tone.

"For what?" she whispered. Sarah's sleeping presence should be a deterrent to intimacy. Instead, it forced them to converse in voices suitable for a darkened bedroom. *Or a church,* she reminded herself. But the darkened bedroom was what came to mind.

Even his smile was soft and intimate. "For not avoiding me. For staying my friend."

She felt herself blushing. "Nonsense." It was terrible to be thanked for something she was secretly ashamed of. She knew perfectly well that she ought to be keeping him at a distance. She simply couldn't bring herself to do it. Her craving for his company was a weakness. A serious, baffling weakness.

He quirked an eyebrow at her. "It's no small thing. When a lady rejects a man's proposal, a little awkwardness between them is inevitable. I'm glad you didn't cut my acquaintance."

"I have taken pity on you," she said mendaciously. "Since I know your wits to be addled."

"Handsome of you."

"Thank you," she said demurely.

She was teasing, but she saw his expression grow thoughtful. "Someday," he said softly, "I will explain myself to you. And you'll see that I'm not quite as addled as I appear."

"You could hardly be as addled as you appear."

He laughed and she glanced warningly at Sarah, placing a finger against her lips. He leaned forward on his knees, bringing his face closer to her and lowering his voice still further. "You may be right. I am unable to give up the notion of marrying you. I keep picturing you as my wife. And I like the picture more and more. Crazy, isn't it?"

Her pulse began to race. She tried to frown, but failed. "A *gentleman* would never mention that subject again."

"This gentleman has no choice. How else am I to change your mind?"

She wished it were possible to say, *You won't change my mind,* and put an end to the discussion. Unfortunately, Natalie was too honest. The words wouldn't come. She did manage to look cross, at least. "My dear, sir, this is hardly the time or place—"

"Oh, I'm not planning to ambush you with another offer of marriage. I merely thought it was high time we discussed the topic like rational creatures."

"What topic? Marriage?"

"That's right. Marriage in general. Not our marriage in particular."

Our marriage. A tiny thrill ran through her at the words. What a goose she was! It was ridiculous to let this man invade her dreams the way he had. But she couldn't help it. She was only human. She had felt drawn to Malcolm from the moment she met him. He was prone to inexplicable behavior from time to time, but still . . .

Besides, there was something about receiving a marriage proposal from a man that inevitably altered a lady's perception of him. She had received not one, but two offers from Lord Malcolm—if she counted that absurd remark he made on the first night they met. Three, if she counted this silly encounter.

Lately, she could not see him without remembering his offer. She could not think of him without thinking of it. The idea was, to be perfectly frank, preying on her mind. It was even keeping her awake at night.

She couldn't let him know how his offhanded proposals had affected her. The last thing she wanted was to find herself suddenly engaged to a man who would marry her for all the wrong reasons.

She felt a craven need to put more space between their bodies. She leaned against the low wall of the boat's side, easing her body to the edge to trail her fingertips in the water. "I see," she said, although she didn't. She kept her eyes on the ripples her light touch sent across the water. "Is that supposed to make me feel more comfortable? Discussing marriage in the abstract?"

She saw, out of the corner of her eye, the disarming smile he bent upon her. "I hoped it would help," he said. "I don't mean to press you—"

"Yes, you do," she muttered.

"—but I would like to know what your objections are. It has occurred to me that it may be marriage, itself, that you object to. Not specifically marriage to me."

She looked at him then, amusement warring with exasperation. "Why would I object to marriage? It is the foundation of civilized society."

He looked chagrined. "Then it is me you dislike. May I ask why?"

There were times, she thought, when she simply wanted to shake the man. This was one of them.

"I don't dislike you," she said patiently. "I like you. But not enough to marry you. Is that so hard to understand?"

It wasn't strictly true, but she had sounded convincing enough. He shifted in his seat, and the boat rocked beneath them like a cradle. "Frankly, yes. I hope you are not one of those females who—" He stopped abruptly, as if cutting himself off before he could say something offensive.

Natalie stiffened. "Who what?" Her eyes narrowed. "Who hope to be married for their own sakes, rather than for *practical* reasons?"

"Well, I wouldn't put it that way," he growled. "But I will tell you, Miss Whittaker, speaking as one who has some experience of marriage, that practical reasons are the best reasons to marry. These so-called 'love matches' are usually more wretched than blissful."

A chill struck at her heart. Was he speaking of his marriage to Catherine? Had he loved her? He must have loved her. And had she made him miserable? Natalie did not dare ask. She took a deep breath and kept her voice steady. "When the marriage is based on fleeting attraction, I grant you, misery is often the result. And unrequited love also is miserable. Or so I hear."

Ah, there it was. Lines of pain appeared in his face. He seemed to withdraw from her, his eyes turning cold and bleak. "Indeed it is," he said. "Unrequited love can drive one mad."

This definitely sounded like the voice of experience.

Natalie felt a keen stab of something that felt suspiciously like jealousy. She sternly repressed it. Lord Malcolm's feelings for his late wife were none of her business. And they were supposed to be speaking of marriage in the abstract, not the particular. She returned to her theme. "But true affection between man and wife—"

"Friendship. The affection of friendship is best in

marriage. Liking is a stronger foundation than love, or what people call love."

"Friendship should be part of it. But I disagree with you; I think it should not be the whole. Marriage should be based on something deeper."

He appeared genuinely agitated. "Miss Whittaker, forgive me, but you are talking nonsense. Sentimental twaddle! It's plain you know nothing of the matter. Love is a trap. A delusion. I have never seen it lead to anything but pain."

"Again, you speak of infatuation. Or of that silly state where people long so deeply to fall in love that they *fancy* themselves in love, generally fixing their emotions on some unsuitable, or completely incompatible, person. I am speaking of"—she took a deep breath, knowing before she said it that she was going to sound like an idiot—"true love."

He stared at her in disbelief. And, she thought, disappointment. It pained her to see him look disappointed in her. "What a bag of moonshine," he muttered disgustedly. "Have you ever been in love?"

She glanced again at Sarah, but the little girl slept soundly. "No," she said, very softly but very firmly. "I have not. But I will not marry without it."

He leaned forward again, earnestness in every line of his body. "Miss Whittaker, you're a sensible woman. I beg you, do not waste your life crying for the moon. Do not stay single, waiting for a man who does not exist. I offer you honest friendship. And loyalty. I will promise to honor you, respect you, and cherish you. You will want for nothing. And we will talk together like rational creatures, not fancying ourselves injured over trifles. I promise you, friendship like ours is superior to *love* in every way." His voice dripped with contempt when he said *love*.

Oh, this was terrible. How could she make him understand? She shook her head, her emotions in turmoil. "I would be unhappy," she managed to say. "Do not press me further. I cannot marry without love. I will not marry without love." Anger suddenly licked through her. She lifted her chin and stared coolly into his eyes. "And if you badger me about this once more, Lord Malcolm, I will be forced to redraw the boundaries of our friendship. I cannot allow you to see me alone if I must continually fear a renewal of your suit."

He went very still. The lines around his mouth drew tight. "I beg your pardon," he said stiffly. "I will not embarrass you again with my unwelcome proposals."

"Thank you."

She had won. Why did she feel as if she had lost? A twinge of despair made her wish she could crawl into a hole somewhere and have a good cry. She *hated* behaving like a tight-laced prude. But what else could she do? If he continued to press her on this, she would go mad.

She shouldn't keep seeing him alone like this—or as good as alone, since a sleeping child hardly counted. The problem was that she looked forward to seeing him. Her heart lifted every time he came into view. She supposed she had been lonely, all these years. At any rate, having a friend was such a treat, she could not bear to give him up simply because he had proposed to her a time or two. Or three. Holding herself aloof would punish her as well as him. What was the point of that?

She studied him covertly as he adjusted the neglected fishing line. He was frowning at the fishing line, not at her, but it was clearly she who had annoyed him. Her heart sank.

She had angered him with her prissy refusal to discuss the subject. This was no way to win his regard.

Not, of course, that she knew the first thing about it.

What makes a man fall in love with a lady? Natalie mused. She had no idea. Were there books on such subjects? Did women learn it from one another, sharing secrets in a sisterhood from which she had somehow been excluded? Or were some women simply born with the knack, a God-given talent that others—like herself—lacked?

And how could *anyone,* let alone Natalie Whittaker, make this particular man fall in love? A man who claimed to believe that the kind of love Natalie longed for did not exist? A man who, if he did believe in love, thought it was a dangerous aberration rather than a desirable state? Oh, it was hopeless.

And yet, the more time she spent with Malcolm Chase, the more certain she was that if he *could* love her . . . if marriage to him offered her something more than a sort of permanent governess post . . . she would be strongly tempted to accept his offer. She had begun to suspect that behind his odd, abrupt shifts of mood and impulsive behavior lay a heart full of intense emotion. He seemed to feel so deeply that he scarcely knew how to contain his feelings. Such a man, if he loved, would love passionately.

If he loved. That was the catch. The *if* was a towering obstacle.

She knew it was commonplace for couples to marry without love; she wasn't completely naive. Some couples married while barely acquainted with each other. And the higher up the social ladder a family was, the more common it was to choose a mate in much the same way one chose a horse. Still, from clues that he had dropped, she suspected that he had loved Catherine to distraction. Indignation rose in her at the thought. How little he must think of her, if he expected her to play second fiddle to a ghost! And how little he knew her, if he thought she would consent to such a degradation!

What had Catherine done, she wondered, to make him love her so? And what had she done that had made him so unhappy? And why had he decided that love itself, not Catherine, was to blame? Could he ever love again, or was his heart utterly unreachable? She wished she knew. Because if it were only possible, if there were a single shred of hope that he might, someday, love her, she was strongly inclined to try for it.

The task seemed daunting, indeed. He seemed determined to think of her as a friend, and nothing more—even if he married her.

To make a man fall in love was enough of a challenge. To make him fall in love against his will seemed impossible.

Malcolm strode up the wooded hill, scowling. He vented his feelings from time to time by whacking at the underbrush with his walking stick when it impeded his progress, but for the most part he brooded. He was in a very black mood.

He had acted like a complete dunderhead out on the lake with Natalie. He had promised himself—and her, confound it!—that he wasn't going to blurt out another marriage proposal, and then, ten minutes later, out it had come. If it happened again, he would lose her utterly. He couldn't risk that.

It wasn't just Sarah who had grown dependent on her, he had to admit. He was all but addicted to her himself. But that didn't matter. His feelings didn't matter. What mattered was Sarah. He needed to remarry. The devil! He *wanted* to remarry. And Natalie was the perfect candidate. Now that he had found her, he would not let her slip through his fingers.

This was no whim. He had planned to remarry almost immediately after Catherine's death. But first the prescribed period of mourning had to be observed, and afterward it had proved unexpectedly difficult to find the right lady. Most unmarried ladies fell into two camps: too young and too old. The ones that were the right age, if they had anything to recommend them at all, were already married.

He remembered the Season in London he had endured, eighteen months after Catherine's death, and shuddered. He had dragged himself down to London and dutifully danced with all the children paraded before him by the matchmaking mamas, but couldn't picture himself married to any of them. Some giggled, some were awkward, some were too forward, some too shy. And all were so young that they made him feel like a graybeard. No dewy-eyed chit fresh from the schoolroom for him, thank you. After the sufferings of his first marriage, he wanted a partner and an equal.

He had met several interesting women with whom it was no punishment to converse, but they were all married except one—a widow a few years older than himself. Unfortunately, it wasn't practical to offer marriage to an older woman. He needed a lady with most of her childbearing years ahead of her.

Children were important, especially now that it was clear that Arthur would never produce a boy. It was up to Malcolm to secure the secession. He needed a son, and the sooner the better. Natalie may turn up her nose at "practical" reasons to marry, but the practical reasons

were damned good ones—and they had nothing to do
with falling in love.

Love! He snorted at the thought. The word itself irri-
tated him. Catherine had clung like a millstone around
his neck, prating of love, mewling and whining and
making herself ill. For years, he had felt guilty that he
could not return her regard. For years, he'd endured her
endless reproaches and her sad, sad eyes, feeling mean
and small because he didn't love her, couldn't make
himself love her. Eventually he began to suspect that all
her tears and megrims had been trumped up to manipulate him. It was disgust with her petty machinations that
had led him to . . . ah, God, he could not think of it. It
did no good to think of it.

Which version of his past was true? That he had
bruised and broken his wife's heart, or that she had had a
mania for controlling him? Did the truth lie somewhere
in between? He supposed he would never know the answer. All he knew was that the very mention of *love*
caused a miasma of disgust to rise up and choke him.

He emerged from the woods at the top of the rise,
breathing hard but feeling better. Nothing like exercise
to clear a man's brain. He halted to look down at the
view. Below him on the left were the roof and chimneys
of Crosby Hall. From this vantage point, it was possible
to trace exactly where the Tudor portion ended and the
more modern sections had been added. It was an archi-
tectural nightmare, he supposed, but it had a certain
homelike charm. Around it, neat fields stretched as far as
the eye could see, dotted with tenant cottages. Crosby
Hall was obviously a working, prosperous estate. It
fairly bustled with activity.

By contrast, down the hill on the right stood his own
home. Larkspur, gracefully poised atop a gentle rise, was

elegant and self-contained. Its pretty, useless park contained no tenants, no spreading acreage bursting with grain, no livestock. Larkspur was a rich family's plaything, not a farm. It was purely ornamental. Much like his own life, he mused. But marriage and children—a son—those prizes, once he obtained them, would lend purpose to his existence.

But how to obtain them? He frowned, unseeing, at the landscape. He had never guessed that the reason why Natalie remained single was that she cherished these idiotic schoolgirl notions about love. She seemed a level-headed female, and she was demonstrably intelligent. Why would any rational creature cling to such delusions? And, more to the purpose, how could he convince her to abandon them?

It would be hard to woo a woman who was determined to marry for love, and only for love. Hoaxing her was out of the question. The very notion of pretending to feel emotions he did not feel was repugnant to Malcolm. An honorable man shouldn't sham such a thing—even if he could, which was doubtful. He had certainly never fooled Catherine on the rare occasions when he had tried. But how could he win Natalie's hand without it?

It was clear that mere argument was not going to change her mind. Showing her the absurdity of her views or attempting to reason her out of her sentimental illusions would only raise her hackles. No one, not even a female, enjoyed being proven wrong. If finding herself still on the shelf at her age hadn't given her pause, obviously there was nothing he could say or do to pluck the cobwebs from her brain.

Or was there?

An idea occurred to him. A risky but interesting idea.

Natalie was a woman grown. She was no shrinking seventeen-year-old. She had needs. Every healthy woman is capable of desire. But Natalie was so untouched she probably wasn't even aware of that incredibly significant fact.

But he was aware of it. And knowledge, as they say, is power.

Could he use her own instincts against her? Did he dare? Would it be honorable? Hah! All policy's allowed in war and love, he reminded himself grimly. The gamble was, she might very well send him packing the instant he touched her. But he couldn't convince her to marry him as it was, so he had little to lose.

He strolled back down the hill toward Larkspur, thinking hard. He couldn't just grab Natalie and kiss her. She'd probably slap his face, and that wasn't the outcome he had in mind. No, the art of seduction required a certain atmosphere. His experience with women was not vast, but at least he knew that much. Kisses had to be coaxed, not bludgeoned. Timing was everything. He could wait forever for the perfect moment to arrive on its own, or he could seize the day—or night, as it were—and create the moment.

High time, thought Malcolm, that he repaid a few social obligations. It was a pity that a bachelor couldn't host a ball, but an elegant dinner would be doable at Larkspur. And a little informal dancing afterward, simply as a means of entertaining the company, frequently occurred at dinner parties. Even dinner parties hosted by widowers. He couldn't invite people for the express purpose of dancing, but if dancing sprang up, seemingly on the spur of the moment . . .

He might not be able to offer Natalie the true love she craved, but he could damn well dance with her. He could flirt with her—if he remembered how. He had already established their friendship. Now he would supplement that with music and romance and good, old-fashioned bodily contact. And with a little luck, he would make her see that that was enough.

Chapter Twelve

"I don't know what you mean," said Natalie demurely. She cast her eyes modestly downward and took a delicate sip of punch. She did, in fact, know—or at least suspect—what he meant. He was right. She had been avoiding him all evening with a circumspection so elaborate that it bordered on the comical.

Lord Malcolm's brows lifted. "Oh, I think you do. You understand English pretty well. Why won't you stand up with me, for instance? It's only a country dance."

If anyone were to glance their way—and she knew that covert glances had followed her all evening—she hoped she looked bored. She wasn't bored. Her heart pounded every time Malcolm approached her. And he had approached her with embarrassing persistence tonight. But it would kill her if anyone guessed her feelings. It would just kill her. She gave him a polite, distant smile. "Thank you, Lord Malcolm, but I do not care to dance."

"Confound it!" He looked as sulky as a thwarted toddler. "I arranged this entire affair just so I could dance with you. Don't make me beg."

She was so astonished she scarcely knew where to look. "You're joking."

"Hardly," he snapped. "And it wasn't easy, believe me, to hire a couple of competent violinists out here in the middle of nowhere."

"I would have been glad to play on the pianoforte—"

"I daresay! And then I never would have been able to dance with you at all. Fortunately, the pianoforte had stood idle for so long that it was out of tune."

She bit back a laugh, secretly pleased that he had gone to so much trouble. "You did it very artfully," she observed, shaking her head in admiration. "I had no notion you planned on dancing. It all seemed to occur spontaneously." She pointed across the room. "Look at Anne Farnsworth urging the violinist to play another cotillion! I'm sure she thinks this is all her idea."

"Well, it isn't," he said mulishly. "I had to dance with her first because she's the squire's wife, but I'll be da— I'll be jiggered if I lead that bucktoothed Beasley woman out next. Have mercy, Miss Whittaker. Dance with me."

She gave a little spurt of laughter and relented, setting down her punch glass. "You put it so beautifully, how can I resist?"

"That's more like it," he grumbled, but she heard the amusement beneath his growl. She laid her gloved hand lightly on his arm, her bland expression masking the swirl of pleasurable excitement she felt, and docilely followed him to where the line of couples was forming. She had, naturally, been dying to dance with him. She simply hadn't known how to accomplish it without adding to the whispers buzzing round the neighborhood. Still, as he had promised, it was only a country dance. They would be one of several couples. They would not be conspicuous in any way—or so she told herself.

This assessment turned out to be overly optimistic.
She dropped her hand from Malcolm's arm the instant
they joined the set, and was careful to bestow her smiles
equally among the persons surrounding her. She touched
him when the dance required it, but no differently than
she touched the other gentlemen. She kept a modest distance between herself and her partner at all times. All
this caution was a plaguey nuisance and took most of the
pleasure out of dancing with him. And it was all for
nothing; *still* she felt exposed!

Out of the corner of her eye she saw the knowing
glances following her, and the few ladies who were not
dancing whispering to each other behind their hands. By
the end of the dance she was flushed with annoyance as
well as exertion. It had been a mistake to dance with
Lord Malcolm. She would not do it again.

She drifted away from him, trying to make her movement seem natural and aimless, but he pursued her. Desperate, she took to the floor with Jasper Farnsworth and
galloped through the Sir Roger de Coverley. Malcolm
was right behind her every step of the way, with Mrs.
Beasley in tow. At the end of the reel, breathless, she accepted a fresh glass of punch from one of the servants
and edged toward the terrace door. Jasper waylaid Malcolm briefly, but soon he broke away and, like an arrow
loosed from a string, headed straight for her. She fastened her gaze on the opposite wall and drank her punch,
wishing she could fade into the wallpaper.

He joined her. She gave him a cool nod and returned
her gaze to the opposite wall. It was an effort to maintain
her bored expression when Malcolm's eyes seemed to be
burning a hole right through her. "What do you hope to
accomplish by treating me as if we were strangers?" he

asked her abruptly. "Everyone here is aware of our friendship."

Her bored expression slipped a little. "That is precisely the problem," she said crisply. "There are many interested eyes upon us this evening. I am determined to give them nothing whatsoever to discuss over their breakfast cups tomorrow."

"They will discuss your standoffishness, and draw from it precisely the conclusions you seek to avoid."

No one was looking at them at the moment, so she took the opportunity to scowl at him. "Certainly they will, if you continue to show me more attention than you should. For heaven's sake, go and talk to the vicar. Talk to Hector. Talk to anyone but me."

"But I like talking to you," said Malcolm plaintively. "And I dislike talking to Hector."

Natalie, in the act of taking another sip of punch, choked. Malcolm patted her helpfully on the back. She looked daggers at him. "Thank you," she managed at last. "There's no need to pound me. Will you kindly stop making me conspicuous?"

There was a decided twinkle in his ice-blue eyes. "I'm not responsible for the stares, Miss Whittaker. Tonight all eyes would follow you regardless of what I did. You are beautiful."

She looked uncertainly at him. Was he making sport of her? Apparently not; the gleam of admiration in his eyes seemed genuine. Flustered, she returned her gaze to her punch cup. "Rubbish," she said woodenly and took another sip.

"It's not rubbish. You outshine every other lady in the room."

She could not suppress her smile, but she hid it against the rim of her cup. "I shall try not to become too puffed up in my own esteem," she promised him, "now that you have clarified your statement a trifle."

He looked surprised, then broke into a grin as he apparently caught her meaning. The other ladies present had little claim to beauty. Two were ancient of days, Mabel was obviously pregnant, Mrs. Beasley was indeed bucktoothed, Anne Farnsworth had always been homely, and poor Miss Spivey had the protruding eyes and wet mouth of a fish.

He rubbed his chin ruefully. "I do this sort of thing badly," he confessed. "I meant to compliment you."

This time, she lifted her chin and looked directly at him. "Why?"

She had hoped to knock him off balance, but his grin only widened. "Come out to the garden with me and I'll show you."

Heat shot through her, flushing her cheeks. She looked away, shaken and furious. "Stop teasing me," she ordered, willing her voice not to tremble. "For pity's sake, sir, go away. You have other guests."

"None as interesting as you."

Natalie felt as if she were suffocating. "Stop it. You'll ruin everything." She hadn't meant to say that, but it slipped out. It was a mournful cry, straight from her heart. She tried to recover by saying lightly, "It is bad enough, sir, that you propose to me several times a week. Until now, we have been able to keep that peculiar habit of yours private. If you dance attendance on me in public, I will be forced to withdraw from you." And that was the last thing in the world she wanted to do. *The second-last thing,* she reminded herself. The *very* last thing she wanted to do was enter a loveless marriage. For some reason, that grew harder to remember with each passing day.

An arrested look had banished Malcolm's teasing smile. His brows knitted in a swift frown. "Thunderation, woman, what are you worried about? Your reputation is safe. Your standing in the community is safe. You won't even let me pay you for your work with Sarah, so you are now, officially, nothing more than a friend of the family. What could be tamer than that?"

She dropped the pretense and faced him fully, her heart in her eyes. "Don't you see, sir, that I cannot remain your friend if everyone believes that you are courting me? If you follow me about, trying to catch my eye—if you corner me and engage me in conversation at every opportunity . . ."

His frown deepened. "You are too obsessed with decorum. All this hairsplitting and hand-wringing over nothing—"

"It is not 'nothing' to me!"

"Sorry," he said curtly. "I don't mean to make light of your feelings. I know the community is small, and gossip runs rampant in such places. And I know you care what these people think of you; you've lived here all your life. But I can't worry about what others think, every time I converse with a lady I find interesting. I don't give a tinker's damn what people say over their breakfast cups. And frankly, Miss Whittaker, you shouldn't, either."

"I can't explain it to you," she said stiffly. "But—"

"You can't explain it to me because it's nonsensical." His voice had lowered to a deep rumble. "Live your life, for God's sake. Follow your heart. Make your own choices. I know you, Natalie. Your natural inclinations are decent and kind. Anyone who finds fault with you must be either malicious or stupid. Why should you court the good opinion of such people? Your friends will never think ill of you. They know better."

Confusion swirled through her. He had used her Christian name, but it seemed the wrong moment to chide him for it. Besides, it had secretly thrilled her to hear her name on his lips . . . and to be flattered with such obvious sincerity. *Decent,* he had called her. *Kind.* She knew she would remember and cherish those words, turning them over and over in her mind. They would warm her heart on many a lonely night.

Nonplussed, she tried to rally. "There are rules," she said feebly. "Despite what you say. A single lady must be exceedingly careful."

"Those rules were written to protect the giggling children thrust into society every year. You are a woman, not a brainless schoolroom chit. You are so decisive in every other area of your life that it's incongruous to see you deferring to dictates that no longer apply to you."

She tried to smile. "How rude of you," she murmured, "to point out that I am no longer in the first blush of youth."

Sly humor glinted in his eyes. "It can't be news to you."

That forced a chuckle out of her. "No," she admitted. She thought for a moment, frowning slightly. "There is a point," she said slowly, "at which an unmarried woman no longer draws attention to herself by behaving freely. It is supposed to be a great relief to reach that age." A faint smile lifted the corners of her mouth. "I have just discovered that it isn't."

There was understanding in his smile. "I imagine most women would feel as you do. No one likes to be reminded that their salad days are behind them. But you are not quite decrepit, you know."

"Thank you," she said politely, and his rare grin flashed.

"I'm a charmer, am I not? Hang it all, Na— Miss Whittaker, I've never been good at this sort of thing."

She regarded him warily. "What sort of thing?"

He looked uncomfortable. "Courtship and, er, things like that."

She took a deep breath. "I will try one more time," she said carefully, "to make myself clear. Lord Malcolm, do not court me. I do not want courtship from you. Nor do I want, er, things like that," she added, copying his words. "I will not make a marriage of convenience. How many times must I tell you so?"

He looked both angry and perplexed. "I've done it again!" he exclaimed. "I never meant to bring it up at all."

His chagrin was so heartfelt it was comical. Natalie choked back a laugh, shaking her head. "Well, you did," she said severely. "And after I expressly warned you that it would drive me away. Now, what am I to make of that?"

Genuine alarm flitted across his features. "Make nothing of it," he said hastily. "Forget I mentioned it. Come and dance with me again."

"No." She sounded firm this time. "Truly, Lord Malcolm, it would cause a sensation. You must dance with Miss Spivey next."

His chin jutted stubbornly. "I want to dance with you. Bear in mind that I planned the entire evening just so I could dance with you." He winked. "Crafty of me, wasn't it? Although I had to invite the entire parish to give me cover. And feed the lot of 'em! You'd stare if you knew what I paid for those lobsters. Shall I tell you what

I spent, and catalogue for you all the trouble I endured? I daresay you'd feel sorry enough to dance with me then."

Natalie refused to be entertained by this. "No. Go away," she said crossly. "The next set is forming. You must dance with someone, sir. For pity's sake, you are the host!"

He tried to take her hand and drag her back toward the center of the room. She pulled away, scandalized, and swatted at his hand. He was laughing. Why, oh, why, could she not make him understand? Part of her wanted to laugh with him, but she was too agitated, too ashamed at unexpectedly finding herself the center of attention tonight.

He left her then, shaking his head and still laughing at her, and obediently led Miss Spivey onto the floor. Miss Spivey looked thrilled.

Natalie saw her chance and walked out onto the terrace to cool her burning face and regain a little of her composure. She dared not stay there, however; she was too afraid that Malcolm would neglect his guests again to pursue her—and that *would* cause a scandal. When she heard the musicians bring the music to a flourishing close amid the laughter and applause of the company, she slipped back into the room. This time, she sat on one of the spindle-legged chairs that lined the walls, hoping to escape notice. In vain, of course. Malcolm strolled nonchalantly over and propped himself against the wall beside her.

"I danced with Miss Spivey," he reported. "Did I finally win your approval?"

"Yes," she said, in a suffocated voice. "You may add to it by going away again."

"I like it here."

Perverse man! "Then stay here," she said stiffly and

rose to walk away, wishing it were possible to hide from him somewhere.

"You misunderstand," he said, following her. "I like it where you are."

"Lord Malcolm, *please*," she moaned, her voice trembling a little despite her best efforts to control it. She rounded on him, desperate. "If you care for me at all, if you care for my friendship, do not make me a laughing-stock."

He halted in his tracks, looking appalled. "Who will laugh at you?" he said roughly, looking as if he would tear the laughter right out of the throat of anyone who dared.

"Everyone will laugh," she said, still in a low tone. They were away from the rest of the company, and no one seemed to be looking at them at the moment, but she dared not risk being overheard. "Or they will pity me, if they see you pursue me—and then see that your pursuit has come to nothing. No one will believe that you asked and I refused." Her mouth twisted wryly. "No one will believe that I declined your very flattering offer. The world views these things as you do."

"The world is right," he countered. "And so am I."

She set her jaw stubbornly and shook her head. "I will not argue with you. We are destined never to see eye-to-eye on this, it seems."

"Come into the garden with me," he said softly. "And let me prove you wrong."

She looked up at him, surprised. There was something seductive in his voice, something low and rough and vibrant. His eyes scalded her with their intensity. What on earth did he mean by it? His invitation was positively loverlike.

Incredulity sharpened her voice. "Haven't you heard

anything I've said to you tonight? I cannot do such a thing." A painful thought occurred to her. "And if you plan to compromise me, you are a villain."

Now he looked angry. And, she noted, guilty. "You insult us both with that remark," he said wrathfully. "I am no cad. Just because I'd like to—" He broke off suddenly, then audibly ground his teeth. "Do you really think I would try to force your hand with such tactics?"

Her face burned with a deep and painful blush. "N-no," she stammered. "I suppose not. I am sorry. I spoke without thinking. Let us argue no more. We attract attention, sir, and I cannot bear it."

"Natalie Whittaker, you are twenty-four years old," he said, carefully enunciating each word as if speaking to a baby. "Don't you know you are an adult?"

Her jaw dropped. "What?"

"A child must be governed by rules because a child cannot think for himself. You, however, have not been a child for some time. Use your God-given brain. It is not *logical* for us to stay here; we cannot talk privately. Come out with me where we can be alone."

She stared at him as if he were a madman. "People will *talk*."

He raised his brows and gave her stare for stare. "People will talk regardless of what you do. They have always talked. They always will talk. Let them. Adults do not fear the opinions of others. They do as they please."

Anger stiffened her spine and narrowed her eyes. "Do you think it *pleases* me to be alone with you? Do you think I *want* to be cornered by you and harangued without mercy?"

"Yes, I think you do. If you don't, you should." Devils danced in his eyes. "It'll be fun."

Furious, she stabbed his chest with her index finger.

"Your behavior is *insufferable*," she hissed. "And everyone is looking at us now. My only consolation is that they will all see how angry I am with you, so perhaps my reputation will survive after all."

His low laughter followed her as she marched away, her cheeks burning. She was so upset that she sat beside Mabel and listened for ten minutes to a steady stream of complaints, not hearing half of them but making sympathetic noises from time to time. Her mind was busy elsewhere, gnawing on the strange, maddening encounter with Lord Malcolm. What outlandish advice he had given her! An adult she surely was, but what did he mean by that? Did adulthood truly give her license to disregard gossip?

For the first time in her life, Natalie wondered whether she had crossed the invisible line that separated modesty from prudery. Had she become an old maid already? Did she appear, to him, purse lipped and fussy and timid?

It was a lowering thought.

Was it possible that Lord Malcolm might actually be *right*? She tried the notion on for size, and felt surprised—and a little disturbed—when it fit. Live your life, he had told her. Make your own choices. And why shouldn't she? It was her life, and no one else's.

Why, after all, should she explain her conduct to anyone? Why should she care about things said behind her back? She wouldn't be there to hear them. It was silly to curb her desire to spend time at Lord Malcolm's side. It was more than silly; it was dishonest. She liked him. And why should she hide her enjoyment of his company? They had done nothing wrong. At least . . . not yet.

Would he have kissed her in the garden? Almost certainly.

At the thought, Natalie felt her toes curling inside her satin slippers. The idea of Malcolm kissing her made her dizzy with terror and desire. And, yes, she feared his kiss—feared it even more than she longed for it. She had a strong notion that it would be impossible for her to guard her heart, impossible to hide or deny her feelings for him, if he went so far as to actually kiss her. The flirting was bad enough. She knew that there was nothing behind his teasing and flummery, no genuine feeling of attraction to her; he never denied that what he wanted from her was a marriage of convenience. And still the things he said, and the way his touch often lingered on her, kept her awake at night. If she had a kiss to remember, too, she might never sleep again. He had warned her himself, had he not, that unrequited love could drive one mad?

Natalie sighed. Mabel's sharp voice cut into her thoughts. "What's the matter with *you*?" she said rudely. "You've nothing to complain of."

"I wasn't complaining."

Mabel turned fretfully to Hector, on her other side. "May we not go home? I vow, I am quite ill with fatigue."

Hector's lip curled in a sneer. "You *would* come tonight. No one could convince you that you ought to stay home."

"Well, you needn't punish me for it! I only wanted to see a few new faces. I'm bored to tears at Crosby Hall."

"Look your fill, then. I'm not tired, and neither is Natalie."

"I'm a little tired," said Natalie quickly. "If Mabel wishes to leave, I've no objection."

It seemed a heaven-sent excuse. But when they went to take early leave of their host, the look of disappointment on his face made Natalie feel absurdly guilty. Absurdly, she told herself, because there was no reason for her to feel guilty at all. Mabel's condition was obvious; it was only natural that she should tire easily. And the rest of the Whittaker party could hardly send Mabel home alone.

While waiting for their carriage, Hector and Mabel wandered out to the foyer where they could continue bickering in private. Malcolm touched Natalie's arm in a silent request for her to stay behind a moment. She paused in the act of following her brother and looked enquiringly up at him.

"I've made a mull of this wretched party," he muttered, looking disgusted with himself. "The evening has not gone according to plan."

She was surprised. "Why, what can you mean? The dinner was perfect. And I believe everyone is having a splendid time. The Farnsworths, in particular, are very fond of dancing."

"I am happy to have entertained the Farnsworths, of course," he said dryly. "But what I was most looking forward to has not occurred."

She opened her mouth to ask him the obvious question, then closed it again. No, indeed; she would not fall into *that* trap! Whatever it was he had been looking forward to, it had probably involved luring her into the garden. She gave him an overbright smile and pretended to misunderstand him. "I'm sure, however, that if you ask, the musicians will gladly play it." She extended her hand in a friendly way. "A very pleasant evening, Lord Malcolm. I shall see you tomorrow morning at the usual time. Good night."

Appreciation gleamed in his eyes. He took her hand and bowed over it in a highly improper way, holding it just a trifle too long. She thought she heard him growl, "Minx!" as he bent—but she could not be sure. She pulled away from him and hurried to join her family before he could see the delight in her face. No one had ever called her "minx" before.

Some of this nonsense, she had to admit, was rather fun. Especially the part where she escaped from his nerve-wracking presence and had leisure to smile over it all in private.

It occurred to her that she was enjoying, for the first time in her life, an actual, bona fide flirtation. The thought pleased her. Everyone should experience this at least once, she decided. Really, it added an amazing luster to an otherwise ordinary summer.

She mustn't let it get out of hand, of course. And it could not, alas, go on forever. But while it lasted, she was determined to enjoy it.

Yes, she was determined to enjoy it. At least when it wasn't shredding her nerves, casting her into gloom, or keeping her awake at night.

Chapter Thirteen

It was like a game, a dangerous game where the careless turn of a card might cost a player everything. Malcolm pursued and Natalie eluded. Each became more ingenious, Malcolm at pursuing and Natalie at eluding, and neither could claim victory as the weeks progressed. The game went on, and the stakes grew ever higher.

Natalie often wished she had the inner fortitude to call a halt, but somehow she couldn't bring herself to do it. *Just a little longer,* she would promise herself. The thought of ending her first and only flirtation made her unutterably sad. She would miss the laughter, the constant state of exhilaration, the sweet, hot sparkle that cast a new glow of excitement over her life. From the moment she opened her eyes in the morning to the moment she fell into a feverish sleep at night, she was in a swivet . . . but the torture was too delicious to resist. No, she would not call a halt. She knew she was a fool, but she was a fool in love—and she was determined to have one summer, this summer, to remember all her life.

What complicated matters, however, was her growing

attachment to Sarah. That was the one thing that truly gave her pause. It was bad enough to endanger her own heart, but she was also risking Sarah's happiness. She very much feared that when the game ended, as it inevitably would, Sarah might be devastated.

Sarah Chase had blossomed into an entirely different child from the tense, sad creature Natalie had first met. She still had odd mannerisms and was often clumsy as well, but her pinched little face had filled out and she smiled much more frequently. Her anxiety had noticeably lessened, and Nurse reported that the "wee thing" slept better, falling asleep more readily and suffering fewer nightmares. How terrible it would be, Natalie thought, if her own careless behavior renewed Sarah's pain. She even wondered if it would be worth it, after all, to marry the father and give fragile Sarah the security she craved. The notion became, unexpectedly, rather tempting.

And yet, as the summer days unwound, Natalie became more firmly resolved—not less—to hold out for what she really wanted: Malcolm's heart. Was it her imagination, or did his face light up when he saw her? Was it wishful thinking, or did he seem every bit as obsessed with her as she was with him? Of course, men saw these things differently. It might very well be the game itself that he enjoyed. It might be the pursuit of an elusive quarry that put that gleam in his eye.

She was still wondering (although "wondering" was too mild a word for the agony of suspense into which the question threw her) one balmy afternoon in August when she and Malcolm were strolling idly down the drive together. The avenue of trees lining the carriage drive provided dense shade, making it the choicest destination for taking the air on a summer day. They frequently walked there in the afternoon—generally with Sarah, but today Sarah was with Nurse. Mrs. Bigalow had taken her to the village to choose fabric for making up "suitable" frocks and pinafores. Since Malcolm had already proven himself incapable of knowing suitable from unsuitable where Sarah's clothing was concerned, Nurse had instructed Natalie to keep the man occupied while she, alone, took charge of Sarah. Natalie had agreed to this arrangement with a show of indifference that fooled neither herself nor Mrs. Bigalow. Nurse had looked at Natalie very hard over her spectacles, but had confined her observations to a sarcastic sniff.

At any rate, Malcolm and Natalie were walking alone. Despite the fact that they were out of doors and, therefore, technically in a public place, it *felt* private. There was no one else in sight. The air between them seemed almost to shimmer with delicious possibility.

For a few minutes the only sounds were the light crunch of gravel beneath their feet and the rustle of a nearly imperceptible breeze in the leaves overhead. The trees whispered and danced, backlit by the sun, forming a backdrop green as Eden. Eventually Malcolm remarked, "It feels like Bordeaux."

"Bordeaux?"

"Wine country. Southern France. Summer afternoons there are typically warm and lazy, like this." He slanted a smile at her. "Heat makes the grapes sweeter."

Something in his smile definitely hinted at heat—and sweetness. She tried to look prim. "I should think the heat would wilt them."

"Not at all. They love it. Wherever the heat touches them, they ripen and blush like clusters of sun-kissed maidens."

"Very pretty," she said approvingly. "But you're wrong about blushing maidens." She tried not to become one as she spoke. "Most of them dislike too much heat."

His voice dropped, low and teasing. "Maidens, by definition, know nothing about it."

Natalie choked back a scandalized laugh. "I'm sure I don't know what you are talking about."

"I'm sure you do. In a limited way, of course, due to your inexperience."

She looked severely at him. "I have never been to France, you mean?"

He chuckled. "Yes," he said mendaciously, "that's exactly what I mean. You will have to take my word for it—when I describe the charms of Bordeaux."

She bit her lip. "And the sweetening effect of heat."

"That's right." The intimate, teasing note in his voice made her tingle with suppressed delight. He leaned slightly closer to her. "It's one of the great, beautiful mysteries of nature. Even the greenest fruit, once properly kissed by the sun, begins to soften and swell."

"And, eventually, rot," she suggested brightly. "What a lovely picture you paint."

He laughed out loud. Then: "I try," he said modestly. "You know, I have seen far more of life than you have. I shall be happy to relate any of my adventures that seem interesting to you. Is there anything I have experienced, that you have not, that you would like to learn about?"

She looked askance at him. "I'm sure you have experienced many things, Lord Malcolm, that I am happier knowing nothing about."

"Perhaps a few," he acknowledged. "On the other

hand, I can think of a few experiences I have had, that you have not, that might actually make you happier. Shall I describe them? Or, better yet, demonstrate?" There was a wicked spark in his eye.

"No, thank you," she said hastily. "I have frequently heard it said that ignorance is bliss."

He was clearly about to contradict her, but at this moment they both heard a shout, as of someone eagerly hailing them. They looked up as one to stare, surprised, at the open gates at the end of the drive. It was a young lad on a horse, galloping toward them, hatless.

"Who is that?" asked Malcolm, startled.

Natalie shaded her eyes with one hand. "Daniel Call," she said, as puzzled as he. "Our groom's boy."

He was upon them then, reining his horse in so abruptly that the flying hooves sprayed them with gravel. "Beg pardon, miss," he cried, gasping for breath. "My lord."

Something in the boy's face rang warning bells, and the afternoon seemed to change in a twinkling from dream to nightmare. Malcolm seemed to sense it, too. She felt him tense beside her. "Yes, what is it?" he said sharply.

Daniel gulped nervously. "Sir—my lord—it's your little girl, sir. I'm frightfully sorry, but she's taken a bad fall. They thought it best not to move her, sir. Mrs. Bigalow sent me to fetch you—"

"Where is she?" Malcolm's voice was thick with dread. He had gone so white around the mouth that Natalie instinctively laid her hand on his sleeve in a gesture of comfort. His opposite hand came up and gripped hers with painful intensity.

"She's at the inn, sir. It happened in the High Street. They carried her as far as the inn, but—"

"Give me your horse." He barked it as an order, shaking off Natalie's hand.

"Yes, sir." Daniel slid off the saddle quick as thought, and Malcolm seized the reins and placed one foot in the stirrup.

"Lord Malcolm, wait!" Natalie clutched mindlessly at his leg, forgetful of the proprieties. "Wait for me."

He stared at her as if she were a stranger, his eyes bleak, the lines in his face suddenly appearing deeper. "I cannot wait." He wheeled the horse round and urged it into a gallop, lying almost flat across its mane to encourage more speed as he headed it back the way it had come.

She watched his figure recede in a cloud of flying dust. "Of course," she murmured, dazed. "Of course you cannot wait. Good heavens, what was I thinking? Daniel!"

"Here, miss."

Her wits returning, she rounded on him. "Come back with me to his lordship's stables and help me saddle the hack. No, Lord Malcolm will not mind a bit, and neither will Delaney! I must tell Mrs. Howatch what has happened. She will know what to do. Is Sarah badly hurt? Should I bring bandages or—or something?"

Daniel shook his head. "No, miss. That is, yes, miss, but you needn't bring anything. The surgeon's been called, and Mrs. Bigalow is with her."

"Thank God," said Natalie fervently. She had forgotten that. Wee Sarah was not alone; her nurse was with her. The knot of anxiety that had formed in her belly loosened slightly. No one more competent, no one better in an emergency than Nurse! Indeed, Natalie would probably arrive to discover that there was nothing for her to do, that Nurse had seen to everything already. She took a deep breath. "Nevertheless, I will go," she said steadily. "Lord Malcolm may need me, even if Sarah does not."

As they walked swiftly toward the stables, she questioned Daniel about what had happened. He had not seen the whole and had been sent for Lord Malcolm almost immediately, so his information was sketchy. From what he understood, Sarah and Mrs. Bigalow had been walking along High Street when Sarah somehow missed her footing and tumbled down a flight of stone stairs. Natalie knew the stairs well; they led from the edge of the street down to the churchyard, nestled in a dell in the lower half of the village. They had been built as a pedestrian shortcut; one could either use the stairs or walk the long way round on the road, which took a sharp turn at the top of the hill to curve back down to the church.

"But the stairs are in plain sight! How could she miss them?"

Daniel scratched his head. "P'raps she was talking to Mrs. Bigalow. Had her face turned the wrong way."

Or, just as likely, Sarah had simply been thinking of something else. Natalie knew too well the utter concentration of Sarah's imagination. Horror seized her as she pictured the stairs; they were terribly steep. And stone was an unforgiving surface upon which to land.

"Did she break any bones?"

"Don't know, miss." Daniel looked apologetic. "She was out cold."

Natalie's heart pounded with fear. "Good God. She must have fallen headfirst." She broke into a run. She knew it was idiotic to run; running served no useful pur-

pose. It didn't matter whether she arrived in twenty minutes or thirty. But she couldn't help it. Every instinct
urged her to hurry.

Daniel obediently trotted beside her. She was grateful
for the sureness and speed with which he led out Lord
Malcolm's hack and saddled it for her, and grateful for
the surprising strength with which he helped her onto the
horse. Natalie was not accustomed to riding such a large
and powerful animal, and she wasn't wearing a riding
habit, but her anxiety to make haste left no room for
lesser fears. She gathered up the reins and headed for the
village, heedless of the expanse of shin her rucked-up
walking dress revealed. *This,* she told herself defiantly,
is why someone invented stockings.

As it turned out, she arrived even before the surgeon
did. The front of the inn yard was empty save for the
sweating mare Lord Malcolm had ridden in, tied haphazardly to a hitching post and gulping water from a bucket,
and a huddle of local citizens, conversing animatedly in
the hushed tones reserved for sickrooms and funerals.
The small crowd parted respectfully when Natalie approached. A few of the men politely averted their eyes
when they saw that her ankle was exposed, but the inn's
sole ostler, a cheeky lad, stepped gleefully up to hand
her down and take her horse.

Natalie hopped off the mount with what dignity she
could muster, nodded to the vicar's sister, and sailed past
the throng into the inn. She could hear the avid whispers
follow her: ". . . nearest neighbor, after all . . . been very
kind to the little girl, from what I hear . . . they *do* say as
he fancies her . . . poor thing, did you see her face? . . ."

She closed the door and shut the whispers out, then
paused to allow her eyes to adjust to the dim interior. No

one had met her, and no one came to usher her in. Indeed, the entire ground floor appeared to be deserted. Overhead, however, she could hear footsteps and low, urgent voices. She climbed the stairs, afraid to call out for fear she would disturb Sarah, and fearing what she would find when she reached the upper chambers.

At the top of the stairs she saw that one of the chamber doors was open. From within, she heard Nurse's authoritative voice: "Whatever you do, don't jostle her. That rag will have warmed by now, my lord. Dip it again. Wring it out, but not too much. Tsk! I'll do it. Hold her hand, sir—gently, now. No movement. That's right."

Natalie tiptoed to the open door. Sarah lay on a narrow bed by the window. Malcolm huddled on a stool between the window and the bed, his tall form folded nearly in half to accommodate the lowness of his perch. All his attention was fixed on his child, stretched motionless before him. His face was nearly as white as Sarah's, his expression grim. He held her little hand as gently as if it were made of eggshell. Nurse was briskly wringing out a cloth she had just dipped in a basin of cold water. The innkeeper's wife hovered nearby, looking helpless.

As Nurse laid the cloth gently on Sarah's head, Natalie heard a thin whimper. Sarah must be conscious. *Thank you, Lord.*

"May I help?" she asked quietly.

Malcolm's eyes lifted to hers immediately, filled with a relief and gratitude that pierced her all the way across the room. Even in her anxiety for Sarah, she felt a rush of gladness. She was right to have come.

Nurse glanced at her only long enough to give her a

brisk nod. "Come you in, Natalie child. I'll be grateful for another pair of hands." In an access of tact, she turned to the innkeeper's wife. "I'm sure you've other matters to tend, Mrs. Hubble, but we'd be grateful if you'd brew the mite a posset."

Mrs. Hubble brightened. "That I will." She bustled past Natalie and quitted the room with every indication of profound relief.

Nurse lowered her voice. "I hope you don't mind, my lord. There's some as can help in a sickroom, and some as can't. Mrs. Hubble does wonders in a kitchen, but it frets me to have her underfoot up here. Miss Whittaker has more talent for nursing."

Malcolm gave her a strained smile. "I doubt if Sarah will be in any shape to consume a posset, but I'll drink it myself if it keeps Mrs. Hubble at bay. I confess, I had rather have Miss Whittaker's help than the landlady's."

Natalie shot him a grateful look, then approached the bed. She studied Sarah's small, still figure with concern. Sarah's eyes were closed, but she was plainly awake. Lines of pain and fear were etched on her pale countenance. Beneath the cold cloths on her head, a lump as large as a hen's egg had formed.

Natalie opened her mouth to ask if the head injury was the worst of it, when her eyes fell on Sarah's left arm. Her stomach rolled at the sight; it lay in a most unnatural position. Natalie had tended many an illness, but she had never seen a broken bone before. She hoped she never saw one again. She looked hastily away, and took a deep breath to banish the queasy sensation.

"Has anything been given her for the pain?" It seemed safer to speak of Sarah in the third person, rather than address her directly and put her to the trouble of answering.

"A little brandy," said Malcolm. His voice was tight with strain. "Mrs. Bigalow was afraid she couldn't keep it down, did we give her more."

"She kept it down like a champion," said Nurse bracingly. "Sarah dear, did it help you? Will you drink a bit more?"

Sarah neither moved nor opened her eyes, but her eyebrows knitted. "Nasty," she whispered, in the thread of a voice.

"Perhaps the Hubbles have laudanum drops," suggested Natalie.

"I asked," said Malcolm curtly. "They haven't."

"I daresay the surgeon will bring some, sir." Nurse dipped another cloth in the cold water and wrung it vigorously. "I'll be glad to have his advice, too, before dosing a child her age. Not certain whether we should, so soon after she's been unconscious. But Mr. Carter will know."

"Where the devil *is* he?" muttered Malcolm, casting a fierce glance at his pain-wracked daughter. But a minor commotion in the hall belowstairs indicated that the long-awaited Mr. Carter had, that moment, arrived.

"I'll go," said Nurse gruffly. She handed the wet cloth to Natalie and was out the door in a twinkling.

Natalie bent over Sarah, glad to be doing something. As she gently lifted the warm cloth from Sarah's head, replacing it with the cold one, she could hear low voices in the passage outside the door. The words could not be deciphered, but Natalie knew that Nurse was explaining to the surgeon, in her concise, no-nonsense way, exactly how the accident had occurred and what she deemed Sarah's injuries to be. Soon Mr. Carter entered the room, rubbing his hands together in a cheerful way.

The surgeon's professional demeanor of genial opti-
mism was so reassuring that one scarcely noticed the
ominous black bag he carried or, when he set it on the
bedside table, the terrifying clink of the instruments and
vials it contained. Natalie swallowed hard and gave Mr.
Carter a rather weak smile. He was an estimable man,
and she had every confidence in his expertise, but despite her nursing talents she had an unshakable horror of
all things medical.

After being introduced to Lord Malcolm, Mr. Carter
glanced at her with a sympathetic twinkle in his eye. "I
believe Miss Whittaker would rather be anywhere but
here while I examine your daughter, my lord. Shall I
send her to fetch Mrs. Bigalow back to us?"

Relief swamped her. "I would be glad to do that," she
said gratefully.

For the first time, Sarah's eyes opened. Her pupils
were huge with pain. "No," she said in a surprisingly
strong voice. "Miss Whittaker?"

Natalie bent over her, gently touching her shoulder.
"I'm here, sweetheart," she said soothingly.

"Don't leave me." The desperation in the little girl's
whisper twisted Natalie's heart into knots. "Don't go
away."

Natalie had been eager to get as far from the scene of
the medical examination as her feet could carry her.
Now, she felt, wild horses could not drag her from the
room. "I won't go, darling," she promised. "If you want
me to stay, I will stay."

A measure of relief lightened Sarah's drawn face. She
did not move her head, but her eyes traveled to where
Malcolm sat, still holding her uninjured hand. "You, too,
Papa."

Malcolm's deep voice rumbled with emotion. "I will never leave you, precious girl."

Sarah's features relaxed a little more. She almost smiled. But then the examination began.

The first thing Mr. Carter did was to pull back the curtains and unshutter the window. The splash of light made Sarah wince. Mr. Carter clucked sympathetically. "Makes your headache worse, does it? Miss Whittaker, pray sit at the head of the bed and shade Sarah's eyes. Mind you don't cast a shadow on the rest of her, if you can help it."

Natalie gladly did as she was bid. Malcolm remained beside the bed, on Sarah's uninjured side. Mr. Carter kept up a soothing babble of comments and observations as his hands and eyes moved deftly, gently, over Sarah's battered body. He did not touch her broken arm. Natalie supposed he was checking for less-obvious injuries, to ensure that nothing was missed. His examination of the swelling on her head was particularly close and thorough. He checked to make sure she could lift and turn her head of her own volition, and although she complained fretfully, vowing that her head ached too much to do so, she obeyed the surgeon's commands. When Sarah demonstrated her ability to touch her chin to her chest and place either cheek upon her pillow, Natalie and Malcolm sighed with relief.

Mr. Carter eventually nodded his satisfaction. "That's it, then," he said briskly. "A few bruises and scrapes, some nastier than others, and a knot on the head. Oh, and one broken arm." His eyes glinted with humor. "Frankly, I was more worried by the head injury. Bones heal quickly at your age, young lady. If you plan to break an arm once in your life, do it as early in childhood as possible. That's what I always say."

The surgeon's gentle flow of chatter was distracting, but not distracting enough. Natalie bit her lip as Mr. Carter, still talking in his falsely comfortable way, rummaged in his black bag. *Sarah needs you,* she reminded herself sternly. Whatever horrors were in store, Natalie must stand by and witness them for Sarah's sake. The first thing he pulled out was not too alarming: a glass bottle containing an ugly-looking fluid. He filled an eyedropper with this, encouraged Sarah to open her mouth for a moment, and, quick as winking, shot the fluid down her throat. Sarah's face immediately screwed up into an expression of revulsion and outrage.

"Peppermint drop?" Mr. Carter offered. "I think you deserve it. You've been a brave girl."

The peppermint drop seemed to pacify the child, at least a little. Leaving her in peace to suck on her candy, Mr. Carter drew Lord Malcolm and Natalie aside. "You've probably guessed, but I just gave her a sedative. We'll wait until she's drowsy before I set the bone."

Set the bone! The surgeon went on talking to Malcolm, and Malcolm, seemingly unperturbed, questioned him about what he had found and what must be done. Natalie heard none of it. She was almost as distressed as if it were she, not Sarah, who must face the ordeal. It was terrible indeed to watch a much-loved child suffer. This was a new kind of pain to Natalie.

It was not possible, of course, to send Sarah back into oblivion for the operation. Mr. Carter explained, regretfully, that sufficient opiate to render her unconscious might accidentally result in death. A surgeon's knowledge of physic was limited, but he assured them that not even a physician of the Royal College would know how to accomplish that trick safely. The most that could be done was to put Sarah into a dreamy, almost drunken state, and hope that however much she suffered while her arm was manipulated, she would remember little of it later on.

They returned to take their places. Malcolm's grim expression mirrored Natalie's emotions; her heart pounded with anxiety while she forced herself to remain outwardly calm. Malcolm's assigned task was, she thought with a pang of compassion, more difficult than hers—she was only to soothe Sarah as best she could, while Malcolm must prevent his little girl from moving during Mr. Carter's ministrations.

Sarah seemed unaware that she was being tied to the bed. By the time this necessary task was completed, her face was slack. She said something, but Natalie could not make it out. She bent over her, gently stroking Sarah's cheek. "What did you say, darling?"

"Hurt me?"

Natalie glanced at Mr. Carter. He had not yet touched Sarah's arm, but was studying it carefully, tapping his chin as if thinking out the best way to proceed. "Yes, I may hurt you for just a moment, sweetheart," he said, with that same ghastly cheerfulness. "But it will soon be over, and then you can get well. You'll like that, eh? We'll be as quick as ever we can, and soon you'll feel much better."

Natalie's gaze immediately went to Malcolm, fearing that he would object to Mr. Carter's honesty—many people thought children should be lied to, in cases such as this—but Malcolm, although frowning, was looking at the surgeon with dour approval. Sarah's eyes did not open. For a moment Natalie thought she had not comprehended what the surgeon had said, but then she murmured, faint but clear, "I will be brave."

Natalie's heart swelled with love. "That's my good girl," she whispered.

The actual setting of the bone must have taken less than a minute, but it seemed to last for hours. Malcolm held Sarah's legs down with one strong arm, while with the other he pressed her uninjured shoulder to prevent her struggling against the ties. His face was white with strain, an agony of pity written on his features. Natalie held Sarah's head—gently, gently—and sang.

She knew not where the impulse came from. It seemed an instinct dormant until this moment, as if generations of mothers, singing lullabies to crying children through the centuries, had unexpectedly bequeathed it to her. Sarah cried out, and Natalie sang. The response of song to tears seemed as natural as breath. She sang softly, and Sarah's cries dropped in volume, the better to hear her. The little girl seemed to cling to Natalie's voice like a lifeline, her eyes wide and staring, her gaze glued to Natalie's face. She panted and gasped, trying not to scream. It was only afterward, as Sarah sank into an exhausted slumber, that Natalie realized what the child had been doing: trying to bring her massive powers of concentration to bear on the pain, willing herself into that private world of hers, where pain could not follow. The attempt had obviously been unsuccessful, but the very act of making the attempt, using Natalie's lullaby as an anchor, had helped Sarah to bear what must be borne.

She really was a remarkable little girl.

Mr. Carter recommended that Sarah be left where she was until the next day. He left instructions with Natalie and Mrs. Bigalow on the use of laudanum to keep the child comfortable, but warned them that someone must watch over her at all times. "We walk a fine line, here," he cautioned. "She's very young, and she's suffered a concussion. Under normal circumstances I wouldn't recommend a sedative, but if you will carefully watch her, I think we can try it. It will certainly relieve her pain."

"Then we will try it," said Nurse, folding her arms like a sentinel.

Mr. Carter nodded. "Very well. Do not leave her alone, even for a moment. The drug will give her strong dreams, and she may thrash about or try to rise. She must be prevented from reinjuring that arm or dislodging the splint. And you should also be conscious of her breathing. If it becomes labored, open the window and wake her. Dash cold water on her face if you must, but wake her."

"Between the three of us, I am sure we can manage," said Natalie staunchly.

Nurse looked sharply at her. "Two of us. You may go home, Natalie. Lord Malcolm and I will stay with the child."

Mr. Carter coughed. "Forgive me, Mrs. Bigalow, but if Miss Whittaker is willing to stay, I recommend that you allow her to do so. Her presence seemed to calm the patient earlier, and Sarah specifically asked for her to remain during the worst moments."

"Hmpf." Nurse looked skeptical. "There's already been talk, and I mislike giving the village cause for more. I'm Sarah's nurse, and Lord Malcolm is her father. No one will wonder at it if we stay with her."

Natalie lifted her chin. "I refuse to consider such piffle at a moment like this. I am staying, Nurse. Three pairs of hands will be better than two. And no one will make mischief if you and Mrs. Hubble are here to guard my reputation."

"She's right, Mrs. Bigalow." Mr. Carter's eyes twinkled. "And you ought not to overrule me when I make a medical recommendation."

Nurse grumbled a bit, but Malcolm smiled—and Natalie stayed.

It was a long night. Malcolm refused to leave Sarah's side except to heed nature's call, but the two women took it in turns to rest. Sarah slept for the most part, breathing heavily, but she did suffer spells of disquiet as the surgeon had warned them she would. Natalie, after resting for several hours, came to relieve Nurse at three in the morning. There were lines of exhaustion in the older woman's face. She met Natalie at the sickroom door.

"How is she?" asked Natalie in a low tone.

Nurse shook her head. "I'll be glad to see the sun rise," she said tiredly. "Seems that any sort of pain or illness is at its worst this time of night." She filled Natalie in on the dosing schedule and Natalie, giving Nurse's arm an affectionate squeeze, sent her off to her well-deserved nap.

Natalie approached the bed as noiselessly as she could and took Nurse's place on the opposite side of the cot from Malcolm. A lamp burned low at the head of the bed, shaded so the light would not fall on Sarah's face. She looked tiny and pitiful with her splinted arm lying stiffly against the coverlet.

Natalie could detect no weariness in Malcolm. His body was taut with alertness, his frown of concentration as fierce as when she had left the room at midnight. He did glance up, smiling slightly, as she sank down onto the chair.

"You needn't be so careful," he said quietly. "She sleeps deeply." His frown intensified. "Too deeply, I think."

Natalie studied the small, slack face on the pillow. "Her breathing seems regular," she whispered.

"Yes, but she dreams." The dim lamplight cast shadows on his face but caught the glitter of despair in his eyes. There was a bleakness in his expression that Sarah's condition could not account for. Natalie, her intuition sharpened by the intimacy of the moment, felt a dark horror emanating, almost palpably, from the depths of Malcolm's spirit. "The laudanum is supposed to lessen her misery, not multiply it," he said hoarsely. "I know Sarah. She would rather lie awake and feel the pain than dream such dreams."

"Are all her dreams nightmares?"

"I don't know. I fear so. She moans and mutters, but I can't make out the words. Once she cried out, 'Bird!' and tried to rise. I suppose she meant to fly." He exhaled, shaking his head. "That was a bad moment."

"But such behavior is not uncommon," she said quickly, trying to comfort him. "Mr. Carter specifically warned us that she might try to rise. Perhaps the drug has so freed her from the pain that she is no longer aware of her injuries. You must not distress yourself over trifles."

He looked sharply at her. "Trifles? You do not know—" He broke off in midsentence, seeming to struggle with dark emotions. His gaze dropped back to Sarah's wan face. Eventually he finished with "You do not know her as I do."

Natalie was certain that that was not what he had originally started to say. "I cannot force you to trust me," she said softly. "But I wish you would."

He looked up, startled. Natalie met his gaze levelly. "There are reasons, I think, why you believe that all of Sarah's dreams are nightmares."

She did not phrase it as a question, but it was. The atmosphere in the room changed subtly. Awareness pulsed between Malcolm and Natalie. The only sound in the room was Sarah's drugged breathing: In. Out. In. Out.

The silence lengthened, and Natalie waited, holding her ground. There were secrets in this family. Something had happened, something no one talked about, that had helped to shape Sarah's oddness and Malcolm's reticence, his black moods, the despair he often seemed to feel. She wanted desperately to understand. *Tell me.*

For a heartbeat or two, she thought he would. She saw the emotion welling up in him, emotion so strong she thought it must spill out at any moment. Electricity seemed to crackle in the air between them. He opened his mouth to speak but was interrupted by Sarah's voice, weak but clear.

"Mama," she said.

As one, Natalie and Malcolm turned to her, everything forgotten save for the little girl stretched on the cot between them. Sarah's eyes were wide open. Her gaze was fixed on Natalie, but her eyes were unnaturally dark and strange. "Mama," she said again, tonelessly.

Natalie placed her hand, featherlight, on the hot little fingers plucking at the coverlet. "It's Miss Whittaker, darling," she said gently. "You're dreaming."

Sarah's odd, fixed expression did not change. "Mama. Don't fall. Careful, Mama. Don't fall."

In the confusion of a laudanum-laced dream, Sarah seemed to believe that her mother, not herself, had fallen. But even as the child's eyes drifted shut again, Malcolm dropped her other hand and rose jerkily to his feet. Natalie looked up at him, surprised. When she saw the look on his face, genuine fear shot through her.

"What is it?" she whispered. She had never seen such torment on a human face. He looked as if all the demons of hell had invaded his soul and were tearing him apart from the inside out.

He turned and walked away from her, almost as if he did not know what he was doing, or why. He walked out of the light and into the shadows, halting by the dressing table at the other end of the room. He stood there for a moment, staring down at the top of the table, his back rigid, his hands fisted at his sides. Then, with an obvious effort, he turned around to face her.

"Sarah's mother died in a fall," he said. His voice rasped as if the words were being pulled, unwilling, from his throat. "Sarah was with her."

A frisson of shock rushed through Natalie. No wonder Malcolm had reacted with such fear when Daniel brought him the news of Sarah's fall. Another memory danced in her brain: Sarah tripping in the grass and lying still, afraid to move. *No wonder. No wonder.*

Natalie, struck dumb with pity and horror, strained her eyes to read Malcolm's expression across the shadowy room. He said, still in that hollow, jerking voice, "Sarah must have seen the whole thing." He scrubbed one hand over his face as if trying to wipe the memory away. "But she was too small to describe what happened. At least, not clearly."

She stared at him, still speechless, as a ghastly smile writhed across his features. "Thank God she couldn't. The coroner brought in a verdict of accidental death."

Natalie's hand traveled to her cheek in an instinctive gesture of dread. "Did your wife . . ." Her voice faltered, and she cleared her throat. "Do you think she fell on purpose?" She could not say *jump*. She could not say *suicide*. Those words were too stark, too terrible.

But there were worse words, she learned. Malcolm was about to use one.

He looked at her, and the tiny bedchamber seemed to stretch between them like an unbridgeable gulf. "I never meant to kill her," he whispered.

Chapter Fourteen

Every instinct Natalie possessed, every prompting of her intuition, rose up in protest. "No." Her voice sounded high and breathless. She shook her head in vehement refusal. Denial gripped her like an ague; for a few moments she could not stop shaking her head. It seemed to wobble on her neck like a broken doll's. "No," she repeated more strongly. "You are not capable of such a crime. You are good and decent and honorable."

Malcolm's shoulders shook with silent, mirthless laughter. He walked back to the bed and sat across from her once more. "I will tell you the story," he said tiredly. She had never seen him look so defeated. "I suppose it was useless to try to keep it from you."

Natalie went very still. "What story?"

"The story of my marriage." His mouth twisted bitterly. "My so-called marriage."

She must have looked even more shocked, because some genuine humor crept into his twisted smile. "Oh, the marriage was real enough—according to church and state. But we had no"—he paused, searching for words—"no accord. No marriage of minds. Catherine and I were like a badly harnessed pair of mules, always pulling in opposite directions."

So that was what he had meant, that day on the lake when he had told her that love made people miserable. She took a deep breath, then let it go. "I see."

"No, you don't." His jaw tightened. "How could you? I've described it badly. It wasn't that we fought—although we did. And it wasn't that our opinions differed—although they did. It was . . ." He shook his head slowly, obviously remembering. The memories seemed painful.

Natalie couldn't bear it. She burst out with "But you didn't *kill* her. It's absurd!"

"Not on purpose." His eyes met Natalie's, and she could feel the dark emotions roiling like a whirlpool in him, inescapable and dangerous. She shivered involuntarily. He acknowledged her reaction with a slight, wintry smile. "You do not understand me. I shall have to start at the beginning, if I hope to make you understand."

He glanced down at Sarah, frowning as if he hesitated to tell the tale in her presence. "She will not hear," said Natalie softly.

Malcolm gave a brief nod. "Right." He lowered his voice, however. And he kept his eyes on Sarah's face, ready to stop talking the instant she stirred.

"I married Catherine in the spring of '94," he said, speaking so quietly that Natalie had to lean in to hear him. "I thought she was, in every way that mattered, an excellent choice of bride. I had known her all my life—not well, but our parents had been friends. I had reached a suitable age, and so had she, and we both wanted to marry. She seemed attractive enough. Biddable enough.

Our parents approved of the match. Everyone approved of the match. You know how these things go."

Natalie nodded, loath to interrupt him.

"I was making a marriage of convenience—and, I thought, a good one. Everyone congratulated me on my sensible, well-chosen alliance." He gave a snort of bleak laughter. "I congratulated myself, for that matter. I looked forward to a life of unruffled domestic harmony. Nothing exciting, no dramatic highs and lows. What I desired was a peaceful sort of life, with a trusted partner at my side." His eyes lifted to Natalie's, filled with irony. "Catherine, unfortunately, believed she was making a love match. And I did not discover this until after the ceremony."

Natalie was so surprised she did not know what to say. She stared at him, open-mouthed. Her picture of Malcolm's first marriage had been completely upside-down. "Oh, dear," she said faintly.

Malcolm gave her a wry smile. "Indeed. There was no end to the difficulties caused by this . . . misunderstanding. If that's what it was." His expression turned bitter. "I came to believe, over the years, that there was nothing personal in Catherine's attachment to me. She would have drummed up the same imaginary emotions for any man who married her. Enacted him the same scenes. Whipped herself into the same froth of agitation. Bent upon him the same mournful, accusing eyes. Made his life just as miserable as she made mine."

His anger seemed genuine and appeared to run deep. Natalie was bewildered by it. "You seem to believe that it was all a fiction. That she did not really love you."

"She didn't."

Natalie blinked. "Oh, but surely—why shouldn't she love you? She did. Of course she did."

He shifted impatiently on his chair. "At first, that is what I believed. I knew nothing of love—this romantic love that poets describe. I honestly believed that Catherine was sick with love for me, and I was, for at least a twelvemonth, riddled with guilt. She begged for my affection. She made herself ill. She would lock herself in her room and refuse to eat. It was ghastly. I tried very hard to return her regard." He shrugged helplessly. "I couldn't. She wept and whined and made demand after demand upon me. She used her adoration of me like blackmail, forcing me to dance attendance on her out of pity." His mouth set in anguished lines. "The result was the opposite of what she wanted. I respected her less with every passing month." A deep sigh shook him. "You will think me hard-hearted. Perhaps I am. Try as I might, I—I could not love her." His voice had sunk to a whisper. He buried his face in his hands, massaging his temples tiredly. "I could not."

Natalie's heart filled with compassion. She reached across Sarah's small bed and touched Malcolm's sleeve. He lifted bleak eyes to hers. "You are not hard-hearted." Her voice was soft but filled with conviction. "Only a kind heart would have tried so hard. Only a generous soul would have felt such empathy. But love cannot be forced."

A flash of humor briefly lightened his aspect. "You seem very sure of that, for a woman who has never been in love."

The irony of the situation suddenly struck her. She *was* sure of it. Love could not be forced. And yet she hoped to achieve exactly what Catherine had hoped to achieve: She hoped to win Malcolm's heart. Was she as much a fool as Malcolm's star-crossed bride?

She withdrew her hand and tried to smile. "I have interrupted your tale."

His eyes darkened once more. He glanced down at his sleeping daughter. "There is not much left to tell. Except for Sarah." Malcolm's expression softened. "Sarah was the one bright spot, the shining, precious thing that made our ill-fated marriage worthwhile. She arrived after several long years of trying. Those years were . . . unpleasant. In addition to the emotional tug-of-war we endured, Catherine blamed her miscarriages on me. And when Sarah was born, she told me that if I had truly loved her, we would have had a son."

Natalie gave a tiny gasp, and Malcolm's jaw tightened. "Ridiculous, isn't it? But by that time, you must understand, Catherine was a woman possessed. She perceived my failure to worship at her feet as the root cause of everything that went wrong in her life. She brooded on it day and night. She would have blamed the weather on it if she could." He looked up at Natalie again. He seemed to be bracing himself for what he was about to tell her next. He took a deep breath. "And then, after Sarah was born . . . I compounded the problem."

"How?" Natalie feared that he was about to confess the obvious: that he had taken a mistress. Her father had made both his wives miserable with his infidelities. Perhaps all men were like that. She hoped not—oh, she hoped not.

But what Malcolm said defied her expectations. He said, simply, "I adored my baby girl from the first moment I saw her."

He looked ashamed! Natalie cocked her head, puzzled. How could loving your child possibly be a *bad* thing? And then she saw, in a flash, what the problem had been. A desperate, unhappy wife, morbidly obsessed with her husband's indifference, had given birth to *her own rival.*

She swallowed hard. "You don't mean— Is it possible that Lady Malcolm was jealous of her own daughter?"

He dropped his head in his hands. "All my fault," he said, his anguished voice so muffled it was almost inaudible. "I loved the child but not the mother. I could not love my own wife. I failed Catherine utterly."

Natalie sank back in her chair, unnerved. For half a heartbeat, she felt intensely sorry for Catherine Chase. And then the reality of the situation sank in. Why, Lady Malcolm must have been a monster of selfishness! Malcolm was right; she hadn't truly loved him at all. Natalie tried to picture giving birth to Malcolm's child—an easy image to conjure—and then tried to picture resenting his love for that child. Her imagination failed her. No. Impossible. Even if she married him, loved him, failed to earn his love in return, but bore his child—oh, she would be glad, *glad,* if he loved their baby. She shook her head, silently marveling that any woman in her right mind could feel differently.

But perhaps Catherine hadn't been in her right mind.

"Lord Malcolm," she said hesitantly.

"Call me Malcolm, for God's sake." He scrubbed at his eyes, then lifted his head, giving her a slightly twisted smile. "You are practically my confessor now."

She returned his smile, albeit tentatively. He was right; it was time. She had thought of him as *Malcolm* for many weeks now. "Malcolm, then, at least when we are alone. But, Malcolm—was your late wife ill, perhaps? The behavior you have described to me seems . . . well, a trifle unhinged. Perhaps she wasn't rational."

"No," he said tiredly. "I don't think she was insane, if that's what you're inferring. But I think she had a—" He paused for a moment, frowning. "A mania for control, if such a thing is possible. All this nonsense about love, her bouts of weeping, the times when she would starve herself . . . it all seemed calculated to manipulate those around her. Me in particular. That's why I began to believe that she did not actually love me as she claimed. It struck me that she used her supposed love for me, and my supposed withholding of love from her, as a means to gain—and keep—the upper hand." His smile was cynical. "It made her forever the dutiful spouse, you see, and I the heartless villain."

"I do see," said Natalie slowly. She quirked an eyebrow at him. "I imagine that you gave her a great many material things? To mend her broken heart?"

His cynical smile widened. "As usual, Miss Whittaker, your perceptions are exactly on the mark. Since I was unable to give my wife what she most wanted—in theory—I gave her everything else her little heart desired. Catherine had her own way in everything. It seemed the least I could do."

"But it did not make her happy."

"No. Far from it." His cynical expression faded. He sighed heavily. "I should not be telling you of her faults. It isn't right. My own shortcomings eclipsed hers. Poor Catherine! Who am I to say she did not love me? Who am I to pass such a judgment on her?" Pain moved across his features. "I never understood her. Not then, and not now. Perhaps she did love me as she said she did. What do I know of love? Even the poets say it is a kind of madness."

"As is unending guilt," said Natalie softly. "I think you have paid too high a price for whatever fault you bore in your marriage. Malcolm, you did not kill your wife. What made you say such a dreadful thing to me?"

He gripped his knees, his knuckles whitening, while a spasm of shame turned his face almost rigid. "I did not push her off the parapet," he said, his voice strained. "I was standing on the lawn, far below. I wasn't even looking at her. But I . . . goaded her." He rolled his head back and stared at the ceiling as if he could no longer bear to meet Natalie's eyes. "I will never forgive myself. She called out, to draw my attention upward. It was the anniversary of our wedding day. She threatened to jump. As God is my witness, I never dreamed she'd do it. I thought it was just another ploy. I looked away, so that she would have no audience to play her scene to. And my last words to her were . . . God forgive me . . . I said . . ."

His voice was wholly suspended; she saw the muscles jump and work in his throat, but no sound came out. Natalie, hardly knowing what she did, rose and flew to his side. She felt unable to watch his agony another instant. By the time she reached him he had stood, and she dove into his arms as if she belonged there. He crushed her to him and she gasped.

"It doesn't matter," she told him through sudden tears. "Don't tell me any more. Don't tell me what you said. It doesn't matter now."

A shudder wracked his long frame. He clutched her mindlessly, as a drowning man clutches at his rescuer. He was speaking, but the words were so choked that Natalie could not make them out.

She didn't care. She didn't need to hear them. Whatever terrible thing he had said to his wife, whatever he had said that he believed made her jump, she did not want to know. What mattered was that it had haunted him ever since, that he had gone over and over that moment in his mind until he had rubbed the memory raw, and over time the memory had festered and fevered.

She had always sensed a constant throb of pain in Malcolm, a dark undercurrent to his every mood. There had been times when he seemed to forget for a while, but it had always returned, gnawing at him in every idle moment. She had seen it and wondered at it. And now she knew the source. She longed to pull that memory out of his head like a splinter from a sore thumb, and leave him free to heal. Was such a thing possible?

"Natalie." His voice was rough, his mouth pressed into her hair. "Natalie, do you understand?" He pulled back and seized her head, cupping her jaw in his hands so he could stare into her eyes. The intensity of his expression was overwhelming. "It is no insult to you, dear girl, that I have turned my back on love. You are everything a man could want in a wife. But I—"

"No, no, I understand." She placed a light hand over his mouth, trying to keep him from saying the words she did not want to hear: *I could never love you in the way you want to be loved.* She swallowed her tears and forced a wavering smile to her lips. "I understand. The last thing in the world you want is a wife who fancies herself in love with you. I imagine the very mention of *love* is repulsive to you. After what you have been through, I cannot wonder at it. You needn't apologize or explain."

"How can you be so accepting?" he whispered. A strange little laugh shook him. "I tried so hard to keep the truth from you. I wanted to believe that even if you married me, you need never know what happened to Catherine. I've kept my head firmly buried in the sand for months, and now it seems I was hiding from a mere bogey. I've told you after all, and you still stand my friend."

"I will always stand your friend."

He was still holding her face in his hands. His eyes searched hers, wonder and pain reflected equally in the blue depths of his gaze. His thumbs traced her cheekbones. Natalie held her breath. And then he did the oddest thing: His gaze traveled to her hair, and he reached to wrap a loose strand of it around his finger. He stared at the curl hugging his finger, his expression rapt and fascinated. "I've been itching to do that since the first time I saw you," he murmured.

Natalie was confused. "Do what?"

"Touch your hair. All those maddening little curls." His gaze traveled back to her eyes. "They are even softer than I dreamed they would be."

Electricity suddenly seemed to arc through the air between them, a hot crackle of need that jolted Natalie like a lightning strike. She was utterly unprepared for the knee-weakening power of it. She felt her eyes widen with shock even as her eyelids drifted down. Through the haze of feeling she sensed his face coming nearer, his head bending to hers. She instinctively tilted her chin to lift her mouth, fully in the grip of desire's blinding force, helpless to resist it.

"Papa," whispered Sarah in the low bed beside them. The two adults froze in place at the sound, Natalie still with her face uptilted, Malcolm's mouth hovering inches above hers. "Papa, I'm thirsty."

Natalie's eyes flew open. Malcolm's face, slightly blurred from its closeness, wore a look of chagrin that was almost comical. She bit her lip, fighting an almost hysterical urge to laugh.

"The pitfalls of having children," he muttered, pulling back from her with obvious reluctance.

Natalie, now seized by a wave of embarrassment, hastily turned to Sarah. The little girl's eyes were closed, and a fretful frown creased her forehead.

"Are you awake, lamb?"

"Yes. Thirsty."

Natalie moved back around the foot of the bed to her own place, where a carafe of water and a small tumbler stood on the nightstand. "I'll pour you a little water, Sarah. You mustn't try to sit up. Let your papa help you." She was glad that her voice sounded normal. She felt extremely rattled.

Malcolm carefully lifted Sarah and Natalie helped her to drink, then quickly fluffed her pillows. As he laid her gently back down, Malcolm said gruffly, "How are you feeling, poppet? Shall we give you a little more medicine?"

"No," said Sarah peevishly. "Makes my head hurt."

"You've a bump on the head, darling," said Natalie softly.

"Makes it worse."

Natalie and Malcolm exchanged glances. Malcolm frowned. "She may be right. I took laudanum once, and it gave me a ferocious headache."

Natalie smoothed the hair back from Sarah's forehead, being careful not to touch the swelling. "What about your arm, sweetheart? Don't you want the medicine for your arm?"

Sarah murmured something indistinguishable, but it sounded distinctively negative. She was already drifting back to sleep. "The last dose is still helping her," Natalie said as quietly as she could. "And it's almost morning."

"Thank God for that."

"Will you move her back to Larkspur tomorrow?"

He smiled a little. "Today, you mean. Yes. I think my traveling coach is well-sprung enough to give her an easy ride. It hasn't rained for a while, so the roads are probably in the best shape they will ever be. I'm anxious to have her safe at home."

Natalie nodded. "Yes, she'll be more comfortable there."

"Natalie."

She looked up. Malcolm was gazing very seriously at her. "Thank you. For everything."

She felt herself blushing. "I was glad to help. You needed an extra pair of hands."

"That's not what I meant," he said softly. "Not entirely."

She looked away, her cheeks burning. "It has been a long night." There were times, she thought wretchedly, when she wished she were French. Or Italian. What *was* it about the English? The hardest thing in the world was to acknowledge emotion, and she couldn't for the life of her understand why. She took a deep breath. "I am glad you confided in me," she said softly. She looked down at her hands for a moment, then realized it was cowardly to refuse to meet his eyes. She looked up. "Thank you," she said steadily, "for telling me about your late wife. It was not an easy thing for you to do. But I needed to know."

His mouth twisted wryly. "I have destroyed whatever chance I had to win your hand, but I suppose it had to be done."

She smiled. "Oh, quite the contrary. If I ever do marry, I would rather have a husband who confides in me than one who does not." It was true, but she hated to see the gleam of hope her words kindled in his eyes. She shook her head at him, almost laughing. "I said *if.*"

He had given her much to think about. She felt closer to him than ever.

But the sad truth was, the better she understood him, the less likely it seemed that he would ever care for her in the way she already cared for him.

Chapter Fifteen

Natalie was standing before the mirror in the foyer, pulling on her gloves, when Hector strolled in from the library. He scowled at her. "So there you are."

"Were you looking for me?"

"Yes, as a matter of fact I was. Mabel and I see precious little of you these days. Where do you think you're going?"

Natalie raised her eyebrows. "I *think* I'm going to visit Sarah Chase, as I usually do in the mornings."

His glance flicked contemptuously down her person. "Fairly natty dressing, to call on a child half-wit."

Natalie flushed with annoyance and embarrassment. She was, in fact, very prettily gowned. And it was not, as Hector had obviously guessed, for Sarah's benefit. But that was none of Hector's business. "There is nothing wrong with Sarah's intellect," she informed him coldly. "It is only her arm that is broken."

"That's not what they say in the village." Hector leaned casually against the doorjamb, folding his arms across his chest and studying Natalie through narrowed eyes. "People say there's something wrong with her."

She finished buttoning her gloves and picked up her

hat, shaking out the ribbons with an angry snap. "I don't give two pins for what they may say in the village."

"Oh, it's obvious that you don't," he said, with false pleasantness. "But you should."

"Rubbish. People will say anything."

"I daresay they will. They did say, not so long ago, that you had taken up a governess position at Larkspur. Mabel and I nipped that little rumor in the bud, of course. Since you assured me that you wouldn't. And hadn't."

Natalie felt a blush stealing up her neck. She set her hat on her head and watched herself in the mirror as she adjusted it, carefully avoiding Hector's eyes. "What I promised was that I wouldn't leave your roof. Pray notice that I do still reside here."

"Yes, but you're scarcely ever home during daylight hours. I think you had better tell me, once and for all. Are you *working* at Larkspur?" His tone was insulting. "Or are you not?"

She concentrated with great care on tying her ribbons. She hated answering to him, but Hector was, when all was said and done, the head of the family. "I am not Sarah's governess," she said at last. "I am her friend. And, I suppose, her teacher. But Lord Malcolm and I have no formal arrangement—"

"Oh, I'll bet you don't," he said contemptuously.

"A governess is paid for her services. I receive no payment. Ergo, I am not a governess." She met his gaze in the glass and lifted her brows at him again. "Satisfied?"

"Hardly," snapped Hector. "If you aren't Sarah Chase's governess, what the deuce are you doing at Larkspur all day, every day?"

"Visiting." She closed her mouth firmly, determined to say no more.

Hector's voice was silky with menace. "Visiting . . . whom?"

"My neighbor. My neighbor's child. What difference does it make?" She set her jaw stubbornly. "Make of it what you will. I am doing nothing wrong."

He straightened then, abandoning the elaborately casual pose. She saw his hands curl into fists and knew he was truly angry. "I'll tell you what they say, Natalie, these people in the village whom you choose to ignore! They say that you and Lord Malcolm are *flirting* with each other. And that's the polite way of putting it! Don't think it went unnoticed, the fact that you spent a night at the inn with him."

Natalie gasped. She whirled to face him. "How dare they? How dare *you*? Nurse was there! We were tending Sarah that night, the three of us."

Hector's eyes were hot and beady. "I'm just telling you what people say. And they say something else, too. They say I ought to demand that Lord Malcolm marry you. I'm beginning to think they are right."

"No!" Natalie swallowed hard. She must not let Hector guess how important this was to her, or he would never let go of it. She must not give Hector such a potent weapon to use against her. She tried to speak calmly. "Do not make a spectacle of yourself, Hector. Lord Malcolm has not compromised me. If you stir up trouble in this quarter, you will only look foolish."

She saw Hector's crafty look appear and knew she had made a misstep. She had overreacted. He had guessed, after all, that he had found a sore spot he could use to torment her.

"Oh, I don't know," he drawled, studying her.

"There's a deal of talk in the village. I daresay he's expecting to receive a call from me by now. If I fail to make a push, he might think I'm shirking my brotherly duty. Might think he was at liberty to insult you in whatever way he chose."

Natalie tried to laugh. "Oh, very amusing. So you will ride over to Larkspur and bully Lord Malcolm into offering me marriage?"

"Why not? I know it's a stretch, but after all, nothing ventured, nothing gained. And it might very well work."

Alarm prickled all over her. *He is talking idly,* she told herself desperately. *He is only trying to needle me.* But it was working. She was thoroughly ruffled. She could not keep herself from blurting out, in a high-pitched, breathless, voice, "Don't do it, Hector. I warn you, you are putting your foot in a hornet's nest. If you think there is gossip now, that is nothing compared to the gossip that will ensue if you browbeat Lord Malcolm into making me an offer. You'll look like a nincompoop when I decline it."

"Decline his offer?" Hector stared at her. "Are you mad? No, even you would not be that imprudent! Good God, what are you thinking? What difference does it make *why* he offers, as long as he offers? I was only half serious, but I'm beginning to think—" He broke off, shaking his head as if marveling at her idiocy. "If I did convince Lord Malcolm to take such a step, and you were stupid enough to turn him down, I'd have you clapped in Bedlam."

She managed a rather sickly smile. "You are joking, of course. But one does hear of families who attempt swindles of that nature. Sending their females to deliberately tempt great men, so as to enrich themselves in cov-

ering up the ensuing scandal. I assure you, it's no laughing matter."

"I should say not!" He took a hasty turn about the
room. The foyer was small, so he quickly ended up back
where he began. He rounded on her, looking a little pale.
"If I thought for one moment," he said slowly, "that
Lord Malcolm had *already* offered marriage to you—"
Something in her face must have given her away. The
color rushed back into Hector's face. "Oh, my God!" he
shouted. He rushed toward her and seized her arm in a
painful grip, giving her a violent shake. "It's true, isn't
it? You've turned him down! You've *already* turned him
down! You turned down the most eligible—the wealthi-
est— Bloody hell! A *duke's* son!" Words seemed to fail
him; he began spluttering incoherently.

"Let go of my arm," she said sharply, trying to hide
her fear. "For shame! Hector, control yourself."

His fingers pinched her cruelly, but he fell back a step,
panting as he fought to control his rage. "If this were a
civilized country," he hissed, "I could lock you up for
this. I could starve you into submission. There ought to
be remedies a man could take, by God. Even if I can't
take a buggy whip to you, there ought to be legal steps.
Things I could do to you, to make you see reason."

"Well, there aren't any," said Natalie crisply, anxious
to throw cold water on such talk. She yanked her arm
out of his grip and stepped out of reach. "You cannot
force me to the altar against my will. This is the nine-
teenth century, not the Dark Ages! I am sorry if my decision upsets you, but the choice is mine to make, not
yours."

"Oh, it is, is it? So I'm to be saddled with you for the
rest of my life?" He ground his teeth with fury. "I must
house you, and feed you, and clothe you, and put up

with your interference and defiance! You're at liberty to refuse every man who offers for you—even a duke's son! I must pay your bills forever, eh? I have no say in it *whatsoever*?"

"I was prepared to leave Crosby Hall," cried Natalie, stung. "You stopped me! I was willing to take a governess post to escape this place—do you understand how desperate I was? I felt I would be happier almost anywhere than here." She pressed her hands together to stop their shaking. "It is unfair," she said in a low tone, "for you to hold that against me now, when it was your threats that forced me to stay."

"Everything has changed now," he shot back at her. "Everything! The world condemns a man who turns a spinster sister out on the world. But you are no longer quite the pitiable figure you were! What if I wash my hands of you?" His eyes narrowed. "I daresay no one will blame me at all, once it's known that you refuse to marry."

Natalie stared at him in horror. "You would spread such a story?"

"Why not?" he flung at her. "It's the truth."

"Dastard! Have you no shame?"

She knew immediately that she would live to regret those hasty words. She should have kept her temper. Hector advanced on her, livid, and grabbed her by the shoulders. She cried out as his fingers dug into her flesh.

"I'll give you forty-eight hours," he told her through clenched teeth. "Make up your mind. You will either accept Lord Malcolm's *very flattering* offer, or you will leave Crosby Hall forever. And I don't give a tinker's damn where you go. Or what becomes of you." He flung her from him with such force that her shoulder struck the wall. "I want you out of my house."

Natalie was so stunned that she could not even reply. She held one hand over her mouth, trembling, as she fought to regain her composure. Hector had been gone for several minutes before she managed to stand erect and face herself in the mirror again.

She took a deep breath. The eyes staring back at her from the glass were dilated with shock and fear. And, as she watched, they filled with tears as well. She blinked the tears back, furious that Hector had succeeded in hurting her feelings. *My house,* he had called it. Never mind that she, too, had been born in it. Never mind that she had lived here her entire life, while he dwelled in London with his mother. Never mind that she had cared for it and tended it and loved it, while Hector displayed only indifference toward the family home. It was, in fact, his house, and he could evict her at his pleasure.

Saints alive. What was she going to do?

She considered, for a few seconds, the possibility that he hadn't meant it. That he would change his mind when his temper cooled. But this idea brought her no comfort. Even if he did change his mind, what was to prevent him making the same threat, or worse, in the future? Must she walk on eggshells for the rest of her life, fearing to incur Hector's displeasure? Intolerable.

She walked blindly to the door, opened it, and left the house. Her footsteps headed automatically toward Larkspur—and Malcolm. She did not stop to question the logic of this, nor what words she would use to explain her embarrassing predicament when she reached him. She simply headed toward him as a stray lamb heads for home, instinctively.

Malcolm was in his study when Miss Whittaker was announced. His spirits lifted immediately and he stood with a smile of pleasure, extending his hand as she walked in the door. He noted with approval that she was wearing an extremely becoming frock and a very smart, deep-brimmed hat with wide satin ribbons. He opened his mouth to compliment her on her modish appearance—but then he glanced beneath the hat brim and saw her face.

His smile vanished. "What is it?" He crossed swiftly around the wide desk and went to her side, taking her hand in both of his. "Something has happened."

She gave him a rather wavering smile. "Trouble at home, I'm afraid."

"How can I help you? Tell me. I'll do anything in my power."

Her gloved fingers wrapped around his hand and clutched it, as if she were drawing strength from him. "My dear friend," she said gratefully, "I knew you would say that." Then she gave an almost hysterical little choke of laughter. "It has just now occurred to me, however, that you are the last person on earth I should turn to for help with this particular mess."

"You may turn to me for help with anything," he said gruffly. "Come into the library with me. I'll ring for tea. Or would you rather have lemonade?"

"Lemonade, please." She looked a little better. "Thank you for the thought."

He held her hand as he escorted her into the library. She clung to him like a lifeline. Even when he paused in the passage to drop a word to Howatch about the lemonade, she did not pull her hand from his. That simple fact told him more about her state of mind than mere words could have expressed.

Once in the library, he turned her to face him and untied the wide satin ribbons that held her hat on. As he had hoped, the gesture made her laugh a little. "Thank you, Papa," she said teasingly. "But I think I can remove my own hat." She lifted the straw confection off her curls as she spoke and set it aside on one of the library tables.

"Good. It's a deuced fetching bonnet and all that," he assured her. "But it hides half your face. Sit down, Natalie, and tell me what happened. Did someone move your roses again?"

She obediently sat, but not, as he had hoped, beside him on the sofa. She perched on the edge of a wing chair that faced him—and tried, but failed, to smile at his last sally. "Not that I know of." She heaved a small sigh and stared at her hands, clasped tightly in her lap. "Do you recall advising me, some time ago, to disregard public opinion?"

He was mildly startled. "Good heavens. Did I?"

A faint smile lightened her features and she looked up at him again. "Not in so many words. But that is what you meant, I believe. You told me I should not worry about what people say over their breakfast cups."

His brow cleared. "Oh, that. Certainly. Excellent advice for nearly anyone, I should think."

"Well, I took your advice. And it has come back to haunt me."

"Oh." He rubbed his chin ruefully. "So some impertinent idiot has said something nasty about you. The best way to nip that sort of thing in the bud—"

"No." She shook her head. "That is not the problem." She seemed to have difficulty meeting his eyes. Her cheeks were slowly turning pink. "The problem is that Hector has heard some gossip. And, as I feared, it is gossip about—about you and me. People seem to think we are . . ." She cleared her throat and directed her gaze out the window. "People seem to expect . . ."

He decided to help her out. "An interesting announcement."

"Yes. And Hector has decided . . ." Her voice trailed off again. He saw the delicate muscles in her throat work as she swallowed back whatever emotion was gripping her. Then she turned to face him, distress in every line of her face. "Malcolm, I don't know what to do. My brother is very angry with me. He—he wants me to leave Crosby Hall. Permanently. And by that I mean, he wants to—to wash his hands of me. That is how he puts it. He knows I have nowhere to go. Derek will help me if he can, but I fear he cannot. I will have to hire myself out as—as a governess, or a cook's maid, or whatever I can find."

"What?" His voice cracked like a whip, and Natalie jumped in her chair. "Sorry," he said, trying to bite back the anger that had swept through him. "But what nonsense is this?"

She sat very straight in her chair, hands clasped like a schoolgirl, but her chin was high now and her eyes met his squarely. "Hector wants me to marry you. If I refuse to do so, he intends to punish me. I have forty-eight hours to decide. If I do not accept your offer, he will evict me from Crosby Hall. And I cannot come here as governess to Sarah now. I must seek a post in some stranger's household."

"The devil! Why?"

"Because you and I are . . ." She swallowed hard. "Because our friendship has made us conspicuous. I cannot come to you. I cannot live at Larkspur."

Malcolm stared at her, incredulous. A dozen thoughts and emotions whirled in his brain.

"How am I to take this?" he said at last, shaking his head in baffled amazement. "I understand that you are reluctant to knuckle under to the demands of a petty little tyrant like Hector. Anyone would feel the same. I can even understand that you might think life as a domestic would be better than life under your brother's roof—at least in the heat of the moment," he added dryly. "But if you would rather be a cook's maid than marry me, I must tell you, Natalie, it's hard to take that as anything other than an insult."

Her eyes filled with tears. "Oh, I know. It's not meant that way. I just . . ." She buried her face in her gloved hands. "I don't know what to do."

"This is ridiculous," muttered Malcolm. He rose and, with great firmness, pulled Natalie's hands away from her face and lifted her to her feet. He held her there before him, supporting her by the forearms as she stared helplessly up at him.

There were tears caught in her eyelashes. They glittered like stars. She looked confused and miserable and heartbroken. And beautiful.

He smiled softly at her. "My dear girl, what are you afraid of? There is no question what you should do."

The misery in her face increased. "Malcolm, I—"

"Ssh." He lifted one finger and touched her lower lip, lightly as breath, to hush her. *Odd.* He had not realized how strongly touching her mouth would affect him. A shock of desire struck him, seemingly out of nowhere, at that tiny touch. Her lip felt warm and full beneath his finger. Soft as velvet. Tempting. His throat tightened with a sudden craving. "You are going to marry me," he said hoarsely. "And I am going to make you happy."

"But—"

"No. No more refusals. No more excuses."

He bent to kiss her. *At last!* A mixture of triumph and tenderness filled him as he moved to take her lips—but he was wholly unprepared for what happened next.

Some portion of his soul, unbeknownst to him, had been straining at a leash. For how long? He did not know; he had been utterly unaware of it until his mouth touched hers. At that instant, the leash suddenly snapped and his heart leaped free.

Astonishment jolted him with paralyzing intensity. *Natalie.* Dear God in heaven. Natalie. He was kissing Natalie. He was participating in a miracle. His arms tightened around her possessively: *mine.* This girl. This moment. Unfettered joy rushed and thundered and shouted in his veins.

Something holy and humbling, earth-shattering, life-altering, was occurring. *Natalie.* Malcolm felt his life divide neatly in two: before this kiss, and after it. This, this kiss, was the turning point; there was no going back. This was the cusp of his life. When he lifted his mouth from hers, he would be forever, fundamentally, changed.

At the end of the kiss his lips lingered on hers, reluctant to part from her even by a few inches. He wanted her. His desire for her was so overwhelming it felt like a primal need: He wanted Natalie the way he wanted air. This wasn't lust; it was something bigger. Something deeper.

Reverence and tenderness tempered his hunger for her, illuminating it. Purifying it. In a revelation that hit him like a thunderclap, he suddenly recalled a phrase in the church's marriage vows: *with my body I thee worship.* The image had seemed vaguely blasphemous until now. Now he understood. This woman would be his wife, consecrated unto him, and he would love and cherish her. It all made perfect sense.

He rested his forehead on hers, savoring the wonder of it all. Gladness sang in him like a choir of angels. "Natalie," he whispered, choked with emotion, "I love you."

She went very still in his arms. He felt her muscles tense. Drugged by the kiss, he did not understand what was happening until she pushed him away with her hands. He blinked at her, confused, like a man awaking from a dream.

Her face was white. Her mouth, still soft from his kiss, was set in a tight line. Good God, those were tears on her cheeks. Had she been crying before? She was crying now. Why? He reached for her, needing to comfort her, needing her to come to him. She backed away sharply, shaking her head.

"That's enough," she said. Her voice sounded nothing like herself. "Give me my forty-eight hours."

For a bewildered moment he did not know what she meant. Then he remembered: Hector had given her forty-eight hours to decide whether she would accept his marriage proposal. Give her her forty-eight hours? Why, she must mean she needed time to think. She must mean that she *still* had not agreed to marry him.

He stood, rooted to the spot, utterly confounded, as Natalie moved to pick up her hat and tie it back on her head with shaking hands. He was paralyzed by the events of the past three minutes. He had no idea how to deal with the feelings rioting inside him. He scarcely recognized himself.

She was going! In another few seconds she would be out the door. It was unbelievable. He still could not seem to move, but he forced himself to speak. "Natalie," he said, desperate to reach her. "I thought . . . I thought that was what you wanted. To be loved."

She turned at the door to face him, bestowing upon him a ghastly, overbright smile. "I know you did," she said cheerfully. *Cheerfully!* "I said as much, didn't I? That was foolish of me. Good day."

On her way out, she nearly collided with Howatch, who was carefully balancing a heavy tray as he headed for the library. Malcolm stared at her departing figure, unable to collect his scattered wits enough to call after her. His gaze then traveled, numbly, to Howatch, who stood uncertainly in the doorway with his tray.

When Malcolm failed to speak for several seconds, Howatch cleared his throat delicately. "Lemonade, sir?" he asked helpfully.

Chapter Sixteen

Natalie fled. There was no dignified name for it; she simply bolted, like a coward, from Malcolm's presence. She was halfway home before she remembered two things: She was supposed to visit Sarah; and it was absurd to return to Crosby Hall, from whence she had fled just half an hour ago. If she let her feelings drive her to and fro like this, she would soon be running in circles.

Ashamed of herself, she halted in her tracks and took a deep, shaking breath. Then, resolutely, she turned and headed back toward Larkspur. Her heart was hammering painfully in her chest, but she ignored it. She would visit Sarah. That was what she had set out to do, and she would do it.

As she climbed the grassy rise, the graceful manor house seemed to shimmer through her tears. Faugh! She dashed her gloved hands briskly across her eyes. Tears were for weaklings and babies. Natalie Whittaker was neither, and she would not cry. Her world was falling apart, but she would recover. One day, she promised herself grimly, she would look back on this horrid morning and smile.

What are you afraid of? Malcolm had asked her.

What, indeed. Only a ninny would feel such panic at the prospect of marrying the man she loved. Very well, she was a ninny. She couldn't help it. She dared not tell Malcolm what she feared: she feared destroying their fragile, teasing friendship. It seemed, to her, to hold such promise. Left to follow its natural course, it might one day become what she longed for it to be. But forced into the intimacy of marriage, what would become of it? What would become of her? She dreaded becoming another Catherine.

Oh, there was no chance she would ever jump from a parapet. But to marry Malcolm, loving him as she did, and knowing that—just as before—he sought a marriage of convenience . . . She shivered at the thought. He had despised Catherine. If he knew Natalie's feelings, would he despise her, too?

It was impossible to know whether Malcolm had felt contemptuous of Catherine's emotions, or merely her behavior. It did seem, to her, that much of Catherine's conduct had been manipulative rather than loving. But Natalie wondered how much of her perception had been colored by Malcolm's interpretation, which was, after all, the prism through which she had viewed the tale. Perhaps Catherine's feelings had been genuine, but so foreign to him that he had failed to understand her pain. He might very well have misread Catherine's motives; he had, in fact, admitted to Natalie that that was possible.

And now he believed that the only way to win Natalie's hand was to say he loved her. She cringed, hating to remember that dreadful moment. She ought never to have confided to him the most secret wish of her heart, to marry for love. It had left her vulnerable to just such a ploy. And what was particularly ghastly, particularly unfair, was that his artificial declaration had soiled what had been the most wonderful experience of her life.

She was right, she thought wistfully, to have dreamed of Malcolm's kiss. She was also right to have feared it. It was, as she had dreamed, a halcyon moment. But it also was, as she had feared, too revealing. He had caught a glimpse of her true feelings. And he had felt compelled to respond with that patently false declaration. He wanted her to believe that he *loved* her! Why, the man didn't even believe that romantic love existed, outside of books and plays!

Remembering, she shook her head in disgust. One would think, she told herself indignantly, that after all Malcolm had suffered in his first marriage, he would be the last man on earth to use the word "love" merely to get his way. She had almost said it to his face: *Don't "Catherine" me!* He would have known exactly what she meant.

She reached the house and entered, as she frequently did, through the French windows in the music room, then climbed the stairs unannounced to the nursery. Sarah had made rapid progress since her fall, and it was becoming more difficult every day to confine her indoors. When Natalie peeped in, the little girl was sitting on a high-backed chair, fidgeting, while Nurse brushed her hair. Her arm rested in a sling.

"Mrs. Mumbles believes we ought to go out of doors today," announced Sarah.

"Mrs. Mumbles hasn't anythin' to say about it," said Nurse firmly. "You want to get well, don't you?"

"Yes. But why can't I get well in the garden?"

"Because Mr. Carter says we must keep you quiet. Give over, Sarah, do! You're too big a girl to wriggle about like this."

"I'll be quiet in the garden," Sarah offered. "I'll be quiet as a mouse. You could brush my hair in the garden."

"I'm brushing your hair right here. Hold still, child! I'm nearly done."

"Mrs. Mumbles wants—ow!"

"There, now, what did I tell you? If you sit still, the brush won't pull your hair."

At this point in the game, Sarah's gyrations turned her toward the door where Natalie stood. Her face brightened. "Look, Nurse."

Nurse looked up, harassed, and Natalie smiled at both of them. "Good morning, ladies. Am I interrupting?"

Sarah's face brightened further. "It's Miss Whittaker!" She jumped off the chair and ran to Natalie. "Miss Whittaker, you must come and speak to Mrs. Mumbles. She's frightfully bored."

Something tugged at the edge of Natalie's consciousness. There was something odd about what had just transpired. She couldn't quite put her finger on it. But then Sarah was upon her, tugging on her hand, leading the way to her play area, chattering as happily as if she'd never felt an hour of pain, and Natalie dismissed the nagging thought. She would consider it later, when she had time.

Nurse rolled her eyes comically for Natalie's benefit, indicating that she thought the child was being overindulged—but she refrained from scolding or calling Sarah back to finish her hair. So Natalie went, and obliged Sarah with a little play time.

She knew it was hard on the little girl, having no playmates, and harder still to be injured and told she must rest. And, if truth be told, playing with Sarah did Natalie almost as much good as it did Sarah. She loved to watch

Sarah's expressive little face telegraphing her every thought, and she delighted in the inventive play that was Sarah's hallmark—even when she couldn't quite follow the fantasy or decipher the peculiar rules of every game Sarah introduced.

At one point Sarah suddenly went very still, falling silent in midsentence. Natalie reached to brush the baby-fine strands of Sarah's hair off her forehead. "Does your arm hurt, darling?"

"Yes," she said, almost inaudibly. "Sometimes it hurts worse like this. But it will go away again in a minute." She lifted troubled eyes to Natalie. "Nurse says my arm will soon be well. How long is soon?"

"Soon is a different length of time for different things, but always short."

"It seems long to me, this time."

Natalie's heart ached for her. "I know, sweetheart. Pain makes the time seem longer. Afterward, when your arm has healed, you will look back on this time and think it wasn't long at all."

"I wish afterward was now."

"I do, too."

"Papa says I must be brave."

"You are being brave. We're very proud of you."

Sarah's sweet little smile touched Natalie's heart, but alarm bells rang in the back of her mind. Had Sarah heard what Natalie heard—too late—in her words? She had, without thinking, coupled her thoughts with Malcolm's. That *we* had slipped out so naturally, she wondered nervously how many other times she had used it. Had she fallen into a habit of linking herself with Sarah's father? Had Sarah come to accept it?

Natalie felt as if the walls were closing in on her. Hector's malice, the gossip in the village, her love for Sarah,

Sarah's love for her, Malcolm's persistence—everything was conspiring to shove her into the prison of a loveless marriage. Worse than loveless: a marriage where she loved, but her husband didn't. She was being dragged inexorably toward the moment when she would accept Malcolm's hand and marry him. She seemed powerless to fight the tide that was sweeping her along, willy-nilly.

This, she thought resentfully, *is what comes of trusting the stars.* She had let them pull her into the dance, and here she was, danced into a corner.

She did not care to encounter Malcolm while she was still feeling so conflicted, so she left Sarah and Nurse when luncheon was brought in. She walked home, her thoughts still in turmoil, slipped into Crosby Hall through a side door, and shut herself in her own rooms. There she paced for much of the afternoon, thinking hard and praying for guidance.

By sunset she had made up her mind. Really, she thought with resignation, it should not have taken her so long. Malcolm was right; the solution was obvious. And it was, after all, useless to rail against the stars.

If destiny was truly leading her, she must submit to her fate. She would marry Malcolm. But forewarned is forearmed: She would *not* make Catherine's mistakes. No, indeed. What Malcolm wanted was a marriage of convenience and a mother for his motherless daughter. Very well, she would give him that. That, and nothing else. She would not hang adoringly on his arm. She would not embarrass him with displays of ardent affection. She would do her best to ape the cool, smiling brides of the aristocracy, and give him a wife who would keep a friendly distance. She could shower wee Sarah with loving attention, but with Malcolm she would never cross the line . . . unless and until she found a way to make him love her.

She still did not despair of that. He liked her, that was plain, and it seemed he felt physically drawn to her as well. The kiss could not have meant to him what it meant to her, but at least he had kissed her, and kissed her thoroughly. That would do—for now. If she avoided Catherine's errors . . . if she did her best to be the kind of wife he admired, and gave him the pleasant, uneventful life he apparently wanted . . . that might, if she were patient, do the trick. But she must not pursue or nag him. She must let *him* come to *her.*

At any rate, she had to try. She would try. She would marry the man of her dreams, and one day, God willing, the rest of the dream would come true.

With her decision made, calm descended on her heart. She walked downstairs to find Hector.

Natalie would marry him! She would marry him after all. He would focus on that. It was, after all, the most important point. But what the devil did she mean by making Hector relay the news? It obviously had not been Hector's choice to do so. The poor blighter was palpably nervous, his extreme youth showing in the awkwardness with which he handled the matter. It annoyed Malcolm that Hector had clearly never given a moment's thought to the idea that his sister might, one day, marry, and that he might, one day, need to have his ducks in a row for such an interview as this. He obviously hadn't a clue what to do, and ultimately agreed to let the two families' solicitors handle the details of marriage settlements and "all that rubbish." But he extended a civil invitation for Malcolm to dine *en famille* at Crosby Hall that evening.

The invitation did not include Sarah, even though it

was her fate as well as Malcolm's that would be sealed that evening. The omission rankled, but, as he reminded himself, there was nothing unusual about it. Most dinner invitations did not include small children. It was just . . . something in Hector's face he did not like. Something in his attitude. It raised Malcolm's hackles, but he tried to ignore it; he knew he was overly sensitive about his child's perceived shortcomings.

And tonight would be about Natalie.

Just as well, under the circumstances, that Sarah would not be present. Malcolm's heart thudded with anticipation when he thought about getting Natalie alone—and he thought about it often. She had run from him yesterday and he had not seen her since, but he was willing to chalk that up to maidenly shyness. Or something. Whatever had caused her to flee, he was damned well going to overcome it.

By the time the Whittakers' butler showed him into the drawing room that night, his nerves were pulled as taut as harp wire. He bowed to the room, but his eyes went straight to Natalie. He felt his breath catch in his throat. She looked beautiful. She had obviously dressed with the same elaborate care that had driven his own grooming tonight, thinking to do justice to the occasion. She was wearing a deceptively simple dinner dress of some cream-colored stuff that flattered every curve of her figure. And her hair, twisted and piled and tortured into submission, framed her face with an elegant sophistication he had never seen in her before.

He murmured something, he scarcely knew what, tossed in the general direction of Mabel and Hector—but his feet were pulling him toward Natalie. Her eyes lifted to his, luminous. A shock of excitement went through him. He wanted to stare into her eyes forever. He had known her for weeks, he marveled, but somehow he was seeing her now as if for the first time. All this extraordinary beauty would soon be his. Amazing. The thought made him almost light-headed.

His pulse pounding, he took her hand in his and bowed over it. She gave him a faint, almost nervous, smile. And then his dratted hosts interrupted, pulling his reluctant attention back to the fact that he and Natalie were not alone.

It was difficult to get through dinner. Mabel was effusive in a chatty, girlish way that set his teeth on edge. Hector's idea of being a charming host consisted of making a series of distasteful jokes at the expense of his wife, his sister, and a number of persons who were not present. Malcolm would probably have found this even more irritating than he did, but he was so eager to be alone with Natalie that he could barely follow the conversation. He ate the food set before him, but tasted none of it. It cost him a tremendous effort every time the meal, or the conversation, forced him to tear his eyes from his future bride.

Natalie sat silent and composed across the table from him, seldom raising her eyes from her plate. Whenever she did, however, her eyes went straight to his, and Malcolm felt that same pleasurable rush of attraction that had struck him earlier. Stunning. Miraculous. He had never experienced anything quite like it. His heart rejoiced; he knew in his bones that marriage to Natalie would be heaven on earth.

Before the night was over, he would kiss her . . . at the very least. His whole body seemed to tighten when he thought of it like a racehorse waiting for the starting pistol. The wait was nearly unbearable, the anticipation so keen it was almost torture.

The evening crawled by, but he knew he was heading steadily toward the moment. He felt it on the horizon, drawing ever nearer. The minutes passed with agonizing slowness while he smiled and chatted and bided his time, striving to appear outwardly normal while inwardly champing at the bit. The covers were removed—hallelujah. He shared a tedious glass of port with Hector. The men joined the ladies in the drawing room. Conversation. More conversation, deadly dull. At last, at last, Mabel and Hector exchanged significant glances. They rose, just as Malcolm had prayed they would, pleading some lame excuse to leave Malcolm and Natalie alone.

Malcolm rose politely to his feet, pretending to believe the ruse, and bowed as Mabel passed out of the room on Hector's arm. Those last few seconds were the longest of the evening, but finally the moment arrived: He was alone with Natalie.

He turned to face her, every atom of his being straining toward her like a bloodhound nearing its quarry. She had not moved from her place by the fire. She sat quietly, hands clasped lightly in her lap, back straight, chin level. The shimmering gown glinted in the light, outlining the soft curve of her breast and hip in lush invitation, belying the propriety of her ladylike posture. And that glorious hair of hers—it had started the evening properly confined, but by now it had run wanton, curling drunkenly at her brow, her temples, the nape of her neck. The very sight of it made him smile.

"Natalie Whittaker," he said softly, "you have made me the happiest of men."

The cliché came straight from his heart and rolled out of his mouth as sincerely as if no man had ever said it before. Still, its triteness caused her face to light with demure laughter.

"Very prettily said, my lord."

"Thank you," he said ironically, feeling like a dunce. "But I mean it."

She looked embarrassed. "I shall do my best," she said primly, "to ensure that you never regret your persistence."

"I know I never shall."

She seemed to relax a little, shooting him that fabulous smile of hers. "In that case, I shall devote my energy to ensuring that *I* never regret your persistence."

He returned her smile but shook his head. "That's my role," he told her. "Not yours. But set your mind at rest, Natalie. Your life is about to change for the better."

Her gaze dropped. She seemed as shy of him as if they were strangers. "I did not keep you dangling all summer from mere caprice," she said, her voice sounding soft and anxious. "I hope you know that. I did have reasons for declining your offer. It is only lately that I have come to believe that marriage will, in fact, change my life for the better. And that I can offer you something valuable in return."

He had no patience tonight to sit through a lengthy discussion of what had brought them to this point. All that mattered now was that they had reached it. "At any rate, I'm glad you accepted me in the end."

"So am I."

Good. But was she going to sit in that blasted chair all night? He couldn't get at her. He strolled forward, purpose in every line of his body. Her eyes widened in patent alarm, but he caught her hand and pulled her up and out of the chair before she could protest. He caught her against him, chest to chest. *Yes.* This was what he had waited for.

His body tingled as he felt her relax against him. He

looked into her eyes and saw her expression subtly alter. The atmosphere in the room shifted. The air seemed to thicken. Natalie's eyes were still wide, but the darkness of her dilated pupils no longer seemed to indicate nervousness. As he watched, her eyes went darker yet. No, that was not fear. It was something else entirely. Her face was so close to his that he could see the sweep of each individual eyelash over those heart-melting brown eyes. Her lids slowly drifted down until her eyes were half-closed.

"I suppose this means," she said huskily, "that you and my brother have come to terms."

He felt his blood heat in response to her teasing. "Rot the terms," he growled, savoring the moment. "You will be my wife. If we're all agreed on that, the terms can go hang."

He felt laughter quivering through her body. "Most unwise," she chided him, still in that damnably alluring purr. "Hector will fleece you if he can."

A surge of recklessness made him grin. "I don't care if he does."

Her eyes flew open, sparking with amusement, and her delicate brows lifted. "But I care," she protested. "My dear sir, it's bad enough to make a marriage of convenience—but to marry a pauper? It simply isn't done."

He brought his hands up to her face and cradled her cheeks in his fingers. Tenderness rushed through him as he marveled at the softness of her skin. "With you at my side," he whispered, "I'll be the richest man in England."

She looked adorably surprised, but pleased, too. A blush warmed the cheeks beneath his fingers. "Why, Malcolm," she murmured, "I'm astonished. I had no idea you were such a flatterer."

"That," he promised her softly, "is only the beginning. I have quite a few surprises in store for you."

He felt her breathing quicken. "Will they all be as pleasant as that one?"

Desire leaped and flared in him. He had delayed the kiss long enough. It was killing him. Five more minutes and he'd be a dead man. "I hope so," he whispered, then crushed her mouth beneath his.

This kiss was no gentle exploration. He was too hungry for her, too needy. He devoured her. And, like a miracle, she reacted almost immediately with a heat that swiftly matched his own. He felt her arms snake up around his neck and heard her moan, deep in her throat. Her response maddened him. He had never imagined anything warmer than compliance; to feel her joining his desire as an equal partner was more than he had dared to hope.

When he broke the kiss and came up for air, she gasped and arched her back, throwing back her head. He could not resist the exposed column of her throat. Groaning, he bent to kiss it. The swift intake of her breath told him that he was giving her pleasure. That was all the encouragement he needed. He nibbled up and down the length of her neck, reveling in the tiny gasps his kisses drew from her.

By God, she was quivering! He felt little tremors running all through her. This was definitely the woman of his dreams. He had longed for this woman all his life, without even knowing it. *Natalie.*

He lifted his head so he could look at her. Tenderness and awe swept through him. *Mine.* He ran one hand along the gorgeous sweep of her waist and hip. "You're so beautiful," he whispered, drunk with emotion, and bent to kiss her again.

But she suddenly went stiff in his arms. Was she pulling back? Why? He paused, opening his eyes. Natalie had placed her hands against his chest to parry his advance. She lifted her head, steadying herself against him. There was a crease in the furrow between her eyes. She seemed to be fighting her way back to reality after a brief spell of madness. He watched in chagrined disbelief as the passionate woman in his arms rapidly cooled.

She gave him a strained little smile. "I have already agreed to marry you, Malcolm," she said, with a ridiculous attempt at lightness. "You needn't empty the butter boat over me."

He was too amazed to reply. She pulled herself out of his embrace, self-consciously straightening her bodice. Her eyes were on the floor as she moved away. Then, having reached what she apparently deemed a safe distance, she looked at him again.

An invisible wall seemed to have sprung up between them. Natalie looked as unaffected as if nothing had just passed between them at all. If it weren't for her still-flushed face, there would be no clue that their kiss had even taken place. Her expression was friendly but placid. She looked utterly composed.

Malcolm was utterly *dis*composed.

He stared at her, baffled, as she gave him an amused little smile. "I did say I enjoyed being flattered, didn't I?" she remarked. "*Mea culpa!* I should have warned you that flattery fails once it passes the bounds of credibility."

He didn't know what in blue blazes she was talking about. All he knew was she had broken out of a kiss he could have sworn was mutual, and was now trying to act as if nothing had happened. It made no sense.

And then it hit him. There was no mystery to her behavior at all. *She simply didn't love him.* Dismay shook him to the depths of his soul. It was more than a disaster; it was calamity. He had been so consumed with his own feelings, so wrapped up in the miracle of loving her, that he had somehow forgotten that love was not necessarily a mutual experience. How could he, of all men, have forgotten that?

Because it didn't feel right, that's why.

He frowned, staring at his beloved Natalie across the enormous gulf of her indifference. Her *apparent* indifference. He didn't believe it. He felt the connection between them as surely as he had ever felt anything in his life. It was there, it was real. Surely she felt it, too. How could she not?

But he had never been on this side of the equation, he reminded himself, his sense of dismay deepening. He knew nothing, less than nothing, about love. He had never given it a second's serious thought. He had dismissed the entire notion of romantic love as pure fantasy, a delusion fit only for poets, females, and idiots. He recalled the contempt he had felt for Catherine's clinging and sighing and experienced an inward shudder. Now the tables had been turned. He faced the hair-raising prospect of repeating his first marriage—from the opposite point of view.

But he would not repeat Catherine's mistakes. Whatever he did, he vowed, he would not use his unrequited love as a weapon. He would never bully or reproach his darling Natalie. She deserved better than that. He would respect her privacy. He would honor her and cherish her and treat her like a queen. He would woo her. Carefully. Gently. And then, God willing, if he didn't press her too much, *she* would come to *him.*

The situation did not seem hopeless. They had friendship and, he could have sworn, they shared passion. That was a foundation upon which he could build.

But he had to ask. It was not in his nature to mince words. He started forward, urgently needing to know. "Natalie," he blurted, "did you not enjoy the kiss?"

She looked startled. "What?"

She fell back a step as he advanced, but he gripped her shoulders to halt her retreat, searching her eyes with his. He spoke again, more gently. "I need to know, sweetheart. It seems to me that you do not find me repulsive. Am I mistaken?"

She blushed. "Of course not."

He reluctantly let her go. Friendship and passion. That would have to do—for now. "Good." He managed to give her what he hoped was a reassuring smile. "These things are more important to a marriage than some women realize."

Her blush intensified, but she nodded. "I understand that."

He watched the firelight dance sweetly on the edge of her cheek. Her skin looked lush and touchable. He longed for her, body and soul. "You're not afraid?" His whisper was rough with banked desire.

She lifted limpid eyes to his. "No."

Her simple faith in him, her trust, took his breath away. And there was something deuced erotic about it, too. If he couldn't have her love, he was glad to have her trust . . . but knowing that his bride was willing, he suddenly realized, was going to make the waiting worse.

Bloody hell.

On the other hand, what the devil were they waiting for? A string of stupid parties? A tedious ritual of banns, to which no one would object anyway? The piecing together of a special costume? Nonsense. He'd bet a monkey that every gently born female of Natalie's age already had a wedding dress wrapped in silver paper and tucked into a cedar chest somewhere.

He took her hand and bent to plant a reckless kiss in her palm. "Marry me soon, Natalie," he muttered against her skin. "Will you?"

She swallowed hard. "If—if you wish," she said faintly.

"I do wish."

He straightened, her hand still captured in his. Her eyes had taken on that slumberous, heavy-lidded languor again. He felt his heartbeat quicken. Had his mouth on her skin done that to her? In a few quick seconds? Ah, God. He had to have her soon.

"Come with me to London," he urged, his voice low and rapid. "We can be married by special license. I'll make you mistress of Larkspur next week. Please, Natalie. Please." He pulled her unresisting body back into his arms. "Please," he whispered again and kissed her, softly this time. Just a little persuasion. Just a little.

She nodded like a sleepwalker, seeming dazed by the heat that had sprung up so readily between them. "Very well," she murmured. "If you like."

So polite! He almost laughed, but the impulse died an unmourned death. He had better things to do with his mouth right now than laugh.

Chapter Seventeen

Natalie moved through the next few days in a dream. Nothing seemed real to her. She accepted the congratulations and good wishes of her friends, danced her way through a small, hastily assembled ball in her honor, wrote the requisite letters to Derek, to her stepmother, and to her future in-laws, and stood for hours being fitted for gowns. In an eye-opening demonstration of her abrupt change in social status, Malcolm arranged for a modiste and a team of seamstresses to travel from London to Crosby Hall for the express purpose of enlarging Natalie's trousseau. New gowns were ordered, old gowns were miraculously transformed, and Natalie became, almost overnight, a lady of fashion. She barely recognized the elegant creature staring back at her from the mirror.

Her instinct was to object to the shocking expense to which Malcolm must have gone to achieve this, but she stifled her protest. She would not argue with him. She would not put her own opinions forward. That was the bargain, was it not? She had agreed to a marriage of convenience. She would give him a conformable, submissive wife, and he would give her his title and his wealth.

And his daughter. That, far more than the outward trappings of title and fortune, would enrich her life beyond measure.

One moment stood out from the blur of her brief engagement period: when Malcolm led her in to Sarah and broke the news that he and Natalie were to be married. Sarah's happiness brought tears to Natalie's eyes, and when the little girl flew into her arms with an incoherent cry of joy, she hugged her tightly.

It would remain forever etched in her memory, bright and edged with clarity—the moment when her arms went around Sarah and she smiled up at Malcolm through her tears and thought, *This will be my family.* This man. This child. They were hers henceforward, forever. The enormity of the gift was overwhelming. She had felt, the day she met them, an inexplicable bond that she had never before felt with anyone but Derek. Had it been premonition? Whatever the reason, part of her had known instantly that she belonged with Malcolm and Sarah. And now, incredibly, the informal bonds of rapport and friendship would be tied and sealed in earnest.

She would no longer be Natalie Whittaker. She would be Natalie Chase. Lady Malcolm Chase. The name sounded eerily foreign, but it would be hers. That would be the name carved on her tombstone. It was all very . . . disquieting. Too much to get used to, too quickly.

She should never have agreed to marry Malcolm by special license. She realized, too late, that the decorous three-week wait imposed by the reading of banns was the bare minimum that a lady needed to mentally adjust to the huge changes rushing toward her. Absent the reading of banns, time ran forward like water in a millrace.

At the end of one short week she found herself bundled into a traveling carriage and heading for London, Malcolm at her side.

For propriety's sake, Sarah and Mrs. Bigalow accompanied them, but they sat facing the betrothed couple—it was Malcolm whose body was pressed intimately against hers, shoulder, hip, and thigh. It was difficult to make conversation while tingling with awareness of Malcolm's long, lean body beside her. It was impossible to believe that this would be her lot forevermore; that in future, this was how she and Malcolm would always travel, side by side. Very strange.

London was less than a day's journey at this time of year, and they reached the Chase family's town house in Mayfair two hours before sunset. When Natalie climbed down from the carriage and looked up, she felt almost dizzy. The feeling of unreality intensified.

Oldham House was definitely a ducal mansion. She was about to be installed in a ducal mansion. From this day forward, whenever she visited the metropolis, this is where she would stay. She was to think of this magnificent edifice as home. Merciful heavens. She had admired her stepmother's elegant little flat in Kensington, but Oldham House made Lucille's flat look like a hovel.

She was suddenly very glad of her new clothes. She would have looked like the imposter she was, had she entered Oldham House in the modest attire of a country gentlewoman.

It was all too preposterous to take in stride. Still, Natalie said nothing. She allowed Malcolm to lead her in and introduce her to a few members of the staff. She smiled and nodded graciously, pretending to be what she was not: a manor-born aristocrat. The sense that she was walking through a dream turned out to be rather helpful. She sailed through the unforeseen ordeal with the correct air of cool friendliness, too detached to feel nervous. She introduced Mrs. Bigalow to Oldham House's butler and housekeeper and made no clumsy mistakes whatsoever.

Sarah and Nurse were escorted upstairs by the housekeeper. Natalie glanced up after them, frowning a little. Something had cut through the fog that seemed to be clouding her brain. Once again, something about Sarah's behavior bothered her. It was in the way she clung to Nurse's hand, and the way she proceeded up the steps— head bent, shoulders hunched, even while bouncing with energy and excitement. It meant something, Natalie was sure of it.

The child was, of course, still recovering from her broken arm. Had Sarah become morbidly afraid of falling? Natalie had the oddest feeling that if she only had leisure to stop and mull it over for a few minutes, the solution to some important mystery would occur to her.

She filed the moment away in the back of her mind, promising herself that she would think on it later: In the meantime, Malcolm had left the butler to direct the unloading of their baggage, and wanted to take Natalie on a brief tour of the main portion of the house.

She trailed after him from room to room, murmuring polite admiration. In truth, she found it overwhelming. The public rooms had last been decorated in the middle of the last century, and were, as a consequence, almost ridiculously ornate. Natalie had never seen anything as intimidating as the flamboyant display of wealth and power exhibited in every gorgeous detail. No surface was left undecorated; even the door handles were carved and plated with gold.

Natalie's spirits sank lower and lower as the tour continued. She could not help fearing, foolishly, that her fingerprints would smear the polished surfaces, or that the edge of her skirt would knock some priceless ornament off its perch and break it. And Malcolm had grown up in such surroundings! He took it all for granted. He turned those gold-plated handles with no more thought or care than if they were the leather latches on a tenant cottage.

They finished the tour in the morning room, and Malcolm rang for tea. He then glanced down at her, a slight, apologetic smile lifting the corners of his mouth when he saw her expression. "I suppose it's a bit much," he admitted, looking about him. "No wonder all this gilding and whatnot has gone out of fashion. I'm so accustomed to it that I don't realize how it must strike someone seeing it for the first time."

"It's lovely," said Natalie politely, sinking, with great care, onto a satin-covered settee.

"The bedchambers have been redone in a more modern style."

Bedchambers. Natalie shivered. So many images suddenly swirled in her brain that she could not think of a single word to say.

"You are tired," he said, looking keenly at her. "Shall I have tea sent up to your room, rather than let you wait for it here?"

"Oh! No." She shook her head, embarrassed. "I will drink it here—with you."

Her answer seemed to please him. He came over and sat opposite her, leaning earnestly forward. "I mean to make you happy, Natalie," he said softly.

She gave him a wavering smile. "I know it, Malcolm. And I shall do my best to give you a—a comfortable life. A peaceful life."

He looked surprised, and a little disturbed. He seemed to search in his mind for a moment, as if trying to choose his words carefully. "You had hoped, at one time," he said at last, "for something more than a comfortable marriage."

"Yes." She straightened hastily, afraid she had said the wrong thing. "But I do not require it, Malcolm. We cannot pick and choose whom we will love. It apparently strikes at random, like—like lightning. I will not pine for what I do not have. I value what you have done for me, and I am grateful. I know the terms of our bargain. I will honor them."

She had meant to reassure him, but he did not look reassured. "Grateful!" he exclaimed. "What is it that you think I have done for you?"

She blinked at him, surprised. "Why, Malcolm, don't you know? You have given me a new home. A new family." Sudden emotion rose in her, constricting her throat. "You are sharing Sarah with me. No one has ever given me such a beautiful gift. I promise you, I treasure it."

His eyes darkened with answering emotion. He reached to take her hand in his, lifting it to his lips. It looked as if he were about to speak, but a discreet knock heralded the entrance of the tea tray. Whatever he had been about to say remained unsaid, and Natalie wasn't sure whether to be glad or sorry. She had been treading on dangerous ground.

Don't crowd him, she reminded herself desperately. *Don't display what is in your heart.* Malcolm would have to come to her, not the other way about, or it would never be any good.

She looked tired and dispirited. Malcolm, his appetite vanished, crumbled a biscuit into his saucer. All he wanted in life was to make Natalie happy. This he had known since their first kiss. She was right; this falling-in-love business struck one out of the blue, like lightning. Was there nothing he could do to make her fall in love with him? He longed to set down the blasted saucer, yank her up off of that settee, and kiss her senseless. But he kept his seat—with difficulty.

Don't crowd her, he reminded himself sternly. *Don't display what is in your heart.* Natalie must come to him, not the other way about, or it would never be any good.

Tomorrow was their wedding day. After that, she would be his. His to woo—without distraction. No separation at the end of the day. His home would be hers. Their lives would be joined. And lightning was going to strike, by God, if he had to drag her out in a thunderstorm with a key tied round her neck.

He had reached this point in his cogitations when Derek Whittaker was announced. He barely had time to stand up before an energetic young man bounded into the room, not waiting for a footman's escort. Natalie flew out of her chair with a glad little cry and went straight into the young man's arms, laughing with delight.

"Derek! Oh, I can't believe it! How did you know I had arrived?"

"Why, you named the date in your letter, goose. I've been hanging about Mount Street all day on the lookout for you. Nearly got picked up for loitering, by Jove!

Dashed particular, your new neighbors." He held her at
arm's length, grinning at her. "And then, after all my patience, you sneaked past me when I stepped round the
corner for a bit of bread and cheese."

Natalie was glowing. It gave Malcolm a queer sort of
pang, to witness her happiness in the arms of another
man—even her brother. The polite, depressed young
lady who had inhabited Natalie's person a few minutes
ago had vanished, leaving behind this laughing, animated girl.

"What! All day long?" she was exclaiming. "I am astonished that Lord Stokesdown could spare you."

"Oh, I'm strictly window dressing." He winked. "Not
really necessary to him at all."

Their laughter combined, two bells ringing the same
peal in different octaves. The family resemblance was
remarkable. Natalie had told him that she and Derek
were often mistaken for twins, and, seeing them together, it was difficult to believe that they were not.
Derek was much taller, of course, and his movements
had a careless, loose-limbed freedom that hers lacked,
but these were gifts bestowed by virtue of his gender. He
had the same charismatic smile and expressive brown
eyes. It seemed that his hair was slightly darker, and perhaps less curly than his sister's, but that might, again, be
a gender-bestowed difference. Young men aspiring to
fashion cropped their hair at a length that resisted curl
and tamed it with oil if it refused to obey the mode.
Derek sported a Brutus cut, neatly tailored clothing, and
a well-tied cravat. He looked every inch the young man-
about-town.

He looked his sister up and down and his brows flew
up. "Gadzooks. It's a good thing I bearded you in your
lair, for I'd never have recognized you on the street."

Natalie rolled her eyes at him. "Pish-tosh. I'd have known you anywhere, even in your London finery." She seemed to recall herself, then, and with a startled "Oh! Where have my wits gone begging?" turned to introduce the two men to each other.

To Malcolm's appreciative amusement, there was a distinct air of animosity in Derek's bow. He could almost sense the young man's hackles rising as he took Malcolm's measure, his brown eyes wary and deadly serious. "How do you do, my lord?" he said, with arctic politeness. "I had hoped to know you better before you wed my sister."

"Yes, an awkward business," said Malcolm affably. "But I daresay we can make up for lost time later."

Derek gazed steadily at him. "I'm very fond of Natalie, sir."

Malcolm knew a warning when he heard one. Excellent! He was inclined to approve of young Mr. Whittaker. It was gratifying to find that Natalie had one brother, at least, who was worthy of the name.

He nodded, a faint smile curling his mouth. "I'm glad to hear it," he said. "I'm very fond of her, myself."

Derek did not noticeably thaw. "I would have thought," he said, steel in his voice, "that a man aspiring to my sister's hand might look me up prior to contracting an engagement. I know that Natalie is of age, but—"

"Oh, great heavens!" exclaimed Natalie. "Do you think Malcolm should have asked you for my hand?"

Derek stiffened. "As the eldest of your brothers—"

"Oh, no! Derek, I promise you, it never occurred to either of us! How absurd you are."

He dropped the stiff pose and rounded on her, glowering. "Natalie, someone must look out for your best interests, and Hector's not the man to do so."

"Well, that's true," she admitted. "But I am perfectly capable of minding my own affairs, you know."

He gazed searchingly at her, his brown eyes troubled. "May I speak privately with you?"

"No," she said promptly. "I want you to become acquainted with Lord Malcolm."

"Well, that's just it! I don't know this chap, and neither do you. Not well enough to marry him—and not in such all-fired haste!"

"Nonsense." Natalie's cheeks were turning pink. "I must tell you, Derek—and this is quite my own fault, for not making it plain in my letters to you—that Lord Malcolm and I have become fast friends during the past month or two."

Derek did not look persuaded. His jaw jutted pugnaciously. "Well, since you won't let me say my piece to you in private, I must say it here. There's something dashed smoky about this business. Besides which, any man whom *Hector* chooses for you is liable to be a bounder. I don't mean to offend Lord Malcolm—"

"Well!" Natalie gasped. "If you don't mean to offend him, I suggest you stop being offensive! For pity's sake, Derek, do you think I would marry anyone at Hector's bidding? I am not such a simpleton."

Derek looked harassed. "But I had a letter from Hector, preening himself on your betrothal and implying—" He stopped in midsentence. Doubt seemed to shake him. "Do you mean he was blowing smoke? He seemed to think that you had initially *refused* Lord Malcolm's offer. Gave me the impression that he had coerced you into accepting him."

He shot another hostile glance at Malcolm. "Daresay

I'm behaving scaly. But, if the wedding is still set for to-morrow, there's no time for me to beat around the bush. If your plan is to drag my sister to the altar unwilling, I'm here to tell you that you won't succeed. And I don't give a fig who your father may be."

Derek rose another notch in Malcolm's estimation. He stepped forward and said in a mild tone, "I see no reason why you should. Would you care to sit down, Mr. Whit-taker? My cook has sent up some excellent biscuits."

These were words calculated to win the heart of any vigorous young man. Derek still looked wary, but he sat. "Thank you," he said stiffly. "I don't mean to fly up into the boughs over nothing—"

Malcolm handed him the plate of biscuits. "I would hardly call your sister's happiness 'nothing.' You have every right to feel concern on her behalf."

Derek took a biscuit, hesitated for a fraction of an in-stant, and took two more. "Good of you, my lord," he said gruffly, "not to take offense."

To Malcolm's intense, if silent, gratification, Natalie sat beside him on the high-backed sofa and leaned slightly against his knee. "You will like Lord Malcolm," she told Derek. Her voice was soft but filled with con-viction. "I am giving you a far better brother than Hector has ever been."

Her brother's eyes lit with quick good humor. "Oh, marrying for my sake, are you? What a selfless thing you are."

Malcolm had a sudden flash of inspiration. "Your sis-ter has asked Mrs. Bigalow to stand up with her tomor-row," he said. "I would be greatly honored if you would act as my best man. It's a private ceremony, no guests, but two witnesses are required."

Natalie's hand crept into his and gave it a grateful squeeze.

Derek's eyebrows flew up. "Nurse is standing up with you?" he exclaimed. "Well, that's something. She would never do so, did she disapprove of this union." He looked from one to the other, apparently digesting this information. A slow smile gradually lit his features. "I'm inclined to rely on her judgment," he remarked. "She loves Natalie nearly as well as I do. If Nurse approves of you, I must be making a cake of myself."

He took a deep breath and expelled it. Then he rose and bowed. "Thank you, sir," he said formally. "I would be honored to stand up with you tomorrow."

Chapter Eighteen

Natalie's wedding day dawned in the muted gray of mist. The morning was shrouded in a drifting softness, as if London itself had donned a wedding veil. She scarcely knew whether she had entered a dream so vivid that it felt real, or a reality so fantastical that it felt dreamlike. She rose and dressed like a sleepwalker.

Nurse and one of the Chase family maids helped her, tucking and lacing and smoothing her into her wedding dress. The two women worked with suppressed excitement, exclaiming at Natalie's beauty, which only added to her sense that none of this was happening. She knew she had never been a beauty. A box of hothouse flowers arrived, sent from the hotel where Malcolm had spent the night. When she opened the box, a heavenly fragrance of orange blossoms filled the room. The flowers were too lovely to be real. It was all too lovely to be real. Natalie held the bouquet reverently to her face, drinking in the perfume. And then she caught sight of herself in the pier glass.

A stranger stood there, a slim, dark-haired stranger with enormous, very serious eyes. She was gracefully attired in the most elegant frock imaginable. Her hair was perfect. Her dress was perfect. A veil floated about her like mist from a waterfall. Her expression was dazed but luminous. Sweet. Pensive. And she was holding Natalie's bridal bouquet.

But there was no time to adjust to the sight of herself as the piece of perfection in the mirror. It was time. It was past time. They must go.

Nurse, also decked in clothes that made her look like a stranger, bustled her down the stairs and into the waiting carriage. Natalie caught only a glimpse of it: an alien carriage, waiting for her in an alien street. Too rich, too gorgeous. There was a crest on the door panel. The horses were perfectly matched, like horses in a dream. The driver and footman were wearing the livery of a duke's household. She could not seem to make sense of it. She could not take it in. Everything was happening too fast.

The carriage rocked and swayed. London passed by the windows in shades of gray, filmed with dew. Hanover Square. The carriage halted. The door opened. A footman stood at attention, holding an umbrella. Natalie stepped down and Nurse led her into St. George's.

She had never been here. It was all strange, all unfamiliar. Music played. *Malcolm must have arranged for music. How thoughtful.* She stepped through a door and paused. Derek and Malcolm stood at the end of what seemed, to her, a very long aisle. Across from them stood Nurse. They were all waiting for her. Between them stood a clergyman whom she had never seen in her life.

Malcolm looked wonderful. Derek seemed to be fighting back emotion. Strange; Natalie felt no emotion whatsoever. Malcolm caught his breath when he saw her, as if she were a miraculous vision. Natalie smiled at this agreeable foolishness. She floated down the aisle toward him, utterly serene and perfectly detached.

She handed her bouquet to Nurse. At the vicar's instruction, she placed one cold hand in Malcolm's. Words were said. Prayers were uttered. The sounds seemed to beat and quiver in the air around her, holy and incomprehensible. The candles were smoking. *Someone should snuff them,* she thought.

She looked up into Malcolm's face. His eyes burned down at her like two blue coals, tender but full of fire. He spoke to her, ancient words of love and committal. Parroting the vicar, she spoke to Malcolm, dreamily repeating the words he bade her say. Malcolm placed a ring on her finger. His hands were shaking. Hers were perfectly steady. Nurse whisked out a handkerchief and surreptitiously blew her nose. Was Nurse weeping? *Dear old Nurse.* How queer this all was.

And then it was over. She was a married woman. Malcolm kissed her. Derek kissed her. Nurse kissed her. Nurse kissed Malcolm. Nurse kissed Derek. Derek pumped Malcolm's hand ferociously, beaming with goodwill. Everyone seemed so happy. Even the vicar, or whatever he was, moved toward her, smiling. She drew back instinctively. She did not know this man. For all she knew, he wasn't even an ordained minister. Not a real one.

She could not be married—not *really* married. It had all been too easy. Too artificial. When she married, she would marry in the church she had attended all her life, surrounded by her friends and family and old, familiar things. Reverend Wentwhistle would marry her, just as he had married all her friends. He had married everyone she ever knew since time began.

A pang of hot sorrow reached her through the fog of

unreality. She had made a dreadful mistake. She ought never have agreed to the special license, to London, to this empty church and unknown vicar. In doing so, she had forfeited forever the wedding she had dreamed of all her life. Why had this not occurred to her? Loss keened through her. *Too late, too late.*

More dazed than ever, she signed her name beneath Malcolm's in an enormous ledger. Derek signed as first witness. Nurse signed as second witness. The vicar handed her her marriage lines. She stared at the sheet, uncomprehending. Derek took it from her, saying jovially that he would keep it safe for the time being, but what about breakfast? The others laughed.

As the wedding party stepped through the church door, the sun broke out. Colors sprang to life, and the wet surfaces of London blazed with glittering light. "A good omen," Nurse declared, and everyone laughed again. The air all around her seemed to fizz with high spirits. Why did she not feel merry? What was wrong with her?

Dazzled by the onslaught of brightness, Natalie raised a hand to shield her eyes. There was too much light. It had arrived too suddenly. She didn't want it; it hurt. But Malcolm was at her side, his hand at her waist. He guided her steps toward the carriage that would take them to their wedding breakfast.

It felt strange to allow him to touch her so publicly, so possessively. *But he's your husband.* A little thrill of amazement shivered through her. She tried on the notion another way: *You are Malcolm's wife.* One seemed as incredible as the other.

She floated through the breakfast. It was extremely elegant. Although they had been excluded from the service, Malcolm had invited two of his aunts and their families to the breakfast, and Natalie had invited her stepmother. Lucille seemed completely cowed by the grand company in which she found herself. She barely spoke, for which Natalie was grateful. Meanwhile, Natalie bowed and smiled and accepted everyone's compliments and best wishes as gracefully as if she received such attentions every day of her life. It was easy to remain unflustered. All the kind remarks were addressed to Lady Malcolm, not to Natalie.

Mrs. Bigalow, as a witness to the wedding, was included at the breakfast. Everyone was extremely courteous to her—even Lucille, although it did seem to stick in her craw to be forced to sit at table with her son's old nurse. Champagne was served. Toasts were made. Natalie nibbled at her food and barely touched her champagne. No one seemed to notice her odd detachment.

She wondered if she were feverish, or if someone had slipped an opiate into her morning tea. Neither explanation seemed likely. On the other hand, nothing that had happened to her this morning seemed likely.

She kept staring at her wedding ring. She was very aware of it; it felt heavy on her hand. The gold was beautiful to behold: bright and smooth and flawless. As years went on, she thought, scratches and dents would mar its liquid glimmer. It would not always gleam with the polished luster that it had today. At its heart, however, the gold was incorruptible and would never dull. The thought was oddly comforting.

The meal seemed to go on and on. The day seemed to go on and on. After the breakfast, there was still no time for quiet reflection, no time to adjust to her new situation. Her heart sank, and Malcolm was visibly annoyed, when a stream of visitors descended on them. Somehow, word of the Chase nuptials had circulated.

Natalie knew none of the *haut ton* and, after spending several hours enduring the curious stares of a parade of haughty strangers, she didn't care if she never saw any of them again. Their names and faces were a complete blur to her. The entire day was a blur to her. When there was a momentary break between callers, Malcolm seized the opportunity to tell his butler, "That's it. No more. I don't care if the Prince of Wales is descending from his carriage this instant and sees the last lot departing—Lord and Lady Malcolm are not at home."

The butler closed the door noiselessly behind him as he left. Malcolm dropped onto the sofa beside Natalie, comically feigning exhaustion. "Phew! Getting married is a tiring business."

She could not help smiling. Just to be alone with him lifted a little of the fog that had enveloped her. She peeped sideways at him. "Am I really Lady Malcolm? It sounds so peculiar."

His arm went around her, across the back of the sofa. "What, the name? That's the curse you must endure when marrying a duke's younger son. It could be worse." He winked at her. "How would you like to be Lady Fred?"

She chuckled, feeling more of her connection to reality return. "Fred is not a real name. I would be Lady Frederick, which sounds well enough. But that is not what I meant, and you know it."

She looked up at him, her expression softening. She felt much better when she looked at him. Malcolm's eyes were so kind. She had thought them bleak and remote not so long ago, but the warmth of their summer friendship had melted most of the ice that had once lurked there. He smiled more these days and appeared more relaxed. Had she done this for him? She hoped so.

He smiled at her now, understanding in his gaze. "It must be odd to be a woman, and change one's identity merely by wedding a chap."

So he did understand, at least in part. Gratitude warmed her. "Yes," she admitted. "Although it's ridiculous to feel so, because it's not as if it takes one unawares. A girl knows from childhood how things are. Nevertheless, I've been feeling utterly disoriented all day."

"Shall you miss being a Whittaker?"

"I shall miss . . ." She paused and thought for a moment, and was mildly surprised when nothing specific occurred to her. A slow smile crept across her face. "In truth, I shall miss nothing at all." What a ninny she was being. Some of the tension left her shoulders and she leaned lazily back against Malcolm's arm. "I like your name."

He kissed her, then, of course. Natalie gave herself up to the pleasure of it. *I love you, Malcolm.* She would let her kiss express what she dared not say aloud. She shifted against him, aching with tenderness. How could he not sense it? *Oh, Malcolm, love me. Love me just a little.*

She had learned, during the past week, that he would see nothing amiss in her wanton response to his touch. He seemed to accept her passion for him without reading anything extraordinary into it. At first she had been terrified that her weakness for his kisses betrayed her feelings for him. She soon discovered that it apparently did not, and since making that discovery she had allowed her emotions to relieve themselves in unrestrained outpouring whenever he kissed her.

He didn't seem to notice at all.

His obtuseness had puzzled her mightily—even hurt a

little, although she was grateful for it—until she remembered something she had heard: Men could feel desire for women they did not love. If true, that cleared matters up considerably. For one thing, it explained why Malcolm was able to kiss her so ardently. For another, it explained why he took her response to him in stride. Some women, she surmised, experienced desire separate from love, the way men did. She did not, but Malcolm did not seem to know it.

He broke the kiss and lifted his face a few inches from hers. "Lady wife," he murmured. His deep voice sent a shiver of delight through her. "Do you fear the marriage bed?"

"No," she whispered. At this moment, it did not feel like a lie.

She could feel his need for her rachet up at her denial. Something like a growl sounded in his throat, and his hands came up to cradle her face. The ferocity of his expression was belied by the gentleness of his touch. "Thank God for that," he muttered. "Have you any experience of men, Natalie?"

She almost laughed, the question was so ludicrous. She had no experience of men whatsoever. Malcolm was the first man to kiss her since . . . well, she didn't like to think how long it had been. On the other hand, she *had* been kissed before. Not once, but twice. They had been chaste, respectful kisses, but kisses they definitely had been. That should count for something.

Somehow she doubted that her experience of men had adequately prepared her for what would happen tonight.

She opened her lips to tell him so, then changed her mind. Why must he know that no man had ever touched her? Why should she tell him something that might lessen her worth in his eyes? Men wanted what other men wanted. Let him think she had been desired. Let him think that someone, perhaps a few someones, had wanted her badly enough to give her . . . experience of men. Besides, if she confessed her utter and complete virginity, he might wonder at the passion she displayed in her kisses. He might put two and two together, and arrive at four. He might realize that she loved him. That would never do.

"Experience?" she murmured, stalling for time. "A little." She purred the phrase, dropping her eyelids in a way calculated to obscure her meaning. She would not be dishonest, but at least she could be sly.

A look of rueful chagrin twisted Malcolm's mouth downward. "Don't worry," he muttered, laughing at himself a little. "I won't ask for the particulars. I think I advised you once, long ago, not to ask questions if you don't want to hear the answers."

He stood, dropping a kiss on the top of her head, and walked to the door. She watched him go, surprised by his abrupt departure—but he went only to the door, not beyond it. He turned the key in the lock and walked back to her.

Natalie felt a frisson of excitement that was not quite fear, not quite eagerness, but some odd fusion of the two. Something new was about to happen, she felt sure of it. But surely not . . . surely not anything much. They were in the drawing room, for pity's sake. It was still broad daylight.

But there was an unfamiliar light in his eyes. And then she recognized it: pleasurable anticipation. She felt her pulse begin to race. His lips curved in a half smile. He stretched out his hand to her and she instinctively placed her hand in his. He pulled her to her feet and into his arms.

They were married. The door was locked, and they would not be disturbed.

Malcolm kissed her: He had never before kissed her behind a locked door, and she felt the difference immediately. He insinuated his knee between her thighs as he kissed her, plastering her against his body. Her breasts were crushed to his chest, her pelvis against his pelvis. For the first time, she was vividly aware of his arousal; she could feel the proof of it pressing, almost grinding, against her. She gasped at the novel sensation, then dove back into his kiss, too thrilled to feel shocked.

Even the kiss itself was different. Hotter. Wetter. Her head swam. Her heart pounded. His thigh seemed so much longer than hers, and incredibly strong. She could feel his thigh muscles bunch and strain against her body. His very masculinity took her breath away.

The locked door emboldened her. She writhed against him, eager for more. *Teach me. Show me.* He muttered some exclamation under his breath, then took her mouth again. Delirious with feeling, she clung to him. *Oh, Malcolm.*

His fingers, slipping on the silk of her dress, ran greedily over her. He explored her as a blind man would, seeking to know her every curve and plane. She gave herself completely to the heady feelings his touch evoked. It was more exciting than anything she had ever dreamed of, being touched in this way, by this man. She felt cherished and desired. Desirable. Desiring.

She slid her hands inside his jacket and ran them along his waistcoat, wishing she could unbutton it. She could feel the heat of him through the thin linen of his shirt, but the waistcoat was in her way. She pulled out of the kiss and burrowed her face into his cravat, gasping for air, gulping in the warm, spicy scent of him.

His lips were in her hair. "Natalie," he said hoarsely, then gave a choked-sounding laugh. "How many hours till bedtime?"

Bedtime. For a moment, the sense of unreality gripped her again. Was it the thought of sharing a bed with Malcolm that made her suddenly feel dizzy? Or was this the effect of too many kisses and not enough air? She leaned back against the circle of his arms, still trying to catch her breath. "I . . . don't know."

"Too many." His eyes held a wicked gleam. "I think it's only natural to feel worn down after a day filled with so much excitement. What say you, wife? Shall we go to bed directly after dinner?"

She knew she was blushing. She dropped her gaze to the topmost button of his waistcoat. "If you like," she said, suddenly feeling absurdly shy.

"If I *like*?" Soundless laughter shook him. "What a complaisant wife I have."

She shot him a mischievous look. "I did promise to obey," she reminded him demurely. "Although I don't know what possessed me, to make such a rash promise. You must have caught me in a moment of weakness."

"As long as I caught you, I don't care how." He let out his breath in a sigh. "I'm a lucky man," he said, apparently bemused. "And I never was a lucky man, until I met you." He lifted one hand to her hair, curling a stray tendril around his finger. She smiled at the gesture. It tickled her that he was so fascinated by the curls that had always been such a trial to her.

His eyes searched hers, suddenly serious. "Why did you wait for me, Natalie? Why didn't you marry long ago?"

Oh, she knew the answer to that one: *I never loved till now.* She wished she could say it aloud. Failing that,

what could she say? Malcolm seemed to think her spin-
sterhood was inexplicable, but it had been easy to stay
single, living the narrow life she had led. There had been
few eligible men in the neighborhood. She had had no
opportunity to look elsewhere. Her stepmother had never
expended the necessary energy—or funds—to see that
she was introduced to a broader circle. Lucille had never
brought her to London for a Season. Natalie had never
gone away to school, so she had no friends who might
invite her. In truth, the miracle was not that she had
stayed single for so long. The miracle was that she had
married.

He was still waiting for her answer. She tilted her chin
as if considering, then shook her head. "I cannot account
for it," she said lightly, teasing him. "And I cannot account for your sudden good fortune." Emboldened by
their new intimacy, she reached to push a lock of Malcolm's dark, straight hair off his forehead, then moved
her face very close to his. "Unless . . ." She touched her
mouth to his.

"Unless what?" he murmured, the words moving his
lips deliciously against hers.

She smiled against his mouth. "You finally wished on
the right star," she breathed, and kissed him.

Chapter Nineteen

He shouldn't have left her alone. He shouldn't have let so much time go by. This afternoon, in Malcolm's arms, she had forgotten her maidenly fears. Left to her own devices in his unfamiliar bedchamber, her anxiety had returned—with a vengeance.

Natalie stared at herself in the full-length pier glass. Her new night rail drifted down her body in a cascade of nearly transparent silk. She had never worn tiffany in her life. It felt luscious against her skin, but it made her look . . . a little too inviting.

Actually, it made her look a great deal too inviting.

She swallowed hard. Malcolm didn't need an invitation tonight, she was certain. Perhaps she should don her old bed gown and save this one for a night when she felt more . . . confident?

She devoutly hoped that day would come. At the moment she could not imagine ever feeling comfortable enough to display herself in this night rail. Not to anyone, let alone to Malcolm, whose opinion of her was the most important thing on earth.

Her pulse fluttering with something like panic, she scurried to the enormous wardrobe at the side of the room and threw open its heavy doors. The wardrobe was filled with masculine attire. *Ooh.* She paused, fascinated. The wardrobe exhaled an alluring aroma of leather and polish and Malcolm.

But her own clothing was nowhere to be found. Why? Surely someone would have moved her things from the guest bedchamber. She turned, frowning, and surveyed the room. Everything in sight appeared to be Malcolm's. She remembered seeing an armoire of some sort in the small adjoining room where she had bathed. Perhaps her things were there.

She closed the wardrobe doors behind her and snatched up a lamp, heading for the bath room. The cupboard contained only towels and soap and sponges, but there was another door on the other side of the room. Could it be . . . ? She walked through it and, sure enough, found herself in another bedchamber. Her combs and brushes were neatly laid out on its dressing table—and the wardrobe in this room held all her clothing.

Well, for heaven's sake! Why would a newly married couple require two bedchambers? She chuckled at the self-conscious prudery of the notion. Was it an elaborate ruse for the staff's benefit? How silly. No one would be taken in by it. She could just imagine Malcolm's reaction if she slept here tonight.

Then a sobering thought occurred to her. Perhaps she *was* expected to sleep alone. What did she know of marriage? And besides, this was no love match. Perhaps her marital duty consisted of meeting her husband in his room so he could take his pleasure, then politely withdrawing to her own quarters. It sounded cold, not to mention lonely, but that might very well be what he expected. The staff may have set up the rooms this way at Malcolm's bidding.

Perhaps this was the way the rooms had been set up when Catherine was his wife. Now, that was a thought to throw cold water on the most ardent of brides.

Depressed, Natalie set down the lamp and dug through the neatly packed drawers until she found her old, muslin bed gown, and neatly folded freshly laundered. She tossed it onto the bed and carefully lifted the fragile tiffany over her head.

"What are you doing?" said Malcolm's voice behind her.

Natalie gasped and dropped the skirt of her night rail. It slithered back down over her legs.

"Sorry," said Malcolm. Laughter lurked in his deep voice.

Natalie whirled to face him. "You nearly frightened the life out of me." Her cheeks flamed with embarrassment.

Malcolm stood in the door she had left open behind her, leaning against the frame. He had obviously come to her fresh from bathing. His hair was still damp. She had never seen a man *en déshabille* before, and she found the sight both alluring and scary. He looked dangerous, in her opinion. More like a jungle creature than a gentleman. A gentleman should be well covered, neck to toe. Malcolm had dispensed with jacket and boots and cravat and stockings and . . . well, nearly everything. He wore a clean linen shirt but, without the neckcloth, it fell open to his waist. And although he had tucked it carelessly into the top of his breeches, with no waistcoat to bind it the shirt hung loose, exposing almost his entire chest.

Goodness. She had never guessed that Malcolm was so well muscled. And why did she find that so attractive?

The sight of all that latent power should frighten her all the more. It did, in fact, but on some primitive level it called to her as well.

She stared at him, speechless with confusion. She had braced herself for the well-known fact that a man was built differently, and would look different from a woman. She simply hadn't bargained on all the little, *extra* ways in which that turned out to be true. And she hadn't realized how powerfully all those subtle, unexpected differences would affect her.

Malcolm's eyes traveled to the chaste, muslin bed gown lying on the coverlet. His eyebrows climbed. He glanced back at Natalie, standing foolishly between the open wardrobe and the edge of the bed, wearing a night rail made of gossamer and starlight. He smiled. "Don't tell me you were changing your night rail."

She felt a cowardly impulse to cross her arms protectively across her breasts. She quelled it. "Very well," she snapped, head held high. "I won't tell you."

His eyes traveled down her. She watched as his expression changed. Her pulse jumped and skittered in response to the look on his face. "I like the one you have on," he said. His voice sounded oddly hoarse.

Suddenly Natalie realized that she had set the lamp on the low table beside the bed. The table was behind her now. Backlit, the tiffany gown must be transparent as water. She stepped quickly back, flattening herself against the wall, and picked up the lamp. The light wavered in her shaking hand, and the shadows danced crazily. "It's new," she said lamely, and swallowed. "Part—part of my trousseau."

He didn't speak. He did not seem to have heard her. His expression was so strange! He walked toward her, tugging the shirt out of his waistband so that when he reached her it hung off his shoulders, exposing acres of warm, bare skin. Natalie's eyes dilated at the sight.

Never taking his eyes from hers, he took the lamp from her and placed it back on the table. Then, without a word, he pulled her roughly against him and began kissing her.

Merciful heavens. The shock of skin against skin made her gasp. She could feel the heat of him, the texture of him. She could smell his soap. *Sandalwood,* she thought, distracted.

He smelled good. He felt good. But it was all happening too fast. Malcolm's body against hers, skin on skin, felt like water closing over her head when she had not yet learned to swim. She fought against the tide of unfamiliar sensations—instinctively panicking, almost as if she were drowning.

And the lamp was still lit. He would *see* her. Oh, this was terrible! What if he didn't like what he saw? She had no notion what Malcolm found desirable and what he found undesirable. She was almost certain to look different from whatever it was he had pictured. Embarrassed, she pulled him closer against herself. Anything was better than being stared at.

Now that she was holding him so tightly, she became aware of a deep tremor coursing through Malcolm's body. It was as if he trembled with the effort of holding himself in check. He was kissing her more deeply than he ever had, and yet she sensed a powerful battle going on within him as he fought to keep from ravishing her on the spot. *This is lust,* she thought, fascinated and terrified. She had never been an object of lust before.

And then she realized, with deep dismay, that as Malcolm's appetite for her increased, her own passion diminished. She wanted time. She wanted to sort out her emotions. She needed to think this through, compose herself. She was not yet accustomed to this strange, new intimacy. It was so odd, all this sudden touching and see-ing of each other. She felt vulnerable. Exposed.

She knew, intellectually, that her shyness of him was misplaced. It was false modesty, it was prudery, to seek to hide from one's husband. But, she discovered, one could not instantly shuck off many years of careful adherence to propriety. Her instinct for self-preservation was sounding an alarm that would not be silenced, revolting against this . . . this mauling.

It was her own fault, she thought despairingly, strug-gling to hide her fear and embarrassment. She had delib-erately led Malcolm to believe that she had had some experience with men. How had he interpreted that? she wondered now. He must expect, surely, that she was a virgin. But perhaps courting couples did this sort of thing . . . whatever one called it . . . and he had wrongly assumed that the male form was not unknown to her.

He lifted his face from hers. His breathing came in ragged gasps. He ran his hands greedily through her hair, pulling out all the pins. She heard them strike the floor in a shower of little pinging sounds. "Natalie," he rasped, staring drunkenly at her tumbling hair. "Come to bed."

Fear sent her heart into her throat, where it pounded and fluttered like a trapped bird. *It's wrong to fear your husband,* she reminded herself desperately, and managed a weak smile. She did not trust herself to answer, but he seemed oblivious to her lack of response. He reached be-hind him with one hand and threw back the bedclothes in a single impatient gesture

Here? He meant to do it *here*? She wasn't sure why that mattered, except that it was one more detail for which she was mentally unprepared. She pointed a shaking hand to indicate the still-burning lamp. "The light . . ."

"I like the light." And with that, he tumbled her abruptly onto the sheets.

The bed was soft and smothering. The linens were crisp and scented with rosewater. Natalie longed to dive under the covers. Instead, she forced herself to lie on her back, flushed with humiliation and trying to hide her distress. She wanted desperately to please him. She *must* please him. He would never love her if she didn't please him. But how? What should she do? She had no idea. She wasn't even sure how the male and female parts joined, although she knew that that must soon occur. And, of course, she knew that it would hurt. Every girl was told that much.

Perhaps that part wasn't true, she thought hopefully. It sounded just the sort of thing a girl would be told, to help keep her virtuous.

Malcolm loomed over her. Off came his shirt in one quick move. He tossed it on the floor. His eyes never left her. He looked like a starving man presented with a banquet. She saw him quaking with need. For half a moment her rioting thoughts quieted and her heart swelled with wonder. *Malcolm.* She had never been taught to think of masculinity as beautiful; why was that? His body was magnificent, in the way of some powerful animal. A lion, perhaps, or a racehorse.

But then he was on her, covering her, and her view of him vanished. Her mind raced once more with fright. What must she do? Anything? She struggled to cooperate, to help him do whatever it was he was doing. It was all so confusing. Overwhelming. Eventually her mind completely detached and seemed to float above the bed, looking down in puzzlement.

She did not enjoy the next few minutes. She merely endured them.

The reality of deflowerment was not, she discovered, as painful as the horror stories would have one believe. But it was bad enough. The entire experience was awkward and uncomfortable. What made it worse was the vague sense that this bizarre act should be *pleasurable*. One felt it, somehow—a dim instinct that protested, resentfully, that what she was experiencing was abnormal. That things might have been different. Should have been different.

Afterward, she slipped hastily back into her night rail and pulled up the covers with trembling hands. Malcolm sat, unmoving, on the opposite edge of the bed. His back was to her, his elbows on his knees, his face buried in his hands. The long line of his back was interesting, she thought, still with that strange detachment. She could see each vertebra and trace the powerful outline of his muscles. His body was so different from hers. She could look at him for hours.

She watched as his breath, quieter now, rose and fell in a deep sigh. "That was not well done," he said at last. His voice was dark with disgust.

Natalie's heart sank. She had been a bride for less than a day, and she had already disappointed her husband.

"I'm sorry," she whispered.

His head snapped up. "*You're* sorry?" He sounded astonished. He faced her then. To her dismay, his eyes were filled with self-loathing. It was an expression she hoped she had driven from him forever: "Natalie, for God's sake, you have nothing to apologize for. It is I who bungled it."

She blinked at him in confusion. "What do you mean? Did we—did we not do it right?"

"Not quite, sweetheart." He reached over to her and ran one finger across her cheek. "Not by a long chalk."

Was that *tenderness* she saw in his expression? And he had called her "sweetheart." She held her breath, praying for a miracle.

"Did I hurt you?" he asked, his voice strained.

She hated to tell him that he had, but the moment demanded honesty. She gave him a tiny nod. "A little," she owned.

His disgusted expression returned. "Then I'm a villain." He dropped his hand from her face. "I cannot adequately apologize to you, my dear. I can only try to make it up to you in future."

She had no idea what he meant. She sat up, frowning. "Malcolm, I have always heard that it would hurt. Pray do not blame yourself. There was nothing you could do."

Soundless laughter shook him. "Actually, my innocent, there were several things I could have done. And someday very soon, you will find out what they are." His smile was rueful, but the gleam in his eye hinted at some pleasant secret he meant to share. "There wasn't time tonight because I was"—his smile became almost a grin—"swept away by your charms."

That rather pleased her. She smiled a little. "In other words, I should have worn my muslin bed gown after all."

He stretched out on his side, lying next to her. "It might have helped," he admitted. "But probably not much."

He seemed so comfortable in his own skin, not bothered at all by the lamplight shining on his bare body. She envied him that. She wondered if she would someday expose herself to his eyes with the same lack of concern. Perhaps, she decided. But not tonight. She slid back down under the covers, lying beside his long form. He placed an arm around her and drew her near.

"Shall we sleep here tonight?" he murmured, his mouth close to her ear. "The fire's been made up in the other room. Are you cold?"

Natalie felt as if a weight had been lifted from her mind. They *would* sleep together. She wasn't sure why that made her so happy, except that she loved being with him. She turned her face to smile at him. It was delightful to lie beside him like this, his head so close to hers. "I don't think I need the fire," she told him softly.

"Nor do I." He kissed her again, a slow and languid kiss. The kiss was intimate and tender rather than urgent. She relaxed, loving it. She loved being held like this, feeling him all along the length of her, and being kissed as if he had all night in which to do it.

Perversely, this unheated, unhurried kiss sent fire rushing through her veins in a way his overwhelming passion earlier had not. She became newly aware of body parts she had never noticed before . . . possibly because Malcolm had just introduced them to her. Even in their current battered state, they seemed to awaken and hum with life. It was most peculiar, but not unpleasant.

She felt oddly disappointed when Malcolm promptly fell sleep.

She put out the light and lay beside him for a while, wide awake, trying to accustom herself to sharing a bed with another person. And not just any person: Malcolm. It wasn't easy, despite the fact that it was something she had longed for. He was large and male and totally nude. Every time she began to drift off to sleep, her awareness of him would jolt her awake again, disoriented and flustered.

And then, finally, just as she had fallen asleep—or as nearly asleep as made no odds—something else jarred her awake. Out of nowhere, an idea hit her. An almost-forgotten puzzle her mind had been working on fell into place. Natalie's eyes flew open. She almost gasped aloud.

Of course! Of course.

She knew what was wrong with Sarah.

Chapter Twenty

Malcolm rolled lazily over and reached for his wife. The bed was empty. Not only that; the sheets were cold. The place beside him must have been empty for a while.

He opened his eyes and blinked groggily at the silent room. Bright sunshine slanted through a narrow opening between the carelessly closed draperies. Morning had definitely arrived.

He yawned, stretched, and turned onto his back, hands clasped behind his head. He tried not to think about last night's shameful failure, but the memory would not be banished. Remorse and embarrassment swept through him, two damnably uncomfortable emotions. Bloody hell. He'd behaved like a perfect moonling. Worse: He'd behaved like a lout. He'd *hurt* her. A man of his age and experience ought to have known better.

Never mind. When Natalie came back to bed, he would show her all the tender attention he had failed to give her last night.

He had meant to woo her slowly. He had intended to see to her pleasure before taking his own. If she hadn't looked so damnably alluring in that wisp of a night rail . . . but, no. No excuses. The fault was his, and his alone.

Besides, he had better not remember just now the way she had looked in that night rail. He might lose control yet again.

Where the devil was Natalie?

He gradually realized that she was not, in fact, coming back to bed. He rose and dressed, trying not to feel uneasy. Doubtless there was nothing stealthy about her departure. She had simply awakened early and thought it would be inconsiderate to disturb him. She was probably waiting for him downstairs.

But she was not. The servants informed him that she had departed early, with Sarah. Even Mrs. Bigalow did not know where they had gone.

There was something deuced unsettling about this. Malcolm sat down to a morose and solitary breakfast. Had his clumsy lovemaking last night frightened her away? He winced as the memories intruded again. He had taken her the way a stallion takes a mare. His desire for her had overwhelmed him with its unexpected intensity. He had run mad when he saw her in that thing . . . and when he held her, his nostrils had filled with the scent of her, honey and jasmine and everything he had ever wanted . . . and then when her hair came down . . . thunder and turf! That blasted, maddening hair of hers. Tumbling down her shoulders and into his hands, it had simply robbed him of all rational thought. Even in the clear light of day, remembering that moment, Malcolm had to shake his head to clear it.

But Natalie was no shrinking violet. She had seemed forgiving enough afterward. Indeed, he thought with sour humor, her blessed innocence had protected her from knowing just how badly she had been used. Not that that let him off the hook. He would *not,* he vowed, let his lust run away with him again. She deserved better. She deserved much better.

And he had hoped to make her love him! What an imbecilic way to begin. At that thought he set down his fork, his appetite completely vanished. Damn, damn, damn.

He pushed away from the breakfast table and moodily prowled the house. He was haunted by thoughts of Catherine as well as Natalie. Her ghost dogged his steps, mocking him. Was he doomed to botch his new marriage, as divine punishment for having driven Catherine to her death? He did not deserve happiness, that was certain. *But Natalie did.* Perhaps heaven would be merciful and let him have this last chance at happiness—if he promised to bring Natalie happiness as part of the bargain.

He wouldn't succeed in that endeavor unless he made her love him. And it became increasingly clear, as the morning progressed, that it would be impossible to court her properly in London.

Shortly after breakfast, the knocker began to sound. Malcolm gave orders to refuse admittance to every caller, but it soon was glaringly obvious that he and Natalie would have no peace if they stayed in the metropolis. And on top of the relentless stream of visitors and other diversions, Natalie apparently found the delights of the city overly tempting. Where was she? She had not been able to wait a single day to spend time with her new husband, so eager had she been to gallivant about the town.

He could never compete with the myriad pleasures London had to offer, that was plain. If they stayed, their lives would become a round of social events. A whirl of shopping and dining and theater and parties. They would have little time alone and would be constantly interrupted. She would be distracted. Taken from him. Even when she was with him, her mind would be elsewhere. How could he woo her here?

He gave curt orders to the staff: pack up his family's things and ready the traveling coach. When Lady Malcolm and Miss Chase returned from wherever they had gone, he was taking them home to Larkspur.

Since they had originally planned to stay for several weeks, the housekeeper seemed startled by this change of plans—but after a searching look at Malcolm's face, she hastened to obey. Left to stew in his own uncomfortable thoughts, Lord Malcolm was working himself into a wretched temper.

Time crawled. Where the devil could they be? Noon passed, then one o'clock, then two o'clock. His impatience turned to a formless dread. Natalie knew nothing about London. If anything unspeakable occurred, she would be as helpless as Sarah.

Sarah.

She had taken Sarah with her. Why? He could think of no reason why Natalie would steal Sarah away from him, but it was hard to reason with the anxiety churning in his stomach.

He was not a man who prayed often—he saw no reason why God would hear the prayers of such as Malcolm Chase—but he found himself sending up a silent plea for the safe return of his wife and child, directed at any benevolent spirit who might be listening. If harm befell them, he thought grimly, heads would roll. Beginning with the idiots on his father's staff who let Natalie and Sarah leave the house without his protection.

He was in the library, pacing like a caged tiger, when

he heard the unmistakable sounds of a vehicle pulling to a stop outside the house. He crossed swiftly to the window, filled with hope and fear. It was his father's town coach. Through the glass, he saw a footman letting down the steps and opening the door. Natalie, her face serene, stepped out. Sarah followed. As he watched, Natalie bent and whispered something teasing to the little girl, who laughed and leaned adoringly against her.

Malcolm sagged with relief—briefly. His relief swiftly transformed into an icy rage. He had spent the day worried sick, and all the while Natalie and Sarah had been perfectly safe! He watched his bride and his little girl, quite cozy together, walk unconcernedly into the house. They were obviously unharmed and appeared to have given no thought to Malcolm. Not a hint of guilt in either Natalie's demeanor or Sarah's! No shred of eagerness to find him and apologize! They seemed, in fact, to have had a pleasant time together on whatever unknown errand—or set of errands—they had run.

Sarah could be pardoned, for she was too young to know better. Natalie, however, must have known the anxiety she would cause by disappearing for the better part of the day. How could she appear so tranquil? He had a few things to say to Natalie Chase, he thought grimly.

He stalked into the hall, where Natalie was untying her stepdaughter's bonnet. She looked up from this task when she heard his footsteps, and her face lit with pleasure at the sight of him. She must have recognized the anger in his face, however, for her glad smile immediately faded. She straightened, her expression wary, and studied him. Rather than speak to him, she leaned down to Sarah. "Sarah, here is your papa," she said. Her voice was light and pleasant, but Malcolm was not deceived.

Sarah turned, beaming with unalloyed delight, and bounded over to him. "Papa! What did you do today? You should have come with us."

Malcolm caught his wriggling daughter. "Indeed?" There was a bite in his voice that Sarah would not hear, but Natalie would. "And where have you been? Shopping?"

"A little. At the end." She turned and waved to indicate the open door behind her, where a footman was carrying in a box. "Miss Whittaker bought me a hat. I wanted the puppy, but she thought you might not like it."

"Very astute of her," said Malcolm dryly. It was also astute of her to push Sarah into his arms when she saw he was angry. It forced him to moderate his anger, in order to hide it from the child.

"Does 'astute' mean she was right?" Sarah looked crestfallen. "She thought I should have an imaginary puppy instead, to keep Clara company. But I would rather have a real one. Miss Whittaker says—" She halted in midsentence, looking shy. "Papa," she whispered, playing with a button on his coat, "Miss Whittaker says that is not her name anymore, now that she is married."

"That's right, poppet. She is Lady Malcolm Chase, just as your mother was when she was alive."

Sarah nodded. "I heard people call her that today." Her whisper was barely audible. "She says I may call her Mama now, if you do not object." She lifted pleading eyes to his. "May I?"

Malcolm felt his heart lurch. His anger faded, momentarily forgotten. Should he object?

Poor, jealous Catherine. It would grieve her to know that Sarah wanted to call his new wife Mama. But Catherine was not here to feel the pangs of jealousy. He had a living wife and child whose needs and desires must take precedence over Catherine's. And perhaps death brought understanding with it, in which case Catherine would not object at all.

He squatted down to Sarah's height, bringing their faces level so they could look into each other's eyes as equals. "How do you feel about that?" he asked her solemnly. "Do you want to call her Mama?"

Sarah's eyes were changeable as the sea. At the moment they were green and solemn. "I would like to have a mama again," she said, with great seriousness. "And I do love Miss Whittaker."

So do I. He almost said it aloud, but caught himself. Natalie was standing by, quietly observing their exchange. He glanced up at her. She was motionless above them, smiling a little. Her eyes were moist. She nodded to indicate that Sarah was right, and that she had no objection. Malcolm returned his gaze to Sarah. He brushed a few strands of hair off her forehead, loving the babyfine texture. His own precious daughter. And Catherine's.

And now, Natalie's.

"Then I think you should call her Mama," he said.

Sarah beamed. She broke away from him and danced back to Natalie, jumping and frisking like a puppy. "Mama, Mama, Mama!" she cried, trying the word out.

Natalie caught her and swung her around, laughing. "Yes, very well, that's enough! Pray be careful of that arm of yours. Shall we go and show Nurse your new hat?"

Malcolm straightened. "You'll find that Mrs. Bigalow is busy," he said casually. "Packing."

Natalie's eyes widened with surprise. "Indeed? Why?"

"We are returning to Larkspur tonight." His tone was

crisp. "Pray make yourself ready. We leave within the hour."

He turned on his heel and left before Natalie could question him or protest. In his experience, wives questioned and protested even the smallest assertion of husbandly authority. And he was rather guiltily aware that this was not small. But it was necessary, he reminded himself. Necessary. He just didn't dare explain his reasons to Natalie. He couldn't say to her, "I want your undivided attention, so I can make you love me." Such selfishness on his part would drive her further away from him.

Soon he was handing her into the berline. She had changed into a traveling costume of striped rose and cream. It was obviously one of the modiste's creations. It fit her like a glove, flattered her every curve, and made her look as cool and delicious as a peppermint bonbon. He wished there were time to admire her in it. Best, however, to maintain his distance. There would be fewer questions to answer that way.

She paused on the step, her hand in his. Her brown eyes lifted to his face. Her expression was grave. "Are you testing me?" she asked, her voice low enough that no one could overhear.

He was taken aback. He hadn't anticipated such directness. "I don't know what you mean."

"I think you do." She dropped her eyes. "I think you are punishing me for taking Sarah away this morning. I think you have changed our plans without consulting me, waiting to see if I will defy you or argue with you." She lifted her eyes again. They were clear and luminous. "I shall do neither, husband. If you are keeping tally in your head, pray chalk this one up. And remember it."

She climbed into the coach then, leaving him without a word to say.

Natalie yielded to Sarah's eager entreaty and sat beside her, leaving Malcolm to sit facing them. Mrs. Bigalow was traveling in the second coach with Larkspur's cook and most of their luggage. He watched in silence as Natalie entertained Sarah during their slow, lurching progress through London. She was really remarkable; endlessly patient when Sarah peppered her with questions, endlessly inventive when Sarah grew restless or bored. He still did not know where they had gone that morning, and he still did not ask. But his anger had cooled long ago, leaving room for his heart to swell with appreciation now.

Natalie was a wonder. He had made the right choice. Whether she loved him or no, he had definitely made the right choice.

Soon they were rolling through the countryside, and their progress became smoother. He lay back against the squabs, pretending to doze while still watching them through half-closed eyes. They made a lovely picture, his wife and his little girl. They looked nothing alike, of course, and yet they seemed to belong together. Sarah favored Catherine, with her straight, pale brown hair, fine bones and petite frame. Natalie was tall and lush, with a graceful strength that appealed strongly to a man grown weary of Catherine's nervous fragility. Dark curls. Warm, brown eyes. Curves (he now knew) designed by their Maker to drive Malcolm mad. No, she looked nothing like Sarah. But the two had a special bond of intuitive understanding that made them run together like two drops of water. It was easy to imagine that Natalie was indeed Sarah's mama. He supposed that, eventually, most people would forget that he had ever had a first wife.

He wished he could forget it, as well.

The traitorous thought shot guilt through him. He sat up and stared grimly out the window at the passing scenery. He had no right to resent poor Catherine's memory. He had married her, failed to love her, and driven her to her death. Her blood was on his head; he felt the burden of it every day. And still, *still*, he was angry with her! Angry at her manipulative tricks and all the little underhanded games she used to play. Angry at the way she had blamed him for her unhappiness, when in truth he suspected that Catherine had simply been an unhappy person, and that he had had nothing to do with it. And he was angry at her suicide, which some dark corner of his soul believed had been the ultimate manipulation, expressly intended to visit lasting misery upon him.

Was that really possible? The question haunted him to this day. Would anyone, even a madwoman, kill herself merely to punish her husband? Take her own life, in order to ruin his? It sounded incredible, but he could not help wondering if it were true. Because if it were true, it had worked. It had worked like a charm. He shifted restlessly on his seat, tortured with shame . . . and still angry. What a shallow, self-centered rotter he must be, to harbor such bitter resentment toward his poor, dead wife.

He mustn't think about it any more. He had new concerns, new responsibilities. He shifted his gaze back to Natalie, who was playing some sort of silly finger game with Sarah. The tightness eased in his chest, and he breathed easier. He must concentrate not on the dead wife but on the living child, to whom he had dedicated his life. Catherine's memory was best served by protecting and loving Sarah. And Natalie, his precious Natalie, had miraculously turned out to be the best gift he could give his motherless daughter. Catherine's ghost would have to be appeased by that, he thought wryly. For he wasn't giving Natalie up, at any price.

As if hearing his thoughts, Natalie looked at him. He felt the shock of her gaze shoot pleasure along his nerves. Her features softened into the first smile she had offered him since their earlier meeting in the hall, and he smiled back. Awareness tingled in the short space of air between them.

Sarah, oblivious, placed the index finger of one hand carefully against the thumb of the other. "Pop, pop, peep," she sang under her breath. "Peep, peep, pop."

Malcolm felt his smile widen. He jerked his chin to indicate Sarah. "What a fascinating game."

Amusement crinkled the corners of Natalie's eyes. "Oh, yes. Destined to take the drawing rooms of the *ton* by storm."

"What do you call it?"

"I believe it is known as Peep Pop."

His shoulders shook. Sarah glanced up at Natalie. "Your turn," she said. Her tone was congratulatory.

"Ah," said Natalie gravely. "Where did I leave off?"

They continued their strange game as the light faded outside the swaying coach. Malcolm never did decipher the rules of Peep Pop, and he had a strong notion that Natalie did not understand them, either. She seemed content to follow Sarah's lead, letting the little girl correct her when necessary. Eventually Sarah tired of the game and abruptly called a halt, announcing that the match had ended in a tie. With a prodigious yawn, she nestled beneath her new mama's arm and curled up on the seat, preparing to nap. Natalie took off Sarah's bonnet and smoothed her hair, then leaned back to make room for her. They snuggled comfortably together.

As Sarah's eyes drifted closed, Natalie's eyes lifted to meet Malcolm's steady gaze. The muted light of evening washed her peppermint-striped costume with a lavender glow. She tilted her head quizzically, bestowing a soft smile on her husband. "You are staring at me," she observed.

"I like to look at you."

Surprise widened her eyes. Then she bit her lip, looking both pleased and embarrassed. "I am glad," she said at last.

He shifted his body against the squabs, easing into a more comfortable position. Sarah seemed to be falling asleep already. The carriage was dim and silent save for the rumble of the wheels and the creaking of the springs. The intimacy of the setting seemed to be binding them together . . . and yet there were unspoken issues between them. Some of them he could not voice. Some, he decided, he would.

"You don't really think I changed our plans in a fit of pique, do you?" He kept his voice low, and Sarah did not stir.

Natalie arched a brow at him. "Didn't you?"

His mouth pulled downward. "You've been living with Hector too long. No, Natalie, I did not."

She seemed to weigh his words carefully, mulling them over before she spoke. "But I saw that you were angry with me. When I returned from—from shopping."

"I was angry," he said. "I woke up and you were gone. You were away more than half the day. I was sick with worry. Why did you not leave me word to tell me where you were going?"

Her eyes slid away from his. She stared out the window at the darkening landscape. "I am sorry. It has been many years since anyone worried about me. In future, I shall try always to inform you of my whereabouts."

"And Sarah's," he added dryly.

She looked back at him, shamefaced. "Yes, that was not well done of me."

"I am not an unreasonable man."

"Of course not." She seemed anxious to agree with him. "I have never thought you unreasonable."

"And yet," he said softly, "you think me capable of acting spitefully. Dragging you away from London merely to punish you, or to assert my authority."

She took a deep breath. Her eyes narrowed in puzzlement—or challenge. "Perhaps you are right, and I have lived with Hector too long. But I think anyone might have surmised that you were acting out of temper. Why did you change your mind so abruptly? Why bring us away from London after only two days? I am at a loss to understand it."

How much of the truth should he tell her? Malcolm felt his muscles tense in automatic warning, as if every fiber and sinew knew that he was entering dangerous territory. A misstep would be costly. He had never wooed a woman before—not in any true sense of the word. Not when it mattered. But he had to begin somewhere.

He held her gaze with his, willing her to listen. "While you were out, and I didn't know where you were," he said slowly, "I realized something important."

Natalie's eyes widened slightly. She looked as if she were holding her breath. "And what did you realize?"

"That what I wanted most in the world was to spend time with you. And that London could wait."

She breathed again, visibly relaxing. She even

laughed a little. "You might have spent time with me in London."

He shook his head, smiling slightly. "Not the kind of time I want to spend with you. What! Fritter the hours away dragging ourselves from shop to shop, or chitchatting with people we barely know? No, thank you! I had to go to London to get the special license. Very well; the mission has been accomplished. I married you, and I damn well want you home."

"Malcolm!" Natalie gave a strangled-sounding laugh and glanced at Sarah. The child was fast asleep. She looked sternly at him, then, but her eyes were twinkling. "I was right in the first place. You are behaving very badly, sir. For what is this, if not autocratic? 'Want me home' indeed! Tsk."

He leaned forward, his forearms on his knees. "I'll make it up to you," he promised. "You've never had a Season in London. Would you like one? We'll go back in April and stay until summer. My sister-in-law will trot you round to all the important biddies and make them give you the royal treatment. We'll glut ourselves on parties and balls."

Natalie pursed her lips as if thinking hard. "Hm. I don't know. It sounds exhausting."

"Oh, it is," he agreed.

"And a frightful waste of money."

"That, too. But it's great sport to cut a dash in London."

She laughed. "I would be terrified. So much to learn! I've never led that sort of life." She seemed to catch herself then, and bit her lip. "But of course we will do whatever you wish, Malcolm," she said in a more subdued tone. "I'm sure I shall have a splendid time."

What the deuce? He cocked an eyebrow, puzzled. "Natalie, you goose, I am trying to please you."

She shook her head, looking vexed with herself. "I should not have put my opinion forward. Especially when I know nothing about it! I was talking nonsense."

He straightened, frowning. Was she forcing herself to play the role of dutiful wife? It didn't suit her. Subservience did not come naturally to Natalie. Six months of deferring to him and she'd be heartily sick of it. He didn't want her to resent him. He wanted her to love him.

"So we'll do whatever I wish," he said at last.

"Yes, Malcolm."

"We go to London on my say-so. We leave London at my whim." He waved a languid hand. "We marry, for example, where I choose and when I choose. We live wherever I decide we live. We dine on beef, or on mutton with turnips. And you haven't a word to say about any of it."

She looked cautious. "Well, I may say something now and then," she said meekly. "But I shall honestly try to bend my will to yours."

He couldn't help it. A bubble of laughter formed deep in his chest, shaking him silently for a few seconds, then rose and burst. He laughed and laughed, rocking back and forth in his seat and shaking his head. Sarah woke, grumbling, and sat up indignantly. Natalie looked chagrined, but also looked as if she would gladly join his laughter.

"What is so funny?" Natalie demanded.

"You are," he gasped. "Trying to be the docile bride."

"What is a docile bride?" asked Sarah. "Papa, you are too loud."

"Sarah, hush," said Natalie, putting her arm around the child. "You mustn't correct your papa."

"No," said Malcolm, still choking. "God forbid anyone should correct your lord and master. Phew! That's better. Can't remember when I've laughed so hard."

Sarah yawned. "Are we almost home?"

"No, darling. A few more hours." Natalie's voice was soothing, although she looked very much as if she would like to question Malcolm further. "Would you like to go back to sleep?"

"No. I'm awake now. And the bench is too hard. It hurts my arm." Sarah bounced experimentally on the cushioned seat. "I shall sit with Papa for a while."

Malcolm made room for her and Sarah joined him. Across from them, Natalie relaxed and stretched against the squabs, seeming to enjoy having more space to herself. He marveled at the pleasure it gave him to watch her, even in doing something as mundane as that.

Sarah scrambled up onto her knees, seizing the edge of the window. "Now I am riding backward," she observed. "I hope I won't be sick." Her tone indicated a ghoulish delight at the possibility.

"You won't be sick, Sarah," said Malcolm firmly. "None of us will be sick. Sit still, and I'll tell you a story."

Sarah brightened and snuggled down onto the seat beside him. "I'll help you," she said happily. This was one of her favorite games.

Malcolm hid a grin. "Once upon a time," he began, his eyes on Natalie, "there was a docile bride."

"And a bear," said Sarah.

"And a bear," he repeated obediently. "The bride wasn't always a bride. She was born a princess, as every good fairytale heroine is. She grew up in a castle made of thorns, ruled by a wicked stepmother. She had one good brother and one bad brother, but the bad brother sent the good brother far, far away. Then the poor princess had no one to love her, and the bad brother made her very unhappy—"

"Was she a docile princess?"

"Hm." Malcolm rubbed his chin. "No, I don't believe she was. She only became docile once she married."

"What is 'docile'? Was the bear docile?"

"The bear was exceedingly docile."

"It was a beautiful bear," said Sarah earnestly. "The most beautiful bear in the world. Was the princess beautiful?"

"Indeed she was." He smiled at Natalie. "More beautiful than she knew. But once the good brother was sent away, nobody in the castle of thorns truly appreciated her."

"The bear did."

"Well, perhaps the bear did. But the princess was very lonely."

Natalie made a faint sound of protest. Malcolm looked pointedly at her. "Lonely," he repeated firmly. "Lonelier than she knew. Until, one day, she met a prince who was just as lonely as she."

"Lonelier than he knew," echoed Sarah.

"That's right."

Sarah tapped her chin, looking very wise. "He needed a bear."

Natalie choked. "A bear is a great comfort," she agreed, her voice quivering with suppressed laughter.

Malcolm tried to look stern. "A bear is all very well, in its way," he said firmly. "But the prince and the princess needed each other."

"What the *prince* needed," said Natalie, "was a docile bride."

"Rubbish," scoffed Malcolm. "He never said so."

Sarah looked puzzled. "How do you know what he said?"

"It's my story, isn't it?"

Sarah's brow cleared. "Yes. What did the prince say?"

"He said . . ." Malcolm cudgeled his brain. "He said that what he needed, what he wanted, was the princess's hand in marriage." He shot Natalie a sly look. "The princess only *thought* he wanted a docile bride. He didn't."

Sarah frowned. "But you said she *was* a docile bride."

"Yes, but that was because she was trying to please him," Malcolm explained. "Remember, she had never been docile in the castle of thorns. She tried to become docile so she could make the prince happy. But she wasn't a docile person, so the harder she tried, the more unhappy she became. And the more unhappy she was, the more unhappy the prince was, because—because he wanted the princess to be happy."

"He loved her," said Sarah matter-of-factly. "Did he tell her to stop being docile?"

Out of the mouth of babes. Malcolm swallowed. "He, uh, tried to make it clear that she needn't work so hard at it."

"It was good for her to work hard at it," said Natalie firmly. "Since she was not, by nature, docile—"

"But her docility was bad for the prince," retorted Malcolm. "Docile wives make tyrants of their husbands."

Natalie looked nonplussed but quickly rallied. "Nonsense. The prince was not tyrannical by nature."

"This is Papa's story," said Sarah reprovingly.

"So it seems," muttered Natalie.

Malcolm suppressed a grin. "Very well, Sarah. Where was I?"

"The princess was trying to please the prince, but it made him unhappy. So he told her to stop. Did she stop?"

"Eventually. Once she realized that the prince was in earnest, she stopped being docile and was her own sunny, opinionated self again."

"Did they live happily ever after?"

He smiled. "I imagine they did."

"But what became of the bear? You said the bear was docile, too. Did he stop being docile?"

"The bear continued to be docile, because the bear was docile by nature."

Natalie stifled a laugh. "Now we *know* this is a fairy tale."

Sarah kicked the seat across from her. "The docile bear," she announced, "lived with the prince and princess forever, and they let him play with a golden ball in the garden. How much farther is it to Larkspur?"

Chapter Twenty-one

It was nearly midnight when they reached Larkspur, and Sarah had fallen asleep again. Malcolm carried his daughter up to the nursery while Natalie wearily climbed the stairs to their own chamber. Mrs. Howatch, beaming, showed her the way and helped her undress.

She longed for a hot bath but was too tired to wait for it. Several days of unremitting excitement and tension, followed by her wedding night, a poor night's sleep, a long day jaunting about an unfamiliar city, and an even longer evening unexpectedly journeying home again, had taken a toll. Natalie was tired to the bone. She ached in muscles she never knew she had. Despite the unfamiliar surroundings, she fell into bed and was asleep almost before her head hit the pillow.

She slept dreamlessly. When she drifted awake, daylight on the other side of thick, cherry-colored draperies lit the bedchamber with a muted, rosy glow. She blinked, disoriented. It took her several seconds to realize where she was. Larkspur. She was at Larkspur now, in Malcolm's bed. The strangeness of it brought her fully awake, and her eyes flew open.

"Good morrow, slugabed." The deep rumble, warm

with amusement, came from an armchair near the window. "You've missed breakfast. I was beginning to think you might miss dinner."

"Heavens. What time is it?"

"Half past ten, or thereabouts." Malcolm uncoiled his long body from the depths of the chair and strolled toward the bed. He was wearing a very elegant dressing gown, knotted at the waist with a silken rope.

Natalie raised herself on one elbow. "Slugabed, indeed! You are not dressed," she said indignantly. "How long have you been awake?"

"Longer than you." He sat on the edge of the bed. "I've been watching you sleep."

"Have you? How disturbing." She looked askance at him. "I hope I wasn't snoring."

"Not a whit. You slept very sweetly."

"Well, that's a mercy." She pushed herself up to sit against the head of the bed, punching the pillows briskly into shape behind her. "You really shouldn't do that, Malcolm. It's almost like spying on a person."

"I'll apologize, if you like, but I must admit I enjoyed looking at you." His lips curved into a half smile. "My poor sweeting," he said softly. "You must have been exhausted. It was thoughtless of me to insist on coming home last night."

"Unconscionable," she agreed, yawning.

"I was hoping to carry you across the threshold."

"Never mind. You carried Sarah instead." She smiled lazily up at him. He looked very handsome in his dressing gown.

"There were other rituals I was also hoping to perform." He reached out and curled a lock of her hair around his finger.

Natalie felt her pulse leap. "Rituals?"

He moved closer to her, his eyes darkening. "Traditions," he said huskily. "Traditional celebrations observed by newlyweds throughout history. But you were tired."

"Yes," she murmured. "I was a little too tired for . . . festivity."

He sat beside her on the bed and took her in his arms. "How are you feeling now?"

She shifted against him, warm with pleasure. It felt wonderful to be held by Malcolm. When he behaved so lovingly, she could almost forget that his heart was untouched. "I feel rested," she assured him. "But a little stiff."

He choked back something that sounded like a laugh. "*You're* stiff?" he muttered.

"What?"

"Nothing." He grinned at her. "I know just the thing to help you start the day. Coffee, buttered eggs, and a hot bath."

"Ooh. Lovely."

"Shared, of course, by your husband." He kissed her lightly and moved to pull the bellrope that hung beside the bed.

Natalie looked up at him. "What, the breakfast? Or the bath?"

"All of it." He winked at her.

Her face suddenly felt very hot. "Oh, dear," she said weakly. She was wearing her most modest night rail, white and thick with ruffles. She had put it on last night without thinking. Now she wondered whether some dim instinct had chosen it for her, while her mind was half asleep. She still felt shy about exposing her body to Malcolm's eyes.

Did other brides have this problem? Or was her nervousness connected, somehow, to the secrets she was keeping? She dreaded exposure, in more ways than one.

She hid behind the bed curtains while Malcolm ordered the bath and the tray. After the servant departed he joined her, flopping face down onto the bed with a playful growl. Natalie actually giggled, she was so delighted to see him in this buoyant mood. She longed, again, to tell him that she loved him. She couldn't, of course. Not yet. Someday, but not yet.

It occurred to her that she might feel better if she at least told him about Sarah. It had been impossible to tell him yesterday, but he seemed much more approachable this morning. If only he weren't so touchy about Sarah's little eccentricities . . . But she would have to think about it later. Right now, Malcolm was pulling her into his arms.

He stretched out beside her, grinning down into her smiling face. "You are definitely my favorite wife," he announced.

Natalie, with a scandalized little gasp, pretended to punch his arm. And then he started kissing her, taking her lips in a leisurely, undemanding way that soon had her limp and breathless. By the time the food tray arrived she was in a fair way to forgetting that she had ever kept a secret from him about anything. She had been hungry a few minutes ago, but now the buttered eggs and toast seemed like an irritating interruption.

They shared breakfast in bed, then Malcolm left her to her bath—promising to return in time to wash her back. Natalie, having had time to return to sanity, was relieved to know she would have a few minutes alone to perform her morning ablutions.

Soon after he left her she discarded her night rail, tied her hair up, and sank neck-deep in the steaming water.

Bliss. The soreness in her muscles slowly melted away. She relaxed, lathering herself with fragrant soap. There was something good to be said about nudity after all.

Still, when the door opened to admit Malcolm into her steamy sanctuary, she instinctively ducked her shoulders beneath the water, scrambling to cover herself. He closed the door behind him and leaned against it. She was too embarrassed to meet his gaze.

His voice was unexpectedly gentle when he spoke. "Still so shy of me, sweetheart?"

She blushed. "I'm sorry. I—I can't seem to help it."

Out of the corner of her eye, she saw his bare feet approaching. They were interesting feet, she noted, diverted. Much larger than hers. Strong-looking. Muscle and bone. Yet another area in which men and women differed.

Then he knelt beside the slipper-shaped tub. His dressing gown fell open, revealing his beautiful, masculine chest. She had to tear her eyes away from it and force herself to look into his face.

He was not laughing at her, and he was not angry. His expression was so tender it took her breath away. *Do not hope,* she reminded herself desperately. *Do not dare to hope.* But, in spite of herself, hope stirred in her heart. So much tenderness! She saw it in his eyes. She felt it in his touch. Surely, surely, someday . . .

"Natalie," he whispered. His voice was husky with desire and promise. "Don't think about you, sweetheart. Think about me."

She tilted her head, puzzled. Then he shrugged his dressing gown off, let it drop on the floor, and reached for her bath sponge—and, in a flash, she understood. He was right. When she thought about herself—her fears, her nakedness, what he must be thinking of her, whether or not she pleased him—she froze up like an overwound clock. But when she thought of him—the play of his muscles, the texture of his hair, the feel of his mouth when he kissed her—there was no room in her reeling brain for petty anxieties.

Think about Malcolm. Oh, yes. Yes. Even the simple act of wringing out her sponge worked the sinews of his arm, bringing the line of his muscles into relief and filling her with awe. How strong he was. How beautiful. *Malcolm.* She lifted her hand to trace the edge of his arm with one wet fingertip and watched the water bead up on his skin.

"My husband," she whispered, hardly aware that she spoke. And she sat up out of the water of her own free will and kissed him.

His arms slid around her. She was dimly aware of the sponge in his hand gushing warm water down her back as he kissed her greedily, meeting her passion with his own. Her wet breasts crushed against his chest with a delicious shock of sensation; she had never experienced anything as erotic as the feel of him holding her, flesh to flesh. This was nothing like the encounter of their wedding night. The bath simultaneously intensified the onslaught of feeling and protected her from it; his hands plunging into the water and running over her slick, wet skin gave her exquisite pleasure, yet the barrier of the metal wall between them held him at bay. She reveled in the feelings coursing through her at his touch. Hers was the power, to prolong the encounter or end it.

She chose to prolong it.

Before long he was half in the water himself, leaning far over the tub to embrace as much of her as he could reach. "Natalie," he muttered at last, "for God's sake, either come out of the water or let me in there with you."

She gave a breathless little laugh. "No. I like this."

He growled, deep in his throat, a sound of frustration mixed with amusement. "I can wait," he promised her. "That water will be stone cold in ten minutes. And meanwhile"—his voice became silky—"you can tell me what else you like." He nuzzled her neck, lightly licking at the drops of water an her skin. "Do you like that?"

"Mm." It was difficult to reply, she liked it so well.

"How about this?" He moved his mouth up to her ear and did something, she could not tell what, with his tongue. Natalie gasped and arched her back as pleasure shot through her. "And this?" He slid his fingers across the tips of her breasts and indescribable sensations swirled in their wake. She could not seem to catch her breath. His eyes, dark with hunger, stared at what his hands were doing. "You're so beautiful," he told her, and she could swear he meant it. "So beautiful."

He took her mouth again and, this time, as he kissed her, she let him pull her to her feet and out of the water. It *had* grown a little chilly, after all.

Natalie stretched, catlike, against the rumpled sheets in the warmth of afternoon. Daylight still stole dimly into Malcolm's chamber, since they had never bothered to pull open the curtains. She rather liked the effect. It was strange that that masculine, claret-colored velvet stained the light a very feminine, very flattering, and highly romantic pink.

Malcolm dozed beside her. She turned her head and studied his form where he lay, relaxed and disheveled and unaware of her scrutiny. Her heart swelled with love and sorrow at the sight of him—so dear to her, so desirable. And so unreachable.

How could he make love to her that way, and yet not

love her? It was unfathomable. She was thoroughly aware that her own desire, her response to him, everything that had happened in the past several hours, was inextricably tangled with her love for him. She had no doubt about that whatsoever. She would never have experienced those extraordinary heights of physical sensation absent the emotions that matched them. Without the love that she felt for Malcolm, what would marital intimacy be? She could not imagine it.

At any rate, the question was moot. She did love him. She would never know what it felt like to share physical intimacy without love.

Perhaps this—whatever it was—would be enough for her. She had to admit, it was all rather wonderful thus far. Malcolm could hardly treat her more tenderly or show her more consideration than he did now. He acted, for all the world, as if he *did* love her. It was most puzzling. Had he not told her, point-blank, that what he wanted was a marriage of convenience?

She frowned, trying to remember. It was hard to trust her recollections. A cloud of emotion had risen up to choke her every time he mentioned marriage. Surely he had told her that he didn't want a love match. Surely he had told her that love was nothing but a fantasy.

On the other hand, he had told her once that he loved her.

Natalie's frown deepened. She didn't like remembering that. It had been a particularly painful moment. His mention of love that day was nothing but a ploy. He had wanted her to wife, and had thought that was the best way of twisting her arm. She had made the mistake of telling him what she wanted from marriage, and he had pretended to give it to her. It had been a pathetic ruse, a disgusting attempt to deceive and manipulate her.

Come to think of it . . . that didn't sound like something Malcolm would do.

Suddenly it was hard to breathe. Natalie felt her heart hammering in her chest. She stared at her dozing husband, wondering if it were possible she had been mistaken. It now struck her as unlikely—even disloyal on her part—to think that Malcolm would lie to her at all, let alone about something so important.

What if he had spoken truth to her that day? Could that be possible?

Oh, no—it couldn't be. He had never mentioned it again. But, still . . .

As if feeling her eyes on him, Malcolm stirred and reached for her. "I suppose," he said sleepily, "that it's high time we left our bedchamber."

She went willingly into his arms, but she was still troubled. He opened his eyes and saw her expression. It seemed to shake the vestiges of slumber from his brain. His gaze sharpened. "What's amiss?"

Natalie's eyes slid away from his. "Nothing." She tried to smile. "I am embarrassed to face the staff after lying abed all day."

It was not a lie. But she did wish she had the courage to truly answer his question. *Later,* she promised herself. She sat up, shaking out her hair and combing it with her fingers.

He watched her, an appreciative smile playing with the edges of his mouth. "You have the most amazing hair."

She pulled a face. "It's nothing but a nuisance. All these wretched curls! Try as I might, they never do what I want them to do."

"Yes, that's what I love about them."

Love. The word seemed to hang in the air between

them, reverberating. She paused for a fraction of an instant, then continued her finger-combing, taking care not to meet his eyes.

"Why is it," she said lightly, "that everyone with curly hair admires straight hair, and everyone with straight hair admires curls?"

"One of the perversities of nature," he agreed, lying back against the pillows with his hands clasped behind his head. Natalie stole a glance at him and could not help smiling. The pose brought every muscle in his arms and chest into bold relief. He looked gorgeously male. And very tempting.

She moved off the bed, snatching up her dressing gown and wrapping it about her. "Well?" she said challengingly. "Do you plan to lie there all week?"

He gave her a languid smile. "I'm going to watch you dress and help you with your laces. Since we haven't hired a maid for you yet."

She arched a brow at him. "I wonder why we haven't? Do you suppose it had anything to do with our leaving London too quickly?"

"It might," he said affably. "And since that was my fault, as I'm sure you are ready to tell me, I mean to make it up to you by performing the services myself."

She chuckled. "You'll soon tire of that," she remarked, digging in the trunks thrown open by the window. There had not been time to unpack them last night.

She pulled out stockings, chemise, stays, and petticoat, and was charmed when Malcolm was as good as his word, helping her to put them on. He did a creditable job of it, too. Of course, she didn't care to dwell on where he must have learned those skills. The thought of Malcolm sharing a bedchamber with any woman other than herself, wife or no, was vaguely upsetting.

She was less skillful when helping him dress, but they got through it—with quite a bit of laughter and teasing. And kissing. Really, she had never dreamed that marriage would be so much fun.

When they left the room and strolled down the passage, Sarah pounced on them. "Where have you been?" she exclaimed. "I thought you had gone back to London, but Nurse said you had not."

Malcolm hefted her up. "We didn't go anywhere. We were in bed, goosecap." He planted a loud kiss on her cheek.

Sarah squirmed, giggling, and wiped his kiss off with the back of her hand. He set her back on the floor. "I slept late, too," she announced. "But not as late as you. Would you like to see my paintings?"

Natalie and Malcolm exchanged surprised glances. "Your paintings?" he repeated. "What paintings do you mean?"

Mrs. Bigalow stepped through the open door of the nursery. "It's only watercolors, my lord," she said briskly. "We found a paint box in one of the drawers, and I thought there'd be no harm in the child playin' with it a bit. Seeing as how she's so keen on drawing and sketching and that." Her eyes narrowed, twinkling, as she looked at Natalie—but she said nothing, much to Natalie's relief. For half a second, she'd been afraid that Nurse would inquire outright how her day had gone, or whether marriage agreed with her.

They followed the frisking Sarah into the nursery and over to the table near the window. Sheets of paper lay helter-skelter on its surface, with jars of dirty water acting as paperweights. Natalie bent over the child's work and, as her eyes made sense of what she saw, she felt her throat tighten with emotion. The work was remarkable for a girl of Sarah's age. The child had an astonishing gift. But of the three adults gathered around the table, praising her, only Natalie understood just how remarkable Sarah's gift was.

Would Malcolm be angry at what she had done yesterday? She wished she knew. She would have to tell him before long, but she had not yet decided how best to broach the subject. He invariably fired up at any hint that there might be something wrong with his precious daughter. And after hearing Hector's sneering assumptions that Sarah was feebleminded, Natalie thought he had a right to be touchy. He was trying to protect his little girl from people's ignorance. But if she told him in just the right way, he would understand that there wasn't anything actually *wrong* with Sarah . . . at least, not in the way he feared.

She couldn't speak of it in front of Sarah. She had to explain it to Malcolm privately. But the moments came and went, and the right one never seemed to arrive. The next day passed, and the next, and still she had not told him. He never asked where she and Sarah had gone that day in London, so a natural beginning to the conversation did not occur—and Natalie was preoccupied enough, adjusting to the novelty of being married, that she did not press the issue.

Shortly after luncheon one day, when Malcolm was stealing a kiss from her in the drawing room, a cough sounded in the doorway behind them. The cough was followed by Howatch's voice.

"Beg pardon, my lord, but there's a Mr. Whittaker here to see you and Lady Malcolm. And a pair of ladies with him," he added. "I know you said to turn visitors away, but I wondered if, under the circumstances—"

Natalie and Malcolm turned in unison, Natalie hastily

patting her hair into place. "A pair of ladies?" she repeated in astonishment. "Why would Hector bring a pair of ladies with him?"

Howatch looked slightly offended. "It's not Mr. Hector Whittaker, my lady. I am acquainted with Hector Whittaker, and I don't know this gentleman. Nor, I might add, do I know the ladies with him." Seeing the baffled expressions on his employers' faces, he added helpfully, "It's quite a young gentleman, sir. And, if I might be so bold as to venture an opinion, he bears a strong resemblance to Lady Malcolm."

"Derek!" exclaimed Natalie. "What on earth—"

"Show him into the library, Howatch," interrupted Malcolm. "You were right to admit him, of course. We'll be down in half a minute."

"Very good, sir."

Natalie checked her reflection in the mirror on the wall and absently tugged at her bodice. "How odd of Derek to arrive without warning. I wonder what brings him here? Now that I have a home of my own, mayhap I will invite him to stay here rather than at Crosby Hall. You would not mind that, would you? I own, I would like to have him under our roof for a while. I thought he looked too thin when I saw him last."

"It will be as you wish, of course." Malcolm held the door for her and they started down the stairs together. "Does he make a habit of popping in unannounced?"

"No, it's most unlike him. In fact, he rarely comes home at all. He is kept so busy! Last year he even spent Christmas with Lord Stokesdown."

"I daresay he's just paying a bridal visit."

Natalie looked skeptical. "So soon after seeing us in London? And who could the two ladies be? I confess, I am mystified."

"Well, we'll know soon enough," said Malcolm, standing aside to let her pass before him into the library.

As expected, the young man Howatch had announced was Derek. He stood by the fireplace and looked up when Natalie came in. But she had never seen such an expression on his face—tense and deadly serious. She paused in midstride, surprised. "Why, Derek! How are you? Welcome to Larkspur. What brings you to . . ."

Her voice died away as her eyes fell on Derek's companions. One was an elderly woman of respectable, but modest, appearance who rose courteously to her feet as Natalie entered the room. This woman was a stranger. But the other . . . the lady who remained seated, turning vacant eyes upon her and giving her a vague smile . . . this lady resembled . . .

No. This lady *was*.

A strange roaring sound filled Natalie's ears, and the room suddenly turned gray before her eyes. As her vision dimmed she thought she heard Derek's voice. It was sharp with alarm but seemed to be coming from a great distance.

Chapter Twenty-two

"Catch her, Malcolm!"

Derek had already started toward Natalie as he spoke, but Malcolm was closer. In two quick strides he overtook his swaying wife and held her up. She had turned a ghastly color and was almost limp in his arms.

"What the deuce! Natalie, are you ill?"

"It's the shock," said Derek grimly. "Sorry, but there wasn't time to send word ahead, to warn her. And besides that, I needed to be certain." He took a deep breath. "Now I am certain. Natalie's reaction has confirmed it."

"Confirmed what?" Malcolm's voice sounded sharper than he intended. "If you've harmed her in any way, Whittaker, you'll pay for it. Brother or no." He half carried Natalie to a sofa and laid her tenderly upon it, supporting her head with a fat cushion Derek silently passed to him. "Natalie," he said gently. "Natalie, are you coming round?"

"Yes," she said faintly. "I think I—oh." She lay back against the cushion, still visibly pale. "Malcolm." She clung to his hand.

"I'm here, love."

"Don't leave me."

"I won't," he said with great vehemence. "Ever."

"What happened?"

The elderly woman moved diffidently forward. "If I might be so bold," she said, holding out a small vial she had taken from her reticule. "I've a vinaigrette, if you think it would help the dear lady."

"Thank you," said Malcolm gruffly. He took it and held it beneath Natalie's nose.

Natalie pulled a face, coughed, and turned her head away. "Thank you," she said feebly. "I'm quite all right. Thank you." She opened her eyes dazedly. "Who are you?"

The elderly woman gave a sympathetic cluck. "I'm Mrs. Gilford, dearie, but don't you worry about that now." Her manner was both kind and efficient, and Malcolm instinctively made room to let Mrs. Gilford, whoever she was, perch on the sofa beside Natalie. He was still holding one of Natalie's hands, and Mrs. Gilford took the other in a firm, professional-looking grip and laid her fingers against Natalie's wrist to feel her pulse. "Still a bit rapid," she remarked. "I suggest we let her lie quietly for a bit."

"Right." Malcolm stared at her, feeling almost as disoriented as Natalie. "What are you? A nurse?"

"That's right, sir."

He glanced up at Derek, who was hovering behind the sofa with an anxious expression, his eyes on his sister. "Care to explain?" asked Malcolm dryly.

"Eh?" Derek looked at him blankly, then flushed. "Oh! Sorry. Lord Malcolm, this is Mrs. Gilford, a—a friend of the family. Mrs. Gilford, my brother-in-law, Lord Malcolm Chase. And my sister, Lady Malcolm."

Natalie did not stir, but Malcolm bowed as well as he could from a sitting position, and Mrs. Gilford nodded courteously. He then jerked his chin to indicate the other woman, who had not moved from her chair and seemed oblivious to the excitement going on across the room from her. Derek swallowed convulsively. "I believe," he said hesitantly, "that the other lady is—is my mother."

Malcolm felt his jaw drop. His eyes immediately returned to Natalie, lying white-faced and motionless before him. She seemed to be conscious but still recruiting her strength.

Derek continued speaking, his voice low and troubled. "It sounds incredible, I know. I wasn't sure, myself, until a few moments ago. But Natalie is a year older than I, and I knew her memory of our mother would be clearer than mine. So I brought the ladies here, and . . . well, you see the result."

"Then it's true," said Natalie in a low voice. "I thought I dreamed it." Her eyes fluttered open and focused, more strongly than before, first on Malcolm and then on Derek. "Where is she? Let me go to her."

She struggled to sit up. Mrs. Gilford moved to prevent her from rising, however, saying in a firm, compassionate voice, "Take care, my lady. You've waited this long to see her. You can wait a moment longer. There's no need to make yourself unwell."

Natalie obediently remained seated, pressing one hand to her forehead. "I don't know what came over me. I've never swooned like that before."

"Well, now," said Mrs. Gilford comfortably. "Anyone would. It's a terrific shock you've had, my dear. I daresay your brother would have reacted the same, had he recognized her right off the way you did."

"But it's impossible." Natalie's hand dropped and her eyes traveled painfully to Derek's face. "Our mother is dead," she whispered numbly.

Derek came around the sofa and sat on a hassock at Natalie's feet, bringing his eyes level with hers. He leaned forward earnestly. "Natalie, they lied to us." His warm brown eyes were full of trouble. "Mother wasn't killed when the gig overturned. They wouldn't let us see her, remember? They carried her home and shut her in her bedchamber, and they wouldn't let us see her."

"But—but that was to protect us." Natalie's expression was bewildered. "We were so young. Too young to understand. She lingered for a while, but then she—she passed on. They didn't want us to see her like that."

It was a painful scene, and Malcolm could not bear to see his wife suffer. He put his arm around her and held her strongly, heedless of their audience. Something dreadful hung in the air; this was no joyous reunion. He wished he could protect her from what she was learning today.

Derek clearly felt compassion for Natalie's pain and confusion as well. He placed a hand on her knee, his eyes as sad and pleading as a puppy's. "Natalie, I—I don't know how to tell you this."

"Just say it," said Malcolm. He knew what was coming.

"Mother's brain was damaged." Derek's voice was unexpectedly gentle. "In a sense, our mother *is* dead. She won't know you, Natalie. She doesn't speak. She's not suffering, but she's not . . . herself."

Mrs. Gilford patted Natalie's hand. "That's right, my lady. Don't go thinking they lied to you deliberately, for it's entirely possible they didn't. I daresay your papa meant well. Nobody expected her to live." She looked modestly down. "If I do say it as shouldn't, the physicians underestimated what competent nursing could do for her."

"Mrs. Gilford has been taking care of her all these years." Derek shot a grateful look at the pink-cheeked old lady. "We owe her a debt we can never repay."

"Oh, well, sir, you needn't say *that*. I've been well paid for my trouble," said Mrs. Gilford, fluttering with embarrassment. "I've no complaint to make on that score. Your papa made all the arrangements early on, and never a payment has been missed. But I'd no idea that her children were told she had died, or I promise you, I would have handled this matter differently."

"What matter?" asked Malcolm.

Mrs. Gilford's embarrassment increased. "Well, my lord, as I say, no one expected Mrs. Whittaker to live. My task was simply to make her as comfortable as I could until she died. But, as you see, she hasn't died, so my commission has continued all these years. She's quite healthy, but I'm getting on now and haven't the stamina I once had. I'm afraid the time is nearing when other arrangements must be made. I had been specifically told that I mustn't communicate with her children—although I never dreamed the reason why—but what else could I do? Mr. Whittaker has passed on. I hardly liked to approach his bankers with such a personal matter. There was no one else to turn to." She sighed. "Dear me! I had no notion that everyone believed the poor lady was dead."

Natalie shivered. "How could you think we knew?" Her low voice throbbed with anguish. "All these years, we never visited her . . . we never wrote . . . did you think we were monsters?" She shook off the various hands that were touching her and rose shakily to her feet. "I must see her."

"I'll go with you," said Derek gently. He placed one hand at Natalie's elbow in a protective gesture and walked with her across the room. Malcolm did not move to accompany them; this was a private moment for brother and sister.

As he watched them approach her, he was struck again by the resemblance they bore to each other . . . and, he now saw, to the lady in the chair. Her hair was graying beneath her cap, but the thick waves that framed her face reminded him of Derek's. And her face was Natalie's face, thinner and chiseled but still appealing, despite her vacant expression.

Natalie sank onto the floor at her mother's feet. The expression on her face was heartbreaking. She took the lady's thin hands in hers. "Mama," she said softly. "Mama, it's Natalie. Do you remember Natalie?"

Mrs. Whittaker's empty eyes traveled briefly to Natalie's face, but her vague smile did not alter. No emotion registered on her features. No recognition lit her eyes. She was plainly a hollow vessel, sleepwalking through her days. Still, just seeing her again was obviously a miracle to Natalie; she touched her mother's face with shaking hands, squeezed her shoulders, laid her head in her lap. "Mama," she whispered. "Oh, I can't believe it. Mama." She closed her eyes. Tears slipped down her cheeks.

This scene should not be witnessed by so many eyes, thought Malcolm. He walked over to Derek and touched his sleeve. "Come," he said gruffly. "Let us leave them alone for a few minutes. Mrs. Gilford will look after them." He shot a questioning look at the elderly nurse, and she nodded a placid acceptance from her place on the sofa. Malcolm led Derek from the room.

"Step into my study, where we can be private," said Malcolm curtly.

Derek silently followed him in, and Malcolm closed

the door behind them. He walked to the windows and threw back the curtains. Light flooded the room. He turned and saw Derek standing just inside the door, regarding him gravely. The corners of Derek's mouth were set in grim lines, and his gaze was steady.

Malcolm's former impression of Derek as an engaging, boyish rattle underwent a sudden revision. This was a young man with a head on his shoulders. This was a young man who took responsibility seriously, whether to his sister, to Lord Stokesdown, or to his newly found mother. Malcolm already liked his new brother-in-law very well. It was a pleasant discovery to realize that he might respect him, too.

"Natalie has not thought through all the implications of this," said Malcolm softly.

"Naturally not. There has not been time."

"I'd be curious to hear your thoughts on the matter. Mrs. Gilford's assessment of your father's motives seems, to me, a bit . . . optimistic."

Derek uttered a short, mirthless laugh. "Oh, that's occurred to you, has it? I wonder who is buried in my mother's grave? I daresay it's an empty coffin." He shook his head in grim revulsion. "I wish I could believe that my father's actions twenty years ago were benign. But it's all too obvious they weren't."

"I agree."

Derek shot a troubled glance at Malcolm. "We can't keep that from her, you know. Natalie's too needle-witted. She will eventually come to the same conclusion you and I have reached. Our father deliberately lied. Not only to us, but to the entire community."

Malcolm walked slowly behind his desk, thinking. "There is another implication that Natalie has not yet realized," he said. He shot a keen glance at Derek and raised an eyebrow.

Derek gave a brief nod, a curt acknowledgment of what they were both thinking. There was a strange light in his eyes, and a half smile on his face. A flash of understanding seemed to knit the two men in an instant meeting of the minds. A huge truth loomed large in the room, a truth that both of them had seen and recognized.

Derek took a deep breath. He was standing ramrod straight, yet perfectly relaxed, like a young warrior girding his loins for battle. And then he spoke it aloud.

"Hector is illegitimate," said Derek softly. "I am the master of Crosby Hall."

Chapter Twenty-three

"The question is, my young friend, what will you do about it?"

Derek frowned. "There's no question at all. Crosby Hall is mine. Hector can dashed well take Mabel back to London and live on her dowry; she's a woman of means. Or he can do something useful in future and get paid for it, as I have done. Or he can move his family in with Lucille; her flat is spacious enough."

"Ah. It was my impression that your stepmother's flat was purchased with family money."

An arrested expression crossed Derek's face. Then he shook his head. "No. I mean, it was, of course, but I shan't turn her out on the street. I'll deed the flat to her outright."

"Good." Malcolm waved Derek toward a chair and sat, himself, behind the desk. "You have every right to make things ugly. On the whole, however, I'm glad that your impulse is toward generosity rather than animosity."

Derek sat, still frowning thoughtfully. "I see no point in taking revenge on Lucille. She's never been fond of Natalie and me, and she's done her best to make life hard for us at times. But I've no reason to believe she was an accomplice in this. My father may have kept her in the dark as well."

"Possibly," agreed Malcolm. He thought it unlikely, but approved of Derek's determination to give others the benefit of the doubt.

A smile flitted briefly across Derek's features. "And besides, I've no taste for scandal. The less dust is kicked up about all this, the better."

"Very true. The quickest way to cause a riot is to boot your stepmother out of her flat. But you will, of course, need to boot Hector out of Crosby Hall."

Derek's expression turned grim again. "Immediately. Will you come with me?"

Malcolm's brows flew upward. "Today?"

"Absolutely." Derek's voice was clipped and sure. "This news will spread like wildfire. I daresay the servants are already gossiping about it belowstairs. If Hector gets wind of my mother's reappearance, he'll put two and two together as quick as winking. I'd rather take him by surprise."

"I see." Malcolm tapped his fingers meditatively against his chin. "I think you are right. Prompt action is called for." He sighed. "One hates to think ill of one's relations, but I formed my opinion of Hector's character before I married your sister. And, frankly, I've no doubt that he will thrust a spoke in your wheel if he can. Best to give him no chance to come up with a plan."

Derek grinned. "Why, so I think. Natalie told me I would like you, by the way. I'm inclined to believe she's done me a great favor by marrying you."

Malcolm hid a smile. "She's certainly done *me* a great favor by marrying me. Come! Let us think this matter

through before we act. Who is the local magistrate?
Squire Farnsworth?"

Derek nodded. "I suppose he must be. He is justice of
the peace. Why?"

"It seems to me that we should have an impartial
witness when we confront your brother. And the best
witness to have would be one with some official capac-
ity."

Derek shifted restlessly in his chair. "Blast," he muttered at last. "I'm afraid you're right." He lifted troubled
eyes to Malcolm's face. "You don't think Hector would
offer us violence, do you?"

Malcolm shrugged. "He is bound to become a
little . . . excited, shall we say? He's only human. But
what I was fearing more was that he might actually
refuse to leave. What would we do in such a case? Since
he has busied himself the past few months in replacing
all the family retainers with his own people, I can't think
who would come to our aid, did we try to evict him by
force."

"What a pretty picture you paint," said Derek dryly. "I
can see it now: You and I unceremoniously kicked out
the door by Hector and his merry men, and a protracted
battle in the courts before I take what's mine."

Malcolm spread his hands in an apologetic gesture. "I
don't mean to rain on your picnic. But we'd do well to
consider our response to that scenario and foil him before he acts. Rather than wait for him to act, and then
fight an uphill battle."

"Quite right." Derek waved a hand. "Carry on."

"Possession being nine tenths of the law, I think we
should do what we can to put *you* in possession of the
house. You should sleep there tonight, in fact. I doubt if

Hector will start a court fight. He hasn't a leg to stand on. But it occurs to me that he might, er, remove a few favorite items, if left to pack his bags at leisure."

A muscle jumped in Derek's jaw. "You're right again, confound it. That's exactly what he would do. Steal from me. That, or break things. He's always been a spiteful little blighter." He sighed, then nodded. "Jasper Farnsworth," he said, concurring with Malcolm. "We'll wait for the squire before proceeding."

Malcolm reached for the bellpull. "I'll send a message by my fastest rider."

When the two men left Malcolm's study, the sound of muffled weeping led them back to the library. There they found Mrs. Bigalow, quite overcome with tears, rocking the unresponsive Mrs. Whittaker in her arms. Natalie and Mrs. Gilford stood by, patting and soothing the distraught nurse.

Derek immediately walked over to the huddled group and placed his hand gently on his old nurse's back. She turned away from her former mistress, gasped, and buried her face in his shoulder for a moment. Derek hugged her with one arm. "There, then, Nurse," he said, his voice suspiciously thick. "There, then. How many times have you told me not to cry over what can't be mended?"

Mrs. Bigalow scrubbed her face vigorously with the edge of her apron. She took a deep breath and emerged from Derek's embrace. "That's true, that's true," she said, pulling herself together. "It did come as a shock, that's all. To see my poor mistress again, which I never thought—" She broke off, gulped, and shook her head. "Ah, well. What's done is done."

"It's been a shock for us all," said Natalie. She looked

calm but pale. "Perhaps I shouldn't have called you down—"

"Oh! No, now, none o'that," said Mrs. Bigalow, regaining some of her customary briskness. "I'm glad you did, Natalie. Or Lady Malcolm, I *should* say. I'm glad you did." She whipped out a handkerchief and fiercely blew her nose. "I shall be myself again in a moment."

Malcolm had joined the group by now. He felt he couldn't go one more minute without touching Natalie. He drew her to his side and placed his hand at her waist. She looked up, seeming glad of his touch, then leaned lightly against him as if to confirm it. His heart swelled with protectiveness. "Are you feeling better?" he asked her quietly.

She nodded, giving him a tiny smile. "My life is moving much too fast for me," she confessed. The group's conversation had moved on without them, so she took the opportunity to whisper: "Malcolm, I'm so glad you're here."

He almost chuckled. "I live here, sweetheart."

"You know what I mean."

He could not resist touching her cheek. Her face was soft and warm. "Yes, Natalie," he said softly. "I think I do."

Her eyes were gorgeous. How could eyes as dark and warm as hers be so full of light? A man couldn't help smiling, when handed such a tremendous stroke of luck. He would be able to drink his fill of her, eyes and all, for the rest of his life.

"Ahem!" said Derek loudly, recalling Malcolm and Natalie to the here and now. "Any chance our hostess will remember her duties? Or must her long-suffering brother remind her?"

"Oh!" said Natalie, turning a little pink. "I'm so sorry! In all the excitement— Nurse, will you ring the bell for me? Thank you. I'll have tea and sandwiches sent up, shall I?"

"Better have them make a few extra," suggested Derek, sprawling in one of Malcolm's wing chairs. "Send up a ham, too, if you've got it. You're liable to have Jasper Farnsworth descend on you before too long."

She looked startled. "Squire Farnsworth? Why?"

"Because Malcolm sent for him, that's why."

Natalie turned to her husband, eyes wide with questions. The two nurses, fortunately, had fallen into conversation while helping Mrs. Whittaker back into her chair. They seemed thoroughly absorbed, so Malcolm and Derek went apart with Natalie, drew three chairs close together, and, in carefully lowered voices, gave her the gist of their earlier discussion.

As she took it all in, her eyes grew larger and darker, and her face lost the color it had regained. At the end of their tale, she collapsed nervelessly against the back of her chair and covered her eyes with one hand. The men waited in sympathetic silence for her to digest the information.

"I see," she said at last. Her voice was low and tremulous. "So Hector will be gone, and Derek and I will be neighbors. It is rather terrible, isn't it . . . to secretly wish for the impossible, and then have your wish come true." She took a deep, shuddering breath. "The world is not supposed to work this way. One isn't meant to receive so many of one's heart's desires, one after the other. There's something frightening about it."

Malcolm frowned. He took her hand in a sustaining clasp. "Natalie, love, you are talking nonsense."

"No, I know what she means." Derek gave him a twisted smile. "I feel it, too. But, unlike Natalie, I've had some time to think about it." His voice slowed and softened. "The thing is, none of it is up to us. Sometimes we must suffer a disproportionate portion of slings and arrows. And sometimes, apparently, we must accept a disproportionate portion of God's bounty. What we are called upon to do is to accept what we're sent, with as good a grace as we can."

Natalie removed her hand from her eyes and gave a shaky little laugh. "Well, then, I'm being a ninnyhammer, aren't I? Anyone might complain about ill luck, but to weep over good luck is—"

"Idiotic. And ungrateful." Derek reached across the space between them and gave his sister's knee a friendly shake. "Lord knows, you and I have tried to accept our lot in life with good grace up to now. We'll just have to accept this as well." He grinned. "And while you're busy accepting it, don't bother feeling sorry for Hector. The one to pity is Lord Stokesdown."

That made Natalie laugh. Really, the more Malcolm saw of Derek Whittaker, the better he liked him. He gave his new brother-in-law an approving nod and patted his wife's hand. Natalie smiled up at him like the sun breaking through clouds, and Malcolm felt his heart ease.

When Jasper Farnsworth arrived, his astonishment over the day's revelations quickly transformed into resolve. He shook his head over the concerns that Hector Whittaker might do something ungentlemanly, warning Malcolm and Derek that they must not jump to unwarranted conclusions. On the other hand, however, he agreed that they had done the correct thing in summoning him. "I'll be glad to go with you to Crosby Hall to break the news," he said, glancing keenly first at Malcolm, then Derek. "And I'll stay until I'm satisfied that Mr. Hector understands his obligations under the law."

In the end, it was deemed best that Hector be shown the proof of his illegitimacy at once, to forestall any argument. Hector would not be able to accuse his siblings of foisting an imposter upon him if the squire were there to confirm her identity. The party would, therefore, remove to Crosby Hall and present the unfortunate Hector with a fait accompli.

Natalie supported her mother on one side, with Mrs. Gilford on the other, and they walked the short distance to Crosby Hall. Their progress was slow, to accommodate Mrs. Whittaker's halting steps. Natalie's eyes often fixed on her mother's face with a painful earnestness, as if hoping against hope that returning to her home might trigger some response in her, but as far as Malcolm could tell, it did not. Mrs. Whittaker's expression never changed.

Hector and Mabel's startled butler showed them into Crosby Hall's drawing room. The room fell quiet while they waited for Hector to join them. The squire took a stand by the fire, with his hands clasped behind his back and a very sober expression on his face. Derek stood at the opposite side of the fireplace, leaning one arm on the mantle and staring moodily into the flames. Mrs. Gilford seated Mrs. Whittaker on a comfortable sofa and took her place beside her, the only member of the company maintaining an air of cheerful calm. Natalie perched nervously on the edge of a settee. Malcolm sat beside her, holding her hand and wishing it were permissible to place his arm around her. She seemed to find the grip of his hand comforting, but she still trembled a little.

"This is a terrible business," she whispered to him. "I shall be glad when it is over. Poor Hector!"

He squeezed her hand sympathetically. "Do not distress yourself, sweetheart. Let Derek and me handle it." She gave a silent nod of acquiescence, then looked up at the door as a footstep sounded in the passage outside.

Hector entered, wreathed in false smiles. One sharp glance around the room, however, and his air of forced bonhomie grew even more false. It was plain he sensed something in the wind. Malcolm rose courteously to his feet to shake Hector's hand, but Squire Farnsworth cut through their host's overly jovial attempts to greet them all in turn.

"Sorry, lad," said the squire with an air both kind and blunt, "but your welcome is misplaced. We've some news to impart that I fear will come as a shock to you. Eh, it's been a shock to us all—but to you it will be more than that."

He tried to wave Hector toward a chair, but Hector stood his ground near the door. His eyes narrowed as he looked from face to face. "What is it? You'd better tell me at once."

The squire looked distressed. Malcolm stepped into the breach, laying a friendly hand on Hector's arm. "The squire's idea is a good one, Hector. Sit down, and we'll all—"

Hector shook his hand off impatiently. "What, will you tell me to be seated in my own home?" he jeered. "I can hear you as well where I am as in a chair. What the devil is it?"

Malcolm shrugged. Hector made it difficult to feel

much sympathy for him. "Very well," he said coolly. "I will tell you, if you insist. Mrs. Gilford, pray allow me to present to you Hector Whittaker, ostensibly your host. Hector, this lady is Mrs. Gilford. She is a nurse, and the lady beside her is her charge: Mrs. Whittaker."

Hector's head went up like an animal scenting danger. "Mrs. Whittaker? Who is she? A relation of ours?" He looked at her again. "What's wrong with her?"

"She doesn't speak, sir," said Mrs. Gilford placidly.

Natalie rose shakily to her feet. "I will tell him," she said, pity in her voice.

Malcolm moved protectively to her side. Hector seemed, to him, dangerously volatile. "Be careful, Natalie," he said under his breath. "Don't put your foot in the hornet's nest."

"Malcolm's right," said Derek. "Sit down, Natalie. I'll tell him."

"Tell me what?" Hector's voice was sharp with suppressed fear.

Natalie did not sit down, but she buried her face in Malcolm's shoulder. He held her silently, wishing, for the hundredth time, that he could remove her from this scene.

Derek walked forward, his face impassive, and stood behind Mrs. Whittaker. He placed one hand on her shoulder. "This lady is my mother," he said simply.

Hector cocked his head, looking puzzled for a moment. Then the fear returned to his eyes. His face turned a sickly hue. "Your mother? That's impossible. She's dead."

"No, sir," said Mrs. Gilford gently. "She's unwell, but she's alive. As you can see."

The squire coughed. "I must tell you, lad, that I recog-

nized her at once. This lady is, indeed, the first Mrs.
Whittaker." He looked flustered. "That is—"

"She is the only Mrs. Whittaker," said Derek quietly.
"I'm sorry, Hector."

Hector looked stunned. His eyes darted frantically
from face to face. "What—what—what do you mean?"
he stammered. "What—"

Natalie lifted her head, her composure returning.
"Hector, do sit down," she said. Her voice was soft with
compassion. "You'll make yourself ill. I nearly fainted
when they broke the news to me, and to me it was *good*
news."

He stared at her, his jaw slack, his expression uncomprehending.

The squire cleared his throat. "Whether you sit down
or no," he said gruffly, "it's my duty to proceed." His
voice took on the measured tones of authority. "Hector
Alphonse Whittaker, you are in possession of property
that lawfully belongs to your half brother. Will you relin-
quish it voluntarily, or must I evict you by force?"

"What?" The squire's words seemed to pierce the
trance that had seized young Hector. He whipped around
to gape, wild-eyed, at Jasper Farnsworth. "Evict me?
You're mad."

Malcolm felt a tremor run through his wife. He tightened his arm around Natalie as the squire raised a warning hand. "Now, now, lad, let's be civilized. We're all
gentlemen here. All reasonable men. No need to drama-
tize the situation. No need to go off half-cocked. All I'm
saying is you must leave Crosby Hall—at least for the
present, while things are straightened out. If you think
for half a moment, you'll see the wisdom of that. I advise you to cooperate. I put it higher, lad: I strongly advise you to cooperate. We are all sensible of what you

must be feeling this day, but fact is fact, and the law is the law."

Hector spat out a word so foul that Natalie flinched. "You fat, miserable toad," he shrieked, livid. "You can't evict me from my own home."

The squire's head lowered like a bull's. "It is not your home, and I certainly can," he rumbled. "Come down from the high ropes, Hector. I'm warning you."

"They've always had it in for me!" cried Hector, waving an index finger wildly back and forth at Derek and Natalie. "This is some kind of conspiracy, I tell you— some kind of trick! They've always been ready to do me a mischief if they could. They're jealous of me. Jealous!"

Derek and Malcolm exchanged glances. "I think it might be better if you escorted the ladies upstairs, Malcolm," said Derek quietly. "I'll put Mother in her old room, and Mrs. Gilford in the adjoining chamber. Natalie, you know the rooms I mean. Would you lead the way?"

"Of course," said Natalie automatically. Mrs. Gilford rose obediently to her feet.

"I won't have it!" shouted Hector. His face had gone from white to red with fury. "I won't have them under this roof! You can bloody well take them to Larkspur— this, this *imposter,* this *fraud,* and, and, and, the fubsy-faced old biddy with her! I want them out of my house! Out of my house!"

Natalie's eyes flashed, but she wisely said nothing. Everyone behaved exactly as if Hector had not spoken. He continued to rave as Malcolm held the door and assisted Mrs. Gilford and Natalie's mother through it. He was very glad to close the door behind them. They could still hear Hector ranting and the squire's brusque voice reprimanding him, but at least Malcolm knew he was removing the ladies from further insults.

Natalie led them up the stairs. For a few seconds, they climbed the steps in silence. Then Mrs. Gilford gave an indignant sniff. "Fubsy-faced," she muttered. "Well! I never."

Chapter Twenty-four

The sun hung low in the sky when Malcolm and Natalie left Crosby Hall and walked, arm in arm, toward home. *Home.* How quickly she had grown used to thinking of Larkspur as home! It must have something to do with the accelerated pace of the past two weeks. She had now had so much experience at absorbing rapid changes that she was becoming adept at bending with the wind.

But, to her, *home* would always be wherever Malcolm was. She glanced up at him, her heart filled with love and gratitude. This amazing, wonderful man had ridden into her life like a rescuing knight and, from the moment he arrived, her world had irretrievably changed.

His face was very serious and a little tired as he stared into the distance, but she fancied he had lost the haunted look that had so troubled her. She hoped so, at any rate. She would love to think that she had brought him a little of the happiness he had brought her.

"Malcolm."

His eyes refocused, and he looked down at her, smiling a little. "Yes?"

"What happened just now? After you left us in Mother's room."

His smile faded. "It was not a pleasant scene. Suffice it to say that Hector was persuaded, in the end, to leave. He and Mabel will be spending the night at the village inn. Jasper Farnsworth supervised the packing of their bags."

"Oh, that was clever."

"So I thought. And prudent, too. There's no telling what might have found its way into Hector's valise, had he been left to his own devices."

Natalie sighed. "I hope we are misjudging him, but I fear you are right."

"At any rate, better safe than sorry. The squire bundled them into your brother's gig for transport to the inn and promised to send a team of reinforcements tomorrow to supervise their further packing." Malcolm gave a droll little chuckle. "I hope they are sturdy fellows. I shudder to picture what Hector might attempt, after he has had an entire night to plot and scheme."

She looked back up at him. "How did Mabel react?" she asked softly. "I must tell you, Malcolm, I feel sincerely sorry for her."

"Yes." He looked troubled. "She was completely silent, poor thing. We were all grateful to be spared a bout of hysterics, but it was pitiful to see her so dazed. She married Hector believing him to possess a fair estate and a fair name. This is the worst possible time for her to discover that he has neither. She is within a few weeks, I would say, of delivering his child."

"Derek must do something for her."

"Yes. I think he will." He slanted a small smile down at her. "He's really an estimable young man. I am growing rather fond of Derek."

Her heart gave a happy little skip. Another wish had just come true. "I'm so glad."

They had entered the narrow band of woods where the creek ran. Malcolm held a branch high for Natalie to pass beneath, then led her up onto the footbridge, where he stopped her. She looked up at him, laughing. "What is it? For heaven's sake, don't push me in the water. Or slip a frog down my back."

He grinned. "You have spent too much time down here with your brothers. No, I am going to do something I have wanted to do since the first moment I saw this bridge." He pulled her into his arms and kissed her.

Natalie sighed with happiness and gave herself utterly to his kiss. A breeze ruffled the hair at the back of her neck and caused the trees overhead to whisper and dance. The water beneath the wooden planks chuckled and sang. Heaven.

When the kiss ended, she laid her cheek against his shoulder and relaxed, filled with contentment. "Very romantic," she murmured.

His arms slipped more snugly around her. "Yes, I thought it would be."

She smiled against his coat. "Did you really want to do that when you first saw the bridge? You barely knew me then."

He shifted his body so he could take her face in his hands, then tilted it upward, gently forcing her to meet his gaze. His eyes were so strange . . . still the color of a frozen lake, but burning with intensity.

"I knew you," he said softly. "Don't you remember, Natalie? I asked you to marry me the day we met. I'd been waiting so long for you that I recognized you almost at once."

Natalie felt her breath catch. The world seemed to

fade like a dream upon waking, leaving her alone in a universe that contained only herself and Malcolm Chase. She could hear her heart beating.

"Natalie," he said hoarsely. "I know you wanted to fall in love someday. You told me at the outset that you didn't want to marry until you did. I took that away from you, and I'm sorry. Is there any chance, sweetheart, that I could make it up to you? Is there any chance you could fall in love with a man who is already your husband?"

This was more than a wish come true. This was a miracle.

Natalie felt her knees start to buckle and forced herself to stand upright. She would not collapse into his arms and weep all over his coat. She wanted to see his face. She did not want to miss this moment. And there was something, one small thing, that needed clarification.

"You told me love was undesirable in marriage." Her voice sounded high and breathless.

"I was wrong." His fingers traced her cheekbones, achingly tender. "I was wrong."

He kissed her again. Natalie's emotions rose up in an engulfing tide. She clung to him, riding the waves of feeling. Tears stained her cheeks. Finally she tore her lips away, choking on a sob. "Malcolm. Oh, Malcolm." She buried her face in his cravat. "I could never marry a man I didn't love. Don't you know that? Don't you know that about me?" She lifted her head and raised her shining eyes to his. "I love you with all my heart."

Afterward, she was never certain how long they stayed on the bridge; time was meaningless in paradise. But eventually they returned, if not entirely to earth, at least close enough to solid ground to resume their journey home. Malcolm had suggested that they continue their conversation in the privacy of their bedchamber. This had struck Natalie as an excellent idea, so they wandered blissfully toward Larkspur, arms wound around each other in a way that was brazenly indiscreet. Neither Malcolm nor Natalie cared who saw them. They could not bother with such mundane considerations while in the thrall of so much bliss.

As luck would have it, just as they were about to climb the stairs to their rooms, Natalie's eyes fell on a small, neatly wrapped parcel lying on the hall table. Her eyes widened in amazement. "Already?" she exclaimed.

"What is it?" Malcolm nuzzled the top of her head. He didn't sound very interested in the parcel.

"Something I ordered in London," murmured Natalie, torn between desire to continue upstairs with her husband and curiosity to open the package.

"You can show it to me later." He tugged gently at her hand.

"Yes," said Natalie absently. "Later." But she knew the unfinished business would distract her. She had put off telling Malcolm where she had taken Sarah in London. She could not delay that conversation much longer.

He sensed her hesitation and paused, lifting an eyebrow at her. "Is it so important?"

"It is important," she admitted. She studied him, uncertain where to begin. Halfway up the stairs seemed an odd place to tell him. "You never asked me where I took Sarah, that last morning in London," she blurted.

Silent laughter shook him. "And you want to tell me *now*?"

"I must tell you sometime."

"Very well." He shrugged agreeably. "Where did you take her? Shopping, I thought you said."

"Well, actually, it was you who said that," said Natalie

apologetically. "And since we had visited a milliner, Sarah was not telling you an untruth when she confirmed it. But we had not set out to purchase merely a hat."

A certain wariness flitted across Malcolm's features. "Natalie, what is it? You look as if you feel guilty about something."

"I do." She glanced hastily behind her. It would not do to have the servants overhear them. "Come into the library with me," she urged. "For just a moment, Malcolm. I promise." She darted downstairs, snatched up the parcel, led the way into the library, and closed the door behind them.

"Well, this is all very mysterious." He did not sit but leaned against the back of a tall chair, crossing one ankle over the other and watching her with hooded eyes. She could feel at once that he had withdrawn from her. She didn't blame him. "What's in the package?"

She took a deep breath and leaned her back against the closed door, holding the parcel before her with both hands. "Spectacles."

"What?" He stared at her.

"Oh, I wish there had been more time to think out what I would say," exclaimed Natalie wretchedly. "I never dreamed the package would arrive so quickly. Pray, pray, hear me out."

"I'm listening." He looked stunned.

She walked up to him and laid a pleading hand on his sleeve. "Malcolm," she said in a low voice, "you have always been so protective of Sarah. I know you are sensitive to any . . . flaws people perceive in her. But this is different." When he was unresponsive, she shook his sleeve a little. "This has nothing to do with her *mind*," she said urgently. "Indeed, we both know there is nothing wrong with Sarah's brain. She's cleverer than most children are at her age. Why, she reads beautifully, and draws, and paints, and sews—she's remarkable."

Her eyes searched his frantically, begging for a response. She could not read their expression. His thoughts were utterly hidden from her. His eyes were blank and shuttered. "Malcolm," she said, her voice breaking. "She can't see. I took her to the finest optician in London. It's not her mind that is feeble. It's her eyes."

Malcolm brought both hands up and covered his face. His whole body went rigid with guilt. "No" was all he said. It was a groan of self-reproach.

Natalie hastened to reassure him. "It's not as bad as all that. And she may improve. As she grows, her eyes may change. Even without the lenses, she can tell light from dark, and she can see colors. But . . . apparently the world is all a blur to her."

"Dear God." He dropped his hands. His features were hard and set in lines of anguish. Disbelief. "You're telling me that all these years . . . all she needed was a pair of *spectacles*?"

As if he could not bear for her to witness his emotion, he walked away from her and stood by the window with his back to the room. "Oh, dear God." The words sounded like a prayer, not a curse.

She longed to go to him, to comfort him, but sensed that she must not. She stood her ground, therefore, still clutching the little parcel. "Do not blame yourself, Malcolm. No one realized what was wrong."

Malcolm seemed to be struggling to speak, willing himself to control his voice. "What . . ." he croaked. "How . . ."

"How did I guess?" She took an instinctive step forward, then forced herself to halt. "It came upon me gradually. I knew that something was amiss, but it took me

some time to fit the pieces of evidence together. She
bends over her work so closely . . . I thought, for a long
time, it was just another manifestation of her tendency to
shut the world out." She took a deep breath, then expelled it in a sigh. "But now I think the main reason why
Sarah lives in her own little world so much of the time is
that she cannot see this one clearly. You have seen her
drawings and her watercolors. The details are rendered
with great care . . . but the larger picture is indistinct.
The background of her paintings is nothing but a wash
of color."

"Yes." His voice was almost inaudible.

"I believe that is how she sees the world. Once, I took
her down to the creek to show her the tadpoles. I had the
oddest feeling that she was humoring me . . . as if she
believed we were playing one of our imagination games.
Now I realize that she could not see the creatures in the
water. No wonder she thought I was playing a game."
She was clutching the package too tightly. She set it
carefully down on a low table, running one finger absently along the string. "And finally, one day, I noticed
something odd about her greeting, when she welcomed
me into the nursery. I was wearing a new dress. She noticed me standing in the doorway, but her little face
brightened considerably when I spoke." She cleared her
throat, which had suddenly developed a lump. "Before
she heard my voice, she knew only that she had a visitor.
It was my voice, not my face, that identified me to her."

Malcolm raised one hand to cover his eyes. "The fall,"
he said, his voice tight with sorrow.

"Yes," said Natalie gently. "She has always been a little clumsy, has she not? And fearful of falling. After you
told me about her mother, I thought . . ."

"So did I." He dropped his hand and sighed. "I

thought some corner of her mind remembered the way
her mother had died. I thought that was why she clung to
me when we walked anywhere. I thought that was why
she was so afraid of falling."

"It still may be, you know. At least, part of it."

His head swiveled back to look at her. His expression
was bitter. "But she did not see the stone stairway in the
village. And that, in fact, is why she fell."

"It would seem so," agreed Natalie softly. "I'm sorry."

"What a sad excuse for a father I am," he said. His
voice was harsh with self-loathing. "I should have noticed. I should have known."

"Stop it." She flew to him and put her arms around
him, hugging him fiercely. "You must not reproach yourself."

"She is my responsibility," he whispered, distraught.
"God placed her in my care. I try to do my best, but—"

"Stop, stop! You are a wonderful father. Sarah adores
you." Natalie, thinking of her own father, almost choked
at the irony, the injustice, of Malcolm—of all men—
thinking he was a bad parent. "I cannot bear to hear you
blame yourself. Had I received half the attention from
my father that Sarah receives from you—"

"I love her so much. How could I have missed it?
There were so many clues—"

"No, no, it was never obvious—"

"There were many clues," he repeated bitterly. "You
don't know. I've been standing here, remembering . . ."
His throat worked for a moment. Then he managed to
say, "Did you know that that Thorpe woman used to
punish her? She would insist that Sarah sit up straight.
'Sit up straight!'" He mimicked her. "'Posture, Sarah,
posture.'"

Natalie, understanding what this must have meant,

was horrified. "But Sarah could not see her work if she sat up straight."

"Right. And Mrs. Thorpe knew what Sarah was capable of, so she punished her when her skills seemed to desert her. Harshly. She must have believed Sarah was defying her, being deliberately obtuse . . . oh, my poor little girl."

"Ssh, ssh." Natalie, beside herself with grief for him, kissed his mouth to hush him. "It's all over, now. It's all behind us."

He hugged her tightly. "Thank you," he said, in a low tone. "Thank you for seeing what I did not." He managed a rather wan smile. "Between the two of us, we may yet rear her safely."

Relieved, Natalie smiled back. "I wouldn't be a bit surprised."

They unwrapped the parcel then and sent for Sarah. Mrs. Bigalow brought her down to the hall, where the last light of evening slanted through the tall windows. Malcolm pulled Sarah's nurse aside and, in a carefully lowered voice, told her what was about to occur. Meanwhile, Natalie crouched down to Sarah's eye level.

"Sarah dear," she began, "do you remember the kind gentleman we visited in London?"

Sarah nodded. "He thought you were my mama."

"That's right." She could not help feeling touched; it struck her as so quaint that *that,* out of all the wonders of her visit to the optician, had made the greatest impression on Sarah. "But do you remember all the pieces of glass you looked through? Some of them let you see better."

"I remember." Sarah smiled. "One made everything weensy." She held her fingers in a circle before her eyes and screwed up her features to demonstrate.

Natalie tried again. "But some of them made faraway things look clearer, didn't they?"

Sarah cocked her head, birdlike. "Yes." She seemed puzzled.

Natalie's voice took on a congratulatory tone. "Well, the kind gentleman has made you a pair of spectacles. Fancy that! You will be able to look through those bits of glass always."

Natalie held out the little spectacles as she spoke. All three adults fell silent, watching. They seemed to be holding their breath, waiting for the child's reaction.

Sarah's eyes grew round with curiosity. She took them gingerly from Natalie's hand and inspected them, holding them very close to her face. "Will they fit me, do you think?" Her voice sounded perfectly matter-of-fact. She seemed completely unaware that her world was about to change.

"Oh, I believe they will." Natalie placed the spectacles on Sarah's face and hooked the arms over Sarah's ears, carefully bending the wires into shape and checking to make sure the lenses were level as they sat on Sarah's tiny nose. Sarah closed her eyes during this procedure, as if nervous of having such a device attached to her face. She looked adorable in them, like a miniature owl.

"There, then," said Natalie at last, straightening. "What do you think?"

Sarah slowly opened her eyes. Fear immediately darkened her pupils. She gasped, flinching backward, and her gaze flicked to her father's face. Her small jaw dropped. Her eyes filled with tears.

"She's crying," exclaimed Malcolm. He stooped and picked Sarah up in his arms. "What's wrong, sweetheart? What is it?"

Sarah stared at his jaw. Her small hand cupped his face. "Papa, I can see your whiskers," she sobbed.

Malcolm's eyes met Natalie's, seeking enlightenment. Natalie gave a helpless little shrug. Whatever reaction she had been expecting, it was not this. She hastened to soothe the little girl. "Sarah, sweetheart, do they pinch you?" She stroked the child's hair. "Do the spectacles hurt?"

"No," Sarah wailed. Her wet eyes focused on Natalie's face. She gulped and cringed. "You're too close," she cried, evidently trying to explain. "You're too big."

"Mrs. Bigalow, you wear spectacles," said Malcolm, a note of desperation in his voice. "What is happening here?"

Nurse gave a sympathetic cluck. "Poor dear, it's startling her. That's all."

The voice drew Sarah's eyes to Nurse, who was standing a few feet away, and she cried harder.

"Well," said Natalie helplessly, "Something is wrong. Shall we take them off?"

"No!" Sarah wriggled frantically in Malcolm's arms. "Papa, put me down."

Malcolm and Natalie exchanged glances again. Malcolm shrugged. "Very well," he said, and placed his daughter on the floor.

She stood absolutely still, evidently afraid to move. Her tears stopped. She sniffed a time or two, recovering, but did not cry again. Moving cautiously, as if she had just been injured but wasn't sure how or where, she lifted one foot and set it down slightly ahead of the other. One step. Then she swayed as if dizzy and clutched at her father's coat.

"I'm here, Sarah." He took her hand in his.

"The floor is too close," she whispered. "Papa. I can see *everything*."

It was apparently disconcerting for Sarah to have so much information about her surroundings. To a child who associated details with proximity, being able to see the edge of a carpet, or a floorboard, or an individual step, meant she must be falling.

"I want to go out of doors," said Sarah in an urgent whisper. Natalie had the strangest impression that Sarah thought if she spoke out loud, she might wake up. And she evidently wanted to see as much of the world as she could before the dream ended.

With Malcolm holding one of Sarah's hands and Natalie the other, the threesome left Nurse wiping away a tear in the hall behind them. They walked slowly, slowly, out the door and onto the front step.

Sarah paused, looking down the drive. Her eyes were enormous as she took it all in: grass and trees and gravel and sky. She must have forgotten to breathe at first; after a few seconds of silence her chest heaved, and a huge sigh escaped her.

What was Sarah thinking? Natalie wondered. What did she make of it all? She was sure Malcolm was wondering the same thing. But neither of them spoke. It would have been a sacrilege, somehow, to intrude on this moment.

"May I walk out on the grass?" She seemed subdued and spoke very quietly, but she was no longer whispering.

"Certainly you may." This time Malcolm was whispering, his voice hoarse with suppressed emotion.

Still hand in hand, they all walked down the shallow steps and out onto the lawn. Sarah stared down at her feet. "Grass," she breathed, as if the word were new to her. Then she looked up at the purpling sky. Surprise flitted across her features. "Look, Papa," she said, pointing upward. Her face was filled with wonder. "There are little holes in the sky."

Sarah had never seen the stars.

They stayed out on the lawn and watched the stars come out. At Sarah's request, Malcolm held her up so she could be "closer to the sky." Natalie leaned against him on the other side, resting her head on his shoulder. With one arm around his wife and one around his child, Malcolm talked about the stars as they appeared, first one by one, then blooming like great drifts of wild daisies over their heads. When Sarah's neck grew tired, she lay back against her father, silent and attentive as he told her stories of the twins and the bear and the dipper, all the tales he could recall of the great, unending dance of the stars.

"I do not see them dancing," Sarah remarked.

"No, for it's a slow dance. Too slow to watch with our eyes. But the stars do change places as the months move on."

"I think," said Sarah sleepily, "that they dance up above the sky. Like angels. I think they are wearing shoes with little wee heels, little sharp heels, and they punch holes in the floor as they dance."

Natalie smiled. It was a pretty thought. "So the sky must be the floor of heaven, and we are looking up from beneath."

Sarah yawned. "Yes."

Malcolm's eyes met Natalie's. Emotion flashed and sparked between them. "And heaven is filled with light," he said softly. "I see." He shook his head in slow amazement. "My daughter is a poet. When Sarah looks at the stars, she sees divine radiance pouring through tiny rips in the firmament."

Sarah's sleepy voice sounded again. "Do you think Mama is up in heaven, Papa? Can she peek through the holes and see me?"

"I don't know, poppet. Perhaps she can."

"I hope so." She yawned again. "I hope she can see me right now. I think she would like to see us so happy."

Natalie felt tears welling up. "I'm sure she would like you to be happy, sweetheart."

Silence fell again. Then Sarah, barely awake now, murmured sorrowfully, "It was a very bad bird."

Natalie looked at Malcolm. He mouthed, *Dreaming*. But Natalie didn't think so. She leaned forward and peeked around Malcolm to see Sarah's face. Her eyes were closed now, but she seemed awake.

"What bird was that, sweetheart?" asked Natalie. She reached across and gently tried to remove Sarah's spectacles, to make her more comfortable for sleep—but changed her mind when Sarah put up a hand and clung to them, keeping them on.

"The bird," Sarah repeated, opening her eyes. She sat up. "Papa, you know about the bird."

Malcolm was clearly at a loss. "Do I?"

The silvery light of moon and stars was strong enough to read Sarah's expression. It was puzzled, and a little anxious. "Am I not to talk about it?"

"Talk about what? You may say anything you like." When she still did not speak, Malcolm gently prompted her. "Tell us about the bird."

Visible tension ran through Sarah's small form. "It was the bird," she whispered. "You remember that day. Mama did not want to leave us. Not really. The bird made her fall."

A shock went through Natalie's veins like a dash of cold water. Sarah was remembering her mother's death.

She had been there, and at three years of age she had been old enough to comprehend—what?

Had there been a ledge? Of course there had been, if Catherine was threatening to jump from it. Had birds been nesting beneath it? Malcolm's words came back to her: *I married Catherine in the spring . . . It was the anniversary of our wedding day.* Springtime. Nesting.

A nesting bird would fly out at anyone who came too close to the nest.

Natalie placed a trembling hand on Sarah's little arm. "Did a bird fly out, darling? Did a bird fly out very suddenly?"

Sarah nodded, her face very grave. "I heard it. *Swish.*" She raised her arm and demonstrated, making a fast, swooping motion. "I felt it." Her face crumpled. "And Mama screamed." She buried her face in her father's coat, shuddering.

Malcolm looked thunderstruck. He patted Sarah's back with automatic, soothing, circular movements. "Ssh, poppet. Ssh. It's all right now. Never mind." His dazed eyes sought Natalie's again.

Natalie hugged him as tightly as she could, waves of joy and sorrow pounding her. There were tears in her eyes, but she was smiling, too. "Then the coroner was right," she said. Her voice quavered a bit. "Don't you see, Malcolm? The coroner was right. It was an accident. It was *no one's fault.*" The emphasis was for his benefit; with Sarah there, she could not say aloud what she was thinking: *You, my love, were not to blame. Whatever you said, whatever you did, it doesn't matter now. It never did.*

Malcolm took a deep breath. She saw the very moment when the weight rolled off his soul. He looked as if he could not quite believe it, but Natalie knew that his initial incredulity would gradually fade as the truth hit home. *Thank you, God.* She hugged him again, burrowing her face into his sleeve.

"I'm sleepy, Papa."

Malcolm kissed the top of Sarah's head. "Shall I carry you in?"

"Yes, please." She snuggled back into his arms, laying her head down and closing her eyes. Malcolm removed the spectacles, and this time she allowed it. He folded the little miracle of gold and glass and slipped it carefully into his breast pocket.

Natalie smiled up at him. "Your arms must be tired."

"Not very." The corners of his mouth lifted. "I think nothing could tire me tonight."

She saw a flash of silver light out of the corner of her eye. She turned, looking back at the sky. Malcolm glanced up at the same moment, apparently seeing what she had seen. Wonder stirred in her heart. "Oh," she breathed. "How beautiful."

"A shooting star," said Malcolm. Quiet pleasure rumbled in his voice. He looked back at Natalie. "Make a wish."

She stared upward, overwhelmed. The sky spread its canopy over her, the blackness spangled with silver light like hope triumphing over every mystery, twinkling even more brightly where the dark was deepest. Summer was ending and autumn would soon be here; the breeze carried the fragrance of hay and the warmth in the air was fading into chill. Beside her was Malcolm, her husband. Her love. And he held in his arms a child who was almost as dear to her as he was. Derek was home. Her mother was alive. Sarah could see the stars. Miracle upon miracle had showered down upon her, filling her heart to bursting.

Natalie shook her head. "I can't."

He quirked an eyebrow at her, amused. "You can't make a wish?"

She spread her hands in a gesture of helplessness. "I have nothing to wish for." She sighed with happiness. "Absolutely nothing. You make a wish."

His eyes met hers, filled with understanding. "Natalie Whittaker Chase," he said softly, "if one more blessing rains down on me, I think my heart will crack open from pure joy."

She nodded. "A dangerous brew," she said, with mock solemnity. "Joy."

"Let's leave the wish for someone who needs it."

She smiled. "Will it stay, do you think? Hovering invisibly in the sky . . . waiting for someone worthy to come along and take it?" She rather liked the idea.

"I don't know, my love. All I know is that for either of us to make a wish would be . . ." He cocked his head as if thinking. "Greedy," he pronounced at last.

"Pure gluttony," Natalie agreed, slipping her arm through his. And they turned to carry their sleeping daughter back to the lamplit house.

Read on for a preview of
Diane Farr's next novel

Under a Lucky Star

Coming from Signet
April 2004

May, 1803

The Divine Sophronia was the toast of London. The fever of admiration that had swept the *ton* failed, however, to infect Derek Whittaker. Her singing moved him, all right and tight. But it tended to move him toward the door.

The famous soprano waddled purposefully toward the footlights. An aria was plainly imminent. Derek decided he had had enough. He was positioned, as usual, at the back wall of Lord Stokesdown's box. No one would notice if he simply disappeared. During the orchestra's introductory flourish, he slipped neatly through the curtain behind him and escaped.

There were advantages, he reflected, to being a lowly secretary. Provided he returned at the interval, when Lord Stokesdown or one of his guests might want him, it didn't matter whether he listened politely to Sophronia's caterwauling or spent the evening playing mumblety-peg in the cloakroom.

He wandered down the softly lit passage, enjoying the solitude. The opera sounded faintly through the curtained openings in the wall beside him and echoed with pleasant spookiness against the high, arched ceiling. A little distance muffled the shrillness of

Sophronia's voice, and added a peculiarly haunting quality to the orchestra. He rather liked it.

Ahead of him was an arched doorway where the well-lit passage dwindled into shadow. He glanced guiltily about, then ducked into it, his skin prickling with pleasurable anticipation. There was something indefinably exciting about exploring places where he had no business being. He was a little ashamed of this peculiar hobby, but it had held an irresistible allure for him since childhood. He always carried a flint and a bit of candle somewhere on his person, on the off chance he might need it. Tonight, he did not. The passage stretched the length of the building, lamplight gleaming here and there to show him the way. It seemed a shocking waste of oil. There wasn't another soul in sight.

The passage narrowed, then suddenly turned a corner. He found himself in a small, dusty room. Across from him, a flight of wooden stairs led up and out. At the foot of these stairs yet another lamp hung from the ceiling on a chain, feebly illuminating what appeared to be a collection of disused props stacked haphazardly about. He was idly studying these when a sudden tingle of awareness caused him to turn.

There was a soft footfall on the stairs to his right, and the faint slither of silk. To his surprise, he saw a young woman, all alone, clutching the rickety banister as she descended. When he looked at her she flinched, then froze in place. Her eyes dilated as she stared, motionless, at Derek.

Derek felt his jaw start to drop. With an effort, he reanchored it, keeping himself from gaping at the girl. She could have been any age between sixteen and twenty . . . and she was the loveliest sight he had ever beheld. Her beauty was unbelievable. Almost otherworldly. He had always been partial to blondes, but this girl took blondness to an entirely new level. Her fair hair captured and reflected whatever light was available, shimmering like moonlight on water even in the dim glow cast by the overhead lamp.

It was difficult to discern her station in life, for while the cut and style of her simple, white gown were very much *de rigeur* for a young lady of breeding—the material of which it was fashioned was scandalously revealing. The thin silk clung to every line and curve of her slender form. It was hard to tell whether she was a lady of quality or a bird of paradise.

She was so astonishingly beautiful that for a moment or two he could notice nothing else about her. Then he saw that her eyes were stark with fear.

"Help," she whispered. She stumbled down the stairs toward him. "Help me."

Every chivalrous instinct Derek had ever had rushed immediately to the fore. He moved toward her at once. "Of course," he heard himself say. "Anything in my power."

The girl reached for him in the way a child reaches for its nurse, and he caught her in much the same spirit. It seemed perfectly natural to take her hands in his, then place one arm around her to comfort her. For an instant she sagged gratefully against him. He could not help noticing how perfectly she fit in his embrace. But she was trembling with terror; he couldn't help noticing that, either.

"Hide me," she whispered.

At almost the same instant, Derek heard a door close somewhere above their heads, and footsteps, firmer than the girl's, heading toward the stairs down which she had come. The sharp intake of her breath confirmed that this, whoever the individual may be, was the source of her terror. Quick as thought, Derek pulled the girl into the shadowed stairwell. She clung to him in a way that sent a surge of fierce protectiveness through him.

No harm would come to this girl, he silently vowed. He didn't care who she was. Duchess or beggarmaid, princess or prostitute, if she needed him to slay dragons or walk on hot coals, so be it. He'd slay the dragons while walking on the coals, if that was the only way to keep her safe.

The footsteps on the floor above their heads halted, apparently at the top of the stairs. A dry, masculine voice spoke.

"Cynthia."

The single word managed to convey both command and menace. The tone was redolent of hostility overlaid with silky amusement. At its sound, the girl seemed to stop breathing.

The man would surely come down if he were not stopped. Derek laid a finger to his lips, warning Cynthia to keep still, then let go of her and emerged alone from beneath the stairs.

"Oh, hallo," he said, trying to sound affable and mildly puzzled. He peered inquiringly up at the figure standing at the top of the stairs. "Didn't see you," he remarked, in an explanatory tone. "Were you looking for me?"

There was a perceptible pause before the gentleman answered. "No," he said. His voice was hard, but civil enough. "I beg your pardon."

Derek gave him an airy wave. "Not at all, not at all. Haven't disturbed me a whit." Still aping the amiable vapidity of a young man-about-town, and trying to convey the impression that he had, perhaps, imbibed too much wine, he wandered a bit unsteadily toward a suit of armor made from paperboard. "Just having a look round, you know. Fascinating, all this scenery and what-not."

The man at the top of the stairs did not move. He seemed to be studying Derek with careful suspicion, weighing whether to challenge him or move on. Derek stole another glance at the man. By moving toward the suit of armor, he had positioned himself where the light was no longer in his eyes, and he could get a good look.

He knew the man at once, and had to return his gaze to the wall to avoid displaying his start of recognition. Sir James Filey. Damnation! How had a girl like Cynthia fallen into Filey's hands? The fellow was notorious. Gamester, rakehell, lecher—a thoroughly ugly customer. And besides that, he was old enough to be her father. Older, by Jove!

"I wonder if I might trespass upon your courtesy for a moment." Filey's voice was very cold.

Outwardly relaxed but inwardly alert, Derek turned politely back toward the stairs. "Eh?" he said, swaying slightly.

Filey did not bother to hide his contempt. The sneer on his face deepened. "I'm looking for a fair-haired chit in a white gown."

Hiding his disgust, Derek gave Filey a lopsided grin. "Ha! Aren't we all?" He winked drunkenly.

Impatience sharpened Filey's voice. "Have you seen such a female pass by here, a few moments hence?"

"No, dash it." Derek infused his voice with wistful regret. "Is she pretty?"

"Excessively pretty," snapped Filey.

"Really? By George! I'll help you look for her." He began to stagger eagerly up the stairs.

"No, thank you. That won't be necessary." Filey actually threw out a hand as if warding him off. "I prefer to hunt alone."

He sketched a bow and was gone, his footfalls beating an angry retreat. Derek waited until the footsteps receded into silence, then gave a grim chuckle. "That dragon was too easily slain," he remarked. The vapid drawl had vanished from his voice. He strolled back down the stairs. "What a pity that no fisticuffs were called for! It would have been a pleasure to plant that rogue a facer."

A faint voice sounded from the stairwell. "Oh, on the contrary! I am glad no blows were exchanged."

Cynthia emerged into the light. Her attempt at a light tone was pathetically brave; now that Filey was gone, she was shaking with reaction. Derek saw that she was clenching her jaw to keep her teeth from chattering, and his heart went out to her. All humor fled from Derek's features. It was impossible to make light of the situation, confronted with Cynthia's distress.

"I sent him away through deception," said Derek quietly. "I would have served you better, perhaps, had I faced the villain down."

Cynthia's eyes, celestial blue, lifted to his. Derek felt his breath catch in his throat. A thrill went through him like an electric shock, as if her eyes held divine power.

"You were splendid," she whispered. There was something dazed and wondering in her face, as if the words had been pulled out of her against her will. A sudden stillness seemed to descend upon her. And her trembling simply . . . stopped.

How beautiful she was. But there must be something else, some added element beyond physical beauty, attracting him. Nobody was this beautiful. Nobody could possibly be as beautiful as this girl seemed to him. Crazy thoughts jumbled in his brain; snatches of Shakespeare mixed with heart-pounding emotion, and somewhere above it, a detached portion of his mind was noting, with calm, scientific interest, *so this is what it's like . . . love at first sight.* He had read of the phenomenon, but had assumed it was merely a poetic convention. Such things never happened in real life. Real people did not, could not, fall in love with total strangers.

Except that, apparently, they could and did.

They stared at each other, motionless under the flaring lamp. *Oh, she doth teach the torches to burn bright.* Madness, madness. Knowledge and intimacy, clear truth somehow born in intuition, flashed and pulsed in the air between them. How could such things be? And then, without a word, Derek opened his arms.

It was a crazy thing to do; what did he expect? No decent female would accept such an invitation. But, marvel of marvels, Cynthia walked right into his embrace as if she belonged there.

In the midst of a miracle, reality steps aside. The normal laws of earthly existence, including the rules set forth for human behavior, simply do not apply. Whatever was happening here, it was larger, more important, more compelling, than any code of conduct. For another fraction of a second, Derek drowned in those blue, blue eyes, now so close to his own. Then he surrendered to the inevitable. He bent his head and kissed her.